THE G(

FOURTH IN THE 'HEART OF STONE' SAGA

THE GOLDEN FLEECE

For Pam

with love & best wishes

from Shelagh

x

SHELAGH MAZEY

Matador
9 Priory Business Park,
Wistow Road, Kibworth Beauchamp,
Leicestershire. LE8 0RX
Tel: 0116 279 2299
Email: books@troubador.co.uk
Web: www.troubador.co.uk/matador
Twitter: @matadorbooks

ISBN 978 1789013 986

British Library Cataloguing in Publication Data.
A catalogue record for this book is available from the British Library.

Printed and bound in the UK by TJ International, Padstow, Cornwall
Typeset in 11pt Baskerville by Troubador Publishing Ltd, Leicester, UK

Matador is an imprint of Troubador Publishing Ltd

*This book is lovingly dedicated
to my husband
Barry Mazey*

TABLE OF CONTENTS

LIST OF SAGA CHARACTERS

THE DRYER FAMILY
ALVINGTON MANOR
LORD JOSHUA DRYER (1832)
LADY LOUISA DRYER (1833)
AURORA DRYER (1851)
GABRIEL DRYER (1855)
LYDIA MAY DRYER (1870)

ALVINGTON MANOR STAFF
GARETH WILLIAMS (1798) *Butler/House steward*
MICHAEL PORTER (1800) *Footman*
JOHN MOORE (1827) *Head groom*
BILLY RIDDICK (1832) *Groom*
EDWIN PROCTOR (1841) *Stable boy*
PERCY SANDFORD (1810) *Gardener*
THOMAS HAWKINS (1831) *Gardener*
HENRY HODINOTT (1820) *Handyman*
JOHN BOUCHER (1809) *Gamekeeper*
RAYMOND HAWKINS (1832) *Gamekeeper*
MRS ABBOTT (1802) *Housekeeper*
FLORA BOUCHER (1810) *Cook*
GRACE TWEEDY (1821) *Governess*
BETH PUDDY (1835) *Nanny*
ROSA WARREN (1825) *Lady's maid*
LETTIE BOUCHER (1838) *Parlour maid*
EMILY POTTS (1837) *Housemaid*
RUTH PROCTOR (1820) *Assistant cook*
ELSIE HALL (1833) *Chambermaid*
HARRIETT PROCTOR (1844) *Kitchen maid*
ELLIE PROCTOR (1848) *Scullery maid*
CHARLOTTE HODINOTT (1827) *Laundress*

THE WARREN FAMILY
HOME FARM
ISAAC (1792) & ELIZABETH (1795) WARREN
SIBLINGS: JACOB (1830), LUCY (1836) & BEATRICE (BUNNY) (1844)

THE WARREN FAMILY
HAMLET COTTAGE
MALACHI (1825) & ROSA (1825) WARREN
SIBLINGS: RUBY (1856), ELI (1858) & DAISY (1861)

THE SEYMOUR FAMILY
SUTTON BINGHAM MANOR
COLONEL JEREMY (1803) & MRS HELEN (1808) SEYMOUR
SIBLINGS: RUPERT (1823) & ASHLEIGH (1827)
LUCY (1836) & FRANCIS (1869)
ROBSHAW - *Steward*
MARY ROBINS – *Cook*
TIM JEFFRIES - *Gardener*
GLADYS TURNER – *Parlour maid*
MERCY MEREDITH - *Nanny*

CAMP ROAD FAMILIES – ESTATE WORKERS
RUTH PROCTOR (1820)
SIBLINGS: AMY (1838), EDWIN (1841)
HATTIE (1844) & ELLIE (1848)
MICHAEL (1800) & MAUD (1802) PORTER
HENRY (1820) & CHARLOTTE (1827) HODINOTT
JOHN (1827) & SUSAN (1831) MOORE
SIBLINGS: LUKE (1851) & LILLY (1853)
PERCY (1810) & MARY (1812) SANDFORD
SIBLINGS: ROBERT (1830) & HARRY (1833)
JACK (1805) & MOLLY (1802) HAWKINS
SIBLINGS: FRANK (1823) & THOMAS (1831)

THE BOUCHER FAMILY
KEEPER'S COTTAGE, POUND LANE
JOHN (1809) & FLORA (1810) BOUCHER
SIBLINGS: LETTIE (1838) & TOBY (1846)

THE BONFIELD FAMILY
KNAPP COTTAGE, PRESTON PLUCKNET
ARTHUR (1808) & MARTHA (1813) BONFIELD

THE FAIRWAY FAMILY
CHURCH COTTAGE, STAIRS HILL, IVELL
AMBROSE FAIRWAY (1804) *Solicitor's clerk*
DAUGHTER: CLARA (1834)

THE HAWKINS FAMILY
COBB COTTAGE, DRAY ROAD, ODCOMBE
MRS ESTHER HAWKINS (1805)
SIBLINGS: JEAN (1831) & RAYMOND (1832)

THE MEAKINS FAMILY
SUMMERVILLE HOUSE
LADY ANNABEL MEAKINS (1797)
OLIVIA (1813) & ALISTAIR MCNAB (1802)
AGNES (SENGA) (1860)

THE BRIDEWELL FAMILY
CLIFTON MAYBANK MANOR
SAMUEL (1791) & EDITH (1795) BRIDEWELL
SIBLINGS: SERENA (1820), KEZIAH (1822) &
ALICIA (1824)

THE TOMPKINS FAMILY
THE BOROUGH, IVELL
WILLIAM (1808) & BETTY (1814) TOMPKINS
SIBLINGS: HARRY (1834) & BOBBY (1835)
AMY PROCTOR (1838)

THE YATES FAMILY
HATHERLEIGH FARM
ROBERT (1816) & LILLIAN (1821) YATES
SIBLINGS: VICTORIA (1840) & DONALD (1850)

PORTLANDERS
VIOLET STONE (1814) *Joshua's mother*
MATTHEW STONE (1811) *Joshua's stepfather*
REBECCA STONE (1838) *Joshua's sister*
BENJAMIN STONE (1832) *Joshua's half-brother*
JEM STONE (1866) *Joshua's nephew*
ANNIE STONE (1810) *Ben's mother*

THE KELLY FAMILY
SAMUEL (1836) & ANGELICA (1834) KELLY
SIBLINGS: CAMIRA (1863) & CONNOR (1864)

THE DAVIES FAMILY
HUGH (1808) & SARAH (1811) DAVIES
SIBLINGS: LEWYS (1836) & GWYNETH (1839)

THE THOMAS FAMILY
BRYN (1812) & NELL (1814) THOMAS
SIBLINGS: OWEN (1837) & RHYS (1839)

RESIDENTS OF SANDHURST
FREYJA BRUNSVOLD (1837) *Emporium*
JETHRO TULLY (1800) *Landlord Eureka Hotel*

SUPPORTING CHARACTERS
IVELL
SERGEANT GUNDRY
DR GILLINGHAM
DR JESSOP
ALBERT TATTERSHALL, SIMEON BROWN,
MORGAN AND JETHRO *Factory workers*
WILLIAM BELL *Owner of Catkin Mill*

REVEREND DAVID PHELPS *Local vicar*
MR GOSNEY *Wedding photographer*
HENRY BRAGG *Blacksmith*
SUPERINTENDENT MUNRO
DETECTIVE SUPERINTENDENT McKINLEY
WILLIAM FANCOURT TOMKINS *Surgeon*
MRS CREED *Midwife*
WINCANTON
MORTIMER BATHHURST *Owner Lattiford Lodge*
WALTER RODBER *Groom at Lattiford Lodge*
NOAH BOSWELL *Gypsy*
FLORICA PETULENGRO *Gypsy*
LEON PETULENGRO *Florica's father*
KING DUFFERTY *King of the gypsies*
URIAH LEVI *Bookie*
JARVIS POCKET *Bookie*
SNODGRASS & BLAKELY *Pocket's minders*
NE'ER-DO-WELLS *Lanky, Ginger, Shorty & Beefy*
MAURICE FELTHAM *Ginger*
IVAN HOCKEY *Lanky*
LUCKY JOE MINTERN *Stable owner*
JAKE *The ploughman at Hatherleigh Farm*
FRED MEADEN & SON OSCAR *Moorhayes Farm*
FRED OATLEY *Constable in Wells*

MENAGERIE
ALVINGTON MANOR
Hercules, Perseus *Shire horses (brown)*
Capricorn *Josh's horse (black stallion)*
Andromeda *(brown)*, Cassiopeia *(grey)* & Capella *(bay)*
Paddy & O'Malley *Irish Wolfhounds*
Dottie & Dash *Border Collies*
HATHERLEIGH FARM
Samson & Delilah *Shire horses*
Melody *Pony*
Bay Rum & Conker Queen *Racehorses*
Porky & Podge *Victoria's pigs*

Ned *Noah's horse*
BINGHAM MANOR
Skipper *Papillon*
Dolly *Exmoor pony*
BENDIGO AUSTRALIA
Rhiannon *Lewys's horse*

THE PROLOGUE *(October 1866)*

Trudging down Mill Street at the end of the day, Raymond Baker is well pleased with his day's work. The gas lights sputter, creating patches of light between the dark shadows, and the October wind blows the leaves from the trees and rustles the bushes, as he tramps through the muddy puddles towards the bridge over the River Cale.

He has been careful to avoid the more astute of his customers, but the small increase in each person's payment should go unnoticed by the others, and due to his cleverness, his boss should be none the wiser. Since starting his little scheme he has been proud give his wife enough to buy new shoes for all his children, plus some extra coal, now that winter is drawing in. He pulls up his collar against the wind. The road is rutted and he feels the discomfort of gravel pressing through the soles of his old boots. Maybe next month he will be able to replace them, too.

He senses a rapid movement behind him, a sudden searing pain crashes through his head and he staggers under the impact. He is cudgelled again and collapses to the ground, blood running down his neck. The pain is intolerable and he shakes and trembles, unable to focus his eyes, unable to move his limbs. He thinks, *I am done for!* as the blows rain down on him. He feels his skull crumbling, as his blood and bone are propelled into the night air.

Large hands lift him up and he is hauled off the roadway towards the river. Although drifting in and out of consciousness, he can make out the muffled sound of two men talking. They drop him into the undergrowth and go through his jacket pockets, ripping the cloth in their hurry to grab his purse. Then something is bunged into his mouth and the effort to continue to breathe is too much for him. He realises that all his big plans will come to nothing, as his life ebbs away and his blood mingles with the river water.

CHAPTER ONE *(October 1866)*

BILLY LEAVES FOR PASTURES NEW

On Sunday morning Billy Riddick pops into the kitchen for breakfast with the other staff. They are all seated around the scrubbed wooden table while the cook, Flora Boucher, and Elsie hand out the platters of fried egg and bacon. Billy loves Sunday breakfasts, and his mouth waters in anticipation. The family have all been catered for in the dining room and now the staff can relax. The footman, Michael Porter, has just picked up Friday's discarded Western Flying Post. "I want to read about this body they've found in Wincanton."

Flora nearly drops the frying pan. "Body! What do 'ee mean, body!"

"It says here: *'The deceased body of an unidentified middle-aged man has been found in undergrowth on the banks of the River Cale, in Wincanton. The local police have issued a statement saying the man was murdered and are asking for people to come forward, if they have any information that would help in identifying the man, or lead to an arrest of the perpetrator'.*"

"Oh dear! The poor fellow!" says Lettie with concern.

"I'm glad it's not round here. I'd be afraid to go up the hill home tonight, if it was," says young Elle, the scullery maid.

"Well, it's not, so you mustn't worry," says her older sister, Hattie.

1

Michael continues scanning the other pages and Rosa, the lady's maid, looks over his shoulder, as she waits for Flora to dish up her hot food.

Suddenly Rosa exclaims, "Oh my! Look at this! Our Lucy and Ashleigh Seymour have announced their intentions to marry on 5th May next year."

Immediately Billy pushes back his chair. "I've just lost my appetite; someone else can have mine!" He feels sick to his stomach. He marches out; back to the stable yard. Although he had spent some time socially with Aurora's nanny, Beth, it was not the same as his unfulfilled, long-standing adoration of Rosa's sister-in-law, Lucy Warren. Lucy was the love of his life. *Now I've lost her forever to that pretentious prick!*

Later, Lettie finds him mucking out. She sighs at the sight of him angrily jerking the manure fork to and fro. "Billy, I know you liked her, but you like Beth too, don't you?"

"No, Lettie. Not like I feel for Lucy. Beth is a good friend and fun to be with when we're all together socially, but I truly love Lucy, even though she's never given me a second glance. Do you remember when we all went to the St Leonard's Day Fayre and all the girls were taken with them gemstones? Malachi and Rosa bought rose quartz and malachite from the shaman, and Raymond bought you one too. Well, I offered to buy some for Lucy, but she rejected me. She's a sensible girl who wants a man who can provide well for her and her future family. Why would she look twice at me? I was just the stable boy."

He chucks his fork into the corner of the empty stable and Cassiopeia next door stamps her feet and snorts at the sudden noise. "Now I'll have to put up with her being driven around by that silly article; I'll have to be here working and observing them when she visits her parents at Home Farm with their many wonderful children. I just can't stand it, Lettie. It's going to hurt so much… I think I might have to leave here and start afresh somewhere else, where I can try to forget her. I don't want to; this is all I've ever known since the poor house and I love it here, but I can't see any other answer."

"Come on, Billy, it's not going to be that bad. You'll just have to keep out of their way. I'm sure you'll find someone else to love and care for before too long."

"Well, I'm not!" he snaps back. He turns away from her to shovel some more muck and then slowly turns back. "Sorry, Lettie, I didn't mean to snap your head off." He quickly rubs his sleeve across his eyes. "Would you do me a favour, when you go back in? Would you bring out the newspaper for me to check the job vacancies, when they've finished with it, please?"

"Of course I will. I'll go and check now."

He watches her go, as she rushes back into the kitchen for him, and sighs. *This place has always been like home to me, and the staff my family. How will I ever find anywhere as good as this?*

She returns with the newspaper and they sit on the mounting block, side by side, her wild curls confined under her mob cap and his mousy locks under his tweed cap almost touching, as they peruse the advertisements. Lettie, quicker at reading than he is, having had more schooling, soon spots a position as 'groom and trainer' immediately available at Hatherleigh Farm, near Wincanton. "Oh dear, it's miles away. We'll never see you, Billy."

"Well, that's the idea, isn't it?"

"I s'pose so. But Wincanton was where the man was murdered!"

"Well, that's not going to affect me, is it?" He laughs at her.

"Hopefully not." She smiles uncertainly, her dimples deepening. "Do you think you'd like being a trainer, as well as a groom?"

"Yes, I think I would. I've heard John Moore talking about how they have huge, well-organised race meetings somewhere near Wincanton, on Easter Mondays."

"Well, if you really think you'd enjoy it, perhaps you should compose a letter and apply for the position."

"I will. Would you help me, Lettie, by checking my spelling? Two heads are better than one."

"I'll do my best. Do you have some writing paper?"

"No, I'll have to ask Gareth for some, and he'll want to know what I want it for."

"I'll get you some, Billy, when no one's looking. You don't really want everyone knowing your intentions, until you've been offered a position, do you?"

"No." He pauses, daunted by the prospect of leaving. Then he looks up at her. "Thank you, Lettie. I'm very grateful for your help."

Billy is surprised when a few weeks later he receives a letter. It is the first letter he has ever received. Gareth looks intrigued as he passes it to him in the kitchen with everyone there looking on and filled with curiosity. He looks at Lettie and she smiles encouragement. He takes up a knife and slits the envelope open. His whole life could change depending on the contents of this letter.

4

He reads the contents and doesn't know whether to laugh or cry; he has been offered the position. He shows the missive to Lettie, who hugs him. "I knew you could do it," she whispers.

"Is this something you'd like to share with us, Billy?" asks Gareth diplomatically.

"I've been offered a job at Hatherleigh Farm, near Wincanton, and I have to decide whether or not to take it."

Gareth, realising that Billy is shocked, responds. "Perhaps I might suggest you discuss it with Lord Dryer, before you make any hasty decisions, Billy."

"Yes, sir, might you organise this for me please, Mr Williams?"

"Leave it to me, Billy."

John Moore looks offended. "You kept that under your cap, lad."

"I'm sorry, John. I didn't want to tell you or Edwin, until I knew whether or not I'd got the job. There was no use stirring up the pot, if it was all to come to nowt."

"We've been a good equestrian team, we three. You'll be sorely missed, Billy, lad. Do you have to go?"

"It's for personal reasons I feel I must go and seek new pastures. Nothing to do with my job here. I've always loved it. You've been a good friend and teacher to me, John, and Edwin has been a good mate, too. I'm gutted I should leave, but I think it'll be for the best. I'll speak to His Lordship first, though, and see what he recommends."

Billy stands before Lord Dryer later that day, his heart pumping with anxiety, lest His Lordship might think him ungrateful, throwing the security of a good job and living quarters back in his face. Gareth, who has shown him in to Lord Dryer's study, remains standing to attention beside the door.

Lord Dryer leans back in his chair regarding him. Then he speaks softly, "Billy, I'm very sorry to hear you're thinking of leaving us, for you've been a good and loyal member of my staff, ever since I first came to Alvington Manor fifteen years ago and you'll be sorely missed by us all. Is there anything I can do to persuade you to stay?"

He plucks up the courage to look his boss in the eye. "That's most kind of you, my lord, but it's for personal reasons that I'm considering leaving here. Even though this job will be an advancement, as I'll also be a trainer, I wouldn't be looking for new pastures if it wasn't for my final acceptance that the love of my life is lost to me forever, to a man I despise."

"I've no wish to pry into your private business, Billy, but you're still a young man and things may feel raw now, but surely in time you'll feel ready to set your sights on another. You may find more consolation in having your friends around you."

"I've given it a lot of thought, my lord, and I believe I need a fresh start. Making new friends and settling into a new job, and new surroundings, will help keep my mind off more depressing matters."

"I understand and I'd like to say now, that if this new position doesn't work out for you, you'd be welcome to come back here. I'll not need to replace you, as Edwin, who has been our excellent and adaptable 'Man Friday', can take on all your duties working with John. When are you intending to leave?"

"Well, my lord, as soon as you give me leave to go, really."

Joshua looks at his calendar. "There is only just over a week to the end of this month, so shall we say the 31st October, Billy? Would that suit you?"

"Yes, my lord, it will give me time to make all the arrangements."

"How are you planning to travel there?"

"I was hoping to hitch a ride on the mail coach."

"There will be no need to do that. John can drive you there."

"Thank you, my lord, that is a load off my mind."

He addresses his butler. "Gareth, as it will be All Hallows' Eve, I suspect Flora and the rest of the staff will want to arrange a party in Billy's honour that day."

He blushes in embarrassment. "Oh no, my lord, I don't want no fuss."

His employer continues regardless. "Well, I think that is a matter for you, Gareth. I'll leave it in your capable hands."

This sentence has a sense of finality and Billy bows respectfully. Gareth nods his head in acknowledgment. "Of course, my lord."

"A party is the least we can do, Billy, to show you how much you'll be missed as a member of the team here."

Flora, proud to be cook, busies herself baking soul cakes, gingerbread, and doughnuts. Billy enters the kitchen that morning overwhelmed by the tantalising aromas of ginger, nutmeg and cinnamon. He watches her stirring the raisins into the mixing bowl. Hattie, the kitchen maid, dusted with flour, rolls out the pastry for egg and bacon, pumpkin, and apple pies, while Ellie, the scullery maid, prepares the pumpkin and cooking apples at the sink. Billy swallows, tempted by the mouth-watering, sweet-scented foods.

"Are you excited, Billy?" asks Hattie.

He sighs, "A mixture of anxiety and excitement, I'd say, Hattie, but it'll be an adventure and will hopefully prove a happy distraction."

Hattie looks up from her kneading. "I hope so, Billy. For 'tis a big step, leaving us after all this time. How many years have you been here now?"

"Umm, must be nigh on nineteen, Elsie."

"It won't be the same without you, Billy," says Flora. She puts the tray of soul cakes into the hot oven.

The remainder of the staff wander in for their morning cup of tea, and all comment on the wonderful smells pervading the kitchen. Lettie hugs her mother. "You're doing us proud, Ma, as always."

Her mother whisks the bowl away, before Lettie can sample the uncooked cake mix. "Oh, Ma!" she protests.

"Guest of honour's perks," she replies, passing the wooden spoon to Billy with a cheeky wink.

The following morning, riding pillion beside John, Billy reflects on the warmth of his farewell party. He had enjoyed rather a lot of mulled cider, and had danced and kissed Beth Puddy in a way that probably gave her the wrong idea, considering he was thinking of Lucy all the while. It was sweet of Miss Aurora and Master Gabriel to join them and the apple bobbing had been great fun, especially when Edwin had tried his best to push his sister's head under the water and she had tipped the bowl of water and apples all over him. Although everyone had burst out laughing, Mrs Abbott was none too pleased, but Edwin picked up all the apples and mopped up the water from the flagstones and they all began again.

Billy smiles to himself at the memories. The gamekeepers, John Boucher and Raymond Hawkins had roasted nuts for them all and Lucy's family from Home Farm, Isaac and Beth, Jacob and Rosa's husband, Malachi and their little ones all came to say goodbye to him, the children proudly holding aloft their jack-o'-lanterns. For him it had been merciful that Lucy was over at Bingham Manor with Ashleigh, for otherwise she would have come with her family and that would have meant for him a painful parting. All the folk from the tied cottages on Camp Road wandered down Pound Lane to join in the fun, and much mead, apple cider, mulled wine and mulled cider was consumed, along with all the tasty food.

He had been shocked when, at the end of the evening, Lord and Lady Dryer had come downstairs with a farewell gift for him. He had unwrapped the present self-consciously and was thrilled and overwhelmed with gratitude to discover they had presented him with a brand-new riding crop, a pair of leather, short-top riding boots, plus an additional month's salary.

They are on the last leg of their journey, travelling down Lawrence Hill, when Billy spots the sign to Hatherleigh Farm ahead on his right and anxiety knots his stomach. They turn off the main road and find the farm track to be bumpy and rutted, not as well maintained as the carriageways around Alvington Manor and his anxiety increases, as they see the farmhouse, stables and outbuildings. Then he spots a young woman outside feeding the chickens, who waves to them cheerily. *Perhaps it will not be so bad after all.* The young woman must be in her mid-twenties and she walks across to greet them. Addressing John Moore, she says, "Hello, I'm Victoria, who shall I say is calling?"

Billy answers her assertively, "Good morning, Victoria, I'm Billy Riddick, come to start my new job, and this is John Moore, who has kindly brought me."

"You'd better come inside and see me ma. Pa is over in eight-acres field, fixing some fencing with my brother."

The two men clamber down from the gig, stiff from their journey. They stretch their limbs before following Victoria into the farmhouse.

Victoria's mother is baking in the kitchen and the agreeable pastry smell wafts out to meet them as they walk through the ground floor. Billy looks around him at the highly polished furniture, scatter rugs, comfy cushioned sofa and matching armchairs. They enter a large square kitchen with an oak dresser overflowing with a variety of colourful chinaware. Mrs Yates is a good-looking woman with her chestnut hair tidied in a neat bun and her clothes swamped by a large floral apron. She turns and smiles, as they enter her domain.

"Ah! There you are! Pleased to meet you, Billy. I won't shake your hand, dearie, or you'll be covered in flour."

"Pleased to meet you, ma'am. This is my friend, John Moore. I was wondering if you might spare a drink for him before he returns home."

"Of course, take a seat both of you and I'll wash

my hands and serve you up a ploughman's. How long have you been on the road?"

"We left at sun-up, so not bad going at all really. At least the weather has been clement."

The food tastes delicious; home-baked bread still warm from the oven, tasty homemade pickle, and butter and cheese made from the milk of their own cattle. Nothing less than he would have received from the kitchen at Alvington Manor. He is feeling quite optimistic when the door opens and Mr Yates and his son enter. Both are of a similar stature to Billy himself, who has always felt dwarfed by other fellows, so he is pleasantly surprised to feel something in common with this family. Although the farmer appears stocky and muscular, his son's physique is immature, but they both have the same unruly curly brown hair, though the father's is thinning and going grey at the temples.

"Good morning, gentlemen. Which one of you is Billy Riddick?"

He stands up. "I am, sir."

"Good to meet you, lad. You're a sight for sore eyes, that you are. It looks to me that you're the ideal size and weight for the job." They shake hands and he feels the effects of muscles developed over many years working the land.

He turns to John. "And this is John Moore, the head groom from Alvington Manor, who has kindly delivered me, sir."

"Good day, John. We are indebted to you."

John also stands to shake hands with the farmer. "It's my pleasure. Billy has been a real blessing over the years at Alvington. He has an instinctive understanding of the horses in his charge and I'm sure he'll be a great asset to you, Mr..."

"Yates, Bob Yates, and this is my sixteen-year-old son, Don."

"Pleased to meet you, Don. I hope we'll all get along very well together." Billy shakes hands with the young man, a little disappointed that he doesn't make eye contact. He assumes the lad must be shy.

"Once we've eaten I'll show you your cottage, Billy. It's at the other side of the racecourse, back near the entrance onto the London Road at Lawrence Hill. You'd have passed it on your way here."

"How long have you been holding race meetings here, Mr Yates?" asks John Moore.

"Well, as far as I know, they've been having meetings here ever since the turn of the century, with regular Easter Monday fixtures and other matches in between. I believe it was my great, great uncle who organised an event to celebrate his son's twenty-first birthday and invited his pals and local farmers and landowners to take part. It was so successful that it has evolved into the Wincanton Hunt Steeplechases, which now have to be run under the 1865 National Hunt rules."

"It sounds most exciting, sir. What exactly will my duties be?"

"Well, Billy, we have four horses, two shires, Samson and Delilah, for heavy work such as the ploughing, a pony for the trap, called Melody and our bay thoroughbred racehorse, Bay Rum, which can be traced back to the foundation sire, the Darley Arabian." Bob Yates sits down at the table next to his son. "Donny here will help with the mucking out sometimes, but he does have other duties around the farm with the dairy herd, so you're responsible for the horses' well-being. You'll need to ensure that they're kept well-groomed, clean and healthy and their coats and hooves are in the best possible condition. I expect you to spend most of your time with Bay Rum and assess her emotional needs on a day-to-day basis. You'll be responsible for Bay Rum's exercise schedule and making sure she's in the peak of health when due to perform, or alert the veterinary surgeon should any problems occur. It's your job to wash her down after a race and gently exercise her by 'cool walking' her, after being on the track. You and she need to build up a rapport, because, considering you're the ideal size, I think, if things go well, you'll likely be called upon to be her jockey."

Billy, wide-eyed, looks at John Moore and grins.

John's eyebrows are raised in surprise. "Well, mate, that's a turn up. I wasn't expecting that. I can't wait to tell Edwin! He'll be greatly impressed."

Back at Alvington Manor, Edwin has been left in charge of the stables while John conveys Billy to his new employment. He has been working as a Man Friday for ten years now and knows the estate and all its nooks and crannies well, but he loves working with the horses and, although he will miss Billy terribly, he is happy to be able to step into his shoes. He hears the crunch of the carriage wheels on the gravel and steps outside to help John.

"Hey, Ed, how has it been?"

"No problems, John, all is well here. How did Billy get on?"

"I think the lucky sod has fallen on his feet there, Ed. The family all seem very wholesome and supportive, and the old man, Bob Yates, reckons Billy will be their jockey, if he takes to it." Both men and horse are puffing out misty breath, as the night chill descends and they are busy unhitching Perseus.

"Saints alive! I bet he was tickled pink."

"I think so, Ed. He looked a bit happier than he has been lately, when I left him, so perhaps he has made the right decision after all." John leads the horse into the stable. "I reckon he'll be made to feel like one of the family there, and that's something he's always longed for."

Edwin follows him in and fills the manger with oats for the animal. "I hope so. If anyone deserves to be happy, Billy does."

In Ivell, the butcher, Bobby Tompkins is leaning against a gas lamp post in Addlewell Lane, waiting patiently for his sweetheart, Amy, to leave work, when he catches sight of her with Jean Hawkins, chatting merrily as they exit the glove factory building, followed by a stream of men, laughing and wolf-whistling at the two girls. Amy's face is animated as she ignores the catcalls and talks to her friend, before Jean clambers up into the works wagon that will take her home to Odcombe, and Amy waves goodbye.

Bobby feels a warm glow of happiness as he watches her. He has loved her ever since they first met, when he used to deliver meat to Summerville House and she was the kitchen maid there. Now, having escaped the clutches of the evil Nathan Meakins with the help of her friend, Jean Hawkins, she lodges with his family in the borough, while she and Bobby are saving hard to get married. He smiles to himself. *How wonderful would it be to get a place of our own, to start a family and to see Amy happily surrounded by our children?*

Suddenly breaking into his thoughts one of the young men calls out, "How about you meet me in

Grope Lane later, Amy. I'll give you something to remember me by." He has his hands at his crotch rubbing himself crudely.

Bobby bunches his fists in anger, his heart thumping as the adrenalin rushes through him. He steps forward to take Amy's arm and pulls himself up to his full height to focus on the impudent upstart. "You come anywhere near her, you'll have me to deal with," he growls. "She's not some cheap slut who'd consider going with the likes of you!"

The man snorts, "Huh! You don't look like no member of the upper classes yourself, me old mate. What makes you think you're better'n me, I'd like to know?"

Amy pulls him away, saying loudly, "Ignore him, Bobby, everyone else does. He's new, brought in from the workhouse and hasn't learned his manners yet, but someone's sure to put him in his place sooner or later. The bosses won't tolerate him for much longer."

"He needs to watch his step, or I'll be the one to teach him his manners," Bobby replies at the same volume, his eyes still on the insolent lout. Then lowering his voice, "Who is he, anyway?"

"Come on, let's not hang around and cause a commotion that'll attract the bosses," she says. They walk on up Mill Lane and follow Back Street, up into Wine Street.

As they go, Amy tells Bobby, "He's Albert Tattershall from the Ivell workhouse." Amy glances over her shoulder and then whispers, "And he bullied my brother, Edwin, for the short time he was an inmate there, until Lord Dryer took him on."

"Well, he'd better not think he can bully you, Amy, for I'll not stand for it. Promise me you'll tell me if he tries anything like that again."

"I promise, Bobby, but please don't worry. I'd never go near him when I've you to take care of me." She reaches up to plant a kiss on his burning cheek, then looks over her shoulder, relieved to see that Tattershall has sloped off somewhere out of sight.

Unbeknown to Amy, Bobby decides to discuss the situation with her brother, Edwin, and the next time his butcher's delivery route takes him near to the manor, he calls in to speak with him. He finds Edwin at the back of the stables loading a wheelbarrow with matured horse muck to be put around the roses. "Morning, Ed. Do you have a moment to talk with me about Amy?"

Edwin leans his pitchfork against the barrow and moves away from the ripe smelling manure heap. "Of course I do. Why, what's wrong?"

"Do you remember a fellow called Albert Tattershall?"

Edwin sighs, "I'll never forget him. He's a nasty piece of work, he is. Why?" He frowns. "What's he got to do with our Amy?"

"He's started work at the factory and it seems he's taken a shine to her. He was calling out obscene suggestions and upsetting her, as she left work the other night and I want to nip it in the bud, before things get more serious. He needs to be put back in his place, Ed. I fear for Amy's safety while he's around."

"I agree with you, Bobby. He was the bane of my life for the short while I was in the workhouse. If only we could get him sacked from the factory, the women would be safer."

"Perhaps if we kidnapped him, so he couldn't turn up for work, he'd be disciplined then."

Edwin laughs. "True, but so would we be, for he'd never keep his silence. I don't think you've thought this through, have you, Bobby? Where would we hide him for a start?"

Bobby shrugs. "I'm desperate, Ed. But I truly think all bullies are weak cowards and if we could beat him up and teach him a lesson, then maybe he'd respect us and leave Amy alone. He might be too scared to tell on us then."

"True, but Bobby, I can tell you now, he has a mean streak and we'd have to do him over good and proper to intimidate him sufficiently."

Bobby ponders, "If only Billy hadn't left; we could do with an extra man now." Suddenly he grins. "I know who could help us, Ed! Your mate, Malachi! He could give us some boxing lessons, so we could really show the bastard we mean business."

"That's not a bad suggestion, Bobby. I'll speak to him tomorrow and see if we can't arrange some coaching for both of us."

For a few weeks, the two men train secretly with Malachi in the hay barn. They both enjoy the rough and tumble of wrestling together and despite a few bruises they learn a lot of good basic pugilism techniques and a few clever tricks. Malachi has them doing some weightlifting to further develop their muscles, plus skipping and jumping. They soon feel fitter and more confident, but eventually Amy notices how her brother and her beau are going missing regularly and the next time it happens, she challenges him. "What are you and Eddy up to, Bobby. You're both as thick as thieves lately. Where do you both go every Saturday afternoon?"

Bobby hesitates before confessing, "Malachi has been teaching us some self-defence moves and we're joining him in his fitness training. Do you see the difference it's making?" He holds out his forearm for her to test his muscles.

"Hmm, very impressive." She looks at him suspiciously. "What has brought this on?"

"Oh, your Eddy and I were chatting the other day and we thought it would be good for us to get fitter, and we've both really enjoyed working out with Malachi. He's such a great bloke."

Amy has always been in awe of the farmer and bare-knuckle boxer, The Magnificent Malachi, and although Bobby's developing muscles do not yet compare with Malachi's, there is no doubt she can feel the change in Bobby, when he holds her in his strong arms, and she is not averse to feeling the strength of those muscles.

"Just don't you go getting too cocky, Bobby, and getting yourself and our Eddy into trouble."

"You've no worries on that score, sweetheart, you know we're not troublemakers, but it would be nice to think we can defend our loved ones if the need arises." He gives her a warm hug and she nestles in his arms, grateful for his love and protection.

The next time they are all together, Malachi is punching the suspended grain sack swinging from the rafters of the barn, demonstrating the upper cut, left and right hook, the jab and the knock-out blow, which he tells them needs to be aimed up under their opponent's chin.

They each have a practice and then Beth Warren interrupts proceedings by bringing them out a plate of bread and cheese. They all take a break and sit on a pile of corn stooks to eat, while a few chickens bravely return to peck the ground around them.

"How are things progressing with the wedding plans, Malachi?" asks Edwin.

"Ma's very busy stitching the handmaidens' gowns for my sister, Bunny, and my little uns, Ruby and Daisy, and they're all very excited, as you can imagine. I think everything's going to plan, although in many ways I wish it wasn't."

Bobby looks surprised. "Oh! Why's that?"

"Well, between you and me, I think both Ashleigh and Rupert Seymour are arrogant toffs with no ambition, who are lazy and usually drunk. Therefore, I don't consider Ashleigh Seymour a good enough match for our Lucy, regardless of how well off they're purported to be!"

"What exactly do they do?" asks Edwin.

"Good question. They're a couple of idlers who seem to spend all their time either at the races, cockfighting, or at the Black Panther Club, drinking and gambling with their side-kicks. Lucy goes along with them to the club sometimes. She likes to play the piano for them, but I can't see how it will have a happy ending, when she's at home with her children and he's always out carousing."

Bobby exclaims, "The family must be loaded, if neither of the sons are working!"

Malachi shrugs. "Rumour has it that they've established an informal bookmakers' business at the club and with all their fox hunting and cockfighting cronies they're making a mint."

Edwin feels sorry for Malachi, knowing how he would feel if his sister, Amy, was betrothed to someone he loathed. He tries to console him. "Well, your Lucy is a sensible lass, she must be confident he'll always care for her. But I must say that Billy

19

worshipped her. If only she could have loved him back, I know he'd never have let her down."

Bobby interjects, "But he couldn't have provided her with a big house like the Seymours have."

Edwin thinks about this and counters, "No, true, but if she's going to live there, she'll be under the influence of Colonel and Mrs Seymour, as well as her husband and won't be mistress of her own home. At least if she'd married Billy they'd have had their own place," he nods towards Malachi, "even if it was a tied cottage like you have with Rosa."

Bobby says, thoughtfully, "Well, there's no explaining why some people fall for each other, and it seems to me women often fall for the rogue rather than the regular guy, like poor old Billy."

Malachi stands up and shakes the crumbs off his overalls. "She's made her decision and there's nothing I can do to change that, but I'll have something to say, if that toff doesn't look after her."

CHAPTER TWO *(May 1867)*

ASHLEIGH AND LUCY'S WEDDING

At Alvington Manor, Louisa has given her lady's maid, Rosa, the day off to prepare her children for the marriage of their Auntie Lucy, to Ashleigh Seymour. Therefore, Nanny Beth helps Aurora and Gabriel dress for the occasion, while she herself copes alone, going through her closet to find an appropriate outfit that will complement her daughter's beautiful aquamarine frock.

She finds a jade gown with matching mantelet, which she has always thought particularly lovely and after enlisting Lettie to help lace her corset, she dons the gown. She then tries to contain her unruly red curls with a neat little bonnet and hatpin. Rosa would have made a much better job of it, but it's the Warren family's day today and she must manage as best she can.

As the time draws near to leave, Aurora and Gabriel are summoned down to the front hall and Joshua appraises them with a glint of pleasure in his dark eyes. "You all look delightful. Are we ready to go?"

"Yes, Papa," says Aurora.

"I've been ready for ages," says Gabriel despondently.

She adjusts Gabriel's collar and cravat and smiles. "Come along then. It's a glorious day. Let's climb aboard the landau. John is driving us there and will call back later to collect us."

They set off up Pound Lane towards Camp Road with the morning sunshine glinting on the polished brass of the carriage. They pass number three and wave at Luke and Lilly who are helping their mother in the vegetable garden.

While they travel along the lanes together, Louisa decides to broach a subject she has been dreading, certain that her daughter will vehemently resist the idea. "Aurora, your papa and I have something to discuss with you." She pauses and looks at Joshua for encouragement. "We've been thinking that it might be the right time for you to consider a finishing school for young ladies and we wondered if you would like to go off to Switzerland for a year, starting this September, to Lausanne Manor? It's in the centre of Lausanne and the school grounds have views of the Swiss Alps and Lake Geneva. It sounds beautiful. Doesn't it, Papa?"

Joshua smiles. "It does."

"What do you think, darling?"

Aurora looks horrified. "No, Mama, I don't want to leave you and Papa. I'm happy here with Miss Tweedy. She is teaching me French and all the other things I'll need, to find myself a fitting husband."

Joshua intercedes. "Don't be too hasty, darling. All the Bridewell girls attended there and their parents were singing its praises the last time we saw them."

Louisa tries a little persuasion. "Besides, look how many new girlfriends you'd make, dear."

Aurora's brows are predictably drawn together in a stubborn frown. "But I don't want to go off all on my own to a foreign country."

She tries to reassure her. "You need have no fear, darling. They teach in English and French and your French will improve immeasurably with this extra tuition. I believe they also take you to St Moritz to learn to ski."

"What use will that be, living here!" Aurora protests. "It'll be a waste of money, Papa. Please don't send me away."

She looks at Joshua apprehensively, and he says, "Look, Aurora, we don't intend forcing you to go, but we both believe it will be in your best interest and so I want you to think about it carefully. In the meantime, I'll send for a prospectus, so you'll be able to see all that the school has to offer."

Louisa adds, "The Bridewell sisters may be at the wedding and if so, you can talk to them about it and see how much they enjoyed it."

Joshua also continues trying to persuade his daughter. "These finishing schools are designed to give you confidence, Rora."

"Yes, darling, look how well Keziah's doing; she was even brave enough to go off to the Crimea to nurse with Florence Nightingale and has returned betrothed to Captain James Blakely. I doubt she'd have been so brave, had she not already travelled abroad to charm school."

Aurora shakes her head. "But I'll miss you all so."

Louisa puts her arm around her daughter, and says gently, "It'll only be for one year, but don't distress yourself now, let's wait until Papa has more information for us."

There is for the rest of the journey an uncomfortable silence. The coach travels through East Coker and then turns right onto the Corscombe road, where they pass under the new railway bridge and across the causeway to the other side of Sutton Bingham Lake. Here they all disembark outside the little church and John Moore returns to Alvington Manor with the coach.

The church of All Saints at Sutton Bingham is colourfully decorated with large purple rhododendron blooms, white azaleas, pink foxgloves and blowsy blushing peonies along with greenery, trailing ferns and ivies all cut from the gardens of Bingham Manor.

The small thirteenth-century building, set in a tranquil spot close to the shores of Sutton Bingham Lake, is part of the Bingham estate. Generations of Ashleigh's family have been christened, married and buried there.

Lucy had helped with the pedestals and supervised the floral arrangements decorating the font and the windowsills the previous evening. Now, as she walks down the aisle on the arm of her father, she is overcome by a feeling of foreboding as Hattie's saying, 'Married in May and rue the day' sneaks into her subconscious mind.

She follows her flower girl, five-year-old Daisy, who sprinkles the aisle with rose petals, before her. In a procession trailing behind her is Eli, her nephew, page boy and ring-bearer, with his older sister Ruby, and her own younger sister Bunny, as handmaidens.

Ahead of her stands Ashleigh and his older brother Rupert, as best man. She is sure she loves Ashleigh, but like the rest of her family she is superstitious and cannot believe she had never heard the ominous rhyme, before the wedding date was set and the invitations all sent out. Now she cannot help worrying that their nuptials will be cursed. Her hand trembles on her father's arm and her legs feel unsteady as she walks towards her future husband.

Then he turns and smiles at her and a warm glow of happiness pushes aside all her fears. He looks so handsome and dapper standing beside his older brother, in his black morning coat, white embroidered waistcoat and lavender doeskin trousers. His cravat and gloves are of a slightly darker shade of mauve. Both men have buttonholes of white roses and fine ferns. Little Daisy steps to one side, as she and her father draw level with the two men, and the vicar commences with the ceremony. She stands beneath the wide, dog-tooth carved archway, the shafts of light flooding in from the stained-glass window above the altar and the perfume of the sweet peas and lily of the valley in her wedding bouquet wafts around her.

While they are repeating their vows, Lucy is conscious of all her family and friends sitting behind her and Ashleigh's too behind him, but she does not hesitate. She is on the brink of a new and exciting life and a silly superstition is not going to stop her from enjoying this wonderful day.

Ashleigh looks at his future bride, in one glance taking in her modest wedding gown with its layers of lace-edged taffeta and its high-necked, delicately appliqued, sweetheart bodice and he cannot wait to undo all the tiny buttons down the back. He has never seen her naked and from this day she will be his to do with as he wishes. No longer will he have to pay for the whores at the club; he is going to have a loving wife who will be happy to do all they did and more because she loves him.

He grins at her and is rewarded with a radiant smile just visible beneath her fine gauze veil. His little Lucy is going to make him the happiest man alive!

Ruby trembles with excitement. This is the best day of her life thus far. She has never worn a veil and coronet before. She smooths her white muslin gown and looks down at her new lilac shoes and stockings that match her ribbon sash. She has a long gown like Bunny's even though she is only ten. Her little sister Daisy looks so cute in her shorter version, sitting next to their mama, shuffling her feet and fidgeting, until Mama has a quiet word with her. Younger brother, Eli, dressed in a purple velvet suit with white silk hose and black buckled shoes stands to attention with the purple velvet cushion holding the rings held before him, patiently waiting for his big moment.

Ruby looks at her papa. He is her hero and she is pleased to know how proud he is of his family today, because when they were all ready to leave their cottage, he had lined them all up in their passageway and standing before them with his arm around Mama, he had told them he had never been prouder.

Her little brother steps forward with the rings and the vicar proceeds to bless the rings by saying, "Heavenly Father, by your blessing let these rings be to Ashleigh and Lucy a symbol of unending love and faithfulness, to remind them of the vow and covenant which they have made this day through Jesus Christ our Lord."

Ruby says 'Amen' with the rest of the congregation. She watches Ashleigh placing the smaller ring on the fourth finger of her auntie's left hand, and holding it there, he says, "Lucy, I give you this ring as a sign of our marriage. With my body, I honour you, all that I am I give to you, and all that I have I share with you, within the love of God the Father, Son and Holy Spirit."

Her auntie next takes the remaining ring and repeats the promise.

The minister then says, "In the presence of God and before this congregation Ashleigh and Lucy have given their consent and made their marriage vows to each other. They have declared their marriage by the joining of hands and by the giving and receiving of rings. I therefore proclaim that they are husband and wife."

The minister joins their hands together and says, "Those whom God has joined together let no one put asunder." Then he looks at Ashleigh and says, "You may kiss your bride."

Ashleigh lifts Lucy's veil and kisses his wife triumphantly and then, as husband and wife, they kneel for prayers.

Ruby is thinking how romantic it is, when she spots a large black beetle crawling in her direction. She watches in horror as it slowly nears her left foot and is about to climb onto her pretty lilac shoe. She steps surreptitiously to one side, looking up guiltily lest anyone has noticed, but thankfully, all the congregation are focused on the ceremony and, with their eyes closed, they are praying, but the stupid beetle has changed course and is still aiming for her left shoe. She is so focused on dodging the beetle that she misses most of the ceremony and soon the blessing of the marriage is over and the vicar leads the bride and groom and their parents to one side to sign the marriage register.

Folk relax in the absence of the minister and some of the congregation move around to chat with friends. In the process the beetle is squished and Ruby feels sorry she didn't rescue it, but she didn't want it climbing on her, so in a way it is a relief.

When they all return from signing the register they sing 'Praise my Soul the King of Heaven', then there are more prayers until finally they say the Lord's Prayer and Ruby knows this one by heart.

There is one more prayer from the vicar and it is all over. The organist plays some pretty music and Ruby follows her auntie and her new uncle out into the sunshine.

Outside the church Lucy throws her bouquet high in the air towards the gathering young ladies waiting to catch it. Aurora is there, as well as the Bridewell sisters, but Clara Fairway grasps it triumphantly. Lucy and Ashleigh are then bombarded with handfuls of rice as they all process across the lane and into the grounds of Bingham Manor where there is a long tent set out with tables for the feasting, and a tintype collodion photographic booth for the guests.

She and her new husband welcome all the guests before their serving girls pass around glasses of Pimms No. 1 Cup, as everyone gravitates towards their friends to natter and gossip.

Rupert taps a spoon against his glass to get everyone's attention. "Before we all gather for the wedding breakfast, the wedding party is going to pose for Mr Gosney to take their likeness, with his tintype camera, so please meander and enjoy the lakeside grounds and enjoy the Pimms. Once the main photographs are taken, I'm sure Mr Gosney will be more than happy to take further family groups if anyone wishes to purchase them." He turns to his brother. "Come, let us organise ourselves. Ash, you stand to the left of me, and Lucy beside you; come, handmaidens and young Eli, arrange yourselves around us. Mr Gosney, we'd like the lake to be in the background, if you please… that will be perfect… thank you."

Mr Gosney then instructs them, "You must all stand very still," as he makes some adjustments under the blackout cloth. They all stand frozen in time for what seems like ages. Suddenly there is a blinding flash, a loud bang and a puff of smoke from the flash-lamp and the photographer rushes off to his orange booth. The children are excited to see the result, but Lucy is concerned that maybe little Daisy did not stay still enough, for she could sense her moving slightly.

It is not long before Mr Gosney returns with a perfect image of the wedding group on a thin piece of japanned iron. Lucy is delighted and calls for her immediate family to gather around her. "Come, Mama and Papa, and you, Malachi, Rosa and Jacob, join me and the children for a Warren family picture." They are all eager to see this magic repeated and remain statue-still until the final flash and bang.

Lucy is pleased to see how surprised, delighted and impressed her brother, Malachi, is with the result. "I'd never have thought it possible to get such a clear impression of the whole family together like this, Luce. How much are they?"

"Mr Gosney says that this size will be ten shillings and sixpence."

"Crikey, that's a lot of money, but I think it's worth it. I'd like one and I'm sure Ma would like one too."

While Ashleigh organises his own relations, Lucy speaks to Mr Gosney. "Thank you so much, Mr Gosney. We're all very pleased with the photographs. They're a perfect memento of our wedding day."

"Well, my dear Mrs Seymour, you are most fortunate, for this is the first time I've used my new camera, with the right-angled prism, which means you get a true image, rather than a mirror image as before."

"How fortuitous, Mr Gosney. I was wondering though, whether it would be possible for us to have more than one copy of each photograph?"

"Of course, madam. However, this will mean you posing again."

"Very well, I will gather my relations together again. In the meantime, please don't let me detain you, as Ashleigh's family are awaiting their turn."

Mr Gosney hurries off to prepare for the Seymours' photograph and Lucy calls for her group to be ready for the next opportunity. Then she spots Lord and Lady Dryer, with Aurora and Gabriel, chatting to Ambrose Fairway and his daughter, Clara, who still clutches the wedding bouquet. She wanders over to them and dips a curtsey. "Are you going to pose for a portrait, my lord?"

"Well," he turns to Louisa, who eagerly nods her head in assent, "we would certainly like to, if there is time."

"We will make time for you, my lord. Come, you will be first in the queue, after our family. How about you and Clara, Mr Fairway?"

"We actually had one taken in Mr Gosney's studio last month to celebrate Clara's thirty-third birthday, so we'll stand aside for others to take advantage of this beautiful setting, but thank you, Lucy."

Eventually Mr Gosney has repeated the main wedding group and both sides of the family several times and his work is completed.

It turns out that each of the Warren group photographs are slightly different, but Malachi and Rosa, especially, are thrilled with their copy.

Malachi proudly shows his mother. "To have captured all the family together, three generations all dressed in our Sunday best, with our three little ones looking particularly handsome in their wedding costumes in the foreground, is amazing."

They are comparing images, when Rupert announces that the guests might take their seats for the wedding breakfast. They all sit down to a sumptuous feast with champagne for the toasts and the long tent buzzes with the happy chatter of the progressively more inebriated guests.

At the end of the best man's speech, Rupert surprises everyone by announcing that he is to set sail for Cape Town in a matter of weeks. Ashleigh is stunned by this devastating news and later takes his brother to one side. "What's going on, Rupert? You haven't said a word about this to me. How long have you been planning this?"

He is satisfied to note that Rupert is suitably abashed. "I'm sorry, old chap, but Pa met with an old colleague of his recently in London. This man is looking for adventurers to travel to South Africa where he says a huge diamond has been discovered on the south bank of the Orange River in the Northern Cape Province. It's been called the Eureka diamond and it weighs over four grams. Pa has some money he'd like to invest in land over there too, and wants me to investigate in the area between the confluence of the Vaal and Orange rivers. This is my chance, Ash, to make some serious money. Please don't mess it up for me."

Ashleigh sighs. How he'd have loved to go on such an adventure with his older brother, but it's too late now. He's made his vows and he has a wife to care for. It wouldn't be appropriate to take her away from her family to a savage land, where his brother will most likely be living in a tented community, as in the Californian gold rush.

Rupert takes his arm. "Look, Ash, you've been preoccupied with your wedding to Lucy. I didn't want to distract you in any way from that. You're not the only one who I'm going to be disappointing. When poor Clara caught Lucy's bouquet she gave me such a happy, meaningful glance, but she's going to have to wait until I establish myself over there, before I even consider whether there'll be a future for us together."

Clara feels completely neglected sitting at the banqueting table beside her father, with the scent of the wedding bouquet wafting around her. Her beau is preoccupied with his best man duties and now this latest bombshell! How could he announce he is leaving without even having mentioned it to her? He is supposed to love her. It has, in effect, terminated their engagement, for there is no way she would be prepared to leave her dear papa on his own, to travel to God knows where with Rupert to face an uncertain future in a foreign land.

Louisa and Lord Dryer approach them and she stands up and curtseys. Lord Dryer takes her father off to one side and Louisa sits down beside her. "You're a dark horse, Clara. I didn't know Rupert was going abroad to work!"

Clara replies, "No, neither did I, and I'm most perturbed that he didn't think me important enough to confide in, before blurting it out so publicly. His love for me must be fading fast, if he can't be troubled to keep me informed of this devastating plan of his. I feel so upset and angry with him."

"Oh, Clara, don't be disheartened. Maybe his trip will be short-lived and he'll return home sooner than you think."

"I still feel it would have been kinder to break it to me, before everyone else. I'll miss him so, Lou Lou."

"I know, my dear friend, but you still have us to look out for you and your dear papa."

"This is the thing, Louisa. If Rupert decides to make his life over there, I'll not leave my papa over here all alone. I couldn't do it. He must know this and not even care."

"I think he needs to make his way in the world. He's getting nowhere, drinking and carousing with Ashleigh all the time. Maybe this is a good thing, Clara. Maybe he'll quickly make his fortune in South Africa and return to Somerset an affluent man. Give him a chance to talk to you and tell you his plans, before you let him see how unsettled you are."

"He's had plenty of chances, but I fear he's avoiding me."

While Louisa and Clara are talking, Mr Fairway confides in Lord Dryer. "I'm afraid my selfish prospective son-in-law has upset my dear Clara with his untimely announcement."

"You mean she was unaware?"

"Yes, Joshua, she had no idea until he mentioned it earlier. I know she is quite overcome and I don't know how to comfort her. Since Lucy and Ashleigh

33

first announced their wedding plans, my Clara has been imagining her own marriage, and as Rupert is the eldest she's been worried that if he was serious, they'd have been the ones to wed first. Now it would appear he has other things on his mind and no intention of making her his bride."

"If you'd take my advice, I'd encourage Clara to think she's had a lucky escape, for both those boys are self-centred, wild and irresponsible and she's worth far more than Rupert Seymour is likely to offer."

"I'll do my best, but she's a sensitive soul and I fear she'll have no peace of mind after this." He looks across at his daughter and sees the tears welling in her eyes, as she confides in Louisa. It would not be the right time to join them and so he suggests they refill their glasses instead and return later with drinks for the ladies.

Finally, the children are permitted to run free and play in the grounds. Ruby oversees her siblings and they are happily letting off steam, playing tag. Gabriel, however, is curious about the orange photography booth and has sneaked off to take a peak. He has parted the blackout curtain, stepped inside and is looking at all the bottles of chemicals, when he is halted by the sound of Mr Gosney's angry words. "What the devil are you doing in here, lad?"

"I… I'm sorry, sir, I was just looking. I didn't touch anything, honestly."

"This place is out of bounds to the public, especially nosy young boys who might knock something over. I'm afraid I must report this behaviour to your father."

"Yes, sir. He is still in the tent, I believe, sir."

"Come, let us find him."

Gabriel is embarrassed that Mr Gosney is going to make an example of him in front of all the guests, but he has been taught to face up to his misdemeanours and so follows sheepishly behind the photographer. They pass by his sister, deep in conversation with Keziah and Alicia Bridewell. They find his father and mother, still seated next to the Fairways, talking together, so when Mr Gosney interrupts them, Lord Dryer looks down his nose at the man.

"I fortunately caught this young man inside my photographic laboratory before he was able to do any damage, but I wanted you to understand how important it is to keep the public from having access inside the booth. There are poisons in there enough to kill a man, like potassium cyanide."

"Thank you for bringing this to my attention, Mr Gosney, but surely it's your responsibility to prevent this, not mine?"

Mr Gosney is immediately defensive. "Well, I do have a sign saying 'No entry' on the booth."

His father replies with the authority of a Justice of the Peace, "Considering we have a certain percentage of the population who are unable to read, I trust that all poisons are locked in a secure container within. Otherwise I believe you would be in dereliction of duty, and I would be well within my powers to prosecute you."

Gabriel watches the man becoming flustered. "No, no, my lord, you're quite correct, the poisons are locked away, but my equipment is very expensive, and I don't like anyone touching it."

"I understand that, Mr Gosney." He turns to his son. "Gabriel, my lad, I trust you didn't touch anything?"

"No, Papa."

"And you have apologised for this intrusion?"

"Yes, Papa."

He smiles and turns back to the photographer. "Then no harm done."

The matter closed, Mr Gosney wanders off to find Ashleigh Seymour to be paid for his services.

Not long afterwards, John Moore arrives with the landau and the family gather together to say farewell to their friends and thank the bridal party and their hosts for inviting them to such an enjoyable celebration.

Days later, as it is overcast, Aurora has dressed in her prettiest embroidered poplin gown, and has walked up Pound Lane to wait outside John Moore's cottage for Luke. When he returns home from working in the solicitor's office with Mr Fairway, he spots her and breaks into a run, a huge smile brightening his face. *At least he seems pleased to see me.*

He reaches her, panting breathlessly. "What a nice surprise, Rora. What have I done to deserve this?"

She stands before him and puts her arms around his neck. "I just wanted to see you. I couldn't wait until Sunday." She can feel her eyes brimming with tears and sees a look of concern flick across Luke's face, before he takes her in his arms for a reassuring cuddle.

He looks down at her. "Tell me, whatever it is that's upset you?"

"Ma and Pa want to send me off to Switzerland to a finishing school." His mouth drops open in surprise. He's as devastated as she is. "I'm going to miss you so much, Luke. I don't want to go."

"How long will you be gone for?"

"A whole year!"

He sighs. "It will seem like ages while you're gone, Rora. I'll be so lonely without you."

"Pa says he won't force me, but they're both so sure it'll be the best thing for me, I can't see them giving up on the idea easily."

"What's so special about this school?"

"Well, I was talking to Alicia and Keziah Bridewell at the wedding on Sunday and they told me they both loved it and they made so many new friends. Apparently, they taught them etiquette and manners, dancing, music and French. Also, how to cook and host balls and soirées, because they train the girls to be able to help their future husbands manage their social life with business partners, clients and friends. They even taught them to ski and it seems that Serena Bridewell is extremely good at it."

"It does sound like a wonderful opportunity for you, Rora."

"I know, and I know I should be grateful because it's awfully expensive, but I can't help feeling hurt that they want to send me away." She blinks away some tears. "Since I've discovered I'm adopted, I can't help wondering if they'd still be sending me away if I was their own child, like Gabriel."

"Oh, Rora, of course they would. They've loved you to bits, ever since Rosa found you under the clock tower. You mustn't think like this." He holds her away from him and looks straight into her eyes. "I don't want you to go, because I'm selfish. They're being totally unselfish. They only want you to go because they want the best for you. Even I can see that! But what bothers me the most is that I don't want you fitting so well into high society, that you'll no longer have any time for me."

She grins. "I'll always have time for you, Luke. We've always been close ever since we suckled at the same breasts."

He looks embarrassed. "Err! Don't say that it makes us sound like brother and sister, which would make the way I feel for you quite illegal."

They both laugh and Luke says, "At least I've managed to cheer you up. Come on in and say hello to Ma and Lilly and have a drink before you go on back."

"All right, I am feeling rather thirsty."

Mrs Moore dips a curtsey as Luke enters with Aurora. "Good evening, Miss Aurora, I wondered what was keeping our Luke." Always pleased to see Aurora and catch up with her latest news, still feeling the bond that developed between them sixteen years ago, when she was her wet nurse, she watches the lass making herself comfortable at their kitchen table.

"Please join us for supper. Help yourself to some bread, cheese, ham and pickle, my dear." She passes her an extra plate. Luke tells his mother all about Switzerland.

She listens carefully, placing a Victoria sponge and the prepared tea tray on the table. She wipes her hands on her apron and joins them. Steam rises as she pours out the tea for each of them. "Well, it sounds like a wonderful opportunity for you, lass, and it will only be from September until the end of July; less than a year."

"I know, Nanny Susan, I should be happy about it, but I really don't want to leave everyone I love behind. I'll be so anxious going all that way all on my own."

She helps herself to some cheddar cheese and a hunk of bread. "I'm sure someone will be travelling with you, either your mama, or Miss Tweedy probably, and once you're there, you'll soon make friends with the other girls and then it won't be half so bad." She watches Aurora to see if she enjoys her pickle recipe and is rewarded by her tucking into some more.

"I know it sounds like a fabulous opportunity and to be fair to Mama and Papa, I promise I'll reserve judgment until I've seen the brochure Papa has requested."

Luke leans over to whisper in Aurora's ear. "If it's less than a year, I can bear it, Rora, even though I'll miss you terribly."

His mother can just make out what is said, but she turns a blind eye, even though their close relationship has been worrying her for some time now. She is fearful her Luke will end up being hurt, even more so, now that Aurora is being groomed as a debutante before coming out.

CHAPTER THREE *(May–June 1867)*

POST-WEDDING BLUES

Ashleigh and Lucy spend their wedding night in Lucy's new home, the beautifully appointed east wing of Bingham Manor. Lucy is filled with a mixture of eager anticipation and nervous unease, knowing what to expect once the candles are extinguished, having lived on a farm all her life, but her disappointment is heartfelt with the lack of all gentleness and consideration for her well-being, and the lamentably selfish way her new husband approaches the whole business of consummation. She tearfully hopes it is his enthusiastic partaking of a variety of alcoholic beverages throughout the day, that makes him tactlessly remove her nightclothes, rush the lovemaking and go straight for the act itself, then fall asleep and snore loudly until dawn. She silently retrieves her nightgown from the floor, then re-clothed, she lies on her back listening to his regular snoring, resenting his ability to sleep soundly after such brutality and lack of tenderness and worrying that this does not bode well for her future happiness.

The following day, after little sleep, she removes the rags from her hair, washes and dresses in her marine blue going-away outfit, chosen to enhance her blue eyes, and goes down to breakfast. Ashleigh is already there talking to his father; his mother will not rise before ten of the clock.

After they have all eaten, Ashleigh impatiently paces the floor, regularly looking at his gold pocket watch, a gift from his parents on his twenty-first birthday. She dons her travelling paletot and places a matching blue bonnet, decorated with tiny cream flowers, on top of her brown ringlets and ties its ribbons beneath her hair, before they set off on the bridal tour.

Jeremy Seymour has two elderly brothers who had been unable to attend the ceremony, one living in Plymouth and one in Truro and thus Colonel and Mrs Seymour have arranged for the bride and groom to visit them after the wedding, for Lucy to be introduced to them and their families.

Lucy's father-in-law takes them and their luggage to the Ivell town railway station and Lucy cannot help feeling anxious, facing her first journey by rail. When they arrive at the station the huge black locomotive is pulling up to the platform belching out smoke and steam. The porter takes their luggage to place in the guard's van and Ashleigh opens the door of a carriage for her to climb inside. They settle into the comfortable upholstered seating and set off together, in the hands of the *London and South Western Railway Company.*

Ashleigh takes out a silver hip flask and offers it to her. She declines. "No, thank you, we've only just had breakfast!"

"Suit yourself, but I'm on my honeymoon and still feel like celebrating." He takes a large swig and then unfolds his newspaper, placing a barrier between them.

Lucy ignores his regular imbibing throughout their journey to Exeter, content to watch the pastureland rushing by, with its streams and ponds, small villages and farm animals. However, she is unable to relax knowing her husband is becoming progressively more inebriated and fearful that, by the time they disembark in Plymouth, he will be unable to ensure they both arrive safely at his uncle's house.

At Exeter, they change trains into a compartment coach on the *South Devon Railway Company* line, built by Isambard Kingdom Brunel, to go onwards to Plymouth. She particularly appreciates this part of the journey, as the train travels close along the Exe estuary and the Devon coastline between Exeter and Newton, before going inland to Plymouth, and the seabirds, waterfowl and panoramic views are wonderful to behold.

Despite her anxiety, they arrive safely at his uncle's home in Plympton. During their stay, Harold and his wife, Mavis, are both very accommodating and invite their extended family over for supper to meet Lucy. They are shown the sights of Plymouth and enjoy a stroll along the promenade the following day. That evening at Ashleigh's suggestion the four of them go to a music hall in Stonehouse and she and Mavis are shocked by the scantily-dressed chorus girls and the extremely bawdy songs, but her husband loves it.

On Wednesday, after saying farewell to Harold and Mavis, they catch another locomotive, this time with the *Cornwall Railway Company*, to continue to Truro. She wrings her hands anxiously when the train approaches the timber trestle viaducts of the Royal Albert Bridge that crosses the Tamar River, but the view from there is splendid and they are over it so quickly, she has nothing to fear.

They hire a hansom cab at the station and at last they arrive at the home of Walter and Winifred Seymour in St Mary's Street, not far from the sixteenth-century parish church of St Mary's. The cab driver unloads their luggage for them and Ashleigh pays the fare. Lucy strokes the horse, wondering what Uncle Walter and Aunt Winifred will be like.

The door opens and they are welcomed in with open arms and she immediately feels at home. Aunt Winnie is warm and affectionate and Uncle Walter very down to earth and friendly. He made his money when he was young, as a tin miner, but now he is retired and their terraced house is cosy and comfortable. Later that day their children and grandchildren arrive and Lucy is much in demand with the little children running around offering her a variety of sweetmeats.

When they have all left, she is overwhelmed with tiredness, after travelling so far and a busy day meeting all the relations, and so she excuses herself and Winnie shows her up to their guest room. It is a neat and clean room with chintz curtains at the window and a jug and bowl on a marble-topped dresser. The large bed looks very welcoming. She undresses and washes before sliding under the blankets, sinking into the feather mattress and falling into a deep sleep.

Much later she is jolted awake by Ashleigh entering the room, none too quietly. He places a candle on the bedside table beside her, which flickers annoyingly in her face. *Surely he is not thinking of ravishing me in the home of his aunt and uncle!* She watches him covertly, wavering unsteadily as he undresses and she feigns sleep, feeling too exhausted and sleepy to respond to any possible advances. But he has other plans and they don't take into consideration her feelings, or those of their hosts.

Without a word of endearment, he pulls back the bedclothes and pushes her over onto her front, at the same time plunging his hands between her legs and parting them roughly. He pulls her up into a crawling position and is quickly behind her thrusting into whatever aperture he can find and despite her best efforts to avoid it, he finds the wrong one. She wants to scream out against this violation, but she is in a stranger's home and so she muffles her cries of pain in the feather pillow. It seems ages before he reaches satisfaction and withdraws, slumping back on the bed with a loud triumphant sigh. Lucy collapses, frightened to move, lest he tries to start again. He is treating her like a whore, and is far from the loving husband she expected him to be. She cannot discuss this with him while they are guests in his uncle's home, but will she be strong enough to challenge him once they are back at Bingham Manor?

For Lucy, her honeymoon is a huge disappointment and she is relieved to arrive back in Ivell, where at least her family and friends are near at hand. Robshaw collects them from the station in the brougham but by the time they arrive home, the household has retired for the night. She dreads her husband joining her in bed and is relieved when he finally turns in, snuffs the candle and immediately falls asleep.

The following morning, both he and Rupert are already gone about their business when she comes downstairs for breakfast. She joins her father-in-law and during their casual chatting she asks him if he has any objection to her playing the piano.

"Of course not, my dear. This is your home now. You must feel free to do whatever you wish."

"Thank you, Father." She feels strange calling him this, but she calls her own father, papa, and it sounds more respectful than calling him Jeremy.

Later, she settles herself at the piano, placed within the large bay window area of the drawing room, so that while she is playing she is overlooking the garden and the lake beyond. She picks out the music score for the *Chopin Concerto, No. 2 in F minor* and loses herself in the lyrical, romantic music.

It is not long before she hears the voice of her mother-in-law, imperially sending out instructions to the staff. She continues to play, the music soothing her nerves and enhancing her mood.

Eventually, her mother-in-law enters the room with Skipper, her small lap dog in her arms, and addresses her, interrupting her flow and irritating her. "Good morning, Lucy, I trust you enjoyed your trip to Devon and Cornwall."

She spins slowly around on the piano stool to face her, stands and curtseys, smiling politely. "Yes, thank you, mother-in-law; although I'm also happy to be home again."

"Please call me Helen; mother-in-law is such a mouthful. Did you find the relations hospitable?"

"We did. They were most kind and made us very welcome."

Helen Seymour sits down in the opposite corner of the bay window and before she takes up her tapestry frame and needle, she allows the little Papillon to settle comfortably on her lap. "You play well, considering your background. Who was your tutor?"

She ignores the slight, lifting her chin with pride. "I'm self-taught actually; we had a spinet at home, but this grand piano is a wonderful instrument to play, with such a lovely tone."

Helen looks pensive. "It was my mother's, but I never had the patience to practise and so I was a great disappointment to her. Please play some more;

the melody is a pleasant background, while I do my tapestry."

She sits once more, turning back to the keyboard and finding her place, she continues with the second movement of the concerto.

When Ashleigh and Rupert return home it is nearly supper time. Ashleigh strides into the room and places a quick peck on her forehead. Lucy cannot help thinking it is more for his parents' benefit than for hers.

"What's for supper? My stomach fears my throat's been cut," says Rupert.

His mother replies, "I believe Mary is preparing some fish that Robshaw caught in the lake this morning."

Ashleigh asks, "Can I pour anyone an aperitif?"

"I will have a small sherry, dear. How about you, Lucy, will you join me?"

"Yes please, Helen, I'd like that, thank you." Ashleigh pours the two sherries and places them beside the ladies on occasional tables.

"Gentlemen, would you care to join me in a gin, or would you prefer a vermouth?"

His father replies, "Gin please, my boy, with a drop of Indian tonic water."

"Whatever you're having, Ash," replies his brother.

Ashleigh pours three drinks and passes them around, then takes a large swig of his own. Lucy is unaccustomed to drinking alcohol with every meal, but she enjoys the formality of it and sups happily at her sherry.

Shortly, Robshaw announces that supper is served. The meal is most enjoyable, the fish fresh and the vegetables straight from the kitchen garden. However, the conversation is stilted.

Helen asks in her cut-glass voice, "How did you get on today, boys? Have you made any money for a change?"

Ashleigh is enthusiastic. "I did, as it happens. Made a killing on a nice little filly that showed all the other horses her tail."

"Does that mean you will be able to repay some of the money you owe your father?"

"I'm afraid not, Mama. I've other more urgent demands on my purse at present."

Helen asks, imperially, "What could be more urgent than repaying your debts to your father?"

Rupert laughs. "Repaying debts to someone who is not quite so understanding and who may well use force to prise the money from him."

Ashleigh scowls at his brother. "Have no fear, Mama, I'll not forget my family obligations either. I'm quite certain my ship will come in soon and all my money worries will be over."

His mother looks to heaven. "I wish I shared your confidence, Ashleigh."

A fortnight later, Rupert is preparing to travel on the train to Bristol to embark on his journey by sea to Cape Town, South Africa. "I'm travelling on the *SS Great Britain*, an iron-hulled, screw-propeller steamer, designed by Isambard Kingdom Brunel himself."

His father is impressed. "My goodness, is there no end to this man's talents? Designing bridges and railways and ships, it is all so diverse."

Lucy can see he is extremely excited, but also that her husband is terribly upset to be saying farewell to his only brother.

His mother, demonstrating the typical English upper-class, stiff upper lip, kisses him on his cheek, and says, "God speed, my son. Please write to us when you arrive there and keep us informed of any developments. We will, of course, be on tenterhooks until we hear from you."

"Goodbye, Mama."

He also kisses her cheek. "Goodbye, little sister. Look after Ashleigh for me; he's not as self-reliant as he seems and will, I'm sure, miss me."

"I will, Rupert. Good luck in your venture and come home soon. I know someone else who will truly miss you."

"I know, I spoke to her yesterday, but she'll be needing your support too, I'm afraid. She was very upset when I couldn't give her a timescale for this trip, and so I gave her leave to call off our engagement if she would rather not be held to it."

She is astounded. "Did she?"

"No, not for now, but I think it all depends on what decision I make about coming home for good, or staying and setting up home over there. For she will not leave her father."

"Oh dear, poor Clara. I'll go and see her soon to try and cheer her."

Rupert then slaps his brother on his back. "Don't be too downhearted, Ashleigh. You now have a beautiful wife to take my place and take care of you." Lucy feels herself blushing. Rupert continues, "Hopefully I'll make a fortune for Pa, and return to Somerset a rich man myself, which can only benefit us all." He holds out his hand to Ashleigh and he grips it staunchly. "I'll miss our riotous carousing and revelry, Ash, but it had to end sometime and I think it's time we both took on a bit more responsibility. You've started by taking yourself a wife, and I by following a new and sober path, hopefully to our salvation."

Ashleigh mumbles, "It'll not be the same without you, Brother. Enjoy your adventure, but please don't stay away too long. I'm afraid there's no one else who could possibly step into your shoes."

Lucy's heart sinks.

Rupert looks uncomfortable at this comment, and quickly responds, "I promise I'll write, as soon as I tread land at the Cape of Good Hope. Let us hope it is aptly named and all our ambitions are fulfilled."

He gives his brother a bear hug, clambers up into the brougham beside his father and, without more ado, they set off to the railway station at Penn Mill, on the other side of Ivell town.

Later that evening Lucy is preparing for bed when her husband bursts in. Having spent the evening supping Madeira wine with his father, he is inebriated as usual, but she can see by the expression on his face that he is in a bad humour.

She realises straightaway he's in a lustful mood and that it wouldn't be the right time to talk to him about his callous disregard of her feelings. She bites her lip as he once more takes her in any way he pleases, in such haste that he doesn't bother to strip her this time.

CHAPTER FOUR *(August–October 1867)*

HOW TO DEAL WITH BULLIES

Malachi has been enjoying training Bobby and Edwin. He has shown them tips like how to pickle their hands in spirit to harden the skin before a fight and now, when the two of them spar together, they have the correct stance and look like genuine pugilists. Their confidence is growing daily and woe betide Tattershall should give them any excuse to teach him a lesson.

Bobby questions Amy regularly about Tattershall pestering her. He can see she is adversely affected by his presence there in the factory, but she remains stoic. On one occasion, she is helping prepare the dinner table for their evening meal while Bobby's mother is cooking the food and she sighs. "I wish he'd never got the job there, Bobby. At every opportunity, he makes crude, embarrassing comments to me, that make me feel very uncomfortable."

Irritated that he cannot be by her side protecting her all the time, he manages to hide his frustration. "Just ignore him, Amy. He's not worth getting upset about."

"I do try, but whenever he comes within a few yards of me I can smell him." She seems to shudder. "Working in the tanning department he has the unpleasant odour of that occupation about his person; a mixture of urine, rotting animal flesh and gore. It's quite revolting."

"If you're working in the office, he shouldn't be coming anywhere near you. Maybe you should complain to the bosses."

"Don't worry, Bobby, he's a loner and unpopular with the other men. He gets no support whatsoever from them. I'm sure I can handle him; I just wish I didn't have to."

He takes her in his arms. "If he ever so much as touches you, come straight home to me and I'll deal with him." He kisses her tenderly, trying to push his thoughts of revenge to one side.

Louisa has accepted an invitation to visit Lucy for afternoon tea and she is pleased when it turns out to be a warm sunny day. Edwin is charged with delivering her and Rosa in the landau. She hasn't had an outing with Rosa for ages and they are both looking forward to some girlie chatter and to catch up with Lucy's news.

They are shown into the drawing room where they find Lucy playing the piano. She doesn't recognise the piece, but it seems a bit sad and dreary and she is concerned for her friend's mood.

However, Lucy's face lights up immediately. "How lovely to see you both. I've missed my friends so much, it's so quiet here. Shall we go out onto the terrace for our tea? I asked Robshaw to set out the cushions and parasol earlier."

Rosa smiles, loving the fresh air. "Yes, that sounds a wonderful idea as it's such a balmy day and we can look out over the lake and watch the ducks and moorhens."

Lucy leads them through the French doors and onto the terrace and they arrange themselves around the table, so they are all able to see the waterfowl and overlook the shores of the lake. Louisa cannot help but think they make a pretty sight in their colourful summer gowns, Rosa in her favourite rose pink, Lucy in a pretty purple, decorated with pink sprigs of flowers and herself in autumn gold that complements her auburn hair.

Rosa then asks, "Where is everyone?"

"Oh, Ashleigh is off somewhere as usual, a cockfight or something of the kind, and his parents have gone to Bath for a few days, staying with friends there, which is why I invited you over, as it will be just us and we can chat freely."

Louisa notices a concerned frown etching Rosa's face that matches her own and she asks, "Is there something wrong, Lucy?"

Lucy shakes her head. "No, it's nothing to worry about, it's just that being married is not quite how I imagined it would be. I do believe I see less of my husband now, than I did when he was courting me."

"Where did you go for your honeymoon?"

"Well, it was a bridal tour to Devon and Cornwall by train and it was good to meet my new relations, but it was very tiring and not nearly as romantic as I'd hoped." Her eyes brim with tears and Louisa sees that all is not well. She remembers her honeymoon in Paris with Joshua and it was the most magical time of her entire life. Something must be very wrong if Lucy's honeymoon was a disappointment.

"Come, Lucy darling, it's just us three friends here, please tell us what's wrong. It's not healthy to bottle up one's feelings and you know you can safely confide in us."

She dabs at her eyes with her handkerchief, and sighs, "It's the lovemaking. I'd longed for such tenderness and intimacy, but the whole business is always over in minutes leaving me sore and upset and feeling used and abused. There's no caressing or stroking, to stir my senses and make the whole thing a beautiful experience. He seems to have lost all respect for me. I no longer believe that he loves me, Lou Lou. I believe he simply wanted to possess me, to use as his plaything when the mood takes him."

She takes up Lucy's free hand. "I don't know what to say, Lucy. Perhaps you should talk to him about it."

"I don't think I can. I dread the night-times now. I lie in bed hoping he'll come home the worse for drink and will just want to go straight to bed in a drunken stupor and then I cry myself to sleep because this is not how it should be. I had such high hopes for us."

"Perhaps you could caress him and show him in that way, what you would like yourself."

"I could, but to be honest, Lou Lou, he was so brutal on our first night, I no longer feel like caressing him, or being loving to him. I wish I'd never married him."

Shocked that Lucy's love and enthusiasm could have waned so quickly she tries to strengthen her resolve, by saying gently, "Well, I'm afraid it's too late for regrets now, darling. You made your vows and we women unfortunately will always be subservient to men. They hold all the power, which is why it's so important to make the right decision. It's hard for me to advise you, because Rosa and I are both fortunate, in that Malachi and Joshua are loving, gentle and kind, so we haven't had to put up with such treatment." She shakes her head sorrowfully. "I'm afraid there's no honourable way to get out of this marriage and so I'd advise you to try to make the best of it."

"I know. As Ma would say, 'I've made my bed, so I must lie in it,' but it's a relief to be able to talk about it to you ladies. Things might be better if Ashleigh had a proper job, but he's making his money by taking unofficial bets at the Black Panther Club and all this drinking and gambling is beginning to worry me too; he seems to come home so often in a bad humour, when things have not gone well for him. I'd no idea he was so tied up in it and I fear I was very naive to think this would all turn out well."

Louisa tries to calm her. "Try not to worry, Lucy, and try to talk to him about your concerns. You have some rights as his wife; you should at least be able to speak your mind."

Lucy tucks away her handkerchief and gets up. "I'll go and ring for our tea to be served." She goes into the drawing room to pull the bell cord and summon the maid then re-joins them.

"Right, ladies, enough about my troubles. What's all your news? Rosa, how are my nieces and nephew? They were so good at the wedding and looked so beautiful."

"They're all fine. Ruby and Eli are doing well at school and Daisy is just settling in, after a difficult start, but it has freed me up for Louisa full time again now."

"Talking of school, Aurora has finally agreed to go to finishing school at Lausanne Manor in Switzerland next month. We've persuaded her to think of it as a holiday and the Bridewell sisters had a chat with her at your wedding reception and said how much they both enjoyed it. We've been busy getting together all her costumes and it's been rather like making up a trousseau for her. Anyway, it's a relief the decision has been made. Even though we'll miss her so, I'm sure it's the best thing for her."

Lucy sighs, "She's very lucky. I'd have given anything to be able to go there. What an adventure for her."

With a clink of china, Gladys appears with the trolley, laden with the tea tray and a wonderful selection of sandwiches and fancy cakes.

Lucy dismisses the maid saying, "Thank you, Gladys, I'll serve and pour the tea."

They are all enjoying the refreshments, when a flight of Canada geese swoop down and land on the water, honking and flapping their wings. It is a wonderful sight and they happily eat the food while watching the birds' antics.

Finally, it is time to leave and Lucy strolls with them out to the patiently waiting Edwin and the landau. "Thank you so much for coming to see me. It's been a lovely afternoon. I'm sorry I was a bit maudlin. Things have probably been worse lately, because Ashleigh has been in such a bad humour since his brother left for South Africa, but I'll take your advice and speak to him about my concerns. Please don't be anxious on my behalf, I'm just having a bad day. I'm sure tomorrow things will look a lot brighter."

"I hope so, but let's do this again soon. We've enjoyed it immensely, haven't we, Rosa?"

"Yes, of course. We should make it a regular event. You could come and see me next time. My cottage is a lot humbler than yours, but you know Malachi and the children would love to see you and we could pop over to see your mama and papa and Bunny and Jacob too."

"I'd love that." Lucy kisses them both in turn.

Edwin hands the ladies into the landau then clambers up into the driver's seat, clicks his tongue and the horses set off. They all wave, as the carriage goes down the drive and turns left onto the roadway.

In September, Aurora waits in the hall for John Moore to bring around the landau. Her father has bought her a set of Louis Vuitton trunks, which are filled with all her best costumes and accessories and are piled up ready to load into the carriage. She prepares herself for a tearful farewell with her mama and Gabriel and all the staff.

She hears the rumble of the carriage on the gravel and looks anxiously at her mama. "Oh, Mama, I am going to miss you so."

"Please don't cry, darling. It will be such an adventure for you and your papa, travelling all that way through France to Switzerland, seeing the different cultures of both countries and the wonderful snow-covered mountains of the Alps. Although I'll miss you terribly, I know you'll be having such fun and will come home with marvellous tales to tell us all. Come, give me a hug."

She hugs her mother tightly to her and feels the gentle kiss on her forehead. Then it is Gabriel's turn and they hug each other self-consciously, with the staff gathering around them to offer their goodbyes.

Gareth and Michael collect the luggage to load onto one of the seats of the vehicle and strap them together for the short journey to the station.

She kisses her mother once more, before her papa takes her arm and ushers her out to board the carriage. "Come, Rora, we must delay no longer, we have a train to catch."

The staff follow them outside and wave, as the carriage sets off for their long journey. Aurora's eyes brim with tears, remembering her fond farewell with Luke yesterday. How he held her so close and whispered his constant love for her, promising not to look at another girl in her absence and saving up all his love for her return. She blinks away her tears, hoping that her papa has not noticed. Eventually she finds her voice. "How long will it take for us to get there, Papa?"

"It is hard to tell, Rora. We're travelling by train to London, then changing trains to travel to Folkestone, to board the *South Eastern and Continental Steam Packet* across to Boulogne. We'll stay overnight in Boulogne and the following morning we'll catch the train to Paris. For a treat, I plan to show you a little of the Paris your mama and I enjoyed on our honeymoon, for a couple of days; subsequently we'll catch the overnight sleeper south to Lyon. The next, shorter leg of the journey is north-east by train to Geneva, and I've arranged for the school to send a carriage for us for the final stage, around the lake, to Lausanne Manor."

"I didn't realise we'd be staying in hotels along the way. It'll be lovely to see Boulogne and Paris with you by my side. Thank you so much, Papa."

"You're welcome, my dear. I only wish your mama and Gabriel could have come with us, but it wasn't practical."

"It is going to be a long journey, though. I'd no idea I'd end up quite so far away from home."

"It may be a long way from us all at Alvington Manor, my darling, but the whole world has so much to offer us and these days, with our wonderful railway network, travel is much quicker and safer than ever it was before. This is the start of your adult life, Aurora. Try to make the best of every opportunity, for you only have one life and it can be unexpectedly cut short at any moment."

Louisa is restless all the time that Joshua is away, hoping that the journey went well and that Aurora was happy to be left in Switzerland, when the time came. Joshua didn't tell her exactly when he would be home, only that he would be back before her thirty-fourth birthday and so she anxiously listens out for him a fortnight later and is relieved to hear the coach return from the station late one afternoon. She rushes out to meet him as he clambers down from the carriage and Michael Porter deals with his luggage.

"How was it, Josh? Did Aurora like her school? Was the journey interminable?"

"Slow down, my love, first things first." He takes her in his arms and kisses her ardently. "Oh, my dear, I've missed you so much. As you can imagine, I was thinking of you all the time, especially when we were in Paris. Aurora, I'm sure, appreciated our time together. She enjoyed travelling through France and sightseeing and was impressed with Boulogne and Paris and I must admit to spoiling her a little while we were there."

"Come inside and tell me all about it. I've been on such tenterhooks waiting for you to come home." They go together arm in arm into the drawing room. Louisa tugs on the bell pull and after a few minutes, Lettie enters. "Could we please have afternoon tea now, Lettie?"

"Certainly, ma'am." Lettie dips a curtsey and goes off to organise their refreshments.

Joshua sinks into his favourite armchair. "I was so proud to have Aurora on my arm, my dear. She was so enthusiastic about all the places of interest, loving the many beautiful bridges crossing the river as we sauntered along the Seine, and admiring the work of the artisans. Like us, we walked all the way from the *Arc de Triomphe du Carrousel*, along the tree-lined *Champs-Élysées* to the *Tuileries Palace* and on to the *Louvre*, where she enjoyed all the superb paintings and sculptures, and outside, admired the attractive fountains and statues of the *Place de la Concorde*."

"You're bringing back some very happy memories, my love."

"I thought I would."

Lettie enters with their refreshments. Joshua smiles at her. "Thank you, Lettie. This all looks very appetising. I'm actually very hungry."

They both help themselves to some sandwiches and Louisa pours the tea for them.

Joshua continues with his tale. "You'll remember our sightseeing tour in the horse-drawn charabanc when we went to *Notre Dame Cathedral?* Well, we did that the following day and Aurora stared open-mouthed at its amazingly beautiful rose window. I must admit I've always been even more impressed with the Gothic architecture and its unusual flying buttressing. Then, to Aurora's delight, on the last day, I took her to *Le Bon Marché* and purchased some bits and pieces of her choosing and then on to the House of Worth on the *Rue de la Paix*, to choose a special haute couture summer gown, and matching bonnet, that will be sent to her on completion, at Lausanne Manor."

"It sounds as if you really spoiled her."

"I did rather, but I enjoyed it. She was so happy and grateful."

"How about Boulogne?"

"Well, it doesn't compare with Paris, and as we only stayed overnight, our time was limited, but it's an old medieval walled city, with a handsome castle and we could see the prominent and attractive tower and dome of the basilica of *Notre-Dame de Boulogne* in the process of being built on the site of the original cathedral, from our room in the auberge. It's similar in style to our own St Paul's Cathedral and most impressive."

"I'm very pleased you enjoyed your time together. So, Aurora was impressed when you reached Lausanne Manor, and happy to be left?"

"I think so, and if she wasn't, she hid it well. The principal was most charming and the building and grounds very spacious, attractive and well-manicured. Aurora was introduced to some other young ladies, who seemed to take her under their wing and she happily kissed me farewell and waved me off, before going inside with them."

"So, you think it bodes well then, dearest?"

"I do, and I look forward to seeing the finished result." He laughs. "It will be most interesting. When we've finished our tea, you must come upstairs with me, as I've brought a little something back with me from Paris for your birthday, but we'll need to open it in the bedroom."

She grins at him. "Is this a present for me, or for you?"

Amy is leaving the factory on a cold, wet October evening. The light from the gas lamps reflect in the numerous wind-rippled puddles on her route home through the town. Her friend Jean left earlier for Odcombe in the wagon with the rest of the outlying workers, but Amy was in the middle of packaging up some repairs and left after everyone else. Now the streets are deserted in this squally, inclement weather. Her umbrella is useless in the gusts and she holds the hood of her cloak tight under her chin, to stop it from blowing off and exposing her face and hair to the rain.

At last she enters the Tabernacle Lane alleyway, relieved to be under cover, sheltered from the wind and downpour, and nearly home, when she is abruptly grabbed from behind and shoved against the wall. She lets out an involuntary scream. The offensive smell of the tannery overwhelms her. Tattershall! She feels sick from the obnoxious smell of him. Her heart pumps with fear. He cannot get away with this! She lashes out, scratching and punching him. He tears at her clothing and her cloak rips, as she attempts to pull away from him, but he is stronger than he looks. His dirty fingers reach up her skirt and gouge her legs with one hand, while the other is bruising her arm with a vice-like grip. Then he pushes against her, pinning her against the wall with his chest, while he tries to unbutton his flies with his free hand.

Trying desperately to hold him at bay, she finds her voice, shouting, "Get your filthy hands off me, you revolting, smelly creep."

He is panting like an animal. "You know you want it. I can tell. You're gagging for it."

"Not with you, I'm not." She brings up her knee, hard into his groin and he doubles over in pain.

"You vicious bitch!"

The blacksmith comes out of his yard and calls out, "What's going on there?" She has no time to explain to him. Instead she hits Tattershall hard across his head, and flees, panting in terror into the borough, towards home and safety and her loving, tender Bobby.

Dishevelled, with a large rip in her cloak, she enters their parlour. Bobby jumps up and her eyes fill with tears of relief, as she sinks into his arms.

"Tattershall?"

"Yes, it was, but I dealt with it, Bobby."

61

He brushes stray strands of hair away from her face. "But you're crying and look at the state of you!"

"I'm not the only one who's crying. I think I may have brought tears to his eyes, too. I kneed him in the crotch."

"Well done, Amy love. Where's the miserable bastard now?"

"I don't know, he could still be in the alleyway. He must have been hiding in Hannam's yard, waiting to pounce on me, but Mr Bragg, the blacksmith, came out to see what all the commotion was about, just as I was able to escape. I didn't wait to explain; I just ran."

Bobby turns to his mother and says in a low voice, "Ma, would you take care of Amy for me? She's had a nasty shock and we need to deal with this."

Amy is worried by the angry expression on Bobby's face, but his mother puts her arm around her and ushers her to an armchair. "Come and sit by the fire, Amy. I'll get you a hot toddy," and she is too shaky to argue.

Bobby says, "Thanks, Ma," then turns to Harry. "Right! Come on, Harry, let's sort him out." And they rush off out to seek retribution.

To their disappointment, the alleyway is deserted. Bobby is livid. "He'll get his just deserts, Harry. He'll not get away with this. He's been asking for a good seeing to for long enough and this is the last straw!"

Harry takes his arm. "Let's speak to Mr Bragg and explain what happened. It'd be good to get him on our Amy's side too, as he was a witness."

They enter the blacksmith's yard and knock on his door. It is opened by the big man himself, who exclaims jovially, "Harry! Bobby! Come on in. I was half expecting a visit. I was a bit concerned about what happened earlier. Young Amy seemed to handle herself, but it must have been distressing for her. I was only sorry I was too late to be of much use to her. As soon as he saw me, the bloke hobbled off after her. I followed close behind him into the borough, but by then Amy was safely inside and he was out of sight."

They enter the parlour and Mr Bragg sends his young children upstairs to prepare for bed. "Up the apples and pears, you nippers; your ma will be up to tuck you in shortly."

The two children kiss their father goodnight and leave the room reluctantly. He pretends to chase them up the stairs with a roar and they both squeal and giggle and rush away happily and he closes the stairway door behind them.

"Would you like a cup o' cider, lads?"

"That would be much appreciated, Mr Bragg."

"The name's Henry. Let's not stand on ceremony. Take a seat then and make yoursel's comfy." He calls into the scullery. "Susan, would you kindly bring us three mugs o' cider, please, m' dear?"

He sits down in the largest armchair beside the fire. "What can I do for you, lads?"

"We want to teach that little creep Tattershall a lesson he won't ever forget, so he knows what to expect if he ever so much as looks in Amy's direction in the future. He's been pestering her for months with his lewd talk and she's been anxious for her safety. I know Amy managed to defend herself tonight, but if you hadn't heard the commotion and shown yourself, or if she'd been further away from home, it may have been a different story."

Susan Bragg enters the room with mugs of cider on a wooden tray and hands them around. The men thank her. She smiles, "You're most welcome. I'm going up to settle the children, Henry," and she exits the room via the stairway door.

Henry takes a large swig of cider and wipes his mouth with his sleeve. "Right, let's get down to business. What are you fellows planning?"

"Myself and Amy's brother, Edwin, have been having bare-knuckle boxing lessons with Malachi Warren and either one of us would be a match for him, however evil and cunning he may be. Harry here is also prepared to take him on. We just want you to turn a blind eye, if you should happen to witness his comeuppance."

"Of course I will; the little runt deserves it."

The brothers each drink some of the amber liquid, then Bobby continues, "I'm not sure at this point how we'll manage to get him alone, but we'll be keeping an eye on our Amy, as she goes to and from work. Harry and I will take it in turns, depending on our shifts, to keep a check on her. But I don't want to use her as an enticement; it's too dangerous. Besides, I doubt he'll try it in the alleyway again; he's far too cowardly for that, knowing we'll be on our guard now."

The blacksmith suggests, "Perhaps you should somehow entice him up into the woods at Ninesprings, where there'd be no witnesses, of a winter's evening."

Harry smiles, "That's not a bad idea, but what could be his carrot?"

The blacksmith takes another large swig of his cider. "There doesn't have to be one, as long as you make him believe there's one. Maybe an anonymous note saying something like: *If you want to learn something to your advantage, meet me at the little bridge in Ninesprings on Wednesday night at six of the clock."*

Bobby muses, "Maybe Jean Hawkins could somehow plant the note in his jacket pocket in the factory. I know she'll help us if she can."

Harry is enthusiastic. "It's worth a try, Bobby. He may take the bait and it would mean that Amy is out of the picture and safe."

Bobby is not so sure. "In the absence of a better idea, I suppose we could make a start with that. He may be tempted."

Henry finds a catch. "Can the fellow read?"

Bobby sighs. "I don't know, Henry. He's a workhouse brat, so he'd have had some schooling. They're supposed to have at least three hours a day of reading, writing and arithmetic, but it'd depend on how he applied himself."

Harry says, "Come on, Bobby, buck up. I think it's a good idea."

On Wednesday evening, Harry watches from Brunswick Street as the workmen leave for their homes. He recognises among them Tattershall's grubby brown woollen fustian jacket, collar turned up against the wind, cloth cap jammed on, and blue neckerchief blowing about, as he slinks away from the mill exit towards Dodham Brook. Harry is convinced he has fallen for their ploy. He sets off after him at a safe distance. He observes the man walking along the brook, until he finds a suitable place to cross and watches him leap across and stride up the hill, disappearing into the woodland.

There is a chilly wind, with rust and golden autumn leaves falling, making it slippery underfoot. Up ahead through the trees, Harry sees his quarry hesitate and turn back down the rocky footpath towards him. He must have spotted Bobby and Edwin. Harry pulls himself up to his full height and walks boldly towards the creep, who plunges into the undergrowth to escape capture. But Bobby and Ed are close on his heels. He stumbles and Bobby grabs the collar of his thick woollen jacket.

"Where d'you think you're going, Tattershall?" he asks, confidently. "It's about time you picked on someone your own size, don't you think? Put up your fists and fight like a man."

Tattershall puts up his hands defensively. "I don't want no trouble."

"No trouble at all, man. We won't bother with the new Marquess of Queensberry rules, but we'll take you on one at a time. That's only fair. I'll go first, seeing that it was my fiancée you assaulted." He immediately punches him in the stomach and as Tattershall doubles over he follows through with a sharp uppercut under his chin and the wiry little weasel is knocked off his feet, backwards.

Harry smiles at this rough justice, as his brother grabs the villain by his blue neckerchief and pulls him back onto his feet. "Come on, Tattershall, is that the best you've got, or are you only brave when your victim's a woman?" He throws a left hook followed quickly by a jab and the fellow is down in the mud again. He drags him up out of the dirt and pushes him towards Edwin. "Right, Ed, it's your turn." He turns to Tattershall. "You see, my friend here is just as unhappy as I am, because he doesn't like his sister being terrorised either."

Harry is impressed watching Edwin putting into practice all the moves that Malachi has taught them over the last few months. The fellow is black and blue by the time they have finished with him.

Tattershall staggers around punch-drunk, and Bobby restrains Edwin. He stares coldly up close into Tattershall's swollen face and says, "I think that'll do for now, but I think you can tell, we've had the benefit of training with Malachi Warren and if you ever so much as look at our Amy in future, we'll finish you off for good. Do you understand, you defeated heap of crap?"

The vanquished man nods and hangs his head.

Tattershall is aching in every bone in his body. He stumbles back down the woodland path in the moonlight. He tries to leap Dodham Brook, as he had done earlier, missing his footing and falling backwards into the stream, with water going up his nose, before he can struggle up onto his hands and knees, and finally his feet. He slowly and painfully progresses through the town, shivering in the chill wind, finding no comfort in his wet clothes. *It's going to be a long walk home to the hostel tonight. Why did I ever go near that little tart? She wasn't worth this aggravation. I'll be giving her a wide berth in future!*

CHAPTER FIVE *(November–December 1867)*

HATHERLEIGH FARM RACES

Billy has settled in at Hatherleigh Farm. He is well fed and cared for by the family and enjoys the work with the horses, especially training Bay Rum. She is a magnificent three-year-old frisky bay mare, standing about fifteen hands high, with white pastern and fetlocks and a broad white flash down her nose. She has a willing temperament and is a pleasure to work with.

Don has been helping him sort out the stables and his shyness with him is improving. He has been teaching the lad how to mix the enriched feed for Bay Rum, a concoction of boiling barley for at least two hours and then mixing it together with bran in an old bathtub and adding in a handful of cooked linseed in the form of a jelly to help lubricate the joints. It is hard toil for the lad, but he doesn't complain. Don and Victoria collect nettles throughout the summer months, spread them out on baking trays and dry them out in their mother's range. Billy puts them into an airtight tin as a tonic for adding into Bay Rum's feed during the winter, when he occasionally adds in some small strips of seasonal vegetables such as carrots, parsnips, turnips, beetroot and swede. Bay Rum loves apples and he reserves the right for himself, to give her these as a treat.

He has also had them check over the whole farm, pulling up all the ragwort and buttercups they could find, as they are both poisonous to horses. It has taken all summer to wire fence the pastureland where the horses graze, to keep the livestock away from any foxgloves, deadly nightshade, acorns or privet that might be growing in the hedgerow. Victoria collects all the acorns; although bad for horses, a real treat for her pigs. Yew has already been eradicated.

Bay Rum responds well to his training exercise regime, as he prepares her for the Boxing Day Race meet. Billy loves the regular gallops around the racetrack, but believes she needs another racehorse to compete against. That evening at suppertime he asks Bob Yates, "Is there anyone hereabouts who owns a racehorse, that we could train with?"

"I could ask the groom from Lattiford Lodge at the next farmer's market. I think young Mortimer Bathhurst has some racehorses. If not, he's a keen huntsman and may have something that will give her a run for her money. You should accompany me, Billy, and meet the other farmers from hereabouts."

"I'd like that, Mr Yates. Thank you."

"I keep telling you, Billy, please drop the formalities and call me Bob; everyone else does."

"I'm sorry, Bob. It's just my way of being respectful. I don't mean to be unfriendly."

Billy feels the farmer's hand on his shoulder. "I know that, Billy, lad, but you've been here, working hard for us, for just over a year now and I think of you as family, so I believe it's time you dropped the 'Mr', don't you?"

"I do, Bob, and I'll look forward to a trip out with you, when you go to market. When is the market day?"

"Wednesday. There'll be no cattle or pigs, because of the cattle plague, but they do sell geese, ducks and chickens, and some flax yarn, but it is mostly farm produce, like eggs, butter and cheese. The Bathhursts are big cheese makers, so I'm sure they'll be there and Walter Rodber will be driving them."

On Wednesday morning after breakfast, Billy sets off with Bob Yates to the Wincanton Market. He turns up his collar against the wind as they leave the pony and trap safely blocked in Mill Street and climb the hill to the market square. The place is milling with farmers and country-folk of all stations and Bob soon spots Wally Rodber. "Wally! Good to see you, my friend. I want to introduce you to my colleague, Billy, here."

"How do 'ee do, Billy." He shakes Billy's hand.

Bob continues, "He's been doing a grand job of training Bay Rum, but we were wondering whether Mortimer Bathhurst might have a mount that could do with a running partner, so we could put them together to train against each other? What do you think?"

"Not a bad idea, Bob. Conker Queen could do with an incentive and we could work on 'em together before the Boxing Day meet and see if it helps."

Billy grins. "That was exactly what I was thinking."

"I'm sure Mr Bathhurst will think it a grand idea. When would be a good day to bring her over?"

Bob looks at Billy. "Well, if your boss agrees, as soon as possible, I suppose."

Billy nods his head in accord. "It makes no odds to me; just turn up with her tomorrow if you can." He rubs his hands together wishing he had brought his gloves today.

"I'll mention it to him if I get the opportunity this morning and let you know, if you're still here."

"Thank you, Wally, that's much appreciated."

"Well, it'll work both ways, Bob. It should benefit Conker Queen too." He slaps him on the back and wanders off to find his boss.

Bob says, "I'm just going to check out the butter and cheeses on sale. I'm wondering if my Lillian might set up her own stall. There's a lot of competition, but we could sell our eggs as well." He wanders off towards all the dairy produce and Billy casts his eye around to see if there is anything that might attract his attention in the meantime.

He is looking around at all the people when he spots a young girl with her shawl wrapped tightly around her, who has a white ferret peeping out from beneath the woollen material. The creature is wriggling around as if trying to escape, but the girl has it held firmly. He thinks, *she'd be an attractive young girl, if she wasn't so unkempt.* An older youth joins her and they go off together arm in arm, black curls almost interlocking they are so close to each other. He wonders if they are gypsies, as both have dark-olive skin and deep-brown bold, flashing Romany eyes.

He wanders a bit further on to look at the livestock and spots a group of young lads idling against the wall and wonders why they are not working at their ages. One is exceptionally tall and thin with a receding hairline, another has red curly hair and freckles, the third is heavily built and looks rather sullen and the last lad is small and wiry and Billy cannot help thinking he would make a good jockey. The farmers are busy bartering and he can see why they all gather together on market day, but these boys look a feckless lot and he avoids them instinctively.

71

Bob catches up with him. "How do you fancy a mug of mulled cider in the Bear Inn to warm us through?"

"That sounds like a grand idea, Bob."

"Come on then, lad, I'll treat you. This inn is an old coaching house, dating back to 1720, when it was rebuilt after having been burnt down in the great fire of Wincanton."

A huge blaze roars away in the inglenook at the end of the room and the bar staff are busy with customers, this being the busiest day of the week for them. The aroma of baked pies, ales and ciders and a fug of tobacco smoke waft around them. Bob works his way through the farmers to the bar and orders two mulled ciders, while Billy moves closer to the fire. He stands with his back to the flames to warm himself through and spots Walter Rodber entering and seeking out Bob. He watches as they have a quick conversation and then Wally gives Billy the thumbs-up signal before he leaves.

Bob joins him by the fire. "Wally says his boss is fine with you exercising the horses together, and he'll be there tomorrow at about ten of the clock."

"That's good news, Bob, cheers." They chink their tankards together and Billy enjoys supping the steaming amber liquid, as it warms him through.

Bob introduces him to local dairy farmers and race committee members from Holton, North Cadbury, Charlton Musgrove and Bayford, and finally his friend, Fred Meaden, from Moorhayes Farm just north of Wincanton. While they are all enjoying a good chinwag Billy notices the four youths entering the bar. He quietly asks Bob, "Do you know who they are?" He nods in their direction.

"The local ne'er-do-wells, I'm afraid. I'd give them a wide berth if I were you; they're a light-handed lot and not averse to picking pockets."

Bob draws him back into the conversation, which is the fear of the cattle plague that is ravaging the country and confining their cattle and pigs.

The following day, Walter turns up with Conker Queen at a quarter past ten. Billy admires her gleaming chestnut coat, bright eyes and alert ears. Bay Rum canters across the field to greet her and they are introduced over the fence for the first time. Bay Rum bucks and rears happily in her field until Billy saddles and mounts her and Conker Queen is led through the gate by Walter. The two animals appear to be content to be ridden together and Billy has organised for Don to hold a tape across the racetrack and drop it on a count of three to start them off.

Immediately Bay Rum seems more enthusiastic with another horse to compete with and the two animals thunder around the course, leaping the hedges, fences and water jump effortlessly. Bay Rum is easily a length ahead of Conker Queen on the first circuit, and Don checks his father's watch to check the time to compare with further distances. By the second circuit, Conker Queen is beginning to gain on her, which pleases Walter considering she has already been ridden over from Lattiford. They rest the horses and give them both an apple as a reward.

Then they do another couple of circuits before Walter must return to Lattiford. "Well, I think that experiment worked well enough, don't you?"

Billy is pleased. "I do. They both seem to respond to the other's enthusiasm. I think it bodes well. Will you bring her again next week?"

"I certainly will."

"You'd better take some refreshments before you set off home, Wally. Would you care for a mug of small beer and a bite to eat?"

"That would be most tempting, Billy, thank you."

As they walk towards the farmhouse, Billy looks back at the horses grazing contentedly together. "Don't they make a pretty picture; such beautiful animals."

"Well, they're both thoroughbreds, aren't they? Bathhurst tells me that Conker Queen's line traces back to the Godolphin Arabian."

"That's interesting; I believe Bob told me ours was the Darley Arabian, so this should be an interesting experiment."

Christmas is made merry for Billy by the warmth and generosity of the Yates family. He spends the day with them and enjoys being fed and mothered by Lillian, parlour games with Don and Victoria, and warm toddies with Bob. It is a far cry from the large staff party he was used to at Alvington, but just as pleasurable nevertheless, as he is made to feel part of the family. They all enjoy a well-earned rest after all the preparations, not only for the Christmas celebrations, but also for the Boxing Day Steeplechase, when all the farmers, gamblers and landowners from the vicinity will be turning up on horseback, with ponies and conveyances, betting booths, and well-groomed, competing animals.

He and Bob have fenced the racecourse and prepared Clemmy's Field for the entrance, where Jake the ploughman will oversee the entry fees. They have painted a new sign displaying the charges: *One shilling per person, One-horse carriage 2s 6d, Two-horse carriage 5s, and Four-in-hand 10s (Drivers free)*.

The grandstand has been reconstructed near to the start and finish line and alongside it is the race office, not far from his cottage. The competitors will gather in the race field, beside the grandstand field. The distance of the course is one mile and two furlongs, with a run in of about a furlong. The two-mile, four-furlong race starts and ends right by the grandstand, with starts in the country for both the shorter two-mile race, which sets off just before the water jump, and the three-mile race, starting beyond the water jump.

He cannot wait for the spectacle to begin, because he will be riding Bay Rum himself. Bob has explained to his previous jockey that as Bay Rum is so used to Billy, he will be his rider from now on. He hopes there will be no hard feelings. He wanders back to his cottage on Christmas night, glad that he has had a few mugs of mulled cider and wine, for without it he would never fall asleep, he is so excited. He and Walter have decided to put Conker Queen and Bay Rum into the two-mile, four-furlong races, but not to run against each other. There are two races at this distance and they will each be in a different one, which will give them both a chance at first place.

The following morning dawns crisp and frosty and the turf will be hard going. He goes outside to the water pump, his breath misty in the cold. He shivers as he pumps out a pail of water and rushes inside to hang it over the fire to warm, before washing. He is too excited to eat breakfast.

He dresses in his normal clothes; his purple and gold silks are hung up ready for later. He polishes the leather riding boots from Lord and Lady Dryer, and puts them with his riding crop, then goes off to the farm to help with any last-minute chores.

There is so much to do, the morning flashes by and soon people and carriages are pouring through the farm gates into Clemmy's Field, many clutching binoculars and copies of the pink *Sporting Times*, *The Sportsman* and *The Sporting Life*. The race committee, consisting of local farmers, including Bob's friend, Fred Meaden, and some of the others he met at the Bear Inn, are acting as stewards and race officials, while the front field is filling up with hawkers, peddling food and drink, and a line of betting booths are bordering the course.

The committee has put Fred Meaden in charge of the bullhorn for the announcements. Bob, and Fred's son, Oscar, are to oversee the starting flags. The competing horses are taken from the entrance on Lawrence Hill, around the back of the grandstand field and into the race field to avoid the milling crowds.

Billy is explaining to Victoria, "There's a programme of five races, starting with Walter's race at one of the clock, with a mares' novice hurdle race for four-year-olds and upwards…" His voice fades away.

"What's wrong, Billy?"

He shrugs off his shock and disappointment. "Oh, nothing, I just spotted a ghost from the past, that's all." He cannot believe his nemesis has followed him here. Ashleigh Seymour is among the crowd with a large group of vaguely familiar men hailing from Ivell, some of them with gaudily-dressed women draped on their arms. The Black Panther Club must have organised a charabanc for the outing. *That is all I need!*

He turns away from him and joins Victoria, observing Walter calming Conker Queen by walking her around the field while the announcements are being made, before joining the other seven mounts at the starting point. The horses are arrayed in a straggly row, some side-stepping and frisky and Fred inspects them until they all line up and he drops the flag. Billy then watches to see if Oscar, a hundred yards along the track, keeps his flag down, but all is well, and Conker Queen is sensibly positioned fourth, running on the outside of the group.

She takes the first two hedges easily and is approaching the water jump when another mount veers across her path and puts her off, but she regains her position and is gaining ground when the group thunder past the starting point for the second circuit. The leader lands badly over the next fence and throws its rider, Walter manages to ride around the fallen jockey and is in second place when Conker Queen reaches the water jump. She is over it with ease, confident from her regular practice over the last few weeks and Billy is absolutely thrilled when she streaks past the winning post in first place. He rushes to congratulate his friend while other folk are rushing to the bookies to pick up their winnings.

"Well done, Wally. You and Queenie make a good pair."

Walter leans forward and pats the horse, grinning widely. "I like it – 'Queenie' – it suits her. She did well, didn't she?"

"She certainly did. I hope I do as well with Bay Rum."

Walter nods in the direction of his boss. "Mortimer and Malcolm look rather surprised. I don't think they expected that."

"Do you know what your bonus will be?"

"No," he laughs, "but I think Queenie deserves a bonus more than I do."

Fred Meaden announces the results of the first

race and Edward Woodhouse from the Hall and Woodhouse Brewery shakes hands with Walter and his boss and then presents Mortimer Bathhurst with the winner's plaque. The crowd cheer and clap enthusiastically, then Fred announces the time of the next two-mile novice race, three-year-olds and upwards, at a quarter to two.

Billy decides to go and check on Bay Rum back in her stable. He walks into the stable-yard and hears a female giggling from the barn. Surely he has just seen Victoria and her brother over by the roast chestnut stall. He looks cautiously through the barn door and catches the two gypsies in the act of pinching Bay Rum's apples.

He is indignant. "Hey, what do you think you're doing?"

The girl looks up, her large brown eyes filled with fright, and stammers, "S... sorry mister, we didn't think you'd miss a couple; you've got loads racked up here."

"It's still stealing, and you shouldn't be back here, it's private property."

The girl speaks to the boy in their Romany language then the boy finds his tongue. "I'm sorry, mister, we normally wouldn't 'ave, but we're both starving hungry."

"Well, I'll say nothing to my boss this time, but I don't want to catch you round here again. Do you understand?"

"Yes, sir."

"What are your names?"

"I'm Noah Boswell and she is Florica Petulengro."

"Well, I tell you what I'll do; if I win my race which starts at half past two, I'll treat you to a jacket potato each. How's that?"

"That'd be grand, sir. Good luck, sir. We'll be cheering you on."

"Now get back to the racetrack and behave yourselves."

He watches them leave and then goes into the stable to check on Bay Rum. She whinnies at the sight of him and he strokes her nose to calm her. He can hear the noise from the crowds and judging by her agitation, she can hear the other horses. He saddles her, changes into his silks and leads her to the mounting block. Once mounted he rides her down the farm track, around the perimeter of the course, along the edge of Moggs Copse and into the race field.

He is met by Don and Victoria who both pat the horse affectionately. "You two shouldn't be in here, it's the riders' enclosure."

"But we live here."

"I know, but the race committee and probably your pa wouldn't like it. We won't be in here long ourselves. I just wanted Bay Rum to get used to the other animals around her. Our race starts at half past two."

Don whispers in the horse's ear, "Good luck, Bay Rum."

"Good luck, Billy," says Victoria, smiling at him, before they both rush off to find a spot along the track rail.

Fred Meaden is announcing the winner of the two-mile race and presenting the owner with their prize. There is enthusiastic cheering from the crowd, then he hears the distorted voice of Fred announcing the line-up of his race, the second mares' novice hurdle race for four-year-olds and upwards, over two miles and four furlongs.

Billy clicks his heels gently to encourage Bay Rum to get into the queue with the other horses for the furlong run in and they eventually line up across the track, eager to go. From his periphery vision, he sees the flag drop and he spurs Bay Rum into action. She leaps forward and goes straight into the lead. He didn't want that, but she is on home ground and eager to leave the field behind her and so he gives her free rein. Oscar's flag stays down, so all is well. She is over the first two hedges a length ahead, then at the water jump she seems to gain another length, the next few fences are soon dispatched and she sails past the winning post for her second circuit. He can hear the crowd cheering them on and his heart races at the thought of pleasing the Yates family by winning this race for them. The field is strung out behind them and as if in a dream he takes her over the jumps again. Soon he hears the noise from the spectators rising to a crescendo and he spurs Bay Rum past the winning post, standing up in the saddle triumphantly, as he sees ahead of him the ecstatic Yates family gesticulating wildly.

Bob, Don and Victoria all rush over to greet him. Bob says, "Well done, Billy, my lad."

Victoria has a bucket of water to quench Bay Rum's thirst and Don has the horse blanket.

He dismounts and removes her saddle and Don proudly asks his father, "Shall we take her back to the stables now and wash her down."

"Yes, lad, good idea, as Billy must come with me to receive the trophy."

Billy is breathless. "What an experience! I'll never forget this for as long as I live!"

"I never thought you'd beat Midnight Rambler!"

"Which one is that?"

"The black mare who came second, about three lengths behind you. It's one of the horses owned by Lucky Joe Mintern, from Templecombe. He brings his horses up on the train. Come on, Billy, they're about to announce us."

Fred Meaden grins at his friend, as he proclaims the results of the third race, and Billy goes with Bob to receive the silver trophy from Edward Woodhouse. They all shake hands and while the head of the brewery is doing the presentation to Bob, Billy is idly scanning the mass of faces turned up towards them, when he spots a chap head and shoulders above the others weaving his way through the people. It is the lanky one of the ne'er-do-wells from the town and he soon sees the other three all separately mingling and moving swiftly through the gathering. He feels sure they are pickpocketing!

The formalities over he turns to step down from the platform, when his stomach churns at the sight of Ashleigh Seymour staring at him. He avoids eye contact and goes to find Florica and Noah to fulfil his promise to feed them. Suddenly, as if out of nowhere they are walking beside him.

Noah says, "You was good, sir. Does that mean we can have a spud each, sir?"

"I'm as good as my word, Noah. Which vendor do you prefer?"

"Follow us. We'd both like one with cheese and bacon, please. We've been considering, while we was watching you lead the field, all the way around the course."

He laughs. "I'm glad I didn't disappoint you." He looks at Florica. "Where's your little white hairy friend, today?"

"Misty? She's back at *vardo*. I didn't want to risk losing her, with all people."

Noah leads them past the bookies, where Billy notes a rather large, rotund, jolly man sporting bushy sideburns and wearing a bright yellow plaid waistcoat, sending tic-tac signals to another bookie who is extremely thin, scruffy and in contrast looks rather morose. The fat man's booth has the name Jarvis Pocket Bookmakers on it and the thin man is identified as Uriah Levi, and Billy wonders what the hand signals are conveying.

They reach the chosen food seller and Billy purchases three bacon and cheese jacket potatoes. They stand together and observe the people around them, Noah and Florica hungrily devouring the food as if they haven't eaten in days.

Billy is curious and he asks them, "How do you two make a living?"

"I breed ferrets. I use them to catch rabbits with my *day*… err, my mother, and sometimes we barter young kits with other travellers for food," says Florica. "My *dat* is *petulengro*, how you say? Black smith?"

"Her *dat* is a horse dealer too," says Noah, "and he's training me with the metalwork. I'm always on the lookout for any old scrap metal that we can use."

"Well, I'll speak to the boss and if he has anything broken around the farm that's beyond repair, I'll let you know."

Noah looks pleased.

"Where are you settled?"

"Our present site is near the River Cale, in the field off Cemetery Lane, but the townsfolk don't want us there and we suffer a lot of abuse, with folk calling us dirty gyppos, pikeys and didikais. We aren't dirty, I expect we're cleaner than they are, as long as we have access to water, but we're dark skinned and they're mistrusting of our foreignness."

"Do you know many local people?"

Florica shakes her head. "Not really, because we don't stay anywhere long. We travelled here after Priddy Fayre, where my *dat* sold a colt on second day, when young horses and ponies are sold between other Romany families. We had good feast that day, didn't we, Noah? Because they roasted half bullock on spit on village green."

Suddenly the gang of ne'er-do-wells appears around the side of the vendor's booth.

"Ah, what do we have here?" says the lanky one.

"Looks like a gyppo lover to me," replies the ginger one.

Billy bristles. "Looks to me like we have some ignorant louts asking for trouble," he responds, stepping forward. "If I were you, I'd keep on walking, before I call the constable and get him to check your pockets. I'm sure you've found some ripe pickings here today."

Shorty looks surprised. "Come on, Lanky, they're not worth bothering with," and he tugs at his pal's arm to draw him away. 'Lanky' gives Billy a dirty look and sheepishly wanders off with the other three lads.

Billy notes Florica's sigh of relief and turns to her. "Don't worry about them; they're a bunch of ill-mannered cowards, trying to make themselves feel big by picking on you. You're both worth far more than they are."

Noah grins for the first time. "Thank you for sticking up for us, Billy."

"You're very welcome, Noah." He takes his last mouthful of food. "Right, I'd better go off and see if I'm needed by my boss. I'll probably see you later."

On his way back to the grandstand, he notices Ashleigh Seymour and his cronies gathered around Uriah Levi's booth, placing more bets, and he is staggered at the amount of money being handed over. *The man must be loaded to be able to afford to risk that kind of money. No wonder Lucy agreed to marry him; she should be financially secure for the rest of her life.*

A letter drops through the letter box with a Zululand postage stamp on it, displaying an image of Queen Victoria's head. A letter at last from Rupert! Clara Fairway's heart races. She uses her father's letter opener to slice through the top of the envelope. A magenta pressed flower falls from the pages as she opens the sheets of paper. How pretty!

She smiles at his thoughtfulness and settles down in an armchair to read.

8th November 1867

Dearest Clara,

I am writing with season's greetings from a small settlement called Hopetown in the Northern Cape Province of South Africa. I managed to obtain passage from Cape Town to Port Elizabeth by working as a deck hand on a fishing vessel and now I am living in a tented community and enjoying the camaraderie of my fellow prospectors. It has been an amazing adventure, travelling around 450 miles by oxen-drawn wagon, from Port Elizabeth, traversing the shifting desert sands of the Great Karoo, across the gorges and valleys of the Drakensburg Mountains, and through the vast veldt and pasturelands to finally arrive here last month. In all it took us around forty-six days. (By us, I mean myself and a fellow prospector whom I have befriended called Jack Penberthy, who has travelled out here from Cornwall.) While travelling through the Karoo, we managed to bag a few rock rabbits for the pot and the occasional springbok along the way. Then throughout the fertile pastureland or veldt we discovered many settlements beside streams or water pans where we were cheerily greeted by the farmers and their families and invited to join them for hot meals. Nevertheless, it is with great relief that we discovered there is a general store here, that not only sells all the fossicking paraphernalia required, but also working clothes, cooking utensils, and tinned and dried foodstuffs such as a dried meat they call 'biltong' and thus I am managing quite adequately.

You would love the wonderful scenery. On the tree-lined slopes of the Drakensburg Mountains we saw the majestic ironwood, the Natal mahogany, and the wild chestnut and on the high plains, there are the feathery fronds of tree ferns, towering palms and the colourful vines of a plant I am told is called bougainvillea. (Small white flower and magenta bracts enclosed.) On the fertile plains, the birdlife is amazing; nearly at every pond, or water pan, we found the elegant blue cranes and in the gardens of the homesteads beautiful plants and birds of all the colours of the rainbow.

However, I am afraid it is no place for a lady. You would hate the communal latrines, and those few women who are here, are married to the prospectors and roughing it along with the men. They dress like the men and work like the men. There is no civilised society here, just day-to-day work and more work.

I miss you, my dear, and I hope that you and your papa are keeping well. I will be thinking of you, especially over the festive season, and look forward to being successful in my quest and returning to you a wealthy man. I have been fortunate in that I

have found some garnets and peridot, but, as yet, no
diamonds. I live in hope.

Your loving fiancé
Rupert
xx

Clara is thrilled to hear at long last from her beau. She has been so worried about him, but now she cannot wait for her father to finish his work, so she can show him the letter. He had suggested to her that she ought to put Rupert from her mind and prepare herself for the fact that he may never return to Somerset, but this letter proves to her, he intends to be true to his word and it has made her very happy.

CHAPTER SIX *(January–April 1868)*

SAD TIDINGS

On the 5th January Lettie is supervising the dismantling of the Christmas tree and fastidious removal of all decorations, when there is a loud knock at the front door. Gareth goes to answer it, letting in the cold winter air, and a young lad says, "Telegram for Lord Dryer, sir."

Gareth takes the envelope and, from where Lettie is supposed to be polishing the hall table, she notices the round red stamp of the *Electric and International Telegraph Company*. Her first thought is for Aurora and she feels sick with anxiety. She goes down to the kitchen to tell her mother and the rest of the staff what has occurred.

"Don't 'ee worry, pet. It may be good news, not bad," says Flora, but her words do not calm her and her mother puts her arm around her. "Don't fret, we'll know soon enough, I'm sure."

Later the staff are informed by Gareth, that there has been a death on Portland and Lord and Lady Dryer are to leave shortly to go and stay there until the funeral on Wednesday.

Lettie, concerned for the family members she has met in the past, asks him, "Who has died, Gareth?"

"It's the master's grandmother, Elizabeth Stone." She breathes a sigh of relief. Lettie has never met Mrs Stone. She feels sad for Lord Dryer, but relieved it has nothing to do with anyone she knows and particularly not Aurora.

"Will Gabriel be going too?" asks Flora.

Gareth shakes his head. "No, he'll be staying here with us."

When Joshua and Louisa step off the train in Victoria Square on Portland, the wind is howling up the platform carrying with it a fine mist that chills Louisa's rosy cheeks. She wraps her mantle tightly around her and follows Joshua and the porter into the Royal Victoria Hotel.

It has been ages since she was last here on the island and she is looking forward to seeing Joshua's family and especially Ben and Becky and their little boy Jem, who must be around eighteen months old by now.

Joshua's parents, Matthew and Violet, have arranged for the immediate family to gather at their home and, as soon as they have both freshened up after their journey, they set off up to Cove Cottages to see everyone.

Once inside the door, they are welcomed with tears and kisses from Violet and Becky, bear hugs from Ben and Matthew and welcoming greetings from everyone else in the parlour. Louisa goes straight to see young Jem who is sleeping like a cherub on some cushions in the corner of the room, oblivious to all the family chatter.

"He is so beautiful, Becky. Just look at those long eyelashes, resting on such chubby, rosy cheeks. You have a bonny boy, my dear, and so like his papa."

"They're always gorgeous when they're sleeping, but you just wait, when he wakes up he's like a mini tornado!"

Joshua leaves the women talking together and takes his stepfather to one side. "I'm so sorry for your loss, Matthew."

"Thank you, Josh. As you can imagine, I'm devastated. She was lucky in that she died peacefully in her sleep." He brushes the back of his hand across his eyes. "She had more than her three score years and ten, so it should have been expected, but these things are always a shock and I wish I'd spent more time with her recently."

"I'm sure you do and I intend to make a big fuss of my own mother while we're here."

"She'll appreciate that, son. I've a few bottles of fine Madeira wine for us all to raise a glass to a good-hearted, hard-working woman." Matthew then turns to everyone. "Please come, fill your glasses and join me in a toast to Elizabeth Stone, my dear old ma."

As everyone raises their glasses, Matthew stands beside his younger brother, Johnny, puts his arm around his sister, Hannah, and says huskily, "To our ma. You will always live on in our hearts, so your spirit will never die."

The folk respond in unison, "To Elizabeth."

Hannah weeps for the loss of her mother and Joshua is filled with compassion for her, unable to contemplate how he would be feeling in her shoes. After a few minutes of silence for more personal memories, Matthew suggests that everyone should help themselves to the food laid out on the table and the hum of conversation recommences and becomes more diverse. Joshua picks up his conversation with Matthew. "On the way here, I noticed from the train that the viaduct spanning the opening of the breakwater is no longer there."

"Yes, that was last year, when we had the most severe storm since the infamous one of 1824, and the structure was carried away by the high winds and crashing waves. But thankfully to everyone's great relief, the permanent stonework weathered the storm, as did we all."

Violet joins them. "It's so good to see you both, Josh." She squeezes his hand. "How is Aurora enjoying Switzerland?"

"Well, Ma, we had a wonderful time together on our railway journey there, spending time in Boulogne and Paris, where I was able to show her most of the sights I had seen with Louisa on our honeymoon. We're both quite heartened, because we've had several letters from her and they all sound uplifted. She's made friends generally and has a special little French friend called Odette."

"I'm glad she is settled and happy. How about young Gabriel?"

"He's doing well too, working hard at his lessons. We'll bring him with us next time we visit, but we thought he was a bit young to be attending a funeral."

"I understand, Josh, but it would have been so good to see him."

"I promise we'll bring him next time. But how are you, Ma? I remember, you were very fond of Matthew's mother. Didn't she help you in the shop with her lacemaking?"

"Yes, she taught me how to do it myself too when I was a young girl, but I was never as good as Elizabeth and so I stuck with the sewing and she and Hannah did the lacemaking for me."

"How is your shop doing?"

"It was doing very well, as you know, but two years ago Henry Russell built a grand drapery emporium in the centre of Fortuneswell, and I am afraid I've lost quite a bit of haberdashery trade to him since then."

"Oh dear, I'm sorry to hear that, Ma."

"Well, it was a mixed blessing really, because this led to other elegant shops opening, which, although means more competition, it also means more fashionable people visiting the island, staying in the Victoria, or the Breakwater hotels and bringing more business for everyone. Besides, I still have a lot of regular customers who prefer my tailoring skills, so we are nevertheless ticking over nicely."

Joshua takes a bite of his sandwich and realises his parents have no food. "Aren't you two eating?"

His mother laughs, her violet eyes twinkling. "I will do, I just haven't got around to it yet."

He puts his arm around her. "Come with me and get some sandwiches."

"That's a good idea." She turns to Matthew. "And I'll get a plateful for you too, Matthew. I think you'll need something to soak up the alcohol today." His mother smiles at her husband and Joshua notices the tiny creases developing around her mouth and forming crow's feet around her eyes, marking the passing of the years, but not detracting from her beauty.

They find Ben at the table piling his plate with food and Violet squeezes in beside him.

Joshua greets him. "Hello, Brother, how are you?"

Ben grins. "I'm good, Josh. Working happily with Matthew and enjoying being a husband, and father to Jem. He is such a cheery little chap." He turns, when Becky quietly joins them from behind and nudges him. "Life is good for us, isn't it, Becky?"

"It really is, Josh. We're both so content." She smiles at her mother. "Ma and I take it in turns watching Jem in the shop and it's working out well."

Her mother links arms with them, looking up at Joshua. "It's wonderful to have us all united again."

Joshua agrees. "I've missed you all too and I'm very pleased for my brother and sister." He grins. "You waited a long time for your baby and motherhood suits you admirably, Becky. It's truly heart-warming to see you both so happy."

Her smile fades. "I wasn't so happy last year mind, when we had twenty-three of those Irish Fenian prisoners confined on Portland, but thankfully they've gone now. It took me back to the transports being landed on the beach when I was a child, seeing them chained together, guarded by soldiers and frogmarched through Castletown, to the convict ship."

Ben reassures her, "You've no need to worry, Becky, the *Hougomont* is on the other side of the world by now in Freemantle." He turns to Joshua. "Their ship was escorted into the channel by the armed *HMS Earnest*, as the authorities had received threats to ambush the convoy at sea."

Joshua's brows raise. "My goodness, it all happens on Portland, doesn't it? I read in the newspapers about the attempt to free one of them from Clerkenwell Prison in London. They showed their true colours when they exploded that bomb and killed twelve innocent people. Over a hundred more were injured, and they damaged property into the bargain. I think there was some sympathy for their fight for freedom from British rule, until then, but their infamous actions have only caused a backlash of hostility. I can see why you were concerned, Becky. They do seem to be completely reckless!"

"Yes, they are," agrees his sister, "and there were those who were hung recently for attacking a

92

police van, trying to release captive Fenians, early last year."

"You mean the ones the Irish call the *Manchester Martyrs*?" queries Josh.

"Yes, them," says Becky. "Who knows what might have befallen us, had the Fenians decided to rescue the ones on Portland, with bombs and the like. I'm glad they're gone. Now, apparently, the authorities are talking of ending the transportation of prisoners to Australia, so we're all praying that the prison will be closed for good soon."

"That'd be the best thing in the world for you, Becky, wouldn't it?" says Ben, laughing.

"Don't mock me, Ben. You know you agree with me."

Joshua quickly changes the subject.

The funeral the following morning takes place at the church of St John the Baptist, Fortuneswell. The ladies are all decked out in their black bombazine, or paramatta silk, with jet beads, and the menfolk are wearing their darkest suits with black gloves, cravats and hatbands. Fortunately, the wind has dropped, but it is still a chill January day.

Louisa shivers as she enters the church on her husband's arm. It is a beautiful building with an attractive floral-shaped window above the altar, and according to Ben, the building was only completed twenty-eight years earlier. Her mind wanders with thoughts of her children and parents, anxious to know they are all safe and sound in their absence, both in Lausanne and back in Ivell. Thus, the ceremony seems to drag on, although the vicar says some nice things about Elizabeth Stone, which is interesting to her, because she had never met her.

At last the service is over and they file outside for the committal. Louisa hates to see Hannah, Molly, Violet and Rebecca so upset and cannot wait for this ordeal to be over. It has been good to spend time with Ben and Becky, and Joshua's parents, but she is ready to go back home now, feeling the sadness overwhelming her.

The wake is held at the Cove House Inn and Louisa is relieved to find the mood lightening. Drinks are passed to the ladies by the menfolk and she chooses to sit beside the fire and have a glass of mulled wine. Becky joins her. "How is everyone at Alvington? I often wonder what Lettie and Lucy are doing now?"

"Lettie is fine. She's replaced Rosa as our parlour-maid and is very happy still with Raymond. However, Lucy was married to Ashleigh Seymour last year, which upset Billy dreadfully and regrettably he's left us to go and work near Wincanton."

"Gosh, how sad. Poor Billy. I remember him mooning over Lucy when I was staying there with you all. What about Clara?"

"I'm afraid her fiancé, Rupert, who is Ashleigh's older brother, has gone off to seek his fortune in South Africa, so she's been feeling hurt and left rather in limbo at present."

"Oh dear, poor Clara."

"I think their engagement hangs in the balance, depending on whether he stays over there, because Clara will not leave her papa on his own. Rosa and Malachi are very happy though and they have three children now, who are all delightful. Talking of children, who has Jem?"

"He's with his Great Uncle Eddie, Ma's brother and his wife."

"Do you think you'll have any more children, Becky?"

"I'd like to, but we had to wait so long for Jem, I'm already thirty, so I think it's doubtful; it's in the hands of the Almighty, I'm afraid. How about you, Louisa?"

"I think it's unlikely too. I'm five years older than you are, but, like you, we'd both welcome it, if it should happen."

Gabriel has been lonely since Aurora went off to her posh school and he has been relying on O'Malley for company. This has worked out well for O'Malley too, who has been missing his brother Paddy since he died last year, but O'Malley is an old rheumatic hound now and all this exercise roaming the estate has been taking its toll.

Gabriel has noticed the dog's hips seem to be troubling him, watching him going around and around, circling his bed before he finally, gingerly lies down to rest. Thus, in a way it is no surprise when Gareth breaks it to him one morning that O'Malley died during the night. Even though it was expected, Gabriel is still devastated, especially as his parents are both absent when he needs them the most. He rushes downstairs in floods of tears, to give his pal one last hug before they take him outside for the gardeners to bury him beside his brother Paddy, in the orchard. He says a little prayer over the grave and places a jam jar of snowdrops in front of a small rustic wooden cross that Percy has provided.

The following day, when he hears the wheels of the carriage on the gravel, he rushes to break the distressing news to his parents.

Louisa greets him with open arms for a hug, but sees instantly that her son is upset. "Whatever's wrong, darling?"

Gabriel tries to explain between his wracking sobs, "It's O'Malley… he has died… he was my best friend… I miss him so much."

"Oh no! I'm so sorry, darling. Don't be upset. He had a thoroughly good life and lived longer than most wolfhounds do."

"Percy buried him next to Paddy in the orchard, and I did a funeral prayer for him, like we did for Paddy."

"That was very kind of you, darling." She looks at Joshua. "Perhaps we should go and see Mrs Brown at Montacute Market to see if she has any more?"

Joshua nods his head in agreement. "Why not? It'll be good company for Gabriel."

"Can we? Oh, thank you, Papa. When?"

Louisa smiles. "On market day next week, if you'd like to come with me and Rosa."

"Yes please, Mama."

"Very well, but don't be disappointed if she doesn't have any presently. We may have to wait some time before she has any puppies that are weaned and ready to be sold on."

"I understand, Mama."

On Valentine's Day, Ashleigh comes home with a prettily wrapped parcel for Lucy. Amazed and intrigued she opens it excitedly, revealing inside a brand-new pair of cream kid gloves. She is astounded that he has been so thoughtful, even selecting the right size for her. "Thank you, Ashleigh. They're perfect for Easter. What a lovely surprise!"

"Well, it is Valentine's Day and I thought I ought to mark it, as it's our first, since our wedding."

Lucy smiles, reminded of the man who courted her. She kisses his cheek. "They are lovely, my dearest."

He puts his arm around her and whispers in her ear, "Perhaps you'd like to thank me properly upstairs?"

Her smile fades. So, he had an ulterior motive. "But it's the middle of the afternoon; what will your mother think?"

"It is none of her damn business. Come on, Lucy, I'll make it worth your while."

She considers quickly, at least he is sober and maybe she can talk to him about her own needs and desires for a change. She takes his arm and they go upstairs together. This could and should be rather romantic.

Once in their private rooms, Ashleigh speedily strips down to his undergarments, then turns and begins to undress her gently. She feels vulnerable with her nakedness being exposed in broad daylight, but he is treating her tenderly, kissing her bare shoulders and stirring her senses, despite her reservations. He leads her to the bed and she lays down, letting him stroke her skin softly, arousing her and himself. Soon he is lying beside her, kissing her mouth, her breasts and her belly, and using his soft hands expertly, until she wants him more than ever before, but he delays until she is writhing with longing. He has stirred the passion within her and can hold back no longer, satisfying her finally with undulating ripples of desire for the first time since their wedding day. *This is how it should always be.*

As they lie together afterwards, Lucy toys with the idea of broaching the subject of his hateful drunken lovemaking, but she is wary of shattering the mood. If only it could always be like this she would be a happy wife.

Eventually, when they have both washed and dressed for dinner, she finds her courage. "Ashleigh, that was truly wonderful. It has been the perfect Valentine's Day for me. It makes such a difference when you take the time to stir my desire beforehand." She kisses him gently on his cheek and, her heart racing, she adds softly, "Unfortunately, you don't usually do so, when you come to me the worse for drink."

Ashleigh's face clouds over with a frown. "Is that a criticism, Lucy? After I have pleasured you all afternoon."

She decides not to back down. "It's an observation, in the hope that you might consider this in the future, that's all, my dear. You've no idea the difference it makes to me when you treat me like a respected and honoured wife, rather than a whore."

He looks like she has just smacked him around the face. "A whore! Whatever do you mean?"

Although trembling, hating any form of confrontation, she is determined to continue. "Sometimes when you are inebriated your lovemaking borders on rape, my dear. I'd simply like you to attempt to get me in the right mood, before you jump on me in the future."

He looks genuinely shocked. "I am sorry, Lucy. I didn't realise," and seems to be completely sincere when he says, "I will try to be more considerate in future."

"Thank you. I'm sure it will make me more responsive towards you too, my dear, and so more satisfactory all round." She breathes a sigh of relief, having feared she'd anger him so much that he might even strike her.

Ashleigh is pleased when Lucy wears her new gloves to church on Easter Sunday. He has tried to be more considerate since Lucy's declaration on Valentine's Day. The following morning, he leaves her playing the piano, when he sets off with his cronies to Wincanton Races. The sun is shining and he is in a good mood. *I'm going to be lucky today, I feel it in my bones!*

The charabanc he has organised is full of the patrons of the Black Panther Club, all noisy and excitable, singing bawdy songs and swigging back tankards of ale from a barrel provided by William Bell, the owner of Catkin Mill. While he checks his notebook to make sure that he has logged everyone's forward bets from the club, his money bag jingles with their coins and the racegoers are perusing a variety of racing papers to see what is running at the course that afternoon.

They arrive at the entrance to Hatherleigh Farm, he pays the ten-shilling fee for a four-in-hand and they find a place to leave the charabanc. They all clamber down, a little inebriated, from the vehicle and wander off in small groups to get their race cards. Most of them, intent on studying the form of the competitors in the first race, end up alongside the riders' enclosure.

He was very annoyed the last time he was here on Boxing Day, having put a large sum on Lucky Joe Mintern's horse, Midnight Rambler, to win, only to watch the outsider, Bay Rum, beating her with ease. He can picture now, Lucky Joe in the grandstand, swearing and gesticulating at his useless jockey. He scans the race card looking out for Lucky Joe's entries and is pleased to note that this time, Midnight Rambler is not in competition with Bay Rum, so he decides to stick with her in the mares' novice hurdle race for four-year-olds and upwards, over two miles and four furlongs, at odds of three to one. For the second race at the same distance, he goes for the favourite, another of Lucky Joe's horses, Shining Star, a bay with a prominent white star on her forehead with odds of five to two.

When Uriah Levi is busy with punters, he surreptitiously finds the jovial Jarvis Pocket's stand and places his five-guinea bet on each of his chosen horses, to win. Jarvis says, "Good luck, my friend," as he pockets his coins.

He hears the announcement of the first race and goes to find a seat in the stand. The going is soft, having had April showers during the previous week, and the seven competing racehorses are getting in line for the off. His heart races with excitement as he watches Midnight Rambler and her competitors at the starting line. *Hang on a minute, isn't that the horse that won at this distance last time? Conker something or other?*

The flag drops and they are off. Midnight Rambler immediately takes the lead, but Conker Queen is on the outside in third place. Ashleigh wants to shout out encouragement for Midnight Rambler, but it is too soon. They have another circuit to do before everyone will start shouting. Both horses take the jumps in their stride and Ashleigh can see that Conker Queen is gaining ground, her ears are up, and she seems alert and full of energy. As they take the water jump for the second time, the crowd begins to scream for their favourite, but Conker Queen overtakes Midnight Rambler after the last fence and to his utter frustration she wins the first race with ease. *Damn! That's my hope for a twenty-guinea win gone!*

Lucky Joe has only entered his two best horses this time, so Ashleigh goes back to the riders' enclosure to check out the form and selects a lively, frisky grey mare called Silver Moonlight, an outsider at twelve to one, for the two-mile novice race for fillies and mares, three-year-olds and above, and for the following race, an each-way bet at nine to one on Neptune, a dark brown gelding, at the same distance, for four-year-olds and upwards. Finally, he chooses a handsome gelding, Trojan Soldier, for the Lord Bath Memorial Cup, the last and longest race, a three-mile steeplechase for four-year-olds and above, at odds of seven to one.

He goes again to Jarvis Pocket to place his bets, once more optimistic. All together his gambling has cost him twenty-five guineas, but, taking Midnight Rambler out of the equation, he hopes to make over 160 guineas when they all streak past the winning post.

He finds some of his group, mostly from East Coker, gathered around the Hall and Woodhouse stand and joins in with a round of ale. He misses his brother terribly; the other men from the club are in their groups of chums, but he feels almost an outsider without Rupert beside him. He wonders where he is at this precise moment and takes a large swig of brandy from his hip flask. Lucy doesn't understand how lost he is without him. She will never understand. *I wonder if he would have lost his money on the first race?*

While supping ale, the group observe Mortimer Bathhurst and his jockey being presented with their prize by Edward Woodhouse and the next race is announced. They make their way, wobbling and bumping into each other and spilling their drinks, squeezing between the spectators at the edge of the track to get the prime spot. It is the two-mile novice race for fillies, and Ashleigh looks out for the little grey, Silver Moonlight. This is his big gamble, five guineas on the nose, because she is a real outsider, but she is so spirited he couldn't resist her.

He spots her side-stepping and bucking as her jockey tries to get her to line up with the rest of the field about two furlongs before the water jump. The starter is waiting patiently, ready with his flag. Down it goes and they are off. *Come on, my little darling, you can do it!*

She is full of pent-up energy and takes the lead immediately, but at the second obstacle she abruptly stops short, sending her jockey flying, to land in a crumpled heap on the other side of the fence. He wants to cry; sixty-five guineas more in winnings have slipped through his fingers in less than fifteen minutes. He turns away. He didn't even get to watch a good race! He takes another large swig from his hip flask and spots some of the chaps from Stoford. He quickly pockets his flask and goes to join them. "How are you doing, Jack?"

Jack Cooper grins. "I won the first race with Conker Queen and my money is on Indian Princess in this one."

Ashleigh slaps him on the back. "Good luck, Jack. I just lost out on a refusal, when Silver Moonlight unseated her jockey."

"My money's on Bay Rum in the next race. Do you remember she beat Midnight Rambler easily on Boxing Day?"

He sighs, "Yes, I do remember, now that you mention it." *I shouldn't have been so quick to back Lucky Joe's horses.*

"I think most of us had a punt on her."

Oh, dear, perhaps I should back her as well?

He is in two minds whether to take from the Black Panther purse or not. He has run out of his own cash and if they have all bet on Bay Rum he will not be able to honour their bets on her, unless he does something quickly. He checks his book and seven out of ten have gone with Bay Rum. At least if he makes an off bet on her himself, he will make some money back.

So, he takes ten guineas from the money bag and places it with Jarvis Pocket. Even though Uriah Levi is the nearest bookie to him, he skirts around his stand, keeping out of his sight line; it being his habit to change bookies periodically whenever his unpaid debts become embarrassing. Bay Rum's odds have shortened considerably during the morning. However, he takes odds of nine to two with Pocket but has promised the Black Panther boys odds of seven to one. He is afraid it is too little too late.

The official announces Indian Princess as the winner of the last race. He checks his book and four of the men have gone for her; not quite as bad as if Bay Rum should win. He remembers recognising her jockey at Christmas, but still cannot place him. He joins Jack Cooper and the Stoford chaps near the starting line, just as the flag drops and watches despondently as Bay Rum is with the front three horses the whole of the way around the first circuit, then she pulls into second place just before the water jump and is neck and neck with Shining Star.

He starts to scream, "Come on, Shining Star. But watches in despair as Bay Rum beats her by half a length. In a foul mood, he goes to pick up his fifty-five guineas from Jarvis Pocket. The bookie removes a wad of notes from the pocket of his customary yellow plaid waistcoat and peels off the required amount. Ashleigh returns the ten guineas stake money to the purse. At least that gives him forty-five guineas towards his losses. If all seven men had bet five guineas at seven to one, he would be paying out 280 guineas. Some must have bet more and some less; he will know for certain when he gets back to the club and can check his book in peace. He takes another large swig from his hip flask.

He watches Bob Yates and his jockey go to collect their trophy, racking his brain to try to remember where he has seen the jockey fellow before. Then it comes to him. *It was at the boxing tournament, when I was first introduced to Lucy. The fellow was collecting the nobbings for her brother, Malachi!*

The third race is announced. His money is on Neptune in this race. *Surely I'm due for at least one winner?*

The seven horses line up before the water jump for the shorter race, and Ashleigh watches Neptune clearing the water easily, but in fourth place. Gradually he gains ground until he is just behind the front runner. Ashleigh feels his heart racing, "Come on, Neptune," he cries. But the horse simply doesn't have the reserve stamina to pass the leader and finishes in second place. *Thank the Lord for that! At least I have a place, which means I've pulled back just under fourteen guineas.*

He goes to pick up his meagre winnings, but while he is at Jarvis Pocket's stand, Uriah Levi, sending the bookie some tic-tac signals, spots Ashleigh being handed some money. He immediately beckons to him with his long, thin knobbly forefinger. Ashleigh's heart sinks. He has no choice but to go and face the man.

"Good morrow, Mr Seymour. I see you have collected some winnings, my dear, and I was wondering when you might be thinking of repaying me some of the money I loaned to you in good faith last year?"

"I'm not doing well today, Uriah, but I've picked up just under fourteen guineas for second place in the last race."

The old Jew holds out his hand for the cash. "Ten guineas will do nicely for now, my dear boy, but please remember the loan is earning interest and the longer you take to repay it, the more it's going to cost you in the long run. I did say I'd expect regular monthly repayments, and if you're unable to comply, I promise you, my dear, I'll get my money back, one way or another."

Ashleigh reluctantly counts out the ten guineas. Even though he has had a small win, he will not be able to explain to Lucy that it was taken by the old moneylender.

The old man looks up at him from under bushy grey eyebrows. "Which is your steed in the last race, Mr Seymour?"

"Trojan Soldier at seven to one. He looks to be a strong, game animal for that longer distance."

"Good luck, my dear. Will you be paying me the forty guineas should he win? It will, after all, only make a small dent in the total owing."

He frowns. "He has to win first." He wanders back to the racetrack without enthusiasm. *Even if Trojan Soldier does win, I'll still not be taking my winnings home with me, but I suppose it will be reducing my debt. I should never have agreed to the loan in the first place; with the interest compounding daily, the bastard is fleecing me dry!*

Unfortunately, Trojan Soldier would have been part of the rear guard in the military, as he came in as an 'also ran' at the back of the field in seventh place. Ashleigh goes to take another swig from his flask, but there is merely a small drizzle left.

Billy spotted his nemesis, Ashleigh Seymour, looking a bit the worse for wear earlier that afternoon, when paying his meagre winnings back to Uriah Levi. He couldn't help wondering how his sweet Lucy could put up with his behaviour.

At the end of the event when the stragglers are wending their way towards Clemmy's Field and he is helping the race committee members and the Yates family to clear up, the Black Panther group are still milling around the Hall and Woodhouse stand, staggering around and singing their silly songs. If anything, Ashleigh seems to be the worst of the bunch.

He watches Bob Yates trying to move them on. "Come on, lads, time to make tracks homeward."

Ashleigh says, "Come on, man, don't be a killjoy. Let's just have one more, before our long journey back to Ivell."

"I'm afraid Mr Woodhouse would not approve, sir," says the barman, busily securing the casks on his wagon.

Bob Yates tries to shepherd them away from the stand. "Please, gentlemen, I must insist. We need to be able to clear the field before tomorrow."

Ashleigh shrugs him off. "All right, all right, no need to get narky," and he moodily staggers after his cronies.

Billy is helping Don clear the site of litter, when he spots a pink page from the *Sporting Times* fluttering in the April breeze, through the gateway into Clemmy's Field. He goes to collect it for his sack and observes the charabanc leaving through the gates onto Lawrence Hill. He is glad to see the back of them, but sorry to think of that drunkard going home to poor Lucy.

It is around midnight when Lucy is awoken by the sound of her husband lurching through the bedroom door, staggering towards the bed and collapsing, fully clothed, across her feet. She knows there is no way she will be able to shift him and so she eases her feet from underneath him and lies crossways across the bed, trying to fall back to sleep, but his loud snoring puts paid to this. Eventually, she indignantly gets up from the bed, fumbles around for the tin of Congreve matches and lights her bedside candle, puts on her oriental dressing gown and goes to sleep in the guest room. *How selfish he is to treat me in this appalling manner.*

CHAPTER SEVEN *(April–December 1868)*

FINISHING AND BEGINNING

Gabriel is excited to be going again to Montacute Market to collect two border collie puppies, promised by Mrs Brown to be ready in the first week of June. His mother has enlisted Edwin to accompany them with the dog basket and Gabriel runs ahead of them, weaving through the stalls and villagers, wanting to be the first one to see their new pets. He hears his mother calling him to slow down and wait for them, but he cannot wait.

He reaches Mrs Brown's stand and is overwhelmed with joy at the sight of eight porky little puppies all scrambling over each other, tails wagging and tongues at the ready to lick any reachable hand. One is standing on its back legs, its furry front paws resting on the side of the container, reaching up to be stroked. It has a white muzzle and a white stripe up to its forehead with three little black splodges over the top of its nose, a white tummy and legs and black back. He is besotted. "Can I have this one, please, Mama," he cries, as his mother arrives beside him.

His mother looks to Mrs Brown for her answer. She says, "He can have any one of these; they are all looking for good homes, my lady."

"Which are boys and which are girls?" asks Gabriel.

Mrs Brown smiles, "The one you have chosen is a little girl."

"Please, Mama, can I have that one? I want to call her Dottie."

"All right, Gabriel. You can have that one for your birthday present in July and we must choose one for Papa whose birthday is next Wednesday."

He spots another puppy nuzzling against his Dottie with matching colours, apart from nutmeg-coloured eyebrows. "How about that one, Mama, with the brown eyebrows?"

"That one is a little boy," says Mrs Brown.

"If you think so, dear." She turns to Mrs Brown. "May we please have those two? My son seems to be smitten."

"Of course, my lady."

He trembles with excitement as his mother hands over the money and places the two pups into the basket held by Edwin. He cannot wait to get them home and watch them frolicking together on the lawn. He knows he has given his mother no opportunity to peruse any of the other stalls, because they must take Dottie and Dash home immediately to settle them into their new surroundings.

Edwin carries the basket back to the carriage, conveniently waiting in the coaching park at the back of the Phelips Arms. Once in the carriage, Gabriel lifts Dottie from the basket and kisses her on the top of her head.

"Put her back, Gabriel, she'll be safer cuddled up with her brother, as we go over the ruts in the road. You can cuddle them when we get home, but you cannot leave poor little Dash alone in the basket until then, can you?"

"I'm sorry, Mama, but I cannot resist her, she's so adorable."

"They are both delightful, but you must remember they will also be scared, having been taken away from their mother and the rest of their litter, so you must treat them gently and let them get to know us slowly."

"I will love them both forever, Mama. Thank you so much for finding them for me."

On the 12th June, Joshua is thirty-six years old and, as well as the gift of little Dash, Louisa organises a trip to the United Kingdom's first ever Aeronautical Exhibition held at the Crystal Palace, on Penge Common in London, as a birthday celebration for him. She has arranged for them to travel up to London by steam train, visit the exhibition and stay overnight at the Grosvenor Hotel.

Louisa is glad that Joshua appears thrilled to be at the Crystal Palace. He is animated when he tells her, "I remember back when I arrived at St Katharine Docks on my return from Fiji in 1851, only to be amazed to see London so busy, due to Prince Albert's first Great Exhibition at the original Crystal Palace in Hyde Park. I was unable to attend in my haste to get home, but London was full of folk of all nationalities."

They stroll together among the other fashionably dressed sightseers, and she is gratified that Joshua is fascinated by all seventy-seven exhibits, studying heavier-than-air models, engines, kites, air balloons, projected plans of machines and in pride of place a model of the triplane designed by John Stringfellow, suspended above them. This model is driven by a small motor and they wait below, until the moment when it lifts off the wire and actually flies.

Joshua is very impressed. They move on and he tells Louisa, "I've met John Stringfellow before, you know. He lived in Crewkerne at the time and was working in Chard making bobbins and carriages for the lace industry."

"Really? He was a local man?"

"He was. Then I read in the *Western Flying Post* that he was building a lightweight engine for the aerial steam carriage, designed by his colleague William Henson and together they had hopes of forming the *Aerial Transit Company*, but despite their efforts, they've not managed to get that off the ground, excuse the pun."

Louisa smiles, as affluent strangers mill around them. Joshua takes her arm and pulls her closer to him, continuing his tale. "The man is credited for achieving the first powered flight in 1848 using an unmanned, ten-foot wingspan, steam-powered monoplane, which was built in the disused lace factory in Chard. His first attempt only managed ten feet before being damaged, but the second managed thirty yards. However, this triplane, with its superposed wings, looks to be far more substantial."

"It is rather beautiful, but I'm not sure I'd be brave enough to risk my life in it," whispers Louisa.

"No, I don't think I would either, my dear, but I can't help admiring the man's bravery, ambition and determination."

"So you're pleased with your birthday surprise?"

"I'm truly delighted, my dear. Not only to see the exhibition, but also to enter this wonderful glass building, designed by Joseph Paxton. Apart from being an amazing feat of engineering, it is also quite magnificent to behold and even more incredible to think it was designed by a freelance gardener."

Suddenly, Louisa feels light-headed and a little faint. "Do you think we might find somewhere to take afternoon tea, my dear? It is very hot and crowded in here."

"Of course. If you're feeling weary, I've seen enough, and would be happy to take you back to the hotel."

They work their way back to the main entrance and Joshua hails a hansom cab to take them back to the Grosvenor. Once settled in the carriage, away from the crowds and chaos of the exhibition, she feels her colour returning and she relaxes again.

On their way, they pass the magnificent Buckingham Palace and Louisa is especially impressed with all the gold, glittering in the sunshine, decorating the Royal crests, lanterns, gates and iron railings. What a wonderful day they are having!

Finally, the horse-drawn cab pulls up at the corner site of the Parisian-styled hotel and the driver opens the door for them to step down. Joshua pays the coachman and takes Louisa's arm. They go up the stone steps and the doorman opens the door into the spacious and opulent hotel lobby. Louisa, who was fascinated earlier with the crystal chandeliers and the marble flooring, pillars and balustrading of the stairs, comments, "It's just as beautiful as Buckingham Palace with the gold leaf decorating the pillars. I thought its Parisian influence would remind you of our honeymoon, darling."

"I'm very impressed. This hotel is only six years old, Louisa. The ascending room is the latest innovation and the first in London. This was a very good choice, my dear, for our first stay in the capital city."

"I thought you'd like it, Joshua."

Joshua asks the concierge to organise afternoon tea in the lounge for them. They sit together, going over all they have seen and enjoying the excellent waiters' service. After relishing a selection of sandwiches, a variety of fancy cakes, displayed on a dainty, tiered cake-stand, and supping China tea, they retire using the ascending room to the third floor, where they relive their Parisian honeymoon by making the most of their large and comfortable four-poster bed.

At the end of July, Aurora returns home from Switzerland accompanied by her little French friend Odette, who has been invited to stay for a few weeks.

Luke is thrilled to hear that she has returned home after missing her all this time and he rushes down to see her on the first Sunday she is back, only to feel frustrated by the charming, but ever-present Odette, preventing him from being able to see Aurora alone. *How could she have been so thoughtless to invite this girl to stay with her, knowing the barrier it would place between them.* Even more so because they both insist on speaking in French all the time, glancing in his direction and giggling together, so he is convinced that they are talking about him.

He decides to leave them to it and returns to his home feeling nettled. He finds his mother preparing their lunch, and he asks her, "Do you know how long that little French minx will be staying with Rora, Mama?"

"No, I don't. Why didn't you ask her yourself?"

"Because I couldn't make head nor tail of what they were saying, as they both insisted on speaking in French!"

"Well, that was rather rude, and not very kind of Aurora, was it? I'm not sure this finishing school has done her any good at all!"

"Neither am I, Mama. I think I prefer her, as she was when she left us, back in September."

Things do not improve as Aurora spends the whole of August enjoying the summer sunshine with her new best friend and Luke feels decidedly left out in the cold.

Lucy has learnt not to expect too much from Ashleigh when he has been out all day, gambling on anything that moves, from cockfights, horse racing, playing cards, wrestling or boxing matches, followed by drinking sessions late into the night with his cronies at the Black Panther Club. He may well be an affable socialite when with his friends, but he comes home to her, a bad-tempered drunk. She is never sure what mood he will be in and soon realises she has married a manic depressive.

One night at the end of September, Ashleigh unusually comes home early from the club. Unbeknown to Lucy, it is because he has run out of cash and William Bell has refused to let him have any more credit. Lucy is pleased to note that he is relatively sober and responds cautiously to his romantic overtures. Once more, he is gentle, considerate and persuasive and she becomes aroused and responsive. They make love into the night.

About six weeks later, she wakes up feeling nauseous. She puts extra rouge on her pale cheeks and ignores her symptoms, going out into the garden to help Tim, the gardener, plant spring bulbs down by the lake.

However, that night Ashleigh comes home in a foul mood. He strides into the drawing room, cursing and kicking his mother's lap dog, as she gets under his feet. The dog yelps. "Get out of my way, you cursed lap rat!"

His mother jumps up and rescues her precious pet. "Ashleigh, how could you! My poor little Skipper!"

"What do you expect, Mama, when she is stupidly trying to trip me up? It's lucky I didn't fall headlong into the fireplace."

"Well, be that as it may, she is tiny compared to you and you should be ashamed of yourself." His mother marches off to bed in a huff, with the tiny Papillon huddled in her arms.

"Stupid bitch!"

His father says, "I trust you are referring to the dog, my boy, and not your mother?"

"Of course, Papa." He goes to the drinks cabinet. "Would you care to join me in a nightcap, Father?"

"No, I don't think so tonight, Ashleigh. I think maybe I ought to go up and console your mother."

"Suit yourself."

"I will, my boy, and I suggest you only have the one, as you already seem to be plenty well-oiled enough." Jeremy Seymour follows his wife and leaves Ashleigh alone with Lucy.

"How about you, Lucy? Will you join your husband in a nightcap?"

"I don't think so, Ashleigh. We were all about to retire when you walked in and I'm feeling especially weary tonight, as my back is aching after helping Tim all morning with the bulb planting."

"Well, that's a nice welcome, I must say! I might as well have stayed at the club, for all the cheer that greets me when I arrive home."

"Don't be like that, Ashleigh. I've been looking forward to you coming home all night, rather than sitting here with just your parents for company."

"What's wrong with my parents? Is nothing good enough for you, Lucy? I'd like to know, what do I have to do to put a smile on that miserable face of yours?"

"There's no need to be nasty, Ashleigh. You know I didn't mean it like that. Why do you have to twist everything I say? I was just saying how I was

115

looking forward to you coming home, but you have to spoil it by being in such a foul mood."

"Go on up to bed then, Lucy. I can't bear the sight of you. All you ever do is nag."

Lucy gets up from the armchair to go upstairs to their quarters. Tears well in her eyes and her stomach is churning with angst, even though she is somewhat relieved to be given permission to retire, so she can escape Ashleigh's drunken rantings.

Her relief is short-lived, however. It is not long before he bursts into her bedroom saying, "So, you were looking forward to me coming home, were you? Well, now is the time to prove it." He rips off the bedclothes and straddles her.

"But, Ashleigh, I did say to you, I've hurt my back. Please don't be offended, but I really cannot do it tonight."

Nevertheless, he is determined to have his wicked way with her. Unfortunately, it is not long before she feels her back painfully going into spasm and she cries out in agony. To her utmost horror, unable to control his frustration he slaps her hard across her face. In addition to her spinal seizure, another sharp pain rips through her head, her dizziness makes her feel nauseous and her face smarts.

She is devastated. *Why, oh why, did I marry him?*

The following morning, she lies in bed, frightened to move lest her back should spasm again. Ashleigh is begging for forgiveness at the sight of her red swollen cheek and black eye. "I'm so sorry, I should never have slapped you, Lucy. It is indefensible. I promise it'll never happen again. You know I love you. Please forgive me." He holds her face in his large, strong hands and strokes her inflamed cheek.

She moves her head away from him on the pillow, unconvinced. "We cannot go on like this, Ashleigh. You've changed into a monster and I can no longer bear it."

"But I'm so sorry, I don't know what came over me."

"Well, if you ever strike me again, please believe me when I say, I'll leave you without hesitation and go back to my family."

He grabs for her hand. "I do believe you and I don't blame you, but I'm truly sorry. I thought you no longer cared for me and I was upset. But I'll never love anyone else like I love you. You're the love of my life."

She pulls her hand away from him. "Well, let us say no more for now. You'd better tell your parents that I'm indisposed for a few days, at least until the swelling goes down."

Ashleigh tentatively suggests, "We could say you walked into the wardrobe door."

Lucy almost sniggers. "I doubt they'd believe that, Ashleigh. They're not deaf and blind! Besides, I really can hardly move for the pain."

Ashleigh sighs, "All right, have it your way. I don't want us to argue anymore."

"Neither do I. Please would you go and arrange a breakfast tray of tea and toast, and bring it up for me, yourself."

"Of course, my darling. Is there anything else I can do for you?"

"No, that will suffice for now."

She is relieved to have an excuse to keep to their quarters for a while, as in addition to her inflamed back, she is feeling nauseous every morning now and is convinced she is pregnant. Whatever happens in the future between her and Ashleigh, they will soon have another person to add to the equation. She is thrilled to be expecting a baby, but worried that her choice of husband is flawed and that regardless, this child is going to tie her to Ashleigh and his family forever.

The week before Christmas, Helen Seymour is handed the mail and she is elated to see a Zululand postage stamp on one of the envelopes. She calls to her husband, "Jerry, dear, we've a letter from Rupert!"

He is nowhere to be seen. She walks through the house calling his name and eventually finds him having a quick tipple in his study. "Jerry, I've been calling you; didn't you hear me? Look, we've a letter from Rupert." She sits down beside him and reads the letter aloud.

1ˢᵗ October 1868

Dear Papa and Mama,

I have glad tidings in that Jack Penberthy and I have formed a fossicking company, aside from my work for Papa's colleague, Neville Frosdyke. I had purchased land for Mr Frosdyke beside the Orange River, just outside Hopetown and when three claims became available on the opposite side of the river about six miles downstream from his, I used your money, Papa, plus his payment for my services, to join with Jack and we've purchased the claims and called our company 'The Hopetown Hopefuls'. There are a lot of silicates and carbon here among the alluvial deposits and so far, we have found some small diamonds, plus some larger pale green peridots and dark red garnets. This means we are scraping a living between us and hoping to find something much larger any day now.

You would love the wildlife here, Mama. The birds are such bright, stunning colours compared to their timid English cousins. The starlings are iridescent blues and greens and the weaver birds are bright yellow or red. There is a bird called a lilac-breasted roller, which is blue and lilac basically, and the bee-eaters are patterned in green and yellow and gold and there is even a carmine one. I have seen yellow hornbills come down to the river's edge to get mud for their nests in November. According to the locals, the female finds a hole in a tree and the male brings bark, leaves and grass for her and she seals herself in with her droppings and the mud brought for her by the male. Then, while he feeds her through a small slit, she moults her feathers for her nest. Her eggs hatch in about twenty-four days and when the chicks are half grown, she breaks out of the nest and helps her mate to feed them.

As you can probably tell, I am enjoying the beauty of this place, even though it is hard work, we are out in the fresh air and feeling fit and well. I am not sure you would like the thunderstorms, however. They seem to be so much more violent than those we sometimes get at home and more frequent, causing the rivers to swell and flooding our claim. We have built a cabin on higher ground, which is adequate for our needs, but there is so much land here, one day I hope to build a fine ranch.

Anyway, enough about me, the purpose of this epistle is to send you season's greetings (I should imagine this letter should reach you by December) and to wish you all the very best for the New Year, 1869. I wonder what fortune this year will hold for us all? I trust you are all well.

With fondest wishes
From your loving son Rupert.

"Well, that's a nice letter, don't you think, Jerry? He seems to be very happy there."

"Yes, he does, although he doesn't mention any return on my capital, does he?"

"Well, give him a chance, Jerry. He had to set it all up first and find the best way for them to survive in that wild land with its variable climate. I'm sure he'll let you know, as soon as he has a significant find."

"I'm just wondering whether my name is an associate of the company, or on the third claim, so that we all have one each; me, Rupert and this Jack fellow."

"Maybe you should write and ask him, my dear."

"We don't have an address for him, do we?"

"Perhaps you could address your letter to the Hopetown postal office."

"I suppose it is worth a try."

On Christmas Day at Bingham Manor, the staff wait on the Seymours, as on any other day, but on Boxing Day they are given the day off to visit their own families. Ashleigh's parents follow the tradition of giving the staff a Christmas box of goodies to take home with them, which may contain a bonus, or a gift and sometimes, extra Christmas food.

Mary has cooked a large turkey, a goose and a joint of gammon, with roast parsnips and roast potatoes, Brussel sprouts, carrots, garden peas, pigs in blankets and all the trimmings for the family and the staff. If they had been entertaining guests, or if Rupert and Clara had been there, she would also have cooked a selection of pies and desserts, but for the four upstairs and four downstairs there is little point. This is followed up with mince pies and plum pudding with brandy sauce. In this way, there will be enough meat for a cold collation in the absence of the staff the following day.

On Christmas morning Lucy is awoken by Ashleigh getting out of bed. She yawns and stretches, pleased that she no longer feels sick. She is going to have to tell them all today.

She watches Ashleigh go to his tallboy and extract a large pretty pink package. He passes it to her. "I hope you like it, I had it wrapped professionally by the young lady in the emporium."

"Thank you, Ashleigh." She accepts the gift and carefully unwraps the ribbons. Inside is a box containing an attractive crystal glass dressing-table set, comprising a galleried tray, a pair of candlesticks and two bowls, all mounted with silver rims. It is exquisite and she is thrilled and impressed with his choice.

"Oh, Ashleigh, it's truly beautiful."

"I hoped you'd like it. I thought it would look good on your dressing table and would be useful too."

"I love it, thank you very much." She kisses him on his cheek. "I'm afraid my allowance doesn't stretch to too much, but I've been busy knitting a small gift for you." She reaches down to her bedside table and withdraws her parcel. "It's not so beautifully wrapped as yours, but it's taken me a long time to make."

Ashleigh rips off the paper wrapping and exclaims, "Ah! It's a cardigan; the very latest fashion, like those worn by the earl; very smart, thank you, my dear. I like the dark olive green too. I'm sure I'll make good use of it. In fact, I'll wear it today." He bends over her and plants a kiss on her forehead. "Come, let us get up and enjoy the day together."

She is pleased to see him in such good humour. "Ashleigh," she hesitates, "I have another surprise for you."

"You do?"

"Yes, I do." She strokes her stomach. "I'm also going to give you… a baby."

He looks stunned. "What! You mean… I'm going to be a father?"

She smiles at his shocked expression. "Yes, you are, and your parents are going to be grandparents, so we must also tell them today."

"When do you think this will be?" he asks.

"I think in July sometime."

He grabs her shoulders and pulls her up into his arms in a bear hug. "Oh my goodness, that's wonderful news, Lucy." He holds her away from him and kisses her lips. "Come, get dressed, we must tell them right away."

Lucy will never forget the look on Helen Seymour's face when Ashleigh announces that they will shortly be grandparents. It is a mixture of confusion, surprise and distaste. It is as if she can see time trickling away before her eyes and she wants to turn back the clocks.

Jeremy, however, is thrilled. "Well done, my boy!" He congratulates his son by shaking his hand enthusiastically, then as an afterthought he turns to Lucy and says, "Congratulations, my dear. Let us hope it will be a boy to carry on the family name."

Lucy replies, "I don't care either way. A little girl would also be good company for me; as long as our baby is healthy, that is all that matters."

They spend the rest of the day relaxing together, eating and drinking, playing parlour games and discussing baby names.

On Boxing Day, Lucy is disappointed when Ashleigh reminds her after breakfast that he is off to Wincanton Races with the club, as usual.

"But, I hoped you'd want to spend time with me, now that I'm having your baby." She lowers her voice to a whisper, "I'll be left here all on my own again, with your parents. Do you have to go, Ashleigh?"

He replies firmly, "It's a club tradition and I'm the one who has organised it. I can't let everyone down by not turning up."

In an instant Lucy makes up her mind. "In that case, I'd like you to take me to my parents for the day, beforehand."

Ashleigh sighs, "Well, you'd better hurry up, for I've arranged for the charabanc to leave Catkin Mill at ten of the clock."

Lucy is enthusiastic. "I'm ready now," she looks across at Gladys and adds, "once Gladys has fetched my gloves, reticule and mantle for me, from upstairs."

Gladys dips a curtsey and leaves the room.

Just before nine o'clock, Lucy taps on the front door of Home Farm and steps inside. "Morning, everyone! Merry Christmas!" Her mother enters the parlour from the kitchen, followed by her sister, Bunny. "I thought I'd surprise you all!"

Her mother throws out her arms for a hug. "Oh how wonderful! What a lovely surprise! It's so good to see you, Lucy."

Bunny squeezes past her mother, for her hug. "I've missed you so much, Luce. It's not the same here without you."

She smiles, glad to be home. "Did you have a good day yesterday, at the manor?"

Bunny nods her head. "It was enormous fun, and such a banquet. You know what Flora and Mama are like; there was enough food to feed an army. How about you?"

"It was pleasant, but quiet with just the four of us. Everything has changed since Rupert left for South Africa. We don't see much of Clara anymore, either."

Bunny says, "She came with her father to the manor yesterday. I was chatting to her and unfortunately she still harbours hope that Rupert will return for her, as he has been writing regularly, but I think she'll be disappointed."

Her mother says, "Come, let me take your shawl and gloves, you can warm yourself beside the fire and tell us all your news." They all sit in armchairs, placed to form an arc around the fireplace.

"Well, I do have some news, but I ought to wait until Pa and the boys are here, before telling anyone."

Her mother looks shocked and puzzled, studying her carefully. "You're not…?"

She smiles, "I am, Mama."

Bunny looks confused. "Not what?"

"I'm going to have a baby, Bunny. You're going to be an auntie."

"Oh my goodness, really?"

"Yes, sometime in July."

Her mother looks tearful. "That's wonderful news, Lucy. I'm so pleased for you, and your pa will be thrilled."

"I've been longing to visit you all for some time now, so I could tell you, and today Ashleigh has gone to Wincanton Races and so I persuaded him to bring me, before they all set off on their journey."

"Well, your papa and Jacob will be in, after they've finished the milking and Malachi, Rosa and the children will be coming here for lunch, so we'll celebrate with a Boxing Day party. Flora let me take home some of the pies that weren't eaten and we have loads of cold meat and a variety of pickled vegetables and I'll do some baked potatoes in the range. Bunny and I also prepared a large plum pudding for today, and this morning we made a treacle tart. So, I don't think we'll go hungry."

"It sounds perfect, Mama. It will be so good to have us all together again."

Soon her papa and Jacob are heard outside in the outhouse taking off their dirty boots. Lucy rushes over to surprise them. The backdoor creaks open and Lucy stands before them smiling at the dazed looks on their faces.

"Lucy!" exclaims her father. "I dreamt about you last night, lass. What are you doing here?"

"I've come to spend the day with you all." She turns to her mother. "Actually, I'd like to stay the night if you'd have me?"

"Of course, I'll go and make up the spare bed in Bunny's room."

"No, Mama, I'll do it," says Bunny, eagerly jumping up to help.

"Thank you, Bunny, and you, Mama. I didn't want Ashleigh collecting me later, as he'll have been drinking and carousing all day with his cronies, so I asked him to collect me tomorrow. We're going to have to take extra special care, now that we have another to think of."

Her brother Jacob is about to give her a welcoming kiss, but he pauses just before their lips meet. "What are you saying, Lucy?"

"Yes, what do you mean?" asks her father.

"We're going to have a baby."

"Congratulations," the two men cry in unison and they each give her a hug.

"This is why I've been longing to come and see you all, to tell you the wonderful news."

Once Malachi, Rosa and the children arrive, all dressed in their Sunday best and looking positively charming, the happy news is relayed once more and everyone toasts the health of the new life developing within her. She feels overwhelmed with the love of her family and has a marvellous afternoon, playing cards and chatting to the adults, parlour games with the children and playing her neglected spinet for a sing-song.

After tea, while chatting to Rosa, she asks after Ben and Becky on Portland. "Jem must be nearly two and a half by now."

"Yes, and, according to Louisa, he was very bonny when they saw him last. She did say she was worried about them, though, because of that dreadful storm we had here last Tuesday. Apparently, it was even worse on Portland because, where they've built the station and the Admiralty has filled in the mere, there's no escape for the flood water from Chiswell now, and the ground floors of some homes were completely submerged. She was reading a very comprehensive report in the *Dorset County Chronicle*, concerned that Ben and Becky's Mermaid Cottage, which is overshadowed by the great beach, must be prone to flooding."

"Oh dear. I hope not for their sakes. That would ruin their Christmas!"

"Well, I remember her reading that a freak gigantic wave, instead of breaking on the shore as usual, continued right to the top of the bank of pebbles, breaking at the summit, scattering vast quantities of stones in every direction, and flooding the houses built near the station. Apparently, the force of this was so powerful that a stone wall, 200 yards long, was demolished and the roadway was rendered impassable, partly by flooding, but also because of the large area strewn with huge pebbles and the water rushed into the harbour with such force that it washed away part of the highway. The final, most inconvenient thing was, the gasworks were completely underwater, leaving the whole island in darkness until the following night."

"Well, I do hope they're all safe. Has Lord Dryer contacted them?"

"I believe he's sent a telegram to ask them to let him know if there's a problem, but I don't think he has heard back yet."

"Oh well, no news is good news, so they say."

CHAPTER EIGHT *(July–September 1869)*

PRODUCTION AND INVESTMENT

For most of the spring, into summer, Lucy is confined and feels like the poor hornbill in Rupert's letter. Early in July, her waters break and her labour begins. She asks Ashleigh to send for Mrs Creed, the midwife, in Halstock. Feeling a mixture of relief, excitement and apprehension, she is eager to see the tiny human result of her last nine months of purgatory. She is apprehensive, lest all should not go well, but she is unafraid of the pain; after all, it is nature and if her mother could give birth to four children, she is sure she can cope with one, but she is in for a shock.

It starts off well, with gentle contractions, but soon she is groaning with pain and doesn't know how to relieve it. She tries numerous different positions and ends up on her hands and knees on the bed. The midwife arrives, puffing with the exertion of the stairs and her long walk from the village; she appears efficient and capable, as she briskly covers the floral counterpane with a canvas sheet and towels. The old woman tries to encourage her, but with wave after wave of agony, she is soon begging for some relief. Before once again being banished from the room, Ashleigh obliges with a bottle of whisky, which the midwife dishes out slightly diluted with water and Lucy soon feels the benefit.

Unfortunately, the labour continues, hour after hour, with her drifting in and out of consciousness, until after forty-eight hours, she hears loud knocking on the bedroom door and Ashleigh shouting, "Should I send for the doctor, Mrs Creed?"

The old lady replies, "I think it would be too late, sir. She is nearly there." She turns back to Lucy. "Come on, my dear, you must push with all your might; you have a large baby and it needs all the help you can give it. Come on, push!"

Lucy summons all her strength and pushes until she is red in the face with the effort. The stout midwife is holding her legs up over her shoulders, and sees she is exhausted. "Right, rest now for a few moments, then when I say so, push again, as hard as you can muster. Now, my dear, push!"

She cannot help but cry out with the effort of this. She feels her skin stretching and a sharp nip as her baby's head is born. "Well done, we have the head; now push gently to give birth to the shoulders and the rest of your little baby."

She makes a final exhausted effort and hears her baby crying.

"You have a healthy little boy, Mistress Seymour."

He's a tough little monster. "I'd known it all along; he's made me sick, he's kicked my insides about and it has been a huge effort to birth him. It had to be a mini man! At least Ashleigh and his family will be pleased."

Mrs Creed cuts the cord, checks the baby over, washes him at the washstand, wraps him in one of the towels and places her son in her arms. While she nurses him she feels the placenta being expelled, and the midwife washing everything away and making her comfortable.

She looks down at him in wonder. "How could you have caused me so much pain, you little rascal?"

129

But she is immediately besotted. "Mrs Creed, would you ask my husband to come in now, please?"

"Of course."

Ashleigh is waiting impatiently, sitting on a chair on the landing outside the bedroom door, and supping nervously from his hip flask. He jumps up as soon as the midwife opens the door and rushes in to her bedside. "What is it?"

Lucy turns towards him proudly holding up their son. "We have a perfectly healthy little boy, Ashleigh."

"Well done, old girl." He kisses her cheek gently and then kisses his son on the top of his head even more gently.

"Shall we call him Julian? I quite like the sound of Julian Seymour."

"I'm not sure, Ashleigh. I was thinking perhaps Francis Seymour would be nice. Also, it would save confusing him with your father's initials. What do you think?"

"Francis Seymour. Yes, I think he looks like a Francis."

Lucy giggles. "What does a 'Francis' look like then, Ashleigh?"

He smiles back, "Our baby boy."

The 14th August falls on the Sabbath and Aurora is looking forward to seeing Luke that afternoon when he and his sister Lilly attend the birthday picnic party her mother is holding for eight-year-old Daisy, on the lawns of the manor.

She has felt a frostiness in Luke's attitude towards her since last summer when Odette was staying. She remembers teasing him by speaking in French and regrets their foolishness. He seems to have been avoiding her since, only seeing him occasionally when he attends church with his family and having no opportunity to see him alone. This is the first time it might be possible and she flushes remembering their first kiss in the woodland at her brother's birthday picnic, several years ago now. She chooses her gown carefully; it must be flattering, but practical, as they will be playing with the younger ones. She eventually chooses an ecru foulard dress, with a ruched overskirt, decorated with sprigs of forget-me-nots and Nanny Beth has braided and pinned up her hair.

Aurora is looking out of the drawing room window when Rosa arrives first, with Daisy, Ruby and Eli. She watches her mother settling down beside Rosa in the deckchairs to enjoy the sunshine. Gabriel is soon playing tag with Eli, and Dottie and Dash are frantically chasing their tails between them. The two little girls are exploring down by the lake. She is patiently waiting for Luke, before she steps outside. It is a tranquil scene, with bees buzzing in the herbaceous border, a pair of buzzards soaring on the thermals and smaller garden songbirds flitting from tree to tree, searching for food.

Ellie Proctor has been asked to serve them. She has brought out a tray of fruit juice for the children and some Pimms No. 1 Cup for the adults and is pouring the fruity concoction into glasses for her mama and Rosa.

She spots Luke, Lilly and their mother, Susan, entering the garden from the side gate. She times her exit through the French windows to coincide with their arrival on the terrace. She dips a curtsey in greeting. "Hello, how nice to see you all. How are you, Nanny Susan?"

"I'm in good health, thank you, Aurora, and you?"

"Yes, I'm very well, thank you. Please, come and sit with Mama and Rosa. Ellie will pour some Pimms for you." They walk down the stone steps from the terrace and Susan settles in a chair beside Rosa.

She catches her mother's eye. "Mama, may we also have a glass of Pimms?"

Her mother checks with Susan. "What do you think, Susan? Is Lilly old enough?"

"Well, she's sixteen now, so I think she might have one glass, don't you?"

"You may all have one glass, but not the younger ones."

"Thank you, Mama."

Ellie pours out the Pimms for each of them and Aurora passes one to Luke. Their hands touch as he takes it and a tingle of excitement runs through her. She smiles, but he looks away.

Gabriel and Eli come running up and Gabriel asks them, "Would you like to play a game of garden quoits with us?"

"Why not?" says Luke.

"I'll go and get them from the orangery." He runs off with Eli and the two pups in hot pursuit.

Ruby, having spotted her friend Lilly arriving from down by the lakeside, also joins them with the birthday girl.

"Happy birthday, Daisy," says Susan Moore, passing her a gift.

"Oh! Thank you," says Daisy, taking the package and ripping off the wrapping. "A new skipping rope! That's just what I need; mine is too short for me now. Thank you, Mrs Moore." She unravels the rope and skips around them expertly twisting and jumping.

"You're very welcome, Daisy. I'm glad you like it."

"I love it, thank you."

Her mother calls her. "Aurora, would you mind getting our present for Daisy? It's in the oak, on the dresser."

"Of course, Mama." She goes inside to look for the parcel.

In the meantime, Gabriel and Eli come back with the quoits and are busy planting the pins. The metal rings are piled up ready to use. Aurora returns with the present and Daisy is immediately at her side with a look of excited anticipation on her face. "I hope you like it, Daisy," she says, passing it to her.

The wrapping is swiftly removed, revealing a small family of colourfully dressed wooden dolls. "Thank you, Auntie Louisa, they're adorable. Look, Ruby, aren't they sweet?"

"I thought that perhaps after our picnic, you might like me to hide them around the garden for you all to find; like hide the thimble. Would you like that, Daisy?"

She nods her head. "Yes, Auntie Louisa, that would be fun."

"Well, in the meantime, perhaps you'd like to join the boys playing quoits."

Ruby and Daisy drag Lilly off to join Gabriel and Eli and there are soon squeals of delight and moans of frustration as the game takes shape. Aurora looks at Luke and says, "I thought you wanted to have a go?"

"I do, I was just finishing my glass of Pimms."

"Come on then, drink up, or we will be left out."

They stroll across the lawn to the flat part where the quoits are set up, but they soon realise Dottie and Dash are disrupting proceedings, by chasing after the rings and either running off with them, or getting hit on the head.

"I don't think this is working out, Gabriel," says Luke, laughing as Dottie makes off with Ruby's ring before it reaches its target.

Aurora suggests, "Why don't we all play hide and seek, like we did last time we had a picnic? What do you think, Daisy? It's your party."

"All right. I'll go first. You all go and hide, and I will count to fifty." She closes her eyes tightly and they all scatter. The puppies continue to play together with the rings.

Aurora watches Ruby and Lilly go around the side of the orangery, Gabriel rushes to hide in the boat, moored at the jetty on the lake, and Luke sets off towards the woodland area, south-east of the house. She doesn't see where Eli goes; she is too busy setting off after Luke. She follows him into the undergrowth and watches him concealing himself in the redcurrant bushes, behind the gardener's shed. Her heart racing, she creeps in after him.

"I've found you," she whispers, looking innocently up into his handsome face.

He looks down at her. "You're supposed to find a hiding place of your own."

"I know that well enough, but I want to share yours."

"Well, there's hardly room," he says, determined to resist her charms.

She presses closer to him. "In that case, we'll have to make the best of it."

She hears his breathing getting heavier and senses his weakening resolve. But he remains quiet. The currant bushes do not have a pleasant smell, but Luke must be wearing some cologne because he smells fresh and wonderful. She cannot bear the silence and confesses, "I'm sorry I hurt you, Luke, by spending all the summer with Odette."

Foolishly she has killed the mood and he responds with pent-up anger. "I didn't mind Odette; in fact, I thought she was rather appealing, but I couldn't understand what you were talking about, and that was damn right rude."

"There's no need to swear at me, Luke."

"Well, you knew I was looking forward to seeing you, after missing you all year and that is how you treated me. I can tell you, Rora, I was right narked."

She feels guilty and uncomfortable. "I'm truly sorry, Luke. We were only having a bit of fun. I didn't mean to scare you away."

He pushes her from him. "I wasn't scared, Rora, I was cross."

"Well, I think you're converting a tiny mole hill into a large mountain. There was no need to send me to Coventry."

"To be honest, Aurora, I felt that you, who had caused the problem, should be the first to make amends, and the fact that nothing has happened until now, speaks for itself."

"Oh, Luke, please don't be like this. I've had my hair braided especially because you were coming and now you are being mean to me."

"So you don't think that you and Odette were being mean then?"

"No; well, not intentionally."

"Well, I'm afraid I still think you've some making up to do."

"Then let me make a start." She moves closer, her head tipped back, her lips puckered and her eyes

135

closed. She can feel his breath on her face, his heart thumping through his shirt and she has butterflies of desire in her tummy.

While the children are hidden and Daisy is searching everywhere, Louisa takes the five dolls and proceeds to find hiding places for them. She keeps an eye on where Daisy is and, when she isn't looking in her direction, she nips across to a hiding place before Daisy spots her. One doll she has hidden in the arms of a statuette, another is sitting on a staddle stone, the smallest is hidden in a climbing clematis and another is peeping over the edge of a stone urn, on the terrace. She decides the biggest male doll should be sitting up in the fork of a tree and she makes her way into the wooded area beside the house.

She is nearing the garden shed, when she spots the forget-me-not sprigs on the ruching at the back of Aurora's frock, just showing among the redcurrant bushes and she sneaks up to make her jump.

"Boo!" she says, rounding the corner, but she is the one who is shocked when she finds Aurora wrapped in the arms of Luke and kissing him ardently. "Aurora, whatever do you think you're doing?"

They spring apart. "I'm sorry, Mama."

She frowns. "I'm disappointed in both of you."

Aurora hangs her head. "I know I should have said something to you, Mama, but I've had feelings for Luke for some time now."

Louisa pulls her away from the bushes. "Well, of course you have feelings for Luke. You've grown up with him. You must love him like a brother."

Aurora shakes her head. "No, Mama, I don't love him like a brother, I love him like a lover."

She turns to Luke. "Luke, I'm surprised at you, taking advantage of my trust like this. You know full well, that it is not appropriate for the two of you to be behaving in this way."

She looks at her daughter, who appears upset and embarrassed. "In future, you will not be allowed to see Luke without a chaperone, Aurora. Now go on back to the picnic and no more sneaking off."

She decides not to hide the doll in the woodland after all.

She confides in Joshua late that night, after everyone else has retired to their bedchambers.

"Joshua, I'm afraid we have a difficult situation developing between Luke and Aurora. I found them this afternoon hiding together in the woodland, locked in an embrace and it's obvious they both have romantic feelings for each other. I've no objections to Luke, we both know him well and he's a charming lad, but they are both very young. Aurora has not been exposed to any other eligible men and I should not like her to make a hasty decision, only to regret it for the rest of her life, like Lucy has."

"Lucy? Is she not happy with Ashleigh?"

"No, she is not, but now that she has his baby, she has to make the best of it. I would hate that to happen to Aurora. I've told them they must not meet in future without a chaperone, but I'm not sure how easy it will be to enforce that."

"She'll comply, I'm sure. She knows how easy it is for a reputation to be ruined and I'm sure the principal and teachers of etiquette at Lausanne Manor will have emphasised this to her. She won't want to let us down, my dear. But just keep an eye on her nevertheless; young passions burn bright."

On a misty morning at the end of September, Joshua receives a letter with a Southern Australian stamp on it, bearing the head of Queen Victoria. He is immediately curious. Opening the pages, he recognises the writing of the gold miner, Hugh Davies. His mind turns back the years to his visit to Alvington when the kindly Welshman had taken the trouble to inform him that his old adversary Nathan Meakins was a thief and a murderer. He had led him to the evidence that finally put paid to the man's mischief and he will for ever be grateful to him. He reads the missive with interest.

June 1869

Lord Joshua Dryer
Alvington Manor
Ivell
Somerset
England

My Dear Joshua,

I hope that you and your family are keeping well. We are all in good health down here; our business is thriving and we are hoping to expand, however we find ourselves in need of more capital. I won't beat about the bush: as a result of the 1855 Act for Better Regulation of Mining Companies and the related Act of 1858, liabilities are now limited to the extent of holdings, which means we can confidently sell shares in our company. This has become more appealing to us since we have purchased a promising claim in the White Hills, between Bendigo and Huntly. The land is ripe for exploitation and the returns, from our initial investigations, look to be extremely promising.

I have discussed this with my partner Bryn Thomas and we have decided we are in need of a reliable partner, who is interested in a favourable return on his capital. We would wish that person to make an investment of £6,000 to be raised by 600 shares at £10 each, to finance machinery, etc. for the future workings.

Thus, I am writing to offer you the opportunity to invest £6,000 in our limited company, Brecon Valley Mines. I realise this has come out of the blue, and please feel free to give it some considerable thought. The land is going nowhere, we have bought it as an investment for the future, but the sooner we can commence sinking shafts and erecting whims the better.

Of course, we will understand if you prefer not to invest, but we would not be offering this opportunity if we did not genuinely believe it would be a worthwhile investment for you and your family.

With kindest regards,
Hugh Davies.

Joshua goes to search for Louisa to show her the letter. He finds her in the orangery checking on the guava and the inca berries. "These will soon be ripe for Flora for her jam making."

"That's good. I love her jams." He pauses. "I've come to find you, my dear, to show you this letter I've received from Hugh Davies in Australia."

"Oh! Is there a reason this may concern me?"

"Yes, there is, my dear. Come and sit with me for a while." He pulls out a comfortably cushioned wicker chair for her and then sits down in its matching partner.

He hands her the document. "If you would care to read it first, then I think we should discuss it." She quickly scans the sheet of paper and then looks up at him questioningly.

"Are you seriously considering this?"

"It's very tempting, Louisa, but I don't think I ought to decide whether to invest or not, without actually seeing their set-up for myself."

"But it's the other side of the world!"

"I know, my darling, but it could be a fantastic opportunity and an exciting undertaking into the bargain. I thought you'd enjoy going on an adventure with me."

"You'd take me with you? On a ship? But we'd be gone for months!"

"Well, it used to take around three months to get there and three months to travel back, but we may be lucky enough to be able to go via the new Suez Canal, which will reduce the time considerably and if we stay for a month to explore the area and discuss the matter with Hugh and his partner, we should be back home sometime in late May, early June. Come on, darling, it will be a marvellous experience for us."

"I'm not sure I'm brave enough to travel over such deep seas on a ship. I'm unable to swim. What if it should sink? Where would that leave the children?"

"I promise you it won't sink, especially now we can go via the canal. It is much safer. Rounding either the Cape of Good Hope or Cape Horn was always known to be quite perilous, but it will be different now. I wouldn't suggest it, if I wasn't confident we would be perfectly secure. Don't forget, I'm an experienced sailor and I will be there to keep you from harm's way."

She smiles nervously. "You seem to be able to counter all my arguments against it. All right, why not? The children are well cared for here with all the staff; they will hardly notice we're missing. We'll just have to make sure Grace closely chaperones Aurora while we are absent."

The following day, Joshua goes into Ivell to purchase a copy of Thomas Cook's newspaper, *The Excursionist* and contacts the company to book two tickets to travel to Melbourne, Australia for himself and Louisa. Then he sends a telegram to inform Hugh of his plans.

The tickets arrive in the morning post a fortnight later and when Joshua shows them to her, Louisa trembles at the thought of this long voyage on the high seas. She can see he can hardly contain himself with glee at the thought of retracing his steps to the Antipodes once more.

She smiles. "Wonderful! I suppose I'd better sort out what I wish to take with me. It will be hot by the time we get there, won't it?" She feels nauseous and retires to her bedchamber to join Rosa and select suitable costumes and travel wear, for Rosa to prepare for her. She opens her closet to make her choices and takes out her travelling paletot and mantle.

"The tickets to Australia have arrived, Rosa. We're travelling on Friday the 5th of November with the *Peninsular and Oriental Steam Navigation Company* on their liner, *Delta* and Joshua is jubilant, because we're going to be their first ship to travel via the Suez Canal."

She watches Rosa with the clothes brush, as she smiles and says, "Don't worry, milady, we've plenty of time to organise everything."

She sighs, "It's really going to happen, and no matter how I may want to, I can't get out of it, without upsetting Joshua."

Rosa is dreamily sorting through suitable costumes for her mistress. "Oh, milady, it will be an amazing experience for you. You'll be able to see the kangaroos and koala bears; surely you're excited?"

Louisa slumps in the little armchair beside her bed. "No, Rosa, I'm actually terrified."

The following morning, Louisa is sick. By the time Rosa has arrived, she has cleared everything away, but she feels dreadful.

"I think I'll stay in bed for a while, Rosa, I'm feeling rather out of sorts."

"Would you like me to fetch the doctor, milady?"

"No, Rosa, I'm sure it is nothing serious. I think it might be anxiety over this voyage. I'll just rest today and I'll be fine again tomorrow."

Louisa feels sick every day for a week and remains in her bedchamber. She must have contracted a sickness germ of some sort. Eventually, after being nagged at by Rosa and Joshua, she gives in and agrees to the doctor being called.

Rosa shows Dr Gillingham into her bedchamber. He places his Gladstone bag on her nursing chair in the corner of the room and examines her. "As far as I can see you are extremely fit and well, Lady Louisa. I can only put this sickness down to one thing. Have you thought you may possibly be pregnant?"

She is stunned. "Of course, I've been so focused on this trip to Australia, that I'd lost track of my cycle."

He smiles benignly. "Do you remember when your last show was, my dear?"

"It was the day after Daisy's birthday party, so it was the 15th August."

"Then I would predict you will be giving birth sometime towards the end of May."

"Oh my! That's wonderful news, Doctor, thank you so much."

"My pleasure, my dear. When you are no longer feeling nauseous, it will do you good to get up and get back to your normal routine." He laughs, "Although I think perhaps a trip to Australia might be rather too ambitious." He picks up his Gladstone bag and says to Rosa, "Don't trouble yourself, I can see myself out," and in an instant, he is out of the door and down the stairs.

Rosa begins to put the gowns she has selected back into the wardrobe.

Louisa sighs, "Oh dear, Joshua will be so disappointed."

"He'll be delighted that you're going to have another child, though, milady."

"Yes, he will, that's true, but for him it has come at the wrong time."

"But for you, milady, it is the perfect excuse."

She laughs. "That's true. I no longer have to fret over that horrific voyage or have nightmares where I'm drowning."

"There's a silver lining to every cloud, milady."

She speaks her thoughts aloud. "Now that he has a spare ticket, it might be a good plan for him to take Aurora with him instead. It would be an enlightening experience for her and she would be able to meet her half-sister, Camira, while they're there, although at present she doesn't even know that she exists."

"Do you think that you ought to tell her all about it, milady?"

"Yes, Rosa, I believe she is old enough now to understand that her father had no respect for women and took them by force and that Camira is the result of one of those relationships."

"In that case, I think this is the best possible opportunity, milady."

Joshua returns home, tired from working all day at the Michaelmas quarter-session. He picks up the mail from the silver salver in the hall and goes into his study to go through it. Before settling at his desk, he pours himself a glass of Madeira and is pleasantly surprised when the door opens and Louisa walks in.

"Ah, my dear, you are recovered. Did the doctor give you a physic?"

She attempts to hide her glee. "I'm afraid it isn't quite as straightforward as that, my love."

"No?"

She replies, "No, my dear, the doctor did call and he examined me and pronounced me perfectly fit and well, except for one small anomaly." She pauses for effect... "I'm pregnant."

"Pregnant!" He jumps up and throws his arms around her, then smiles to himself. "Oh dear, that is most inconvenient!"

She is suddenly crestfallen. "Inconvenient! Is that all you wish to say on the matter?"

Then he laughs out loud. "Of course not. It's wonderful news, darling, but we'll have to cancel our trip and I've paid out all that money on the tickets."

She eases herself free of his loving embrace and sits down in one of the comfortable armchairs. "Sit beside me, my dear, I have a proposal for you." He pulls up a seat next to her.

"You won't have to cancel, Josh. *You* can still go and I was wondering if you might consider taking Aurora with you, in place of me? It might be a fortuitous opportunity for her to learn all about her half-sister, plus it will take her away from her hankering after Luke, to give them both some more time to consider their true feelings."

His big brown eyes are focusing steadily on her. "Are you sure you don't mind?"

She nods her head in assent. "I'm quite sure."

Joshua ponders, "That's not a bad idea, Louisa. She'll be a fine travelling companion and it'll be another valuable experience for her. Besides, you are right, she ought to know about her half-sister and it will be a wonderful opportunity for her to meet her."

Relieved she no longer needs to concern herself with her fears of drowning on the voyage, she suggests, "I think we should tell her soon, so that she can organise her travelling wardrobe. She already has her *Louis Vuitton* travel chest."

"You're right, but we'd better consult with her, before we make any assumptions. However, I think she will want to accompany me. Like you say, it will be an edifying experience for her."

"I suppose we ought to also tell her that I'm pregnant, otherwise what reason could there be for her taking my place."

"Yes, you're right, we must tell her, but ask her to keep it confidential. It's too soon for it to become general knowledge among the staff and I think we should also keep Gabriel in the dark for now."

"As you wish, my dear."

Joshua crosses the room to pull the bell cord and Lettie responds. "Good evening, Lettie. Would you be so kind as to go and fetch Mistress Aurora for us, please?"

Lettie dips a curtsey. "Of course, my lord."

Moments later, Aurora enters. "You wish to see me, Papa?"

"We do, my dear. We have some interesting news for you." He sits down in his leather chair, behind his desk. "Unexpectedly, your mama finds she is expecting another baby."

"My goodness, Mama! So, this is the reason you've been feeling unwell?"

"Yes, it is. But, of course, it means that I'm now unable to travel all the way to Australasia, which means there is a spare ticket, if you should like to go on another adventure with your papa."

"Are you serious?"

"Yes, we both think it will be a wonderful experience for you. What do you think?"

"I agree! It will be amazing! We had such a wonderful time on our trip through France and this will be even more incredible!"

Louisa hesitates, but it is too late now; Aurora has to know everything. "There is also something else we need to tell you, Rora. Come and sit down beside me." When Aurora is settled in the seat beside her, Louisa continues, "You have a little half-sister over there, called Camira."

She looks shocked. "I do?"

"Yes, my dear. Unbeknown to your father, he had another child over there and if you go with your papa, you will have the opportunity to meet her." She looks at Joshua. "I think we should tell her everything, rather than she learn it from someone else, over there." She turns back to Aurora. "The sad part is that her mother, Angelica, named her after a young aborigine friend, who was raped by your father and subsequently died from her injuries. We were asked to keep the truth hidden from your father, because, like Millie, Camira's mother was also badly treated by him, but the fact is, she is your half-sister and you have the right to know of her."

Aurora looks horrified. "Oh my! How dreadful! That is such a shock. Is there no end to his villainy?" Tears fill her eyes.

"No, I'm afraid there is more. It has also been proved that he double-crossed the miners in Australia. When employed as a trooper escorting their gold to the banks in Melbourne, they were attacked by bushrangers, and he managed to escape

146

with their takings, but to achieve this, it is believed, that he also murdered those of the soldiers who survived the ambush."

Stunned, Aurora dabs at her eyes, wiping away her tears. "You weren't exaggerating when you told me he was an evil man." She sniffs. "I realised he was irrational when he trapped me in the loft at Catkin Mill, but I thought his crazy behaviour was all due to the opium."

"The opium didn't help, but he was an unprincipled, arrogant, selfish human being and we are all better off without him."

"I realise that, Mama, and thank you, both of you, for protecting me from this information until now, when you judge correctly, I'm quite old enough to deal with it maturely." She smiles reassuringly at them both. "Although I'm sure you already know this, I cannot say often enough how grateful I am to you, Papa, for taking me in as a foundling, and caring for me all this time." She kisses her mother and then goes to kiss her father too. "I now wish to never think, nor speak of him ever again." She pushes her hair away from her face. "But I can see that this trip will be a wonderful chance for me to meet my half-sister and thank you so much for allowing me to go once more on another adventure with Papa."

Louisa smiles at her lovingly. "It has been our pleasure, darling."

Joshua looks relieved. "Well, you'd better start planning your travelling wardrobe, because we'll be leaving Southampton on the 5th November."

She hugs her mother. "Thank you, Mama. I'm sorry you'll not be able to go with Papa, but I'm so pleased to be going with him instead." Then she hugs her papa. "Thank you, Papa. Are you sure you can put up with me for a whole seven months?"

"No, I'm not sure, but if you prove to be more trouble than you're worth I'll just tip you overboard." He chuckles at her comical expression.

That evening Joshua sits down to write a letter to his mother.

Mrs Violet Stone
Cove Cottages,
Portland,
Dorset

Dear Mama and Papa,

I am writing with the amazing news that Louisa and I are expecting the arrival of another child in May. This is not generally known as yet, but circumstances dictated that we have had to tell Aurora, because, unaware of this development, I had arranged for Louisa and I to journey together to Australia on the 5th November, as I was intending to consider an investment over there. Thus, rather than waste the opportunity, I will now be going instead with Aurora. As you can imagine, she is very excited about the trip and I believe that Louisa is rather relieved to be staying behind with Gabriel.

However, in our absence, I was hoping that you and Matthew, Ben, Becky and young Jem might consider travelling up on the steam-train and coming to stay with them at the manor over Christmas, as I believe they will be feeling rather lonely without us. Obviously, it would be a great relief to me to know that you are here with them and will be able to keep an eye on Louisa in her condition. The staff would make you all very comfortable and look after you with all the festive food taken care of. I am sure it would be a nice break for you. I am only sad that I am unable to be in two places at once!

Please consider it, Mama, as it will be so much more fun for them with you all there. If you do decide to come, let Louisa know in good time and she will arrange for John Moore to collect you from Penn Mill Station in the landau.

With fondest wishes,
Your loving son,
Joshua.

A week passes and he receives his mother's reply.

Dear Joshua and Louisa,

What wonderful news, we are all so pleased for you. I have spoken to Ben and Becky and, like us, they are keen to take you up on your offer. We plan to arrive on the winter solstice, Tuesday 21st December at Penn Mill Station at twelve noon, and stay a week, returning by train on the 28th December. I hope this will be convenient for John to collect us.

We are all looking forward to seeing Louisa and Gabriel and all the friends we have made among the staff. I think a change of scene will do us all good and it is something we all await with pleasure.

Please give Aurora and Gabriel our love and we wish you all the luck in the world on your voyage.

Your adoring Mama xx

Ever since Daisy's birthday party, Aurora is given no opportunity to meet Luke unchaperoned. But determined to say goodbye to him before she leaves for such a long period, she writes him a note on Sunday morning saying: *Please meet me by the gardener's shed this afternoon at 3 o'clock. I have something important to tell you. Love Aurora. X*

With her parents constantly watching them, she deliberately avoids his company after church, but manages to slip the note to Lilly, whispering, "Please pass this secretly to your brother for me, Lilly. It's important."

Her plan works and at three o'clock she is pacing back and forth behind the wooden shed. She hears the crack of a twig and spins around anxiously. It is Luke. He looks so tall and lithe as he approaches cautiously through the woodland and her heart races.

He whispers, "Is something wrong, Aurora?"

She responds at the same volume, "Not really, although I doubt you'll be pleased. I just had to let you know that I'm going off with Papa to Australia next week and I wanted to say goodbye properly, before I leave."

"Australia! That's a million miles away!"

She looks down at her feet. "I know, and I'll be gone for about seven months; three months there and three months back and a month in between."

He pulls her into his arms. "Don't go, Aurora. I'll be worried sick about you. Such a long voyage could be treacherous and I'll miss you so much."

She looks up at him. "And I'll miss you." She strokes his face. "But it will also be an amazing adventure and the time will fly by, like last time. I'll soon be back here and maybe then they'll let us see each other again."

He looks into her eyes and slowly and sensitively he bends down to kiss her. When they finally part he says, "I can see I've no choice but to put up with it, but I'll be counting the days until you return, Rora. Please remember always, that I love you."

"I will." She is delighted; he has never said that to her before. She kisses him again and then whispers, "I love you, too, but I must go before we are discovered."

He hugs her tightly to him, before releasing her saying, "Take care, my love, and safe journey."

"Thank you. Goodbye, Luke. I'll look forward to seeing you again in the spring." She kisses him once more then turns and runs back into the house, unhappily aware of him left hiding there, wistfully watching her go and feeling abandoned once more.

CHAPTER NINE *(November 1869)*

AN EVENTFUL VOYAGE

Thursday the 4th November turns out to be wet and blustery. The wind tears at the trees and rocks the carriage as it traverses along the high road from Ivell to Dorchester. For the first time, it occurs to Aurora that the seas are likely to be turbulent in these squally conditions. She suddenly dreads their long voyage, starting with the crossing of the Bay of Biscay, which is known to be treacherous in stormy weather.

When they reach Dorchester, John Moore drops them off at the railway station and bids them farewell. The guard loads their trunks into the guard's van and they board the train through to Southampton. The train carriage is comfortably appointed and she relaxes as the countryside rushes by, lulled by the rhythmic chant of the wheels on the metal rails. They stop at each of the main railway stations of Wareham, Poole, Wimborne, Ringwood, Brockenhurst and finally they arrive at Southampton West. Joshua has arranged for them to stay overnight at the Dolphin Hotel in the High Street and he enlists a porter with a trolley to help convey their luggage there.

They are served an evening meal in the restaurant, and when the restaurant manager comes to ask if they're happy with their food, the man tells them, "You know many famous people have stayed in this hotel, including our very own Queen Victoria and the courageous Admiral Lord Nelson."

Joshua replies politely, "So we are following in the steps of the nobility."

"Indeed you are, sir. And, before she became famous, the celebrated novelist, Jane Austen, lived in Southampton for three years and she celebrated her eighteenth birthday here."

Aurora smiles at him. "That is most interesting. I love her books and the subtle humour of her irony. She was a very talented lady."

"Are you here in preparation for a voyage, my lord?"

"Yes, we're bound for Australia tomorrow, thus we'll be retiring early tonight, so we're both well rested for the passage."

"Well, I trust you will enjoy your stay with us and bon voyage for tomorrow. I will bid you both goodnight."

"Goodnight," they respond in unison, and he bows and turns away to another table.

The next morning the wind has dropped and they set off with their luggage, following the porter, who knows the shortest route to the dockside. Seagulls screech and wheel overhead, flashes of white against a pewter sky. Aurora turns up her nose at the smell of dried seaweed and rotting fish carried on the salty sea breeze. The jetty is busy with sailors, passengers and porters pushing trolleys loaded with steamer chests and she is anxious to keep up with her father and their guide. She moves aside for a mail wagon, belonging to one of the steam packet companies, as it urgently pushes through the crowds. The porter heads through all this commotion towards a sailor who is calling out, "First class passengers for the *Delta* this way, please," and they are directed towards a small paddle steamer which is to convey them to the larger vessel. A sailor holds out his hand for her and she steps down into the boat. She can see below the leaden sea, lapping against the dockside and swilling submerged litter in an unwholesome soup.

The air is damp with the promise of rain and Aurora is thankful that she chose for warmth her deep green, silk-lined, cashmere mantle with the gold tasselling, and glad to be under a canvas cover, once they have boarded the smaller boat. They watch as their porter passes their chests down to some lascars who are loading all the passengers' baggage into a designated tug. Then they settle together inside the cabin, ready to be transferred to their temporary home for the next few months. The small boat leaves the pier and heads out into the Solent, the sea and sky almost merged together in a foreboding dark grey colour. Aurora looks ahead at the two masts, fore and aft, and the twin black steam funnels of the *Delta*. Two collier ships are pulled alongside her, and their crews are elevating sacks of coal up onto her decks with pulleys. Beyond this she can make out the small shadowy landmass of the Isle of Wight.

She watches one of the collier ships pulling away from the steamer and their smaller boat pulls alongside. The gangplank is lowered and Aurora follows the other travellers, climbing gingerly up the ramp and onto the deck of the *Delta*. Here they mingle among all the passengers from first class down to steerage, impatient to be allocated their berths. Sailors are loading supplies and are shouldering barrels and casks, and descending the companionway to the lower decks. She spots a

154

stack of wire crates containing flustered, squawking chickens and alongside them is a larger container of rather smelly, live pigs. She puts her handkerchief to her nose and drags her father away from them.

Finally, they are shown to their quarters on the port side of the ship, where they each have a single berth. Her father disappears into his and she goes into the one next door. The small cabin is constructed with a solid timber outer door and a louvered inner door. With the porthole open, the outer door may be clipped back, wide open, for the air to circulate through the cabin and the louvre door, into the corridor, when in the oppressive heat of the tropics. Today it is not necessary, with the damp November chill in the air, but it is reassuring nevertheless. There is a wooden bunk bed along the left-hand wall, opposite is a narrow wooden wardrobe and a fixed, comfortably upholstered, bench seat. Immediately in front of her is a porcelain washbowl fixed in a washstand, with drawers below and the porthole above. *This will not be too bad.*

The steward knocks on the door of the cabin and she responds eagerly, hoping it will be her steamer chest. "Good morning, madam. My name is Miles Balfour and I'm your steward for the journey. Welcome on board the *Delta*. I'm reliably informed your luggage will be delivered shortly. In the meanwhile, here is a complimentary copy of *The Daily Telegraph* newspaper and a plan of the ship, showing where the dining salon is, the medical surgery and the access to the promenade deck, etcetera. Is there anything else I can do for you?"

"No, thank you." She takes the newspaper and plan from him and dips a curtsey. "Thank you, Mr Balfour, that is most kind."

She is about to close the door when her luggage is delivered. The porter then knocks to summon her father, who stands aside for the man to deposit his trunk in his cabin. Her father turns to her. "I suggest that after we've sorted our wardrobes, we go up to the promenade deck, where we'll be able to watch for a while, as we leave the Solent, until the English coastline finally disappears."

Their conversation is interrupted when the porter comes back out into the passageway and her father tips him. He touches his cap, says "Thank you, my lord," and goes about his business.

Aurora replies to her father. "All right, Papa, I expect I'll be longer than you will be, so please knock when you're ready to go up."

"I shall. See you shortly."

Aurora has difficulty finding space for all her travel costumes in the small wardrobe. There are some additional hooks fixed on one side of the porthole and she hangs her floral dressing gown, green cashmere mantle, travelling paletot and umbrella on these. Her toilet bag she places on the washbowl and her undergarments in the drawers below it.

She hears her father's knock, dons her mantle and goes to join him.

Up on deck there are other passengers wandering around and they promenade among them. The pewter clouds have moved away to the east and the sun breaks through, creating a double rainbow.

"Look, Papa, isn't it beautiful!"

"It is, my *dear*, and let us hope that it's a good omen and this journey will lead us to our very own pot of gold."

Aurora's fears are realised when the little ship bucks and rolls in a typical November gale, as they travel across the Bay of Biscay. She feels for the poor livestock down below them. To avoid the sea sickness that most of the other passengers are suffering, Joshua persuades Aurora to endure the cold wind and accompany him up on deck. She follows him, hanging on to the handrails on the way, with her skirts and mantle billowing in the wind, but she is rewarded by the briny fresh air.

"If you keep your eyes on the horizon, my dear, you'll not experience the motion sickness."

She hangs onto the deck rail, her body swaying with the rolling ship, but her eyes steady. "You're right, Papa, I feel better already."

"We'll be docking in Gibraltar tomorrow night for refuelling, and you'll be able to rest; then the following day we go on to Marseilles. We should arrive in Marseilles on the 10th November." A thought occurs to him. "Oh, I forgot to mention, tonight we've been invited to dine at the captain's table."

"Oh no! I'm not at all sure I'll be feeling hungry, Papa; and whatever should I wear?"

"You'll be fine, Aurora, we should be in calmer waters by then and your appetite will have returned. I think you'd look perfect in your peach gown, which was made for you in Paris, together with the *Bon Marché* pearls and lace gloves."

That evening they are shown to the captain's table and formally introduced to him and the other three guests. Captain Richardson stands up to greet them and as Aurora is presented, he kisses her gloved hand. "Come and sit here beside me, my dear, with your father next to you. Have you travelled by sea before?" The steward pulls out the seat for her and she sits down.

"No, sir, but my father has crewed a ship, haven't you, Papa?"

"I have, but it was many years ago, when I was just a boy."

"Well, my lord, I think you've chosen well for your daughter's first maritime journey. This trip is going to form part of an important historical event, with the grand opening of the Suez Canal and we plan to be among the vessels that form the first flotilla that navigates it."

"We're both very excited, aren't we, Papa?"

Her father smiles, "Most assuredly. It's obviously a major engineering accomplishment and an honour to be able to travel in the first British passenger liner booked to pass through there. I'm also told it should save us over 500 nautical miles, compared to going, as before, around the Cape."

"This is true, my lord, but it's an even better advantage on the route to India and the east, which has been the motivation for the investment."

While the stewards hover with bottles of red and white wine, the captain introduces them to the other passengers on their table. There is a young married couple, Lionel and Phoebe Southcombe, travelling to Ceylon with the ambition of setting up a tea plantation, and an elderly Frenchman, Monsieur Moreau, who is not fluent in English, travelling home to Marseilles.

The captain says, "It's a shame you'll miss all the pageantry, monsieur. We'll be picking up some French dignitaries in Marseilles, including the British Ambassador to France, Viscount Richard Lyons." He places his napkin in his lap. "I understand the Empress Eugénie, wife of Napoleon III, will be leading the flotilla in the imperial yacht *L'Aigle*, accompanied by the canal's developer, Ferdinand de Lesseps. I believe the ruler of Egypt, Khedive Ismail, has had the Gezira Palace especially built in Zamalek for the empress, during her stay in Egypt."

He passes Aurora the dinner menu. "I hope our chef has chosen a suitable menu for you all. To start, we have various hors d'oeuvres, followed by mock turtle soup, then for the ladies, I can highly recommend the jugged hare with redcurrant jelly and for the gentlemen, the roast sirloin of beef, but of course you must choose for yourselves."

The stewards are serving their table first, and they are soon tucking into the tasty hors d'oeuvres. Then the steward takes their orders for the main course. Aurora smiles, "I'm going to take the captain's advice and I'd like the jugged hare, please."

While joining in with the small talk around the table, Aurora practises her French with Monsieur Moreau. She is gratified to see, out of the corner of her eye, her father looking on with admiration. The mock turtle soup is also most acceptable and she is thankful that it doesn't contain real turtles. She looks about the wood-panelled dining room, admiring the first-class passengers all dressed in their finery and the sparkling cutlery and glassware, lit by the wall-mounted oil lanterns. Then the plates are cleared away and the main meals are served. The captain was right; the jugged hare is delicious and her papa seems to be enjoying his beef.

"This is most enjoyable, Captain."

When they have eaten, the captain surveys all the empty plates. "My chef will be gratified that everyone has enjoyed his menu. You'll see that this is followed by a choice of semolina pudding, gooseberry tart, or plum pudding and brandy sauce."

"I'd like the plum pudding with the brandy sauce, please. How about you, Papa?"

"Me too; I'm feeling hungry now that we're in quieter waters." He dabs at his mouth with the table napkin. "When will we reach Gibraltar, Captain?"

"Should be sometime tomorrow evening, if all bodes well."

Aurora stifles a yawn. "I must admit to feeling quite weary after the rigours of the Bay of Biscay, and I'm looking forward to a good night's sleep in my little bunk bed."

The captain wears a feigned look of disappointment. "But surely after our dessert course, you'd like to join me in a glass of Madeira wine?"

"That would be most agreeable, Captain," says her father.

When, finally, they return to their cabins, the smell of vinegar and chloride of lime is permeating the corridors, where the wooden floors and decks of the ship have been washed down by the sailors, to remove the vomit of the seasick passengers, help prevent the spread of disease and make the ship smell a little better.

On the 8th of November, they pass through the straits of Gibraltar and into the Mediterranean Sea, where they restock and refuel in the British port. The dark green olive and pine trees cover the rock towering above them.

Aurora soon becomes accustomed to the ship's timetable and each day she enjoys a breakfast of Wiltshire, smoked or pale bacon with omelettes or hashed turkey. She usually has pigeon or veal and ham pie, or something similar for tiffin and between meals she enjoys sitting in a deckchair and watching the world and the Portuguese, Spanish and French coastlines passing by. She enjoys practising her

French with Monsieur Moreau and finds him a charming old gentleman, who likes to chat about his family in Lyon. She is sad when they reach the Gulf of Lyon, on the 10th November and the ship docks at Marseilles and she must say goodbye to him.

Phoebe Southcombe joins her at the rail to wave farewell to Monsieur Moreau, and as the ship sets off again, they find two available steamer chairs, side by side and sit together to chat and watch the busy harbour scene. Phoebe is an interesting young woman, she'd guess in her mid-twenties, with deep blue eyes and an attractive smile. Aurora greatly admires her for her pioneering spirit, planning to settle in an alien country to start a new life.

A healthy south-westerly breeze gets up as they skirt Sardinia on the 11th November and the sails are unfurled to take advantage of it. On the twelfth, they navigate past the Gulf of Tunis, where the Mediterranean narrows between Tunisia and Sicily and on the thirteenth, they pass Malta.

On the 14th November they pass between Crete and the coast of Libya, and she and her father join Phoebe and Lionel in a game of deck quoits. They are good company and the four of them dine together for most of the meals thereafter.

When the *Delta* arrives at the newly constructed Port Said on the 16th November, around 160 vessels have gathered for the first religious ceremonies of the inauguration, and they are welcomed by cannons, rockets and fireworks. There are three huge grandstands that have been built for the dignitaries to witness the ceremony, with international flags fluttering above them. Egyptians astride camels, turbaned men dressed in their colourful ceremonial jellabiyas and women in their kalasiris mingle together on the shore. Unfortunately, because their ship arrives unannounced at Port Said, when the purser pays her transit fee, they are allocated last place in the proceedings.

However, in the early morning of the 17th November, to the thundering sound of a cannon salute, they take their place in the sedate procession of vessels, headed by the imperial yacht *L'Aigle*, and file into the canal towards Ismailia, where the main festivities are to be held.

Aurora and her father are up on deck and watch in fascination as their vessel is finally steered through the entrance, at the back of the single file, along the narrow waterway. The fertile, well-irrigated Nile delta and far away the Egyptian pyramids, are on their starboard side and the shimmering deserts of the exotic orient, on their port side. They spend most of their time on the more interesting starboard side, as the port side is mainly mile after mile, of desert dunes. The Egyptian peasant workers wave to them enthusiastically, as they pass serenely by, at the limited speed of $7\frac{1}{2}$ knots.

Regrettably, by the time they arrive at Ismailia they are too late to be allowed to attend the inaugural ball, which is most disappointing for Aurora. Instead of enjoying this spectacle, they dine on board as usual and after dinner, Joshua reads aloud the account of the proceedings to date. "According to the *National Newspaper*, '*Cairo was illuminated with gas lights, and fireworks were sent up from rafts on the Nile and at least eight palaces were set aside for around 1,000 invited honourable guests. Khedive Ismail then set sail up the river to Port Said, followed by Prince Henry of Holland, who arrived on the 13th November. Franz-Josef, emperor of Austria, arrived at the port to a roar of artillery on the 15th November aboard his yacht, escorted by a war frigate. He was followed by Crown Prince*

Frederick of Prussia, Prince Ernest-Auguste of Hanover, Emir Abdel-Qadar of Algeria, and the Russian and British ambassadors to Istanbul, General Nicolai Ignatieff and Sir Henry Elliot.'."

Phoebe comments, "We were indeed among prestigious company."

Aurora is impressed. "Who would have thought we were anchored among all those important people, aboard the ships waiting to pass through the channel at Port Said and into the canal."

"It is a remarkable line-up, no mistake," says her father.

She frowns. "And now they're all enjoying the inaugural ball." Then an idea occurs to her; "Why don't we all go up on deck and sit in the steamer chairs? There's bound to be more fireworks."

Phoebe says, "That's not a bad idea; it's a starry night and no wind."

She says, "Come on, Papa, and you, Lionel, let's go and get our warmer clothes and we can watch the spectacle from up there."

The night is balmy and calm and they sit in a row on the starboard side of the ship and discuss the stars and the constellations. Then they are rewarded by an explosion of light and colourful fireworks and they all enjoy the spectacle. After the finale, Phoebe comments, "At least we can say we experienced some of the celebrations."

"They must have cost a small fortune," says her father.

Lionel has been pondering, and changing the subject, he says, "You know, Phoebe, we must be about halfway on our journey to Ceylon by now. We've got to pass through the Gulf of Suez, down through the Red Sea to Aden and then finally we cross the unpredictable Indian Ocean, before we reach safe harbour at Kolombo. Once we've disembarked, we'll have to organise transport and make our way across the mountains to Bintenne, and our new life will begin, my dearest." He kisses Phoebe and she giggles.

She jumps up and takes his hand. "Come on, Lionel, I believe it's time we retired." She smiles at him with twinkling eyes and then turns to Aurora and her father and says, "Goodnight, to you both; that was a very pleasant evening. We'll see you at breakfast at the usual time."

"Goodnight, sleep tight," says Aurora, thinking of her mother, Louisa, as she does so. She turns to her father. "I'm tired too, Papa. Shall we follow them?"

He gets up and takes her arm, and they step into the companion way to go below.

The flotilla reaches Suez on the 20th November where they restock with the basics such as fresh water, refuel and then up-anchor once more, to traverse the Gulf of Suez. Here they leave most of the flotilla behind them. No longer are they limited to 7½ knots and with a promising northerly wind they set sail and reach 14 knots in places. It takes them four days to pass through the Gulf of Suez and the Red Sea. Thus, they reach Aden on the 24th November. Aurora watches the lascars loading casks of food and barrels of water on board, before embarking on the passage across the Indian Ocean to Kolombo. The trip across to Ceylon is uneventful, thankfully they have missed the monsoon season and the days pass by leisurely with deck games and playing card games in the evening. Her father and Lionel are particularly fond of whist and five-card stud. Phoebe is quite proficient at these too, and Aurora picks up the finer points quickly. By the time they reach Kolombo they have developed a real bond.

When it is time for them to disembark, Aurora shyly gives Phoebe a note of their address in Somerset. "When you're established, promise to write and let us know how you're faring and where you've settled."

"I promise, Aurora." She lightly kisses her cheek and turns to her father. "Good luck with your gold-mining adventure, my lord. We've greatly enjoyed your companionship on the voyage."

Joshua kisses her hand. "Safe journey, my dear, and God speed."

At the same time Lionel kisses Aurora's hand and then the two men turn towards each other and shake hands.

She stands beside her father and watches them walk down the gangplank, with their luggage being shouldered by the lascars behind them. They wave goodbye, as their travelling companions load their trunks onto a porter's trolley and then disappear among the hustle and bustle of Kolombo's busy port.

CHAPTER TEN *(December 1869)*

THE TRUTH BEHIND THE SMILE

Back home in Somerset, everyone is preparing for Christmas. Louisa and Gabriel are looking forward to the arrival of Violet, Matthew, Ben, Becky and Jem. The staff have been busy making up all the rooms and Gabriel is eagerly anticipating seeing his relations and his little cousin once more.

Watching him helping Lettie and Emily decorate the large Christmas tree that John Boucher has planted in a tub in the main hall, Louisa smiles, remembering Joshua's arrival as the grandson and heir of Christian Dryer's estate and his first Christmas at Alvington Manor. He took her and Rosa into the Ivell Christmas Market and allowed them to choose many of the decorations they now keep and use each year. She was only his chambermaid then; today, against all the odds, she is happily married to him and has given him a wonderful son and soon another new baby to cherish, in addition to their adoption of Aurora.

She misses Joshua enormously. Her small round bump is increasing daily, she has felt the fluttering in her tummy, known as the quickening, and this she would like to share with him. Her hair is glossy and her skin glowing, but, nevertheless, she is anxious about how Josh and Aurora are faring on their epic voyage. She will not rest easy, until she receives the promised telegram informing her of their safe arrival in Sandhurst.

As well as the Portland relations, she has invited her parents to stay at Alvington over the Christmas period and the staff are busily planning their traditional banquet. Flora is overseeing the food preparations, with the help of Ruth Proctor and Malachi's mother, Beth Warren. Hopefully everyone will have fun, despite the absence of her husband and daughter, and poor abandoned Gabriel won't be too bored with all the children's games to play, with his friends and his young cousin Jem, and the many sweetmeats to eat.

The Wincanton Christmas Market is full of noise, clamour and commotion and Billy can hear the raucous sound of honking geese, gobbling turkeys and squealing pigs, as he strolls with Bob Yates among the various stalls. Above the animal noises there are the loud cries of folk peddling their wares. Lillian is here with her dairy stall and Victoria is helping her, selling their milk, cream, cheese and butter. She has asked Bob to purchase a dressed turkey and a goose to be stuffed for the Christmas celebrations and he is critically surveying the poultry to make his selection.

As Billy has no family of his own to go home to, he is invited to join the Yates family on both Christmas and Boxing Day. There will only be cold meats on Boxing Day, after the racing, but for Christmas Day Lillian and Victoria have already been busy preparing plum puddings and Christmas cake and more recently, mince pies. The spicy smells have been tantalising him over recent months. Lillian cooked the Christmas puddings in early November, with several silver joeys thrown into the mix, and then they were fed by Bob with brandy, over the weeks leading up to Christmas.

Billy needs to repay the family for all their kindness to him. He tells Bob, "While you're selecting the poultry, I have a few things I need to do myself. Shall we meet in the Bear Inn at around noon?"

"Of course, lad, see you later."

He is curious and eager to look inside Jarvis Pocket's pawnbroker shop, so he moves nimbly through the milling clusters of people towards the entrance of the business. Two of the ne'er-do-wells are lounging against the outer wall of the store. He ignores their insolent stares, opens the oak-panelled door and enters the premises. It is an Aladdin's cave of treasures of all kinds and he browses among the interesting assortment of objects. He cannot help wondering about the unhappy circumstances that led folk to part with all these treasures. He is looking for Christmas gifts for Bob and his family and is delighted to discover a pair of brass and leather field glasses, made by Dollond of London, which are perfect for Bob. Then he almost knocks over a Masons's Chinoiserie ironstone china punchbowl, with its matching cups encircled within and he believes the exotic Chinese decorations will fascinate Lillian and be most suitable for the seasonal celebrations. He will need to barter with Jarvis Pocket over the prices, as nothing in the shop is labelled.

Pocket approaches him with a broad smile. "Good morrow, kind sir. How can I help you this fine morning?"

"Good day, Mr Pocket. Could you please tell me what you are asking for the punchbowl?"

"Ah, let me see, I've only just recently laid my hands on this beautiful set, from a stately home on the outskirts of our fine capital city. I perceive

168

you have a shrewd eye, my good fellow. I'd take four guineas for it; as you can see, it's in very fine condition."

"No, no, that's far too expensive. I could buy new for not much more. How about the field glasses?"

Jarvis Pocket rubs his bushy sideburns and looks at him shrewdly. "I could probably do three guineas on those."

"Hmm, still a bit steep. How about I give you five guineas for the two items?"

"You negotiate well, my friend, and as it's Christmas and I'm in a good humour, I'll accept the five guineas."

They shake hands on it. Pocket wraps his purchases in brown paper and Billy pays him his hard-earned cash.

He is about to leave the pawnbrokers believing he has struck a bargain, when a police constable enters the premises accompanied by an elderly man, and he is intrigued, deciding to browse some more and do a little eavesdropping.

The two men walk up to the shop counter. "Good day, Mr Pocket. This gentleman has come forward claiming that his lead crystal tantalus, that was stolen from his home last month, has been seen offered for sale in your shop." The constable turns to his companion. "Would you be so kind as to point out the item, Mr Musgrove?"

Mr Musgrove locates his treasured tantalus and points it out to the constable. "In the light of this, would you mind accompanying me to the police station in North Street?"

Jarvis Pocket looks affronted. "I must protest, this is harassment. There is no proof that this tantalus belongs to this fellow here!"

The gentleman says, "Well, actually there is, I can assure you. You will discover my initials carved in the base of it, if only you care to turn it upside down."

Pocket frowns. "But I'm trying to run business here. It's hardly my fault if someone brings me things that, unbeknown to me, have been stolen."

Sure enough, the initials are evident, and the constable says, "Come along, Mr Pocket. I presume you keep records of all your dealings. Please, it will not take long. You're guilty of receiving stolen property if nothing else, but we also have further questions regarding the killing of Raymond Baker, three years ago. I understand he worked for you and that you were the last man to admit to seeing Mr Baker alive. I'm also afraid you no longer have an alibi for the time of the murder."

Pocket turns to Billy. "I'm sorry, sir, I have to shut the shop for luncheon. I must ask you to call back later, if there is anything else you wish to purchase."

Billy steps outside and is followed by the three men. Jarvis Pocket turns his sign to 'Closed' and locks the premises.

Unsurprisingly, the ne'er-do-wells are nowhere to be seen.

He wanders off mulling over what he has heard. *Maybe the smiling, cheerful bookie, full of bonhomie, is not all that he seems?* However, he still needs to find something appropriate for Don and Victoria and he pushes these unsavoury thoughts to one side and peruses the various stands in the market on the lookout for two suitable gifts. He spots a stand selling colourful hair ribbons and ornamental slides and he purchases a selection for Victoria. Then he discovers a bone-handled, multi-blade pocketknife for Don and is relieved, as he is running out of time and money.

On Christmas morning, all the family are pleased with Billy's gifts. Victoria wears one of the ornamental slides in her hair for the rest of the day and to his astonishment, when no one is looking, she kisses him under the mistletoe, making his day, but also making him go red with embarrassment. Once the Christmas dinner is cleared away, Lillian fills up the punchbowl for them all. Bob and Lillian give Billy a large hamper containing their butter, cheese and eggs, and a variety of other produce, including chutney, strawberry jam, pork pie, and plum pudding, Madeira wine and cider. Victoria has also knitted a huge horse blanket for Bay Rum in their racing colours of purple and gold.

On Boxing Day, there is a swift breeze and clouds race across the sky, making Bay Rum skittish and frisky. Her ears are erect and she seems to sense the thrill of the forthcoming contest. Around mid-morning, people and carriages crowd onto the farm and take their rightful places as organisers, competitors, spectators, bookies, gamblers, or hawkers.

Towards the end of the afternoon, Billy leads Bay Rum down to the riders' enclosure. The field is busy with the other steeplechase contenders and he feels a frisson of excitement run through him in anticipation of their event.

Once mounted, he can see over the heads of the other racegoers and he soon spots Lucky Joe Mintern with his entourage and Ashleigh Seymour with his Black Panther Club cronies. The race committee members and the usual crowd of gamblers and well-wishers are milling around and among the other spectators he spots the gypsies, Noah and Florica and the ne'er-do-wells weaving among the unwary.

He is so busy looking out towards the grandstand he doesn't notice Wally and Queenie sidling up against Bay Rum. "Hello, Billy, did you have a good day yesterday?"

He grins. "I did, Wally. How about you?"

"I was given the day off yesterday, because of working today, and I was able to spend time with my family, which is always welcome. The children were so excited to see what Old Father Christmas had left in their stockings, they were both up at dawn!"

Billy circles around Queenie giving her a wide berth, not wanting to be kicked. "I came out a bit later today, because we're in the penultimate race and I've been grooming and trying to keep Bay Rum calm, despite the noise from the course."

"She looks alert and confident to me, Billy. Good luck. We're in the next race so I'll see you later."

"Yes, see you later, Wally and good luck to you too."

Billy is riding Bay Rum around the enclosure to help loosen her up before their race, when he spots out of the corner of his eye, Ashleigh Seymour in some sort of contretemps with two burly men. One huge muscular fellow with bushy black hair and sideburns has him pinned in the shadows against the back of the grandstand, while his slightly shorter, but equally beefy colleague is going through Ashleigh's pockets, poking him in the chest, pointing into his face and shouting at him. Ashleigh seems to be trying to reason with the men, but suddenly the shorter one with greasy, lanky hair, punches him in his stomach. He doubles over in pain, as the first man yanks him back against the wall and the second fellow punches him squarely on the nose. The brawl continues with Ashleigh feebly defending himself and consequently taking a lot of punishment. Billy suddenly feels duty-bound to dismount and go and intercede. His heart racing, he loops Bay Rum's reins over the fence and leaps over the railings, before rushing across and calling out, "Hey, what's going on? Leave the fellow be, he's had enough."

The one with greasy hair puffs out his chest and makes a move towards him. "I'll say when he's had enough. You mind your own business and piss off."

The bully waves his arm to warn him off, but Billy summons the courage to persist. His voice shaking, he says, "There's no need for violence. If you don't leave him alone, I'll be forced to call for assistance from one of the constables, here."

The man continues marching towards him menacingly and he notices his deformed cauliflower ears and snake tattoos on his neck. Towering over him he says, icily, "Please yourself, but I recommend you just bugger off and keep your nose out of other people's affairs."

In the meantime, to Billy's relief, Ashleigh takes advantage of the distraction and stamps on his persecutor's foot, breaking free and running off into the crowds. "Now look what you've done. Our boss isn't going to be happy with you. He's obligingly taken on that chap's debts and it's your bloody fault he's got away, still owing a small bloody fortune."

The burly man looks as though he is going to thump him, so Billy backs away, muttering, "There's always recourse through the law; violence isn't the only solution. Your boss should try taking him to court. I'm sure it would be more successful."

With that the larger, swarthy fellow stomps towards him. "My boss don't have the patience to handle things like that. He finds a painful reminder is the best way to get folk to pay up." With that he yanks Billy's arm up his back and marches him ignominiously through the crowds of racegoers, with his shorter companion with the snake tattoos lagging behind them, looking bemused.

Billy panics and struggles to free himself. "Let me go. I've a race to run in twenty minutes. The race officials will be looking for me."

Unbeknown to him, Noah has spotted them and he and Florica are lying in wait behind a betting booth. He is frogmarched past them, and artful Noah sticks his leg out and trips the swarthy fellow, who falls heavily forward against Billy. The man is forced to put out his hands to prevent his face hitting the ground, and in the process, loses his hold on Billy. Relieved, he races off with the two gypsies, leaving the shorter chap trying to pacify his frustrated mate.

They move rapidly through the crowds, racing back to the riders' enclosure and Billy swiftly mounts Bay Rum in readiness for their race. Although his heart is thumping, he feels relatively safe among the other jockeys and mounted high enough to easily identify the men, should they plan further trouble. *Who is this boss they're referring to? Could it be Uriah Levi? I've noticed Ashleigh trying to avoid his betting booth.*

He warns Noah and Florica, "Thank you for rescuing me. I'm truly grateful, but you two need to keep a low profile now, for those bullies are determined to find a scapegoat; if they can't obtain money from Ashleigh Seymour, someone else is likely to pay the price with a beating."

Florica says, "Don't worry about us, Billy. We know all about them two knuckleheads. They're Jarvis Pocket's bullyboys and they've a reputation for being real nasty. But they don't bother with the likes of us, 'cause we're just lowly gypos to them."

Noah grins. "Besides, we're much quicker on our feet than those two lummoxes."

Billy is thoughtful; *so, Jarvis Pocket has taken on Ashleigh's debts, and now he wants paying back he's resorted to brute force. He seemed to be such a jovial chap, but he obviously has his fingers in a lot of pies. So much for that genial smile.*

Billy is shaken by what has happened and finds it hard to focus throughout the race. He knows that Lucky Joe Mintern's best horse, Midnight Rambler, is hard on their heels and he flicks Bay Rum with his riding crop to encourage her to speed up, but she jumps the last fence badly and it throws her a little off course, allowing Midnight Rambler to take the lead and leaving them in second place. Billy notes a few exasperated punters throwing down their betting slips and feels responsible for letting his supporters down. There is no sign of Ashleigh Seymour, who must be hiding away somewhere on the course, unable to leave until the rest of his cronies are ready to go home.

Billy dismounts and Don and Victoria despondently throw the purple and gold blanket over Bay Rum and take her back to her stable to be fed, watered and rubbed down. He watches with the other riders, Lucky Joe Mintern going with his jockey to collect their trophy from Fred Meaden and Edward Woodhouse. As they come back down the steps of the platform, Lucky Joe takes Billy's arm and pulls him to one side. "Just a friendly warning, my friend; I saw you foolishly taking on Jarvis Pocket's minders before the race and, I warn you, they'll be out to get you, to make an example of you to others who might be foolhardy enough to interfere. I suggest you get away for a while, because they're more dangerous than they look and your talk of the constable will have angered them."

"But I've no problems with Jarvis Pocket!"

"You can identify his minders though, should anything untoward happen to that waste of space, Ashleigh Seymour. The constables are still trying to pin them down for the murder of Raymond Baker, the dead man discovered in undergrowth on the banks of the River Cale, three years back."

"But I don't know who they are!"

"Snodgrass has a tattoo of a viper on his neck and Blakely is the bigger fellow. It's rumoured that Baker did the dirty on Jarvis Pocket and that Blakely and Snodgrass went too far with their beatings and are responsible for the man's death."

"Well, I thank you for the warning, Mr Mintern, but I pose no threat to them or Mr Pocket, so I cannot see why they'd be out to get me. However, I'll be on my guard, and I'm much obliged for the tip off, sir."

"You're welcome, lad. I don't like to see decent folk being bullied by the likes of them. Besides, it gives the sport of gentlemen a bad name."

They shake hands and Billy warily sets off back to the farm to check on Bay Rum and change out of his riding kit.

In the meantime, Pocket is tearing a strip off Blakely and Snodgrass. "You need to catch up with that toff and make sure you get back what is owing to me. I can't allow him to cock a snook at me! He needs to be made an example to others. Make sure you leave my calling card, so the message is clear to all those who disrespect me."

"Will do, boss." Snodgrass scratches his snake tattoo.

"Here is his address; you can hitch a ride on Wednesday with Quigley as far as Ivell. The place is between the outlying villages of East Coker and Halstock. I'm told it's beside a lake."

"We'll find it, boss," says Blakely, taking the piece of paper.

"I want this dealt with before the New Year."

"Yes, sir."

Snodgrass is anxious as they walk away. He whispers, "Can you read what it says?"

Blakely shakes his head. "No, I thought you could!"

"Well, I can't."

"We'll just have to show it to someone within the next two days, or when we get near to Ivell. Maybe Quigley will know the place."

Lucy and Ashleigh's parents have already eaten their evening meal and have retired to the drawing room by the time they hear Ashleigh return. He enters the room unsteadily, and they all stare in disbelief at the state of him.

Helen Seymour jumps up and rushes towards him, disturbing Skipper who barks in protest. "Whatever has happened to you?"

"It's nothing, Mama, just a disagreement at the club. I tried to break up an argument and this is what I got for my trouble. Please, sit down. There's nothing to worry about; no bones broken." He instructs the steward, "Bring me a plate of victuals, Robshaw. I'm famished." He strides across the room to the drinks cabinet and pours himself a large brandy. "Would anyone else like a tipple?"

Helen Seymour declines, but adds, "You'd be better off putting some balm on those bruises, Ashleigh. They don't do much for your looks." Then she returns to her needlecraft, with Skipper nestling at her feet.

Ashleigh gives an impatient sigh.

However, his father says, "I'll join you, my boy. A little tipple of brandy will help me to sleep later. My gout is rather playing me up tonight."

Lucy replies, "No thank you, Ashleigh," and continues reading her book in the light from the oil lamp. Ashleigh passes a brandy snifter to his father and looks over her shoulder.

"What are you reading, Lucy?"

"It's *Great Expectations* by Charles Dickens and I've found it to be quite engrossing."

"Obviously!"

She looks up at him, startled by his peevishness. "I'm sorry, do you require my undivided attention for some reason?"

"Not at all, I just thought you might be ready to partake in some intelligent conversation now that your lord and master is home."

"Well, not much of note has happened here today. Francis has a tooth coming through and has been quite fractious, but that is about it. How about you? Did you have success at the races?"

"Not really. I broke even, overall."

"Much the same as usual then," she says sardonically.

"Yes, well, your old friend, Billy Riddick, let me down, by coming in second, when I was anticipating first place."

"That's the trouble with gambling, the clue is in the word."

"There's no need to be sarcastic, Lucy. What do you do to earn money? Sweet nothing!"

Robshaw's entry is timely as he delivers a plate of victuals from the kitchen for Ashleigh, who snaps at him, "About time, Robshaw. What took you so long?"

"There was no one in the kitchen and so I prepared it for you myself, sir."

Helen Seymour gets up. "Thank you, Robshaw, that was very thoughtful." She turns to Ashleigh. "As you are in such ill humour, I'm off to my bed. Goodnight to you all. Come on, Skipper." The little dog jumps up, his tail wagging merrily and follows her from the room.

Jeremy Seymour says, "I'll be up in a moment; I'll just finish my nightcap."

Lucy says, "I think I'm ready to retire now, too." She closes her book and follows in the wake of Helen and Skipper. "Goodnight, everyone."

Half an hour later, Ashleigh stomps into their bedchamber, disturbing Francis who was asleep in the dressing room. He starts to cry and Lucy wearily gets up and puts on her wrap to go and deal with him.

Ashleigh is furious. "Don't you ever make me look small in front of my parents like that again."

"I'm sorry, Ashleigh, but it's not my fault if you're in such a bad humour even your mother comments on it."

Francis's cries are gaining in volume and distress. She goes to him, but her husband pushes past her to get to the bed and she is thrown violently against the corner of the wardrobe, banging her head and shoulder on the sharp edge of the furniture and sinking to the floor. Ashleigh moodily ignores her.

Her head spinning and aching from the impact she drags herself up to go and take care of her baby.

Blood trickles down her ear and tears well in her eyes. *Is this all there is to marriage? Surely there should be more warmth and happiness than this?*

The following day, Billy is in the stable, seated on a milking stool and attending to Bay Rum's hooves. He is painting them with hoof oil when he hears the main stable door being closed and the locking bar sliding into place. He is immediately alert. He silently screws the lid back on the jar of hoof oil and stealthily makes his way towards the food-store at the end of the block. There is a second exit there and luckily it is nearer to the farmhouse. Keeping his head low, he nimbly passes Melody's stall and then Delilah's, until he can see the door into the food-store is ajar. His heart thumping, where he has been holding his breath, he closes the door behind him and rushes outside into the open air. Swiftly he makes for the shelter of Hatherleigh Farmhouse. Lillian is in the kitchen with Victoria and he bolts the back door behind him, then stands concealed by the curtains at the kitchen window. He gasps. His fears are confirmed when he sees Blakely followed by Snodgrass exiting the building.

"Vicky, please go and bolt the front door, quickly." He can see that he is frightening Victoria, and it pains him to do so, but she rushes off to do as he has bid.

"Lillian, I need to talk to you urgently."

"Why, whatever's wrong, Billy? You look as white as a bed sheet."

He explains, his voice low, "I've been warned by Lucky Joe Mintern that there are two villains after me and they've just come out of the stable. Take a good look through the window, Lillian, but don't let them see you. They are called Blakely and Snodgrass. I don't believe they would act in view of others, but I'm reliably informed they are dangerous. You'll see that Snodgrass has a snake tattoo on his neck and Blakely, the other dark, swarthy fellow is much taller. I don't believe it's safe for me here on the farm with you at this moment and I've no wish to bring trouble to your door. If they should call here once I'm gone, don't trust them. I was hoping that Lucky Joe was exaggerating, but I have to take this seriously, now that they are here."

He hears the clip-clop sound of Samson's hooves approaching and Jake the ploughman turns up in the yard. The two men are taken by surprise, but tell Jake they are looking for 'Lower' Hatherleigh Farm and Jake gives them directions. Inside the kitchen, Billy, Lillian and Victoria anxiously watch the two men wandering off. Billy can see Jake cleaning off the plough, before unharnessing Samson, taking him into the stable and coming inside for his luncheon and he realises he must go outside to unbolt the stable door so that Jake can stable Samson, but he is too anxious that Blakely and Snodgrass are still around somewhere.

He waits until Jake begins to unharness the shire and then he slips outside to release the stable door. He looks all around him. There is no sign of the two thugs. He is relieved to have Jake there. He does not feel up to defending himself, let alone two women.

Once Samson is settled, they go inside for their lunch and it isn't long before Bob Yates joins them.

Lillian opens the subject. "Bob, I think Billy has something important to tell you."

"Something wrong, Billy?"

"I'm afraid I've been rather foolish, Bob. I got involved in something unsavoury, when I was trying

181

to be a good citizen and go to the assistance of a man who was being beaten up. However, I now find myself a target for the felons responsible and they came here today looking for me. I've been warned by Lucky Joe Mintern to get away from here, before they get to me. I didn't take it that seriously, but they tried to trap me in the stables this morning. I've no wish to bring trouble to your door, but I fear I must leave for a while, at least until things die down."

"Who was this man you were trying to help?"

"It was Ashleigh Seymour."

"That waste of space; you should have left them to it, Billy. He probably deserved it."

"I know, but he's the husband of my dear friend, Lucy, and what kind of man would I be to stand by and watch him being beaten to a pulp."

"I understand, but we don't want to lose you, lad. How long do you plan to be gone?"

"Can you do without me for a couple of months?"

"Two months!"

"I'm so sorry, Bob, I know it seems a long time, but it will be safer for everyone if I'm no longer here. Perhaps Noah Boswell would help; you know the gypsy who we gave the salvage too last year? He's a good fellow, and they could do with some extra cash. They're saving up to get married. Maybe he could move his *vardo* to the farm for a spell."

Jake interjects, "I could do some more hours, to help out, Bob."

"Thank you, Jake, that's much appreciated. Don't worry, Billy, we'll sort something out. It's better that we should all be safe. If you get your things together I can take you some of the way in the pony and trap."

"Thank you, Bob. I'm very grateful."

CHAPTER ELEVEN *(December 1869–January 1870)*

A HASTY RETREAT

Billy is fast asleep in a heap of straw, his head on his knapsack, when he hears someone coming. His heart thumping, he remains quiet, holding his breath and frozen still, until the person reveals himself to be Edwin. He gasps with relief, "Thank God, it's you, Ed."

Edwin looks aghast. "What the heck are you doing here?"

He shivers as he brushes away the warm hay. "I need a place to hide up for a while, Ed. Some thugs are after me and I had to hightail it away from Hatherleigh Farm, in fear for myself and for Bob's family."

His friend looks concerned. "Whatever have you got yourself tangled up in, Billy?"

"It's complicated, but it's to do with Ashleigh Seymour and some thugs who are after him because of his gambling debts. It's a long story, and to be honest with you, I'm famished. Have you anything you can spare?"

Edwin runs his hand through his hair, as he considers. "I think the best thing you can do is go inside and speak to Gareth. I'm sure the master will take you back, if that is what you want?"

He shakes his head. "No, Ed, I want to go back to Hatherleigh; they've been a real family to me, but I'm forced to stay away for a short while, until it's safe to return."

"Well, I'm afraid the master is away on a trip to Australia, with Aurora, but you can't stay here in the stable, Billy. You can doss upstairs with me in your old room if you wish, but I do think we ought to speak to Gareth first, to make sure you won't get into any more trouble. Come on in with me; I'm going for my breakfast."

He enters the kitchen after Edwin. Flora is amazed and obviously thrilled to see him. "Billy! What are you doing 'ere?" At her words, everyone turns in his direction and there is a clamour of surprised greetings and hugs and questions.

"Come and sit down 'ere and join us for some breakfast."

"I'd love to, Flora. I'm hungry and exhausted. It's been a long walk from Sparkford. Bob Yates took me halfway in the pony and trap, but he couldn't stay away from the farm too long." He sits down at the scrubbed wooden table, beside Edwin. "I need to have a word with Gareth. I'm seeking permission to stay here for a while."

"Go on through to 'is room then, son, while I'm cooking your bacon and eggs."

Billy wearily pushes back the chair, and it scrapes on the flagstones. He gets up stiffly and goes and knocks on Gareth's door. "Come in." He enters tentatively, hoping the butler will be sympathetic.

Gareth appears to be busy with paperwork. Then the butler looks up and sees Billy standing before him. "Well, Billy, my lad, this is unexpected. What brings you to these parts?" The familiar lyrical Welsh accent is comforting.

"I'm here to throw myself at your mercy, Mr Williams. I'm in need of temporary refuge."

"Have you been thrown off the farm?"

"No sir, nothing like that, but I was forced to leave Hatherleigh Farm in fear for my life and for the family who have taken me in, as one of their own. I was being pursued by villains, after interceding in someone else's quarrel and advised to leave the area for a while, until things die down, when I've every intention of returning to my post."

"Well, Lord Dryer is away at present and has left the running of the estate in my hands, so, as long as you're not in any trouble yourself and you're prepared to work for your keep, I'm sure the master would wish me to offer you sanctuary. In the meantime, I'll inform Lady Louisa of your presence here."

"Thank you, Mr Williams. I'm truly grateful."

"Go on then, lad, go and join the others for breakfast and then John Moore can settle you back into your old routine."

Billy bows and exits gratefully, returning to the kitchen where Ruth has plated up his bacon and eggs.

Louisa is discussing the plot of *Lorna Doone* with Rosa, as she pins up her hair for her. "Richard Blackmore is such a clever, romantic writer; you really empathise with his characters. It must be wonderful to own your own secret valley in a wild place like Exmoor. The Doone family are all rogues, but it turns out that Lorna is not a Doone after all, but a Dugal heiress who is finally able to marry her lover, John Ridd."

Rosa removes some hairpins held between her lips to allow her to reply. "It sounds like an interesting story and lovely to think of it being set in Devon, which is not so far from here."

"I think it might be a good excuse to go and see Lucy. What do you think, Rosa? I'm sure she would like to read it."

"Are you thinking of going today, milady?"

"I am. We'll set off as soon as John has the landau ready. Would you mind going and requesting this for us, Rosa?"

"Of course, milady."

They arrive unannounced at Bingham Manor and wait, swaddled in their furs, in the landau, while John Moore knocks on the heavy brass doorknocker to see if they might be received. Before long, Robshaw accepts their calling card, Gladys takes their wraps and they are shown into the morning room, where a flickering fire warms them through. It is a few minutes before Lucy enters the room with little Francis in her arms. She dips a curtsey. "What a lovely surprise."

Despite Lucy's cheery greeting, Louisa is shocked to see the dark bruise and graze across her forehead. "Whatever happened to your face?"

Lucy flushes. "Oh, it's nothing to worry about. I slipped on Boxing night, rushing to pacify Francis; he's teething at present and unfortunately I banged my head on the corner of the wardrobe."

Rosa says, "Oh my goodness, that looks so sore."

Louisa studies her manner, unconvinced by her story.

Lucy says cheerily, "Anyway, it's so good to see you both. To what do I owe this pleasant surprise?"

Louisa holds out the volume. "I've brought you a copy of *Lorna Doone* to read. I know you like to read novels and it's a wonderfully romantic story set on Exmoor."

Louisa can see tears welling in her friend's eyes, but she accepts the book graciously, responding huskily, "Thank you, Lou Lou. I'm sure I'll enjoy it. I'm reading *Great Expectations* at present and I've been thoroughly immersed in that tale, although I've nearly reached the end, so your gift is timely." Then she turns away to cuddle Francis.

Louisa believes she is weeping. "Lucy, what is wrong? I can see that you're troubled and unhappy."

"I'm fine, Louisa, please don't be concerned. It will soon heal."

"But it's not just the marks on your face; you seem so sorrowful, my dear. You know you can tell us anything."

Lucy sighs, hesitating… "I didn't want to make a fuss, but I can see you won't be fobbed off. It was Ashleigh… he pushed past me, knocking me to the floor. He didn't even help me up." She takes a handkerchief and dabs at her eyes. "Your talk of this romantic story makes me even more aware of the failings in my marriage. He has no feelings for me, Lou Lou, and it's breaking my heart."

Determined to bolster her friend, aware she is in no position to stand up against her bullying husband, she says, "Right, in that case I think you need a breather. You must come home with us, either to the manor, or to Home Farm. You need to be cossetted for a while. It's hard work looking after a teething baby, and you need support, not a bad-tempered husband who is cavalier with your emotions. Go and tell your in-laws you're visiting your parents and we'll have you home in time for luncheon."

Lucy appears cheered by their support and without hesitation, she disappears upstairs to her quarters with Francis, to prepare some warm clothes for herself and her son.

Moments later Helen Seymour enters the morning room, erect and prim and adorned in gold jewellery, with Skipper at her heels. "Good morning, ladies."

She and Rosa stand and curtsey. "Good morning, Mrs Seymour."

Helen Seymour looks around the room in surprise. "Where is Lucy and my grandson?"

Louisa answers assertively, "They're upstairs preparing to be taken to visit Lucy's family for a few days. Francis's maternal grandparents haven't seen him for ages and they've been asking after him."

Mrs Seymour sits down in an upright chair; her back is erect and she appears tense. She strokes Skipper, who curls himself into a ball in her lap. "I see. This seems to be rather a hasty decision."

She and Rosa again take their seats and she smiles ingenuously, "Sometimes it does us good to act spontaneously, don't you think, Mrs Seymour?"

"Yes, I suppose there's no harm in it, if her husband is in agreement."

"I cannot see why he should object, can you?"

"No, I suppose not."

Lucy appears flustered when she returns to discover her mother-in-law now in attendance. "Ah, Helen, I've decided to take Frankie over to Home Farm for a few days to spend some time with my parents. Please explain to Ashleigh when he gets home, that the opportunity presented itself and I thought it would be good for the little lad." She hurriedly puts on her kid gloves and before any counter, she rings a bell to summon Robshaw to load their bags. Louisa takes this opportunity to stand up and usher them from the room, with Rosa following dutifully behind them.

Helen Seymour calls out to them, "Goodbye, my dears, and good day, Lady Louisa."

The ladies all chorus their goodbyes and are soon outside in the cold December air and, with John and Robshaw's assistance, they are quickly clambering up into the landau and setting off giggling triumphantly for Home Farm.

Lucy is relieved to be back with her family. After his nap, her sister entertains Frankie for the rest of the afternoon and her mother cooks her favourite egg and bacon pie for their dinner. Her father and Jacob come in from the fields and they all relax as darkness falls.

Once Frankie is settled for the night, Bunny helps her sister make up the bed in her old room. They return downstairs to settle in the parlour where the fire flickers merrily giving off its warmth and all is peace and family harmony. In the lamplight Lucy reads aloud from *Lorna Doone* and is gratified when even her father and Jacob enjoy the magically descriptive words of R. D. Blackmore. The family retire at half past nine, as usual, and Lucy sleeps soundly, only waking once to feed her baby son.

The following morning Isaac and Jacob breakfast early and go off to work in the fields. Jacob is busy with lambing and Isaac is coppicing with Malachi. Lucy has breakfast with her mother and Bunny. She has felt so calm and content with her family. The contrast with how anxious she feels when Ashleigh is around, confirms to her that their marriage is not as it should be. Maybe she should prolong her stay at Home Farm, to make Ashleigh wonder what she is saying about him to her parents and make him think on how badly he is treating her.

She is enjoying helping her mother with some baking and listening to Bunny chatting about her love for Edwin, when they hear the wheels of a carriage approaching the farm.

Bunny looks out of the front window. "It's Ashleigh, Lucy. He doesn't look too happy."

There is a loud hammering on the front door. She trembles with emotion, and her mother goes to answer it. She follows her.

He stands in the doorway looking directly at her. "I've come to fetch you and my son home, Lucy."

Bunny must have understood by the look of horror on her face, her reluctance to comply and she watches her rush off, presumably to fetch her father.

She finds her voice, "But I was planning to stay for a few days, to give my own family some quality time with Frankie. They hardly see him."

"Well, I am your husband and I'm telling you, I want you back home with me, now."

Her mother interjects, "But she's been invited to tea with Rosa and Malachi tomorrow, so that Frankie can play with his cousins, and Lady Louisa has promised to see her home safely at the end of the week."

"Well, I am here now. I've come all this way especially and I too have things planned for my wife and son."

Her mother tries to calm the situation. "Please, Ashleigh, won't you step inside for some refreshments and you can talk it over with Lucy?"

He snaps, "I've no need for refreshments, Mrs Warren, I am in need of an obedient wife."

Several footsteps trudge around the corner of the farmhouse in boots heavy with mud from the fields and she is relieved to see Malachi, Jacob, their father and

Raymond Hawkins, the gamekeeper, approaching Ashleigh, who spins around when he hears the deep baritone voice of her brother, "Lucy has decided to visit her family and she has every right to do so."

She is aware of her brother, looking again at her black eye and grazed face and his darkening expression. He continues, "Your behaviour is totally unreasonable, so I'd be much obliged if you'd get back into your fancy carriage and leave her be."

"Ah! the 'Magnificent Malachi'," says Ashleigh, derisively. "You can't tell me what to do; I'm her husband, and she has made her vows to obey."

"Yes, well, circumstances change, especially when a woman comes home to her family sporting a black eye! You're on our property now and we say what goes on here, so you can piss off home, to wait until my sister is good and ready to return… if ever."

Ashleigh turns to her. "What lies have you been telling, woman?"

Then he makes the mistake of turning quickly back towards Malachi and is rewarded with a single punch in the face, which knocks him backwards into the door jamb. She hears Raymond Hawkins chuckling. She has never seen her brother this angry. He steps forward menacingly. "If you ever lay another rough hand on my sister, I promise you now, I'll kill you."

Ashleigh struggles to remain upright and turns back to Lucy, his hand covering his bleeding nose. "Your brother is nothing but an ignorant lout! How can you let him assault me like this, Lucy? What have you been telling them?"

Malachi is indignant. "She's said nothing; bigger fool her, but I know my sister and I know you and your reputation. I never wanted our Lucy to marry you, because I know she could do much better."

"You insolent oaf! What do you know of me, to offer such offense?"

Malachi then loses his patience and grabs Ashleigh by his lapels and shoves him towards his carriage. "Get you gone, man, you've no business here."

Jacob, her father and Raymond Hawkins, all follow behind, providing unnecessary back-up.

Ashleigh begrudgingly mounts the carriage and cracking the reins he drives off. *You've not heard the last of this Malachi Warren; you'll not get away with threatening me!*

Ashleigh is fuming. *Where is her loyalty to her husband! Letting that gorilla of a brother treat me this way! Who do they think they are?*

He cracks the whip so Dolly is racing through the country lanes back to Bingham Manor. They pass through North and East Coker in record time and once out of the village he slows down. *How am I going to explain this to my parents? Perhaps I should go and calm down for a few hours at the club.* He decides to take the circular route to the Black Panther Club, turning left at Pincushion Corner, following the lane back onto the main thoroughfare. At the junction opposite the needle folly he again turns left. When he reaches the Red House pub at Redmead, he takes Catkin Lane and once more he goes leftward on the final leg of the journey to Catkin Mill.

The doorman says, 'They've caught up with you then?"

"What do you mean?"

"The two fellows who were looking for you."

"I don't know what you're talking about. This was the result of an argument with my brother-in-law."

"Oh, I see. Well, there's been a couple of heavies hanging around outside the club earlier today, pestering the members and asking after you. We gave them short shrift and sent them on their way, but I'd keep a sharp eye out for them if I were you; they looked like they meant trouble."

"Thanks for the warning, Bill. I appreciate the heads-up. I'll stay here for a while, where I'm quite safe and hopefully they'll give up when they find no one will talk to them."

He spends the day drinking with his cronies and lying with the whores and although slurring his words and the worst for drink, he is in a better mood when he decides to return home for his supper.

The sun has set, and the evening is cold and frosty, but there is some light from a nearly full moon and the stars are glittering merrily, enabling him to follow the lane back to North Coker and complete his journey full circle. Dolly is puffing out misty breath as they go and, eager for her stable, she is making good progress when she suddenly starts as an owl swoops down in front of them screeching a warning to its mate, who cries back from a high treetop across the fields. The sudden spooky screeching makes him jump and he grins to himself when he realises it is just owls.

As they approach home, Ashleigh is slumped in the driver's seat, his emotions numbed with alcohol. They pass under the new railway bridge and down the slope to the causeway. He is ready to stumble down from the carriage, drag himself up to his quarters and roll into his bed.

The moonlight casts a silver pathway across the lake, creating shadows on either side. He can just make out a movement and out of those shadows two figures emerge. One hefty fellow leaps up beside him and pushes him from the seat down onto the carriageway. He lands on his right shoulder and his head lurches into the dirt on the grassy verge. The pain makes him cry out and he fears he may have broken his arm, then the second giant of a man grabs him by the collar, hauls him up and punches him in his stomach and face, making the discomfort from his earlier spat flare up again. *It's Pocket's minders! However did they track me down?*

The giant yells, "Where's your damned purse?" impatiently ripping a pocket from Ashleigh's jacket.

He is startled into wakefulness and heart thumping, he mumbles, "I've only small change on me. Here, take it." He hands him his leather purse, but the man checks inside his jacket and retrieves his empty silver hip flask. Then the rogue finds his gold pocket watch and chain in his waistcoat pocket.

His heart sinks. *Pocket has taken over my debt with Uriah Levi and now the cursed man has all my eggs in one very heavy basket.* He can say nothing; he knows he must pay what he owes and time is running out, but maybe these items will hold them off?

His head and arm are throbbing with pain, but he manages to put on an act of bravado, muttering wearily, "You're welcome to it all. Looking on the bright side, with my luck, I'll be able to buy it all back from the pawn shop, once I'm back on my feet."

"Don't kid yourself, mate. We've been instructed to set an example of you to others, to encourage them to pay up on time and not mess with the boss."

To his horror, he spots in the moonlight, the glint of a knife. Before he has time to defend himself, it slashes in an arc and slices through his throat. He chokes on his own blood. The villains drag him to a point where they can lever him over the fence and he plunges into the soggy bulrushes, shaking with shock and feeling his life slowly draining away.

"Wait, Nige, we forgot the pocket! We need to put the torn-off pocket in his mouth as a warning to others, like we did last time. You'll have to climb over the fence."

"What do you mean, 'You'll have to climb over the fence'? You're stood there like a dummy with the cloth in your hands; you climb over."

"All right, give me a leg up then." Blakely bends forward, holding out his hands and Snodgrass steps up and is propelled over the fence, nearly landing on top of their victim. He stuffs the material into Ashleigh's mouth before clambering back, triumphantly. "That'll do the trick."

In his parents' cottage in Odcombe, Raymond is eager to tell his sister, Jean, what had transpired at Home Farm earlier that day and when she returns from the glove factory that evening, he relates the story to her with glee.

"Malachi Warren got his feathers all ruffled earlier today, when that Ashleigh Seymour came to take his sister back with him. He told the toff in no uncertain terms that she was staying put and for him to piss off back home. When the toff argued the point, he punched him on the nose. You should have seen his shocked, indignant expression, as he tried to stand upright in front of us all. It was hilarious."

Jean sits down at the table and wearily rests her head in her hands. "Why didn't she want to go home with her husband?"

"I don't rightly know, but she had a bruise and a graze on her face, so it could be something to do with that. Anyway, he told that Ashleigh, if he ever lays another rough hand on his sister, he'll kill him."

"My goodness, that's not like Malachi, is it?"

"No, but it was no idle threat neither. Hopefully he's guaranteed his sister's safety for the foreseeable future."

Jean knows that Amy at work has a soft spot for the magnificent Malachi Warren and she cannot wait to relay this tasty bit of gossip to her the following day at the factory.

Jean is working with Amy Proctor in the office when she remembers her gossip. "Hey, Amy, you'll never guess what my brother Raymond saw yesterday."

"A purple pheasant?"

She laughs. "Don't be daft! It was a disagreement between Malachi Warren and his brother-in-law, Ashleigh Seymour." She has caught her attention now. "Apparently, Malachi was defending his sister, who wanted to stay for a few days at Home Farm with her family, and when her husband came to fetch her, he punched him on the nose and told him to piss off back home and leave Lucy alone."

Amy is parcelling up some repairs. "What set all this off then, Jean?"

"I think he must have been knocking her about, because Raymond said she had bruises and a graze on her face. Anyway, Malachi tells him if he ever hurts her again, he'll kill him."

"My goodness, he meant business, didn't he? How wonderful to have him to defend and protect you. Lucy is so lucky."

"Not really, Amy; she's married to a bully and Malachi can't be there all the time, can he?"

"True. But I expect her husband will heed the warning, don't you?"

Jean nods. "I think most men would, up against the likes of Malachi."

Amy says dreamily, "He was so good to Edwin and Bobby, teaching them back along. I think he's a hero. We could have done with him, that night we escaped from Summerville House. I was so frightened the witches might get us, or Nathan Meakins would creep up behind us and make us go back with him."

"But we got away, Amy, all by ourselves without anyone's help. We were brave and we're both so much happier now."

"True, but I can't help imagining him, leading us away from danger that night. Just us two and him, alone in the dark."

"Stop it, Amy, you have a loving boyfriend. Shame on you." Amy giggles.

Unbeknown to them, someone else is standing concealed outside in the corridor, flushing red with anger and jealousy as he overhears this conversation.

CHAPTER TWELVE *(January 1870)*

MURDER MOST FOUL

On Saturday Lucy is conveyed home in the landau with John Moore. She shivers in the fresh January air, drawing the travel rug more closely around herself and baby Frankie, and feeling apprehensive, lest Ashleigh decides to take his ill humour out on her, but she knows it is her duty to return to her husband. They are met in the hallway by Helen who appears astonished that Ashleigh is not with them.

"But where can he be? We've not set eyes on him since he went to fetch you, nearly a week ago. We assumed he was staying with you and your family."

She is brusque. "Well, he wasn't. When I told him that I wished to stay longer, he left."

Helen Seymour begins to wring her hands with unease. "Whatever has become of him? He has never been gone this long before." She rushes off to find her husband. "Jerry, Ashleigh hasn't been with Lucy, after all. Jerry, where are you?"

Lucy hears a frail voice coming from his study. "I'm in here, dear-heart."

She begins to shake, the seriousness of the matter sinking in. Her husband has disappeared and hasn't been seen since the day he was at Home Farm. She can hear Helen saying to her father-in-law, "We must inform the police. It has been five days. Wherever can he be?"

Her father-in-law appears in the doorway. "I will go with Robshaw, my dear. Do not fret. First we will go and check out that infernal Black Panther Club of his and ask among his friends."

Her father-in-law rings for Robshaw and they leave together in the brougham.

Lucy takes Frankie up to their quarters to unpack their bags and settle him for his nap. Once alone, she begins to tremble. *This is not like Ashleigh; he always manages to get home whatever condition he may be in.*

Much later that day, Jeremy Seymour returns home with Robshaw. He is weary and goes immediately to his wife to console her with a hug. "There is no sign of him, my dear. We've spoken to everyone at his club and they all say they've not seen him since the same day he went to fetch Lucy. Then we went into Ivell to report him missing to the police. The sergeant is organising a search party and they'll be starting here at Bingham Manor shortly."

"Oh, my Lord, Jerry. I know something dreadful has happened. I can feel it in my heart. He has never been unable to make it home before."

"Don't jump to conclusions, my dear. There might be an innocent explanation."

"You can kid yourself all you like, Jerry, but I know my boy, and something is very wrong here." She gives way to heartfelt tears and Jeremy Seymour is unable to console her. She rushes off to her bedchamber.

Four policemen arrive to scour the grounds of the manor inside and out, looking for any clues as to Ashleigh's whereabouts. They start by searching their quarters and, to keep Francis out of the way, his nanny, Mercy, takes him for a walk in his perambulator. Lucy settles herself at the piano, hoping that her music will sooth her mother-in-law. She plays Beethoven's *Moonlight Sonata* and is soon lost in the music, soothing her fears and restoring her faith that everything will be fine in the long-run.

Mercy returns and brings Francis into the drawing room for a hug. Lucy then follows them upstairs to the nursery to feed her baby, before Mercy settles him for the night. As darkness falls she can see the flaming torches of the policemen moving around the grounds outside. Sergeant Gundry is in charge and it is not long before he is back inside and asking for the family to gather in the drawing room.

As her in-laws join her, she feels sick with anxiety.

Sergeant Gundry clears his throat. "I'm very sorry to have to inform you that we've discovered a body, concealed among reeds on the edge of the lake, close to the causeway."

Lucy is stunned and watches in horror, as everyone takes in the dreadful news. *It must be Ashleigh.* She feels nauseous and her eyes fill with tears, as she remembers happier times spent with him and Rupert.

Helen Seymour sinks into a chair and wails, "I knew it! I told you something was wrong!" She begins to hyperventilate, and gasps, "Jerry… my smelling salts."

Poor Jeremy looks bewildered and wanders off to find the spirit of hartshorn. When he returns, Sergeant Gundry says gently, "We need a member of the family to identify the body."

"I'll do it," says her father-in-law. "But first, I think I need a drop of Dutch courage." He pours himself a tot of gin and downs it quickly, before following the policeman out into the night. As they go through the hallway, Lucy can hear Sergeant Gundry saying, "Prepare yourself, sir, it's not a pretty sight, the poor man must have been there for some days."

Helen Seymour frantically fans herself. She wails, "He cannot have been there all this time without any of us knowing about it. It's too dreadful," then she weeps mournfully. Skipper whines at the door to be let in. Robshaw lets the dog in and it leaps up onto his mistress's lap.

Lucy is mute with fear and sadness. *If it is Ashleigh, and who else could it be, then Frankie has lost his father and I am a widow.*

Jeremy Seymour returns with Sergeant Gundry, dabbing his eyes with a large white handkerchief.

"Oh no!" screams Helen. "Are you absolutely certain, Jerry?"

He sighs deeply, "I'm afraid so, my dear. I'm afraid so."

"Oh, my Lord, whatever will Rupert do without his brother? You'll have to let him know, somehow, Jerry. They've always been so close."

"One step at a time, dear-heart. I will send him a telegram tomorrow." He turns to Lucy. "Lucy, I'm so sorry, my dear, my son's early demise has made you a very young widow. I suggest you ladies both have a small tot of brandy to fortify you." He goes to the cabinet and shakily pours them both a glass of Courvoisier.

He hands her the brandy bowl, and Lucy smiles faintly. Finding her voice, she mumbles, "Thank you."

She sips at the brandy, half hearing the muffled voice of Sergeant Gundry telling them about the police procedures and how he is duty-bound to inform Superintendent Munro. "He will arrive here as soon as he can, but we're not allowed to move the body until then. We've covered the scene with a canvas tent and placed a policeman on guard and we'll get a photographer here, once we have daylight. I am so sorry for your loss. I promise you we'll do our utmost to solve this murder case and bring the perpetrator to justice. In the meantime, I suggest you get some rest. The next few weeks are sure to be rather harrowing."

The location of the crime is photographed and secured, with a range beyond the reeds, large enough to include several footwear impressions leading to and from the area. Casts are taken of those footprints, excluding those of Sergeant Gundry, who is careful not to confuse his own impressions with those of the perpetrators, by stepping into his own footprints, as he leaves the scene. Fortunately, the weather has been cold, dry and frosty for the last week and the footprints remain in good order. Ashleigh's corpse is searched for any valuables and then removed to Borough House in the High Street for the surgeon, William Fancourt Tomkins, to do the autopsy. Rumour travels fast around the locality that Ashleigh Seymour has been found murdered. Then it is front-page news in the *Western Gazette*.

In Hamlet Cottage, over a cup of tea, Malachi reads the article to Rosa: "The headlines are: LOCAL MAN FOUND MURDERED! Ashleigh Seymour, a well-known entrepreneur, gambler and bookmaker has been found dead; his body hidden in reeds at the edge of Sutton Bingham Lake, near to his family's estate. House-to-

house inquiries are being undertaken in Sutton Bingham, Halstock, Closworth and East Coker and other outlying areas in the vicinity. Superintendent Munro is overseeing the investigation and if anyone has any information that might help in this case, they are requested to contact the police station in Union Street.

This incident has similarities with that of the discovery of Raymond Baker, whose body was found in undergrowth, beside the River Cale in Wincanton three years ago. Both men were gamblers. Were they both butchered and robbed for their winnings? Could this be the same murderer? Do we have a serial killer in our midst?"

Rosa slumps into a chair. "Oh, my Lord, poor Lucy!"

"He must have mixed with some real undesirables for him to end up like this!"

"You'd better go and show this to your ma and pa. I expect Gareth has already shown the report to Louisa. She's been so worried about Lucy."

Malachi puts his arm around her. "At least neither our Lucy, nor Frankie, will be bullied by him anymore."

"That's true, but still, she's far too young to be a widow!"

Billy is traumatised when he hears about what has befallen Ashleigh. *Lucky Joe Mintern wasn't exaggerating after all!* He doesn't know what to do for the best.

Edwin finds him sitting on some hay bales, with his head in his hands. "What's up with you, old chap?"

He looks up at his friend and soon they are sitting side by side, and he is pouring his heart out. Finally, he asks him, "Do you think I should go to the police and tell them what I know?"

Edwin runs a hand through his hair. "I don't know, mate. These fellows sound dangerous to me. If they can kill a toff like Ashleigh Seymour, they won't hesitate to shut you up." He mulls it over for a few minutes. "I think if I were you, I'd stay shtum and keep my head down. I'm not saying he deserved to die, but he only had to pay back what he owed, and they'd have left him alone. He was far too greedy and selfish to care about what might befall his family, because of his stupidity. He's not worth risking your life over."

Billy lets out a huge sigh. "If Lord Dryer was here, I'd go and tell him everything, but I'm too afraid they'll think I'm involved in some way, if I go to the police station."

Edwin puts his arm around him. "I don't blame you, mate. Keep your mouth shut and keep out of it, is my advice."

Tattershall is in the pit house at the factory, scraping lamb and kid skins, that might have come from far away Russia, Spain, Italy or Persia, and placing them in tumblers containing alum, salt and large quantities of the yoke of eggs. He is working with four other workers who then transfer the smelly skins to vats where they use long poles to dunk the hides in the preparation known as 'pure', a mixture of meal and water, which softens them and gives them pliability. While they are working, they are chatting among themselves.

Tattershall brings up the matter of Ashleigh Seymour. "'Tis a rum do over at Sutton Bingham, ain't it?"

His colleague, Jethro, is scathing. "Thic toff were asking for it, if you ask me."

He encourages further discussion. "Why do 'ee say that, Jethro?"

Jethro shrugs, "More money than sense, those Seymours."

Morgan joins in the conversation. "You think 'ee was killed for 'is cash, do 'ee?"

Jethro is adamant. "Why else? 'Tis just like that other bloke over Wincanton, according to the *Western Gazette*."

His plan is working. He leads them on. "Mind, 'ee was found close to home. I'd say, this time, it points to someone local."

Jethro wipes the sweat from his brow. "Well, they've yet to say how he was murdered."

"They'll be keeping that under their hats during the investigations, I expect," says Simeon Brown, sagely.

Finally, Tattershall says, "Well, it don't sit well with me, to have a murderer in our midst." He decides then, to call in and make a statement to the superintendent later, when he passes the police station in Union Street on his way home from work. He grins to himself. *There's more than one way to skin a cat. Did they really think he'd take their beating lying down?*

That evening Malachi and Rosa are not surprised when the police come knocking at their door, believing it to be routine enquiries. But their relaxed welcome soon turns to fear when Malachi is handcuffed, arrested and taken away for further questioning.

Rosa tries to calm her traumatised children. "Don't worry, it is obviously a mistake. You stay here, Ruby, and prepare your brother and sister for bed. I'm leaving you in charge, while I go and tell your grandparents what has happened and I'm sure

Grandpa will be able to sort it all out tomorrow."

"All right, Mama, but please don't be long."

"I won't, Ruby, but I have to let them know."

Reluctantly she leaves her tearful children, with fourteen-year-old Ruby in charge, and frantically rushes over to Home Farm to tell the rest of the family of Malachi's arrest. Her breath is opaque in the night air and the searing cold is painful in the back of her throat. She is tearful and distressed by the time she reaches their home. The door has been secured for the night and her fist is sore from hammering before Isaac lets her inside.

She grabs his arm, but cannot get the words out quickly enough. "I don't know what to do, Isaac. I can't think what to do… They've taken him, Isaac. They've taken him away in handcuffs… Malachi has been arrested for Ashleigh's murder, and they've taken him to the lock-up."

"Come in and calm yourself, Rosa." He leads her into their parlour and she sits down in an armchair, beside the glowing embers of the fire, with tears streaming down her face. He pours a small brandy and she gratefully takes a sip.

"They said he'd had a fight with Ashleigh… and he'd been heard threatening to kill him… and they wouldn't listen to him, Isaac… They said for him to say nothing until he's seen in court."

Isaac is furious. He pulls at his beard. "Whatever can they be thinking? They must be desperate to put the blame on someone, but to pick on our Malachi is downright ridiculous."

Beth comes downstairs in her nightgown. "What's wrong?"

He tells her, "They've arrested our Malachi, but don't you worry about it, Beth. It's obviously a mistake." Then he turns back to Rosa. "Don't fret,

Rosa, they won't get anywhere without evidence. I'm sure hearsay alone will not be enough to convict him. Leave it to me; I'll go and see him tomorrow with Jacob and try to get to the bottom of it."

In the morning, in the pouring rain, Isaac and Jacob set off into town. They find Sergeant Gundry at the police station desk and Isaac immediately challenges him. "Whatever are you thinking, arresting our Malachi? He is innocent, Stan. You know he didn't do this. Why has he been arrested?"

Sergeant Gundry speaks confidentially, "My boss, Superintendent Munro's, orders, my friend. We have a witness who swears he was seen punching and threatening to kill Ashleigh Seymour about a week ago."

Isaac frowns. "Who is this so-called witness?"

"I'm afraid I cannot tell you that, Isaac. The best thing you can do, is go home and look out for that family of his. Malachi is being questioned by the superintendent at present, but there's a detective superintendent who hails from Taunton on the case now and hopefully he'll be able to come up with more clues leading us to the real killer."

"As long as you know that our Malachi is innocent. Keep an eye on him for me, will you, Stan? I just wish Lord Dryer was here. He'd soon sort this out."

"I'll make sure he's fed and watered, have no fear, and I'll tell him you were both here."

Jacob asks, "When will we be able to see him?"

"If you call by tomorrow afternoon, the superintendent is off duty and I'll make sure you can see him then."

Isaac shakes his hand. "Thank you, Stan. That's much appreciated."

When they eventually get to see Malachi, he looks bone weary, with a belligerent expression of anger and frustration on his rugged face. He gives them both a bear hug and then says, "I'm sorry, Pa. Please tell Rosa, I'm so sorry, I shouldn't have lost my rag and punched the bloke, but it was just a threat to make him toe the line, nothing more. Who could possibly believe otherwise? It was only us family and Raymond there to hear what was said and I'm sure Raymond knows I wouldn't have acted on it… unless perhaps Ashleigh himself told someone."

"Don't you worry, son. As soon as Lord Dryer gets back from Australia, he'll sort this out." In the meantime, your ma has baked some of your favourite pies for you." He hands him a wicker basket containing two dishes covered with muslin. "You just keep your chin up. They'll need more than an idle threat to convict you of murder."

"Yes, but in the meantime, I'm stuck in here twiddling my thumbs, when you and my family need me the most. This is Jacob's most hectic time with the lambing and you'll be busy with harrowing soon, preparing the fields for sowing the flax and the clover mix."

Jacob cannot bear to see his brother so down. "Don't worry, Mal. You won't be in here much longer; there's a detective coming to investigate and he'll find out the real culprit, you mark my words."

Jeremy Seymour, while in the hallway going through his greatcoat pocket to find his snuff box, is shocked when he overhears the postman gossiping to Robshaw.

"I hear tell, the latest on the grapevine is Malachi Warren, the bare-knuckle boxer, has been arrested for your young master's murder."

"Surely not. He's his brother-in-law!"

"Well, I'm only repeating what other folk are saying."

Jeremy Seymour staggers back into his study, unable to believe that Malachi Warren, Lucy's own brother, has been arrested for Ashleigh's murder. His morning dose of snuff revives him somewhat and once he has recovered sufficiently, he goes to speak to his daughter-in-law. He finds her doing some embroidery in the drawing room.

"Lucy, may I speak with you?"

She puts down her sewing. "Of course, Father."

He takes the seat beside her.

"Why, whatever is wrong, Father? You look stricken!"

"With good reason. Would you please tell me what exactly transpired between you all, on the day my son came to bring you back home from your parents' home? Only I've just heard that your brother has been arrested for my son's murder!" He can see immediately that this is as much a dreadful shock for his daughter-in-law, as it was for him. She blanches and trembles at the news.

Mystified, she mumbles, "But that's impossible! Ashleigh drove off, immediately after Malachi stepped in to prevent him from dragging me home." She looks him in the eye. "I admit he punched him on the nose, Father, but Ashleigh was being totally unreasonable, and my brother had seen the marks, caused by his earlier anger with me." She shakes her head. "He wasn't going to let that happen again.

But I promise you, your son was fit and well when he left Home Farm that afternoon, and my brother is no murderer, sir."

"They must have some reason to arrest him, Lucy. I don't know what Helen is going to say about this."

"Well, I hope she keeps her opinion to herself, for I'm at the end of my tether and cannot promise not to retaliate. Ashleigh has brought all this worry down on my family's head and none of us deserves this." Tears flood her eyes. "You know, as well as I do, he was out of control and I will not have my brother maligned without responding in kind."

He hands her a large white handkerchief. "Don't upset yourself, Lucy. I know he was like a loose cannon, but he was still our son and we had such high hopes for them both, when the boys were small. Who would have thought it would come to this?"

"I'm sure my own poor mama and papa are asking the same sad question about our dear Malachi."

Three days later, Malachi is taken in a horse-drawn Black Maria to Shepton Mallet Prison to await his trial.

CHAPTER THIRTEEN *(January 1870)*

BRECON VALLEY MINES

In the southern hemisphere, Joshua and Aurora have finally disembarked from the *Delta* and are standing in the shimmering heat, debating whether to travel from Melbourne to Sandhurst in a Cobb and Company, Concord stagecoach, drawn by four horses, or opt for the steam train.

While stroking his long bushy beard, the coachman persuades Joshua, "You'll find this carriage far more comfortable than most contraptions on these rough and rutted roads, because our American coaches use thorough-brace technology." He points to the base of the carriage. "As you can see under here, thick leather straps, provide the suspension for the body, rather than the traditional steel springs of our competitors." He grins confidently. "Plus, I know the route to Bendigo like the back of my hand."

Aurora is fatigued with the heat. "I think it will be easier for us to board here, Papa, than to have to find our way to the railway station."

"All right, my dear." He turns to the aborigine porter. "Please load up our trunks."

The driver hands Aurora up into the carriage and she chooses the high-backed, leather upholstered seating at one end of the vehicle, beside the window. Joshua climbs in and sits next to her. There are, altogether, seats inside for nine passengers, but the bench seat in the middle does not look so comfortable for a long journey and if that was all that had been available, Aurora would have preferred to travel by train. As it is, they are the first to board and therefore have the first choice. There is also plenty of room outside, above the canopy, for their luggage.

The journey is surprisingly comfortable, even though the carriage strains and shudders through abysmal ruts, around massive loose boulders and through deep, water-filled fords. Other travellers board and depart along the way and there is the usual polite interchange. The horses are changed every ten to fifteen miles, affording the opportunity for them to take refreshments and use the facilities. Aurora is enjoying the scenery, the flora and fauna so different to that she is familiar with back home. Then to her joy, she sees a troop of kangaroos bouncing across the savannah. They are such strange animals. "Look, Papa! Kangaroos! However did the good Lord come up with such an extraordinary design?"

"I have no idea, Aurora, but they look perfectly adapted for this vast land; just look at the strength in their muscular legs."

She laughs, "They are definitely moving faster than we are!"

They lull back into an exhausted silence as the miles pass them by. She can tell that her father is as exhausted as she is, and both are extremely glad when they see the sign indicating they have reached Sandhurst. However, as they continue, she is dismayed to see a widespread shanty town of canvas tents and wooden shacks of all shapes and sizes. *Surely we won't be staying here?* The land is scarred with holes and heaps from the diggings. Horses are circling around and around within several unfamiliar machines. Then, thankfully, they reach what looks to be the main street with stone-built houses lining the carriageway and the coach finally comes to a halt. Their luggage is placed on the wooden boardwalk and her father looks about him for a native boy to stand guard. Hugh had said that they should send him a message with an aborigine and then wait for him in the cool, inside the saloon at the Eureka Hotel and he and Lewys would come to collect them and their luggage, so, having done so, they cross the road and head for the shelter of the hotel.

The only other customer, seated at the far end of the bar, stares at Aurora with some hostility as they enter. She sits down in a discreet corner, underneath the wafting breeze of a rather noisy mechanical rotary ceiling fan and feels the immediate benefit. Her father goes to the bar and orders two glasses of lemonade. He pays the barman, but the old man squints at him, "You just in off the stagecoach?"

"Yes, sir. We've travelled all the way from the south of England and, unaccustomed to this heat, as I'm sure you can imagine, we're very thirsty."

"Well, I make an exception for newcomers to Sandhurst, but the bar is no place for a lady."

She blushes shamefully as her father explains, "I understand. We're simply waiting for a friend who is meeting us here, before taking us to stay at his house."

The old man puts his head on one side. "Oh aye. Who would that be, then?"

"Hugh Davies?"

He nods his head. "Ah yes, I know him… Brecon Valley Mines."

"Yes, that's right. We met when he came to

213

Somerset, several years back now."

"He's our local hero, is Hugh. He managed to track down the bloke, when he scarpered back to England with all the gold miner's money, having murdered our local troopers while escorting a consignment of gold bullion to the banks in Melbourne."

Her heart sinks as she hears her father responding, "That's right, he was Nathan Meakins. Actually, I was his contact in Somerset and managed to trace the money for Hugh and arrange to have it all reimbursed."

The barman is impressed. "In that case, put it there, sir." He holds out his hand and Joshua shakes hands with him. "I'm Jethro Tully, the proprietor, and I trust you'll take a tipple with me?"

Her father smiles. "Joshua Dryer... Thank you, that is most kind. I'd still like the lemonade, as I am fearful thirsty, but I'll happily join you in a glass of something stronger; what do you commend?"

"I have a very palatable rum, that I can vouch for."

"Thank you, that sounds most acceptable."

Her father glances over at her and she can see he is concerned for her. Jethro Tully pours the drinks and the two men chink their glasses together.

"To justice," says the host.

Her father responds and downs his rum, then excusing himself, he joins her at the table in the corner with the lemonade.

She rapidly fans herself in agitation. "Why did you tell him that? What if they all find out that I'm his daughter?" she whispers.

He responds equally quietly, "Well, don't forget there's already one of his daughters living among them, whether they're aware of the fact or not.

Neither of you should have anything to fear; you cannot be held responsible for your father's actions. Besides, it's none of their damn business."

Aurora takes deep breaths trying to calm down. Perhaps she should have stayed at home with Gabriel and her mother after all. Then the saloon door swings open and Hugh and Sarah Davies enter, looking all around for them.

Hugh seems delighted. "Ah! There thee both are. How good to see thee again, Lord Dryer. Welcome to the land of the golden fleece."

Her father jumps up to shake hands with Hugh, and Sarah steps forward to give her a hug. "And you must be Aurora. We've so been looking forward to meeting thee, my dear."

She has no time to curtsey, the formalities forgotten. The kindliness of this Welsh woman is so genuine, and she smiles, reassured that they will be well looked after during their stay in Australia.

Hugh says, "Come, we've brought a barrow for thy luggage and Lewys is outside waiting to meet thee both."

Sarah says, "There's food and drink prepared at home, and I've brought a parasol for thee. It's only a short walk to Myrtle Street from here, but I know thee'll be feeling the heat."

Aurora follows them. "Thank you. That's very thoughtful."

Outside, the heat hits her and she is very glad of the parasol. Her father tips the young lad who had been guarding their belongings. Lewys is a handsome man in his thirties, with reddish hair and sideburns like his father, but he has inherited the hazel eyes of his mother. Having been introduced she watches with interest, as he takes the weight of the barrow and wheels it along the boardwalk, his manly muscles moving under his calico shirt. Perhaps she did make the right decision to come all this way, after all. *I think I'm going to enjoy staying with this kind family.*

The black natives stare at her as the group progresses along the boardwalk, and she stares back, equally curious to see their half-naked bodies adorned with beads and feathers, some of them the worse for drink. They pass the grog shop and Lewys shouts a warning at the folk lounging about there, to let him pass and they shuffle away in their own slow time.

When they reach the post office, her father pops in to send a telegram to let her mother know that they have arrived safely, and she waits outside on the boardwalk with the Davies family, watching the townsfolk going about their business, before continuing once more.

Once off the main street the roadway is less crowded and less rutted from the carts. Aurora is impressed with the bright colours of the flowers growing around the wooden houses and climbing up the pillars of the verandas. They pass masses of golden laburnum trailing along a fence, crimson vanilla passion vine, the beautiful blue bounty and amazingly colourful scented jasmines. This place seems so exotic compared to the subtle shades of the plants back home.

Gwyneth greets them, as they arrive at the home they will be sharing for the next month. She is a younger version of her mother with her long rich-brown hair, twisted into a chignon and the same eye colour. Her summer-weight gown is a pale sky-blue percale, dotted with sprigs of flowers. The triple flounced skirts and slender basque-waist shows off her youthful figure. She fusses over everyone, finding a cool place for Aurora to sit outside on their veranda under some violet blooms. Aurora cannot help admiring them. "This is very pretty."

Gwyneth smiles. "It's called 'Happy Wanderer'. Kind of appropriate for us settlers." Gwyneth then places a glass of dandelion and burdock beside her on a small wooden table. "I'm just laying the table with some victuals for everyone and then, when we've all eaten, I'll come and sit here beside you and you can tell me all about your journey."

Her father and Hugh also come outside to find the benefit of a slight breeze and she listens to them chatting together.

"Tomorrow, once you're completely recovered from your journey, I'll take thee over to meet my partner and old friend, Bryn, and his family. They can't wait to meet thee both." He looks over at Aurora and gives her a big smile and she smiles back drowsily. She should sleep well tonight.

Shortly, Sarah is calling them in, to find a seat at the table, while she dishes up their food. "We've shepherd's pie, Glamorgan sausage and a variety of vegetables. Then for afterwards, we've some Welsh cakes and some bara brith."

Hugh pulls out a seat for her father to take, at the head of the table, and then sits down beside him to the left.

"What's in Glamorgan sausage?" asks her father.

Hugh says, "Thee will like it, my friend. It's our favourite, isn't it, Lewys?"

Lewys grins. "Sure is, Pa." He takes a seat next to Aurora, opposite his father. She suddenly feels overawed by the physical proximity of this handsome young man, her heart races and she immediately feels tongue-tied.

Sarah smiles. "Well, it's a traditional Welsh

recipe. There's no meat in it. It's Caerphilly cheese and leeks, or some folk may use spring onions, coated in breadcrumbs and rolled into a sausage shape and then cooked."

"Mmm, that sounds very tasty," says her father.

She must join in the conversation and besides, she is curious. "And bara brith?"

"It's a Welsh, spiced fruit tea bread. Our friend, Sam Kelly, calls it Irish brac, but it's basically the same thing." She turns to Aurora. "Would thee like some of everything savoury, Aurora?"

"Yes please, Mrs Davies. It all smells delicious."

"Please, my dear, call me Sarah."

As Sarah piles the plates with food, Gwyneth serves everyone and then sits down beside her mother. Hugh says Grace and then bids them, "Tuck in."

Aurora cannot think of anything stimulating to say to Lewys and so she samples the food hungrily. She is pleased to discover that Sarah could give Flora a run for her money, for her food is delicious. After they have eaten, she helps the ladies clear away and wash up, then they all go outside, onto the moonlit veranda, for a nightcap and to relax. The clear sky is studded with swathes of unfamiliar twinkling stars and to her, the background sound of the cicadas seems very exotic.

She asks Gwyneth, "Is that the Southern Cross?"

"Yes, you wouldn't get to see that in the northern hemisphere."

"It is so different here, Gwyneth. Did it take you a long time to get used to it?"

"Yes, it's true we're literally poles apart, but we were very poor back in Wales and Pa and Bryn have managed to build up their own business here. They'd never have managed that back home and so for us it has been a wonderful experience. I honestly thought the clipper would sink and we'd all drown on the way. Our voyage was terrifying, but we all made it and for us it has been well worth it. It's just as well, because I couldn't face that voyage again."

"You must have gone around the Cape, back then, but we came via the new Suez Canal, which was fascinating, and I believe, overall not so hazardous. Anyway, thankfully our journey was without incident; however, it was still a relief to arrive, sound in life and limb!"

"You must make the most of your stay here. I'll be happy to show you around."

"Thank you, Gwyneth, that's very kind. I'm truly looking forward to it, but I must admit to feeling rather weary now. I hope you won't be offended if I ask you to show me to my bedchamber?"

"Of course not, my dear. Come, you're to share with me." They both get up to leave and Gwyneth says, "Goodnight, everyone, we're both retiring for the night."

There is a chorus of 'Goodnights'.

That night she dreams of a romantic liaison with Lewys, but during the dream he is replaced by Luke and she wakes up in a haze of guilt and confusion.

The following day her father goes off with Hugh to meet Bryn and inspect the mine and the new land claim, while Gwyneth and Sarah show her around Sandhurst. It seems a typical gold-mining town with dusty streets, wooden boardwalks on either side for pedestrians, barracks for detachments of foot and mounted police, a licence tent, the gold receiver's office, extensive stables and the lock-up. In the distance, there is the constant sound of pumping, hammering and drilling. There is also an impressive emporium, plenty of saloon bars, general stores, butchers and bakers. The Bendigo Creek runs down one side and up on a hill there is a hospital and a church. The town is busy with shoppers, prospectors, gold miners, troopers and all nationalities. However, Aurora is shocked to see something you would never see in Ivell; some of the women are even dressed like the men, in baggy trousers, sweatshirts and sombreros.

The day is again hot and dusty, and she is very grateful for the loan of Sarah's parasol. If anything, she is the one who looks out of place here, in her elegant European clothes. They spend some time in the emporium, as the ladies are planning to make a new gown for Gwyneth, so together they peruse the pattern books and then select the appropriate material, silks and ribbons for decoration. The daughter of the owners, a helpful young woman called Freyja, whom the Davies family know well, assists them. Aurora tells them about her experience in Paris when her Papa arranged for her to have her favourite gown especially made by the House of Worth, when they were on their way to her finishing school in Switzerland.

Gwyneth looks envious. "You're so lucky, Aurora. I've never travelled anywhere else but here."

"I hadn't either, until last year, and even then, I didn't want to go. It's quite scary leaving the comfort of your family home for the unknown, but I'm so glad that I did. I had a wonderful experience, and, at Lausanne Manor, I made a very good friend in Odette. It also gave me the confidence to accompany Papa, when poor Mama discovered that she is with child again and was unable to travel."

Sarah gathers together the silks and ribbons

that Gwyneth has selected. "It is such a shame she is confined, but what a blessing to be given another child. She must be so thrilled."

She smiles, "Yes, we all are, but I must admit to being a little worried about her, back home without us to help her. I trust Gabriel will be keeping her company... and she has a good friend in Rosa."

Gwyneth says, "I was looking forward to meeting your mama, but we're thrilled that you were able to come in her stead."

Sarah kindly puts her arm around her. "We hope to make your stay worth the long journey. Later today, I believe you'll be meeting our friend Bryn and his family, who'll be coming to visit us for a barbecue. Freyja is betrothed to his oldest son, Owen."

She looks at Freyja. "So, you'll be coming too then, Freyja?"

"Yes, of course, they are all invited," says Sarah smiling. "We've also invited Sam and Angel and their children. Angel and Nell work together at the school."

She smiles. "Ah, how lovely; it will be quite a party."

"Yes, and the advantage is, the men enjoy cooking all the meat outside and we simply prepare the salads and potatoes, which we can do as soon as we get home."

Joshua is excited to finally be off to see the full extent of the Brecon Valley Mining Company's assets. Hugh takes him up to Eaglehawk to inspect the two quartz mines first.

"Thee can use Lewys' horse; she is a gentle beast and well used to the rocky terrain."

"What is her name?"

"Rhiannon, after the Welsh goddess of the horse, but Lewys calls her Rhia."

Joshua has missed his regular jaunts across the estate on Capricorn and enthusiastically mounts the mare and sets off after Hugh, up the hill, out of the township towards the Whipstick.

Bryn and his sons greet them both at the shaft-head of the Maerdy and they shake hands. "Good day, Joshua. We've put Rhys in charge of operations on this shaft, and Owen oversees the Talliaris; with us, of course, overseeing both boys. If you follow Rhys he'll show you the Maerdy and then when you come back up, Owen will show you the Talliaris."

"Right you are. Lead the way, Rhys. I'm in your hands."

He follows the lads in turn down the ladders to the different levels and sees the impressive glistening quart seams they are following in both shafts. Once back above ground he is again in the hands of Bryn and Hugh and they show him the mining records in the office. After Joshua has spent about ten minutes perusing the pages of figures, Bryn says, proudly, "You can see from the numbers that the mine is prospering."

"I can indeed. Your records appear to be meticulous."

Hugh beckons to them. "Come outside; I'll show thee the steam pump and winch and the working twenty-four-head Berdan steam crusher with its battery of revolving stampers."

Joshua looks down into the bins of glittering crushed ore. Bryn tells him, "We're getting an average of twenty-six ounces of gold to the ton at present, but it has been as high as ninety-two ounces per ton."

"I'm impressed, gentlemen. This machinery

must have cost you a fortune."

Hugh uses a handkerchief to wipe the perspiration from his brow. "Indeed, it has; the ore crusher was over £2,000 and the steam engines for pumping and winding are over £3,000 each, so this is why we need more investment. As I said in my letter, we can sit on the land in the White Hills, but it seems more sensible to keep up the momentum, while we're still fit and young enough to do so."

"I agree." Joshua nods his head, going over all that he has been shown. "Shall we head off to the hills now?"

The sun beats down on them from a cloudless sky. Fortunately, he is wearing a wide-brimmed cowboy-styled hat, courtesy of Lewys, a loose cream calico shirt and light brown moleskin waistcoat and trousers. They drop down through the coarse scrub and rocks, into the California Gully then cross the creek, scattering the Merino sheep as they go. A large flock of dazzling green and gold budgerigars swoop low, aiming to drink from the stream. It is an amazing sight. They continue across the pastureland which eventually gives way to saltbush. A group of about eight emus, all grazing quietly, look up warily as they ride by. Finally, they reach the hills, already scarred by the gold miners' exposing the white clay, that gives the place its name.

Hugh leads them to an extensive unscathed area, covered in blue gum trees. A sign reads: *KEEP OUT - BRECON VALLEY MINING COMPANY.* "This is our claim, Joshua. Thee can see from the fence pegs, it's quite a good size. Plenty of room for shaft, steam engines, machinery and office."

"I'm genuinely impressed, and I'll keep you in suspense no longer, gentlemen. I've decided I'd definitely like to invest the £6,000 you require, in return for 600 shares in your business."

Hugh holds out his hand to shake on it, and Bryn enthusiastically clasps both their hands in his.

"I'm so pleased, Joshua. There isn't anyone else we'd rather join us in this venture, is there, Hugh?"

"No, Bryn. We trust thee, Joshua, and that's essential. Welcome on board the Brecon Valley Mining Company."

That evening, when Bryn and Nell arrive with Rhys, Owen and Freyja, Aurora is heartened to see the warmth of the relationship between the two Welsh families. They must have known each other for many years. Although younger, Rhys is taller and broader than Owen, and she is attracted to his cheeky smile. Then the Kellys appear, and she is fascinated to see her half-sister, Camira. She has the same thick chestnut hair as her mother, Angelica, and it falls in ringlets, just like her cousin Senga's. It is uncanny they are almost identical, even sharing the same expressive pale grey eyes. Senga must be about ten years old now, whereas Camira is younger, but there is no doubt they are all related.

Hugh introduces everyone and Gwyneth and Lewys help their parents by handing around drinks. There is a choice of dandelion and burdock, sarsaparilla wine, Pimms No. 1 Cup, sherry wine, or beer, brandy and rum.

Aurora chooses a glass of dandelion and burdock, being quite partial to the flavour of aniseed. While Camira and Connor play tag with their father, she decides to sit on the swinging chair, beside Angelica, and try to learn more about her and her family.

She smiles, and broaches the subject quietly and tentatively, "I'm sure Hugh has told you in advance

224

that I'm Camira's half-sister."

Angelica seems wary. "Yes, he did warn us that you were coming here, but I don't want Camira told about this, because she believes Sam to be her real father and I really don't think there would be anything to gain by telling her the truth."

She nods. "I understand, but it's wonderful for me to meet her. She's such a beautiful child and a real credit to you. I have a cousin back home who is her double. She is ten in June."

Angelica seems to thaw a little. "Camira's birthday's in June, too. She'll be seven this year."

"They're both Geminis; it will be interesting to see if they share the same character as they grow up." She watches her darting away from her papa, quick as a flash.

Angelica sighs. "Well, thankfully, so far I don't see any signs of her evil father in her."

She answers defensively, "I hope there are no such signs in me either, Angelica, but I believe it was his addiction to opium that was at the root cause of all his problems."

Angelica looks at her apologetically. "I'm sorry. I'm sure you're right. He could be so charming and, in the beginning, I admit, he captivated me."

"As he did my own mother, but he treated all women shamefully. I don't make any apologies for him. I just don't want you to think the evil will be inherited by either me or Camira, because I'm sure it was the opium that addled his brain."

Sam pulls up a seat next to them and sits down with a plate of food. "I'm glad for an excuse to sit down, so I am. It's too hot to be running around after the kiddies. They've too much energy for me."

Camira sidles up to her father shyly and Aurora takes the opportunity to introduce herself to the child.

"Hello, Camira, I'm Aurora. How nice to meet you."

"Hello." She shuffles her feet, leaning against Sam and swivelling her hips self-consciously. Then plucks up the courage to ask her, "Did you come on a big ship like Mama did?"

"Yes, I came with my papa, all the way from England to see you all."

"Is Engeland very far away?"

"Yes, it is; it took us nearly three months to get here."

"What is Engeland like?"

"It is very small compared to Australia, but it is lush and green with lots of small farms, not the big ranches that you get here and we don't have kangaroos, or wallabies or koalas or crocodiles there. You have different birds and different flowers to us too."

"I'd like to know all about Engeland, because it's where my mammy comes from."

"Well, if your mammy agrees, would you like me to write to you when I go back and if you've learned your letters well, you could write to me and tell me all about Australia and what animals you see here?"

Angelica smiles in agreement and asks her daughter, "Would you like that, Camira?"

Camira nods her head. "Yes, I would."

Aurora holds out her hand. "Shall we shake on it?"

The child reciprocates and then rushes off to play with her brother.

Sam says, "You should go and help yourself to some victuals, ladies, while the meat is still hot."

Angelica agrees. "Good idea, Sam," and they both go to the barbecue to make their selection.

Bryn is helping himself to roasted potatoes

and salad, when they reach the table and he says, "Come on, ladies, plenty here for everyone." Then he speaks more confidentially to Angelica. "Hello, Angel, cariad. I hear Sam has heard from his father at last."

"Yes, he is absolutely thrilled. Apparently, he's been working all this time on the Union Pacific Rail Road."

Bryn serves the potatoes and salad to Angelica. "How did he track him down?"

"Well, Sam has been in regular correspondence with his uncle in Ireland since he was at Port Arthur, in the hope that his father will one day contact him, and that is what eventually happened."

Bryn then absentmindedly piles some potatoes on Aurora's own plate and turns back to Angelica. "So his uncle was able to send him your address?"

"Yes. I think the man has a lot of making up to do, abandoning Sam like he did, but he wasn't to know his brother would put him in the care of the Holy Fathers. Anyway, he's apparently making himself a small fortune and is planning eventually to travel to Australia with a view to investing his money over here and getting to know us all."

Bryn passes the salad server to her. "Well, I'm very glad for Sam's sake. He was traumatised as a child by the death of his mother and baby sister and his dreadful experiences thereafter and it all boils down to the deadly scourge of the potato famine and the oppressive politics of the English. His father would never have abandoned him, if he had had any choice."

"This is true, though none of us would be here at all, if only we'd been given a chance for a fair wage. I just hope I like him, and he fits in with our little family."

"I'm sure he will, cariad." Bryn moves on

towards the meat table and the two girls follow him. Angelica says to him, "Bryn, did you realise that Aurora here, is Camira's half-sister?"

"Yes, I did. I wasn't going to mention it, because you have my sympathies, my dear, although I know from Hugh, that your adoptive father is a very honourable man and so in that respect, you have been blessed."

She smiles. "I have indeed, sir. I love him dearly. He is twice responsible for saving my life. No one could have been more loving, or kinder to me."

Angelica says, "I know from my own experience with Sam and Camira, it's not who sires you, but who nurtures and takes good care of you, who matters the most."

Aurora looks across at her father who is chatting to Hugh. "That is so true."

They reach Lewys, who is serving the meat and she smiles, as their eyes meet. "What would you like to try, Aurora?" he asks her.

"May I have some chicken and some sausage, please?"

"The chicken straight from the barbie will be hotter. Pass me your plate." She hands it to him and using tongs, he selects the food for her. "There you go. How's that?"

"Lovely, thank you." She smiles sweetly at him, then follows Angelica, in search of a seat.

The food is tasty and once Angelica has eaten hers and the meat has cooled down a little, she goes to fill two plates for her children. Bryn's youngest son, Rhys, then claims the seat beside her. She looks up at him shyly, and he grins. He has the same devilishly, twinkling eyes as his father and, as the evening progresses, his lyrical Welsh accented words are like liquid gold, melting her heart;

she is immediately lost in starry-eyed, romantic dreams. That night she dreams about Rhys, tall and charming with twinkling, mischievous eyes, shorter, red-headed, muscular Lewys and gentle, kind-hearted, childhood sweetheart, Luke, but which one is the man for her?

CHAPTER FOURTEEN *(January–February 1870)*

ASHLEIGH'S FAREWELL

On the 12th January, Jeremy Seymour sets off first thing with Robshaw to collect Rupert after his long voyage home from Port Elizabeth to Plymouth. Helen Seymour is left behind, beside herself with emotion, crying with sadness for Ashleigh one moment, and happiness at the thought of seeing Rupert again, the next.

Lucy is finding it hard to cope with her mother-in-law's hysterical moods, still feeling desolate herself, over all that has transpired. However, when the front doorknocker sounds, she is thrilled to find her dear friend Clara, dressed in purple and swaddled in furs, standing on the doorstep, with Mr Fairway, her papa, waving and driving off in their gig.

"I couldn't wait any longer to see him. I hope this is all right?"

"Of course it is! Come inside out of the cold. Oh, I'm so glad to see you, my dear. How are you?"

"I'm well, thank you. More to the point, how are you?"

"Much better for seeing you, I can tell you." She turns to the maid. "Gladys, would you please take Miss Clara's mantle?"

Clara shivers as she removes her snug cloak and goes to follow Lucy. "You'll soon warm up. We've a huge log fire burning in the drawing room. While you're here and before the men return, I want you to meet my little Frankie."

The room is warmed through and Helen Seymour is nowhere to be seen. Seated comfortably in matching William Morris upholstered armchairs, placed either side of the hearth, Lucy is relieved to be able to talk freely with her friend, as the fire flickers and crackles before them.

"I'm afraid a dark cloud has hung over the household since poor Ashleigh's untimely death and sadly our black mourning clothes only serve to perpetuate our feelings of loss. But, now that the coroner has released his body, it will be a huge relief at least, to get the funeral over."

"I'm sure it will be."

"If it wasn't for little Frankie, I'd have left and gone home to my own family at Home Farm for good, but how can I take their grandson away from them, at this traumatic time?" She tugs the bell pull and Gladys answers.

"Ah, Gladys, would you please tell Mercy I've a visitor and ask her to bring Frankie down to see us?"

"Of course, ma'am." She leaves the room.

Clara says, "I've been worried for you, Lucy, but I've been kept frightfully busy helping my papa with his office work and running our household. We have no servants and so little free time."

"I do understand, Clara. It must be hard for you with Rupert thousands of miles away."

"Not as hard as it has been for you. I was devastated when I heard of the murder and even more so when your brother Malachi was arrested. Whatever is the matter with the police, that they cannot tell the difference between a villain and an upstanding fellow like your brother?"

"I don't know. It has been a shock for us all, but I know he's innocent. I was there when they argued and Ashleigh was absolutely fine, apart from a bloodied nose, that, to be honest, he thoroughly deserved. He'd been behaving beastly towards me and I needed a break from his bullying. I didn't want to go home with him, and Malachi was defending me. It was as simple as that and look at the trouble it has caused." She is ready to cry again, but Mercy enters with Frankie in her arms and she blinks away the tears and puts a smile on her face. "Here he is; come and say hello to your Auntie Clara."

His fine blonde hair has been parted on one side forming a small quiff and he has the same blue eyes as his mama.

"Oh, he is adorable. What a cutie. He looks like his papa and Rupert."

"Yes, he does. If it wasn't so cold, I'd suggest we take him out in his perambulator for a stroll. It's near to his nap time and the motion soon settles him to sleep."

"I can rock him in the cradle, ma'am. It's good to keep to his routine."

"Yes, Mercy, take him back upstairs, I just wanted Clara to see him first."

Mercy cuddles the child, as she takes him from the room.

"He's the joy of my life, Clara. I thank the Lord every day for blessing me with such a beautiful, sweet-natured baby."

She can no longer hold back the tears and dabs at her eyes with her handkerchief. "I'm so sorry, Clara, I didn't mean to cry."

"Don't apologise, you've been through a dreadful ordeal, my dear."

"I'm crying for what might have been, Clara, not for what was. My marriage sadly did not live up to expectations. If it wasn't the drinking, it was the stress of his gambling debts, making him so unreasonable and tetchy. Unfortunately, he became extremely irascible and difficult to live with."

"Chin up, Lucy. Despite all that has happened, I can see you're truly blessed with little Frankie, while I'm left to watch the years go by, not knowing if my Rupert will ever do me the honour of going through with our promised marriage. Sadly, whilst he is prospecting for diamonds, I can see the prospect of children diminishing daily."

"Please don't you be downhearted too, my dear. You'll be seeing him very soon and he'll be able to update you on all that has happened during his last four years with his partner, Jack Penberthy, in Hopetown."

Clara says, more positively, "Let's trust he has made his fortune and is ready to return home."

"I do hope so, for your sake and mine. Jeremy and Helen are bereft; they need their oldest son back home to take care of things around here. I'm sure Helen will be trying to persuade him while he is here."

Clara looks pensive. "I won't. I need him to make up his own mind. Our relationship would be sure to flounder if I put any pressure on him to return for my sake."

When they hear the carriage on the driveway, they both go to look out of the front window. Lucy is almost as excited as Clara to see her brother-in-law again and looks forward to some life returning to Bingham Manor once more. He looks dapper as he steps down from the carriage and Lucy is reminded why Clara loves him so and of all the fun they had enjoyed together, before her marriage to Ashleigh, and Rupert's untimely departure. She wonders if Ashleigh would have become so volatile if Rupert had stayed here, and he'd been able to turn to him, when things started to spiral out of control.

She and Clara curtsey as he enters the drawing room with his father. He steps forward and takes Clara in his arms in a warm embrace. "Oh, how I've missed you, Clarence." And both ladies smile with the memory of him using his silly nickname for her.

He eventually relinquishes his hold on his fiancée and with his usual charm he turns from Clara to Lucy, taking up her hand and kissing it chivalrously.

She smiles. "It's good to have you back, Rupert."

"I'm glad to be here. It's been a long journey."

Then his mother bursts into the room. "Oh Rupert, my dear boy, how wonderful to have you home. Things have been so ghastly here without you. Your poor, innocent brother murdered in cold blood and we desperate for some answers, but none are forthcoming."

He hugs his mother. "Mama, it's good to see you. I'm very sorry I wasn't here for you all. I can't believe I'll never see poor old Ash again. Whatever mischief he may have got up to, he didn't deserve to die in this reprehensible way."

"No, he did not," says his mother. "And I suppose you ought to know, they've arrested Lucy's own brother for the deed."

Lucy sighs. Sometimes she thinks her mother-in-law is more of a bitch, than Skipper.

Rupert frowns at his mother and turns to Lucy. "Papa told me all about it on the way here. I'm sorry to hear this, Lucy. I don't believe your brother is capable of murdering mine, but, according to Papa, the police seem to be bungling the investigation as usual!"

She smiles with relief, grateful for her brother-in-law's support. "Yes, I'm afraid they are grabbing at straws. Ashleigh was absolutely fine after he and Malachi disagreed that day and I promise you my brother is totally innocent."

"I'm sure he is, Lucy. Don't fret, they'll get to the bottom of it eventually."

Lucy is glad when Jeremy Seymour changes the subject. "I believe Mary has prepared a homecoming buffet feast for Rupert. Shall we go through to the dining room?"

Rupert says, "Good idea, Papa, I could eat a scabby horse."

The day of the funeral turns out to be wild and blustery. The slow toll of the lych bell accompanies the funeral procession. The ladies' black bombazine skirts billow in the wind and the trees wave and bow low above them, as they follow the coffin up the lane and into the tiny church at Sutton Bingham. Lucy leads the procession as his widow, veiled in fine black mesh, hiding her tears, with Mercy following behind, carrying Frankie in her arms. Inside, at the back of the church, as the family and their staff file in and sit in their regular pews, Lucy recognises Superintendent Munro from Ivell among the congregation, obviously there to check everyone out; also, Ambrose Fairway and some of the folk from the Black Panther Club, who she has not seen in years, but is glad they've decided to come and pay their respects.

The service is short with Lucy's favourite psalm, The Shepherd, and two hymns: 'Nearer My God to Thee' and 'Now the Day is Over'.

After the service, they file outside, following respectfully behind the coffin, for the committal. They stand at the graveside, warmed by all manner of furs, and a light dusting of snow begins to fall.

The churchyard is amassed with snowdrops, their dainty white heads wavering in the breeze and although listening to the words of the vicar, Lucy cannot help but notice how beautiful it looks. She did not expect any of her own family to attend, under the circumstances, but nevertheless she misses their support. The committal over, they sombrely file back to the manor for the wake, light white snowflakes floating around them.

Mary, Gladys and a young girl from Halstock, serve everyone with wine for the toast. Rupert then asks them all to raise their glasses to his brother. The Black Panther group are all very enthusiastic and soon the room is filled with laughter and merriment.

Lucy observes Helen Seymour seated in the corner of the room with Skipper on her lap looking very forlorn and her heart goes out to her. She overhears her father-in-law saying to Rupert, "This whole affair has really knocked the stuffing out of her."

"I can see that, Father. Has she seen a doctor?"

"Yes, when it first happened, I got old Dr Robbins from Corscombe to give her a physic, and he prescribed laudanum, which certainly lifts her spirits for a while, but it seems she is soon needing more."

"I think you should wean her off it, Father. It's not good in the long term."

"I've tried, my boy, but you know how your mother can be, once she sets her mind to something."

Clara and Ambrose Fairway come to talk to her, distracting her from her eavesdropping. Mr Fairway asks her, "How are you coping, Lucy, my dear?"

"Not so bad. Today was hard for us all, but hopefully things can only improve from now."

"All these young fellows here, are they Ashleigh's friends from the club?"

"Yes, they are. It was very kind of them to come."

He asks her, "Do you know every one of them?"

"I recognise them all from Catkin Mill, but I cannot say I know them. Not really."

Clara says, "Me too."

"But, you wouldn't say any of them would have been harbouring any malice towards your husband?"

"No, Mr Fairway, not that I'm aware of. Many of them, I'm sure, would have used him for their gambling, but nothing more than that."

"I admit I recognise some of them as sons of the local gentry and cannot think they would have wished him harm."

Rupert, turns to join them. "Forgive me, but I couldn't help but overhear you. I've spoken to all our friends here and they've assured me that Ashleigh didn't owe any one of them a single penny. I know from my experience of working with Ashleigh in the past, that we were always very careful to pay everyone their winnings without exception and I believe that my brother would prefer to pay his debts to his friends as a priority, even if it meant using the services of a moneylender."

"Thank you, Rupert. This was what I was wondering. I think it might be a good idea to mention this to Superintendent Munro."

He turns to look for him among the guests. "I certainly will do. I don't want our friends placed under suspicion, like Malachi." He cannot immediately see him. "He might have already left." He takes out his pocket watch to check the time, before scanning the room again, and spots him chatting to his father over by the chiffonier.

Watching the action, Lucy suddenly realises that the murderer must have stolen Ashleigh's identical gold pocket watch, as they were both given them, inscribed with their initials, on their twenty-first birthdays. She grabs his arm. "Rupert, would you also point out to him that Ashleigh's gold pocket watch, identical to yours, with his initials on, must have been stolen by the murderer, as he always had it with him. I don't know why I didn't think of it before. Come to think of it, he always carried his silver hip flask with him, too. That's two stolen items that might lead them to the killer."

"Well done, old girl. I'll go and tell him now."

Later, once everyone has left, barring herself and her father, Clara is finally able to quietly talk to her fiancé. Lucy has gone upstairs to say goodnight to Frankie and her father is chatting to Mr Seymour.

She asks him diffidently, "What are your plans for the future, Rupert, regarding the Hopetown Hopefuls?"

"Well, all three claims look very promising, we have sifted through all the alluvial mud on the water's edge and found semi-precious gems and a few small diamonds, but now Jack and I are in the process of walling off the river on our land, in order to dig down into the shoreline for the larger stones. I'm sure we're close to the kimberlite, which is usually found about thirty feet below ground level, but it's hard labour and, as yet, we don't have the capital to employ many locals to help with the manual work."

"So, you're intending to return?"

"I'm fully committed now, my dear. I cannot afford to cut and run. Beside, I'd be leaving Jack in the lurch." He looks down at her and she cannot hide her sad expression. "We can still marry, my darling, and you and your father could both emigrate and come live in Hopetown with me. I'd take good care of both of you, Clara."

"He'd never agree to that, Rupert, and to be honest, I'm not sure such a life appeals to me either. I'm not an adventurous type of person. You need to be audacious and courageous to take such a risky chance that will have implications on the rest of your life and I admit, I'm far too timid." She takes a handkerchief from her reticule and dabs at her eyes. "I'm sorry, Rupert, much as I want to be with you, I cannot see myself toiling under an African sky, however rosy you might paint the picture."

She always knew in her heart that he had no intentions of returning to Somerset and that she had no intentions of joining him in the South African bush. In a way, it is a relief that her decision has been made clear, but she cannot help the tears from welling in her eyes and she turns away from him to hide her sadness.

He pulls her back into his arms and says, "I'm so sorry, Clara, it will break my heart to leave you again. Would you like me to continue to write to you?"

She shakes her head, sadly. "No, please forget about me. We must make a fresh start. Here is your engagement ring. You're released from your promise. After all, it's my own fault that we're obliged to call off our betrothal." She turns away from him with tears coursing down her cheeks. Her voice breaks as she says, "Papa, I'm feeling a little jaded, would you please take me home?"

"Of course, my dear."

She dabs at her cheeks and leaves the room. In the hallway, Gladys hands her her fur wrap and they encounter Jeremy Seymour.

Her father holds out his hand. "Please say our farewells to Lucy for us, Mr Seymour."

"I will do, Mr Fairway." They shake hands and Clara curtseys. "Thank you both for coming."

The following morning Lucy encounters Rupert helping himself to breakfast from the chiffonier and she joins him. "Good morning, Rupert. Did you sleep well?"

"Actually, I was a bit too hot, unused to sleeping on a feather mattress. I ended up pulling the eiderdown off the bed and sleeping on the floor with it wrapped around me; then I went straight off like a baby. How about you? It must be strange sleeping alone, after sharing your bed with someone."

"Yes, it is, but it's far more peaceful. He took it out on me, you know. It was as if he blamed me for coming between you both. He would have loved to have gone with you on an exciting boys' escapade and I'm afraid I wasn't enough to fill the gaping hole you left behind."

"I'm sorry, Lucy. Please don't make me think it was all down to me leaving. I really don't want that on my conscience."

"No, of course his death wasn't your fault, but he did change, Rupert, and not for the better."

"I realise this is not what you envisaged as married life and you must be bored out of your mind with just Ma and Pa for company." He moves closer to her and speaks quietly. "If ever you are ready for an adventure in South Africa, just let me know. Now that Clara has broken off our engagement, I am in need of a wife and attractive ladies are few and far between over there. I'd take very good care of both you and Frankie, if you should ever decide you are up to the challenge."

"Oh my! What a suggestion! How do you think my dear friend Clara would feel if I were to do such a thing?"

"She would recover, I'm sure. She will in time find someone more suitable to her temperament, but you, my dear, are a different kettle of fish, as you now have a child to consider, and it isn't everyone who'd be prepared to take on another man's child."

Her face falls and he immediately feels guilty. "It's a genuine offer, Lucy. You and I have always got on well, we already love each other as brother and sister in-law and I believe we could have a real adventure and a happy future together. I'd love to give you more children. We could start our own family dynasty in Hopetown. Please don't dismiss this out of hand. I realise you need time to think about it and maybe Frankie should be a bit older and stronger before dragging him to the other side of the world, but look what an experience it would be for him, compared to his cosseted life here at Bingham Manor. I'm just asking you to give it some serious thought, that's all." He smiles gently at her and continues to pour out his coffee.

Lucy is flushed at the thought of an intimate relationship with her brother-in-law, but they have always been close and, given time, this tiny seed might just germinate and grow inside her heart.

"I promise you I'll give it some serious thought, Rupert. When do you plan to return?"

"I'm here for three weeks. It didn't seem fair to leave Jack with all the work for any longer than that. It's our summer over there and we regularly get the most violent thunder storms and need to be wary of flooding where we are. But you'd love the exotic birds and flowers, Lucy. The only thing that could possibly harm you, would be the poisonous snakes, scorpions and spiders, which you'd need to look out for, but in the main they're more scared of us and keep out of our way. Sometimes we have problems with the bad behaviour of the baboons and naughty thieving monkeys, which can be annoying, if rather amusing. Hopetown is growing rapidly, but it's still at present a shanty town. If you write to me, I'll let you know the progress made. I feel certain it will not be long before Jack and I are in a position to build our ranches. Then you should consider joining me, Lucy."

"It is such a hazardous journey by ship for a lone woman with a small child."

"I know, but if you do decide to take the risk, I promise you I'll make it worth your while."

The door opens and Jeremy Seymour enters, effectively curtailing their conversation.

CHAPTER FIFTEEN *(February – March 1870)*

AN URGENT APPEAL

Rosa manages from day to day with the help of her mother-in-law, taking care of the children for her at Home Farm, while they are not in school. One chilly evening when she goes to collect them, Jacob takes her to one side, saying quietly, "I don't want to upset the children, but I'm afraid the police now have Malachi locked up in Shepton Mallet Prison."

"Oh, my Lord! Poor Mal! Does Lady Louisa know?"

"We haven't had an opportunity to tell her, so I doubt it."

"I will call in at the manor, on my way home."

She quickly dresses her children in their coats, hats and scarves, leaves the farmhouse with them, anxiously trying not to cry, and rushes to confide her fears in her mistress. They discard their coats in the main hall and find Louisa in the drawing room with Gabriel, playing cards, a log fire burning in the hearth.

"Milady, can I talk to you please, in confidence?"

"Of course, Rosa, come into the oak. Gabriel, perhaps you'd like to play with Ruby, Eli and Daisy for a while."

"Of course, Mama." He asks his friends, "Shall we play Happy Families?"

The children chorus, "Yes," and Rosa and Louisa leave them to it.

Once settled in comfortable chairs, Rosa bursts into tears. "They've sent Mal to the prison in Shepton Mallet! Whatever am I going to do? I can't bear to think of him there with such reprobates for company. I'm so afraid they'll hang him for murder, Lou Lou, and him as innocent as a new-born lamb!" Rosa takes a handkerchief from her pocket and wipes away her tears.

"Please don't fret, Rosa. Your children need you to be strong. Besides, I'm sure the detectives will find the real killer, before then." She looks at Rosa's forlorn face and says, "Nevertheless, I think I'll send a telegram to Joshua first thing tomorrow, to let him know his friend is in real danger."

"Oh, thank you, milady. Joshua will know what to do."

"Yes, he will, but sadly he's thousands of miles away. Hopefully, if it's at all possible, he'll make plans to return to us immediately. If he can change his plans, then maybe he can be back with us by April, rather than May. I feel a bit guilty for asking him to curtail his trip, but I'm certain Josh would want to know that Malachi is in trouble; besides, I'm lost without him and need him here as much as you do, Rosa."

The following day Louisa goes into the Ivell post office and sends a telegram with the *Electric and International Telegraph Company*. The telegram reads: *ASHLEIGH SEYMOUR FOUND MURDERED. MALACHI ARRESTED. WE NEED YOU. PLEASE COME HOME. LOUISA X*

When the telegram arrives at Hugh's house on Myrtle Street, he quickly takes it to Joshua to read.

Joshua panics when he sees it is addressed to him. *Oh my God! Please don't let it be Louisa and the baby!* His hands shake as he opens the envelope and he breathes a sigh of relief to see that it is Ashleigh Seymour and not his wife and child who have been lost, but then realisation dawns that poor Lucy is a widow and his pal Malachi is in great danger of hanging.

"I'm so sorry, Hugh, but I've no option; I'm afraid I must make plans to return home immediately. My good friend Malachi has been arrested, on suspicion of murdering his brother-in-law."

"Oh, my goodness; how shocking!"

"I've absolutely no doubt he's innocent, but he's in dire need of my help. Could you please arrange to expedite the legal documentation for the purchase of the shares, so we can all sign it in Melbourne and then Aurora and I can board the next boat back to Britain?"

"Yes, I'll wire the solicitors to that effect, but you may find it not quite so simple to re-arrange your voyage with the shipping company."

"It may be easier to do that in person when we get to Melbourne. I can book into a lodging house, so we are on hand should an opportunity arise."

"Righto, I'll go and sort out the solicitor's telegram. You'd better break the news to your daughter. I'm not sure she'll be too happy about going home early."

"What do you mean?"

"Well, I think she might have taken a bit of a shine to Bryn's son, Rhys, and I think it might be mutual. Having said that, I believe it might also be the explanation for my son's foul mood."

"Well, I'm afraid she has no choice, because I can't let her travel back unchaperoned. I'm also very sorry, if she's offended Lewys. She's very young and not experienced in the ways of handling relationships with men. Perhaps it will be fortuitous all round, if I whisk her away, before too much damage is done. Her mama would never forgive me if she loses her daughter to a betrothal with a man halfway across the globe!"

Aurora is enjoying an early morning ride with Rhys across the expansive veldt, relishing the exhilaration of the speed and the wind in her unruly hair. Gwyneth has been persuaded to chaperone them, but she is not a confident rider and lags a little behind. They rein in their horses to wait for her to catch up.

Rhys is staring at her. She asks, "What is it?"

"The sun is catching the gold and ruby lights among your curls... you look like a goddess. I have to tell you... you're the most beautiful girl I've ever seen."

She smiles. "That's the nicest thing anyone has ever said to me."

"I can't help it, Aurora, you're gorgeous." Then he asks her, more intimately, "How would you like to live over here and experience this freedom every day?"

"I'd love it," she replies smiling at him, confidently.

"I can't believe how quickly you've charmed me, Aurora. You captivated me at first sight. Now I'm totally enslaved. I cannot imagine my life without you, cariad. I don't know what I'm going to do with myself, when you go home in three weeks' time."

"It will be a sad parting."

"Would you like to spend more time with me? Would you consider emigrating, to join me here in Australia, Aurora?"

"I'd consider it, certainly," she says wistfully, "but it would be life changing and it would be hard to tear myself away from my family. My mother would be devastated."

She looks at him, trying to fix the image in her mind forever; his tousled hair, cavalier red neckerchief and mischievous, twinkling blue eyes. "Please don't let's waste time thinking of that now, let's just enjoy the time we have together."

Gwyneth joins them a little out of breath.

Rhys changes the subject. "Would you like to go up to the Whipstick to see our mine and the panoramic views of Sandhurst and the Bendigo creek from there."

"Wherever you like. I'm in your hands, Rhys."

As he flicks the reins, she hears him reply under his breath, "If only."

Louisa rips open the envelope to read Joshua's reply: *PLANNING TO COME HOME IMMEDIATELY. TELL MALACHI CHIN UP. HOPE YOU GABRIEL AND BABY WELL. WILL LET YOU KNOW BOOKING ARRANGEMENTS. JOSHUA X*

She sinks into a chair. *Thank God!*

"Is everything all right, my lady?"

"Yes, Gareth, Joshua is arranging for him and Aurora to return immediately. We'll all feel much better when he's back here and taking charge of things again. Poor Malachi and his family will take cheer that hope is on the horizon. Please let Rosa know for me, will you? I'm a little overcome by it all."

"Of course, my lady."

Gareth leaves the room and she closes her eyes and waits for her heart rate to return to normal. She was anxious enough going through her pregnancy without Joshua, but this added stress has not helped and she has begun to feel sometimes, as though she might faint. There is a knock on the door and she calls out, "Come in."

Rosa enters. "Oh, milady, thank you. I'm so relieved that he's coming back sooner. It will be a load off Malachi's mind to know that he has the master on his side."

Louisa sighs, "How will we let him know? It's a long way to Shepton Mallet."

"I'll ask Jacob to visit him. Hopefully they'll let him see his brother."

"But he's in the middle of lambing. No, Rosa, I think we should ask Ambrose Fairway. They won't argue with a solicitor."

"Very well, milady."

"I'll send a message to him with Luke. Please fetch me my dipping pen, inkwell, sheet of paper, and envelope, and Joshua's stamp and sealing wax."

Rosa goes to the study and returns swiftly with the items on a tray.

Louisa writes her message, places it in the envelope, melts the wax and presses the seal. "Please give this to John Moore, and ask him to give it to Luke, to deliver to Mr Fairway when he goes back in to work tomorrow." She hands it to Rosa. "Also, please ask Flora or Ruth to make a special food parcel for Malachi and give that to John as well. It's the least we can do."

"Of course, milady."

"Thank you, Rosa. I think I'd like to sit quietly and read my book for a while. Would you mind fetching it for me? It's in the oak; only I'm feeling a little light-headed."

"Of course, milady. How about I ask Flora to do you a lightly coddled egg for luncheon?"

"That sounds perfect, Rosa."

When Aurora and Gwyneth arrive back at Myrtle Street, she is dismayed to learn their trip has been curtailed.

"But it's so soon, Papa! We've only just got here!"

"I know, my dear, and I'm sorry, but for Rosa and Malachi it's a dreadfully fearful experience and if I'm able to help them, I must be back in Somerset. I'm afraid we are to leave on the steam train tomorrow with Hugh and Bryn for Melbourne, to complete the business formalities and await an earlier passage back to England. We need to pack up our belongings and prepare for the journey."

She knows there is no use trying to persuade her father that she might stay on alone; besides, she is not brave enough to face the long return trip on her own and she needs to think a lot more about her feelings for Rhys, which have hit her like a thunderbolt. *Surely it is too good to be true? I need more time with him to be sure. It is so unfair!* But could she really see herself married and living with Rhys in Sandhurst? How will she feel about Luke when she returns to Alvington?

In the meantime, she dutifully packs up her belongings, ready for their voyage. In a way, she is excited to be going home, to see for herself how her mother is faring and to tell her, Luke and Gabriel all about their trip, but so sad to be saying farewell to her new-found friends and especially Rhys, who she feels might even, had time permitted, become her soulmate. She wipes away a single tear. Perhaps she can see him clandestinely before they set off tomorrow? She decides to confide in Gwyneth.

She finds her, taking down the dry washing from the line and she helps her, folding it neatly into the wash basket. "Gwyneth, do you think it might be possible for me to have a final private moment with Rhys? I really don't want to leave Australia without saying goodbye to him. We've both become rather fond of each other."

Gwyneth looks appalled. "You don't let the grass grow under your feet, do you?"

"Please, don't be shocked, Gwyneth. I know we haven't had enough time together to be sure of our feelings, but I'm sad to be leaving here so suddenly, maybe never to see any of you ever again. I just want to say farewell to him. Can you help me… please?"

Gwyneth sighs. "I'll suggest we go for a stroll before our evening meal, if you like. But I can't be sure we'll see him, even if we do pass by their house."

She puts her arm around her and gives her a squeeze. "It is worth a try. Thank you, Gwyneth, you're a treasure."

The sun is low in the sky when they set off on their stroll. Gwyneth is quiet and Aurora wonders if she has inadvertently offended her.

"Have I upset you in some way, Gwyneth?"

"No, my dear, of course not. I'm simply saddened that your stay with us has been cut short. It has been a merry distraction, having you here with us."

"It is most unfortunate, I agree, but I can see why Papa would want to get home as soon as possible, for Malachi is his closest friend and he cannot stand by and do nothing to prevent such a travesty of justice."

She glances at her companion; she must be about the same age as Rhys. Could it be possible that she may have had designs on Rhys herself and she has asked far too much of her?

They are nearing the Thomas' family home and Aurora can hear the regular rhythmic sound of water pumping. They pass the end of the property and she spots Rhys in the stable yard, filling a pail and then emptying it over his head. As he draws his hand through his hair to remove the excess water, he opens his eyes and sees her and Gwyneth watching him. His face breaks into his characteristically cheeky grin.

"Why, hello again, ladies. To what do I owe this pleasure?"

Aurora steps forward, her heart beating madly. "I'm afraid I have some bad news, Rhys. Papa has had to bring our trip home forward and he and I are leaving for Melbourne tomorrow."

A shadow falls over his face. "No, you can't go back yet, cariad!"

"I'm afraid I have no choice. I'm so sorry, Rhys. I was hoping we could get to know each other better, but I have come now, unbeknown to my father, to say farewell."

He grabs her hand and pulls her into the stable, with Gwyneth following; appearing unsure of her part in all this. He takes her in his arms and kisses her passionately and she feels as if her heart will break.

"I will never forget you, cariad. I swear I will come to England and find you if I can. Say you will write to me?"

"I promise I'll send a missive as soon as I'm home, to let you know how I fare."

He kisses her again, his strong hand cradling her head as he does so and her eyes close, as the building appears to spin around her. When she opens them, Gwyneth is watching and she can see the pain in her eyes. How could she have been so insensitive? She can only hope she will forgive her, for it is too late to change things now.

Then they hear footsteps approaching and they pull apart. Gwyneth is quickly by her side. Bryn enters the stable and shows surprise at seeing the two ladies there.

Rhys steps forward. "Aurora has come to say goodbye to us, because she is leaving tomorrow with her papa."

"So I understand. It must be very disappointing for you, my dear, having endured such a long journey to get here, but it's been a pleasure to meet you and we all wish you safe passage back home. Come on inside with me; Nell will want to wish you bon voyage, I'm sure."

When Luke delivers the message to Mr Fairway, he lingers to see what could be so important that Aurora's mother has sent instructions to his boss. Mr Fairway meticulously uses his pearl-handled letter opener to break the seal and scans the message. He looks up to find Luke watching attentively.

He puts the young lad out of his misery. "It's saying that Lord Dryer and his daughter are returning sooner than planned, and for me to let Malachi know of this, as it will raise his spirits."

"And mine," grins Luke.

While he goes to the safe and removes some cash, he tells Luke, "I'll be leaving you in charge of any day-to-day business you are familiar with, as I intend to take the pony and trap to Shepton

Mallet. Are you happy to hold the fort for me, for today?"

"Of course, sir."

"If you have any problems, I'm sure Clara will guide you, otherwise, it will always keep for just one day."

"Yes, sir. You can rely on me, sir."

When Ambrose Fairway arrives in Shepton Mallet, he does not hold out much hope of seeing Malachi in person, but he has brought some cash with him, in case he might entice the gaoler, chief warder or governor to let him in.

He starts by knocking up the gatekeeper, who hobbles to the huge gates with a large key in his hands. "What do you want?"

"I'm Malachi Warren's solicitor and would like to be able to see him. I have a message for him from Lord Dryer of Alvington Manor, Ivell, and I have instructions to give it to him personally."

The gatekeeper looks suitably impressed. "I can't just let people in willy-nilly, but I'll go and check." He returns later with the chief warder.

"This is most irregular, sir. Who did you say sent you?"

"Lord Dryer of Alvington Manor in Ivell. His Lordship gave me some money to offer you for your trouble." He holds out two guineas to tempt the man.

"In that case, you may come and wait in my lodge, while the prisoner is fetched."

The gatekeeper turns the large key in the massive lock and swings the postern gate open. He steps uneasily inside the prison walls and follows the chief warder into his lodge.

It is around twenty minutes before he is rewarded with his first sight of Malachi. The poor man looks emaciated and exhausted. They shake hands. "Mr Fairway, how good of you to travel all this way to see me. Do you have any news of my family?"

"I do, Malachi. Rosa has sent word that they are all well and praying for you to be reunited soon." He hands him a wicker basket. "This is a food parcel compiled for you by Flora at the big house, on the mistress's instructions, and I also have a letter from Lady Louisa, which I think you should read immediately."

Malachi removes the letter that Mr Fairway has already read and he even manages a smile when he reads that Joshua is returning to Somerset. Then his current situation overwhelms him and he covers his face in his hands, hiding his contorted features, as he sobs.

Mr Fairway fidgets uncomfortably, unsure how to comfort him, then he says, "Lord Dryer should be back here by mid-April, but in the meantime, I'm working on your behalf trying to keep abreast of the investigation, as well as I can. Your sister helpfully mentioned at Ashleigh's funeral that he would have had both his silver hip flask, and his gold watch on him when he was killed. The watch bears his initials and if the police could track either of these items down, it might lead them to the true killer. Rupert Seymour conveyed this information to Superintendent Munro, so take heart."

Malachi does not seem to hold out much hope. "Come on, lad, enjoy your tasty food before someone takes it off you." Malachi recovers his composure and selects a pork pie from the basket. He bites into it hungrily. "I'm very grateful for your help. Thank you, Mr Fairway."

"Is there anything, Malachi, that you can think of that might help your case?"

"No, nothing. I only know that I was working on the farm all the time Lucy was staying with us, with all the Alvington staff as witnesses. I can't even think of any day when I'd have had enough opportunity to do this terrible deed, let alone the inclination! They say I had motive, opportunity, and ability, but so had hundreds of other people. I can't see how they can get away with incarcerating me in here under the threat of the noose, without the slightest physical evidence." He wraps the food back up into two smaller parcels, placing them in his pockets and hands back the basket. "I don't want to share this with that ungrateful lot; besides, it could cause a riot."

"Please have faith, Malachi. There are a lot of people who believe in your innocence and you must try to trust in God that we will overcome all the obstacles. Please know that Lord and Lady Dryer will do their utmost to make sure justice prevails."

"Thank you, Mr Fairway. I truly appreciate you coming all this way and your message has given me some hope of salvation."

"You are most welcome, son. Please, call me Ambrose."

"Thank you, Ambrose. I suppose I'm going to have to go back on the treadwheel again now. I never realised until I was imprisoned, how blessed I was to live such a happy, open-air, family life of freedom."

"You will again, my boy. Take heart; you will again, I'm sure."

Louisa is unable to read for the headache, unable to leave her bedchamber because of the dizziness and exhausted from the sickness. She has felt unwell now for four days and is frightened for her baby. Rosa has sent for Dr Gillingham. On his arrival, he is ushered upstairs to the sickroom by Emily, who knocks gently on the door. Rosa calls out, "Who is it?"

Emily replies, "Dr Gillingham, milady."

Rosa opens the door. "Please come in, Doctor." She stands aside for him but turns Emily away. Not that she seemed eager to come into contact with the infection. "Thank you, Emily."

Dr Gillingham clears his throat. "Good day, Lady Louisa, how can I help you?"

While the doctor puts his Gladstone bag down on the bedside chair, Rosa helps her mistress into a sitting position and plumps the pillows behind her. "I'm sorry to trouble you, Doctor, but I've been unable to keep anything down for several days and I'm concerned for my baby. Do you think my sickness will cause it any harm?"

"How many months pregnant are you?"

"I am nearly seven and a half months."

"And how many days now, have you been poorly, my lady?"

"I'm afraid I've lost count. How many days is it do you think, Rosa?"

"This is the fourth day today. It all started on Monday, after we received the telegram from Lord Dryer."

Louisa bristles, but her voice is weary. "I hope you're not suggesting that it's an emotional or hysterical reaction, Rosa, because I can assure you my symptoms have been extremely physical and violent in their character."

"Of course not, milady, it simply lodged in my mind, the start of your problems."

Dr Gillingham examines her and palpates her stomach to check on the baby, using a fetoscope to listen for the baby's heartbeat. The beat is strong and although Lady Louisa is pale, she is well hydrated and bears no resemblance to the recent cases of cholera he has seen in Ivell. He asks her, "Can you remember what you ate on that day, my lady?"

"Yes, I can, I had a lightly coddled egg cooked by Flora, because I was already feeling rather frail."

"Do you think that maybe you were feeling frail, as a reaction to the telegram?"

"No, not to the telegram exactly, but to everything else that has happened. The telegram informing me that my dear husband and daughter are returning was a huge relief. But I suppose it did bring it all into perspective and I was feeling rather overcome."

Dr Gillingham looks thoughtful. "So it may have been the egg that upset your constitution. Have you eaten anything substantial since then?"

"No, not really. I've been drinking a lot of glucose water and Flora has occasionally given me a beaker of yarrow tea."

"In normal circumstances, I would recommend yarrow tea in cases of diarrhoea, but it must be avoided while in your pregnant condition, my dear. Apart from that, I believe you're doing the best you can by drinking, to keep yourself and your baby from being dehydrated. I would say you have a case of gastroenteritis. It is a self-limiting disease and usually only lasts a week, so you are through the worst. I believe you and your baby are being well cared for and, apart from the yarrow tea, you should continue in the same vein, but please send for me, should any further symptoms develop, such as a rash, or a high fever."

"Do you think the yarrow tea will have harmed my baby at all?"

"No, my lady, I have examined you and your baby's heart is strong. I'm sure it will be fine."

"Thank you, Doctor. You've put my mind at rest. It was my unborn child whom I was most concerned for."

"I understand, Lady Louisa, and please don't hesitate to contact me should you have any further fears, but I can assure you, from what I see today, it is a case of gastroenteritis and you should feel back to normal in about two or three days' time."

Rosa prepares to see him out, but he says, "Don't worry, I can see myself out. You stay here with your mistress." Abruptly he leaves the room, rushing off to visit his next patient.

"You'd better tell Flora about the yarrow tea, Rosa. But please reassure her that everything is fine with both me and the baby."

"I will, milady."

Billy is working with Edwin in the stables when Gareth comes to find him, accompanied by the detective superintendent. The rays of the low March sun are slanting through the stable door catching the floating wisps of straw and dust particles. Billy spots a spider as it darts into the corner, when the shadows of the two men fall across it.

Gareth asks Billy to step outside and he follows them sheepishly. "Billy, Detective Superintendent McKinley is here to ask you, if you can tell him anything you know about Ashleigh Seymour, leading up to his untimely death."

Billy frowns. How will he handle this? The daylight dims as the sun disappears behind a cloud.

The detective steps forward. "Good morning, Mr Riddick. I understand from our enquiries in Ivell,

Wincanton and at the Black Panther Club that you encountered Mr Seymour regularly at the Hatherleigh Farm race meetings." He pauses. "Is that correct?"

"Yes, sir, it is."

He takes a notebook from his pocket and a pencil from behind his ear. "Can you tell me the last time you saw him?"

Billy scratches his head and then looks up. "I believe it was on Boxing Day, sir."

The detective writes this down. "Did you notice anything unusual about him?"

He hesitates; if he tells the man about Snodgrass and Blakely, they'll find a way to make him pay, but if he doesn't, he'll never be able to tell Lord Dryer, because it will be apparent that he had lied to the police. He takes a deep breath. "It was not unusual to see Mr Seymour the worse for drink, and Boxing Day was no exception. However, I also witnessed him being bullied and attacked by two men." He clears his throat.

"Please go on, Mr Riddick."

"Well, even though he was no friend of mine, I couldn't stand by and do nothing, so I tried to intervene. The distraction enabled Mr Seymour to get away from them, but then they turned on me. The two men took me captive, in lieu of Mr Seymour, and frogmarched me across the racecourse, threatening me with violence, should I reveal what I had witnessed to anyone else. Fortunately, I managed to escape with the help of two friends."

"And the names of these friends?"

"Noah Boswell and Florica Petulengro; they are two Romany gypsies."

"Are you quite certain that Mr Seymour escaped?"

"Yes, I am, because a few days later they were still looking for him and me, which is why I left

Hatherleigh Farm in fear for my life and returned here for sanctuary."

"Did you not think this information would be relevant to a murder investigation?"

"I admit, I did, sir, but I was waiting to tell Lord Dryer, who is our Justice of the Peace. He would know what to do. I was intimidated by these swarthy men, sir. As you can see, I'm of small stature and no match for them, should they seek me out. I was also concerned for the family at Hatherleigh Farm; they didn't deserve to be embroiled in Ashleigh Seymour's unsavoury affairs."

"What do you mean by that, Mr Riddick?"

He stares at his feet, aware, for Malachi's sake, he must tell all. "Well, it was common knowledge that Mr Seymour lived on borrowed time. He had accrued gambling debts with at least two of the bookies, Uriah Levi and Jarvis Pocket, and one of them was impatient to be paid what he was owed."

"Do you know who this benefactor was?"

He looks up at the detective. "I cannot be sure, sir, but I thought it was Jarvis Pocket, because it was his minders who were involved in the attack."

"Do you know the names of his attackers?"

"I was told by the stable owner, Joe Mintern, that they were called Snodgrass and Blakely."

The detective scribbled all this down and then looked up at him. "Thank you for your help, Mr Riddick. It's a pity you didn't see fit to furnish us with this information sooner."

Billy hangs his head. "I'm sorry, sir, but as I say, I truly feared for my life."

A few days later, Billy spots Lucy strolling along Pound Lane and picking primroses, with Frankie asleep in his perambulator. He approaches her warily. "Hello, Lucy. Is your ma making her primrose wine again this year?"

"Yes, she asked me to pick some, while I settle Frankie down for his nap."

He looks down at the sleeping, fatherless child. "I'm so sorry for your loss, Lucy."

"Thank you." She looks at him, with a confused expression on her face. "I thought you were living near Wincanton now, Billy?" She continues to bend, picking the dainty yellow flowers in the same clump.

"I was. I came back here for a while, to escape the clutches of some thugs who were threatening me."

She straightens up. "Why ever would they be threatening you, Billy?"

"Because I tried to intervene when they were assaulting your husband."

Lucy looks flabbergasted. "You did what?"

"I interrupted them. I thought of you and although reluctant, I had no choice but to help him, but he ran off, leaving them very angry with me."

"I can imagine. Do you know why they were attacking him?" She looks thoughtful, as she absent-mindedly pushes the perambulator on down the lane.

"It was because he owed money, I'm afraid."

She stops short and turns to him, concerned. "Have you told the policemen about this, Billy?"

"Yes, I have now, but I was afraid to inform on them before; I was hoping to speak to Lord Dryer first, but then the police come looking for me and I had no choice."

She suddenly bursts forth indignantly, "Well, you should have told them sooner, Billy, then maybe my brother wouldn't have been sent to Shepton Mallet Prison!"

He tries to defend himself. "I know that, Lucy, and I've been shitting myself every day since and praying the police would discover the truth before now, but I've no actual evidence they were responsible; it just seems far more likely it was them, than poor Malachi."

"Small mercies, but at least you've told the police now, so hopefully they'll scour the land until they find the villains. I cannot bear to think of poor Malachi and Rosa and the children all suffering because of Ashleigh and me."

"You cannot blame yourself, Lucy."

"Why not? It was me who decided to seek refuge with my family. If I'd only been stronger, my brother would never have become embroiled in it all." Tears fill her eyes and Billy is at a loss how to help her.

"Please don't distress yourself, Lucy. Lord Dryer is back soon and I'm sure he'll take charge of things. He won't let Malachi take the blame for this, based purely on hearsay."

"You're far too naive, Billy. They'd rather blame anyone, than have an unsolved double murder on their hands. Don't forget the other man who was found dead in the River Cale! Heaven forbid that Mal is blamed for that, too!"

He studies her, while he has the opportunity, and is surprised to see how much she has changed in the last four years, since her marriage. There is an anger in her now; she seems belligerent, whereas before she was so sweet-natured. He suddenly realises, she is no longer the girl to whom he gave his heart and she will never be that person again.

"You must have faith, Lucy. I'm sure the good Lord would not allow an innocent man to hang. I believe the new detective from Taunton is no fool and he'll find the real culprits, you mark my words."

"I hope so, Billy. I truly hope so with all my heart."

CHAPTER SIXTEEN *(April 1870)*

DÉJÀ VU

Joshua and Aurora, having changed trains at Dorchester, arrive at Penn Mill Station in Ivell on the 14th April. Joshua had wired ahead from Southampton and John Moore is waiting with the landau to take them on the final leg of their journey home. The porter loads the luggage, while Aurora takes in the familiar scene before her and sighs. She cannot wait to see her mama and Gabriel, but the anticipation is bitter-sweet. She remembers woefully the warmth of her lover's farewell and the exhilarating passion of his kisses.

She wonders if Luke has truly missed her. Confusingly, she is looking forward to seeing him again too. He has always been her special confidant and she knows he believes her to be his sweetheart. Her feelings are complicated by the suspicion that sweet Gwyneth is also secretly in love with Rhys, and that she may have unintentionally hurt her. Perhaps she will be better able to make her decision when she finally sees Luke again.

There has been a recent rainfall and the foliage glistens in the spring sunlight, lush and green, in stark contrast to the dry grey of the Australian saltbush. They progress through the town, her papa paying the tolls at Goar Knap and Kingston. Little has changed since November, but her mama will have changed, her time is imminent, and she will be so relieved to have herself and papa back home.

On reaching Alvington Manor they are greeted outside by her mama and Gabriel and all the domestic staff lining up to welcome them home. It is heart-warming to see how they have been missed. Joshua helps her down from the carriage and all the liveried men bow and the mob-capped ladies curtsey. Her mother rushes forward to embrace Papa and Gabriel runs to her and hugs her affectionately.

"Come inside and tell me everything," says her mother.

She follows her parents through the main hallway, with the staff following behind them and peeling off back to their duties. Dottie and Dash run around in circles yelping excitedly and jumping up for attention. Papa makes a fuss of them and then takes Mama's arm, commenting, "My goodness, my love, you need to sit down and rest your weary bones, you look pale."

She agrees with him, surprised to see how large and cumbersome her poor mama has become in the months they have been gone and afraid the two dogs may trip her up in their excitement. When they reach the oak, her mother sinks into her favourite armchair and smiles up at him. "I'm fine, my dear. I'm exceedingly pleased to have you both home, safe and sound. We've been incredibly worried about you so far away, with so much happening here in your absence."

Papa sits down beside her and sighs, "That is appallingly apparent, my dear. Have you heard how Malachi is faring?"

"We only know that he's been working a treadwheel at the prison and he looked undernourished and unhappy when Ambrose visited, but he took heart that you were returning sooner."

"Well, I intend to spend some time with my family today, but I'll be going to visit him tomorrow, to bolster him, listen to his story and see whatever I can learn from him."

"I understand, my love. But you must rest after your long journey and I'll enjoy having you all to myself for today. I'll ask Flora to make up another food parcel for Malachi, for you to take with you."

"I'm sure he'll appreciate that. In the meantime, all I want to do, is sit here with you all and enjoy a nice cup of Flora's China tea."

Aurora thinks, it isn't only Malachi who will be needing help and support; she asks, "Do you know how Lucy is coping, Mama?"

"Not really, Rora. Being confined has its limitations, but I believe she and Frankie are staying with her parents at Home Farm at present."

"In that case, with your permission, I'll visit them tomorrow and tell them of Papa's plans."

"Of course, they're all so worried about Malachi, any scrap of good news will be welcome."

"Why don't you give them our presents, Aurora?"

"Of course, Papa." She delves into her reticule and retrieves a small, meticulously wrapped package that she passes to her mother. "I'm afraid the other thing for Gabriel had to go in my portmanteau, as it was too big. I'll go and fetch it in a minute, but I want to see if Mama likes her gift first."

She watches her mother's intrigued expression as she unwraps her present, revealing a finely crafted opal necklace. "Oh, my goodness! It's absolutely beautiful."

Her father says, "We thought you'd like it, as soon as we spotted it, in a little shop in Melbourne. You didn't give us much time to browse, but as your birthday is in October, the opal stones are lucky for you. I thought the necklace would look lovely with all your evening gowns, there are so many fiery colours in the stones."

"You are quite right, my dear, it's beautiful. Thank you so much."

Gabriel looks at her patiently. "Will you go and get mine now, Rora?"

"Yes, of course. I won't be a minute." She rushes upstairs and quickly returns with the parcel. He jumps up eagerly and she laughs, as she gives it to him.

The paper is torn off. "A boomerang! That's amazing. Thank you, Papa."

Her father smiles. "The gift is from both of us."

"Thank you, Rora. I'm going to go and try it out right away. Come on, Dottie and Dash, let's go outside and have a go. If it doesn't come back, they can fetch it for me and I'll keep trying until I get the hang of it."

She spends the remainder of the day with her mama and papa, catching up with all that has transpired in both Ivell and Bendigo Creek.

The following morning, Joshua is preparing for his trip to Shepton Mallet, when Gareth knocks on his dressing room door. On admittance, he explains that Billy Riddick would like a word with him.

"Billy Riddick? I thought he was in Wincanton."

"He was, sir. I made the decision to allow him to stay here in your absence, because I thought it would be according to your wishes, had you been here. This is what he desires to speak to you about."

"Show him into my study, Gareth, I'll be down shortly."

"Of course, my lord."

Billy is waiting on tenterhooks when the door opens, and Lord Dryer enters. He stands to attention.

"Good morning, Billy. You wanted to speak with me?"

He feels himself reddening. "I did, sir. I don't know where to start, my lord… but it's related to Ashleigh Seymour's murder."

"Then I suggest you take a seat and start at the beginning by explaining to me why you are here and not in Wincanton."

Billy selects the seat opposite his master, takes a deep breath and begins, "I'm afraid I was forced to leave Hatherleigh Farm, with their blessing, partly for my own safety, but also for the sake of Bob Yates and his family. It is a long story…"

Joshua listens attentively and at the end of his tale he asks Billy, "Have you told the police your suspicions?"

"I have now, my lord. At first, I was too alarmed to come forward; I was afraid to let on, lest the villains come find me and make me pay for it. I wanted to confide in you, my lord, because you know me well and I know I can trust you, but you weren't here… I was afraid the policemen may think me implicated in some way, but when they came looking for me, I had no choice… I couldn't lie to the detective."

"No, that would have been very foolish, Billy. I'm glad you've told me this, before I go to visit Malachi and I hope it will give him some hope that all is not lost. Thank you, Billy. You may return to your duties now."

"Thank you, my lord." He turns to leave and then turns back. "I'd just like to add, my lord, that I've not left my employment at Hatherleigh Farm permanently. I was simply seeking refuge, while

Pocket's bully boys were hunting for me. Now I've given the detective their names, I imagine they'll be arrested and so it will soon be safe to return."

"I understand and I'm happy to give you refuge here, until you're confident you'll come to no harm."

"Thank you, my lord." He bows his head and leaves the room.

Finally, when Joshua sets off in the gig to Shepton Mallet Prison, he experiences an overwhelming feeling of déjà vu, remembering his last voyage home from Fiji, when he was obliged to travel to Dorchester Prison with Becky to secure the release of his brother, Ben. He prays that this situation will have a similar happy ending, although last time there was no threat of the hangman looming over them.

On reaching the prison, Joshua climbs down, with the food parcel under his arm, and secures Capella to the hitching post. He hammers on the huge oak doors and the sound echoes within. He hears footsteps and the postern door opens cautiously. He speaks authoritatively, "I'm here to see Malachi Warren."

"And who might you be?" is the indignant response.

Joshua draws himself up to his full height, and says with emphasis, "I'm Justice of the Peace, Lord Joshua Dryer of Alvington Manor, in Ivell." He hands the man his calling card.

The man looks taken aback, takes the card and opens the door to allow him entry. "Please come in, my lord." He locks the gate behind him. "I'll have to check with the governor. If you would be so kind as to wait here."

Shortly the governor comes to verify his credentials. He seems satisfied that he is the bona fide gentleman and, handing back his card, he invites him into the governor's residence. The governor instructs his servant to bring tea and he is asked to take a seat while Malachi is fetched.

He is sitting, supping tea, when his friend is brought to him. Joshua is shocked at the change in him. He has never seen him look so emaciated and dirty. Malachi removes the prison hat and stands before him looking very forlorn. Joshua asks the governor for some privacy and once granted, he jumps up and hugs his friend, feeling his bony ribs through the prison duds. Then he hands him his food parcel.

"I'm sorry to find you here, Mal. I've been so worried about you and Rosa since I heard what had happened. I'm most regretful I couldn't get here any sooner."

"I'm just inordinately relieved to see you, Josh. Is there any sign at all that anyone believes in my innocence?"

"Well, I'm sure that everyone who truly knows you, believes you to be above suspicion. I've learned a little more about Ashleigh Seymour's unsavoury connections with the gambling fraternity, from Billy Riddick. He was witness to an attack on him by some Wincanton thugs at Hatherleigh Farm on Boxing Day. He's recently informed the detective in charge of this, so I hope for your sake, some progress is being made with regard to that."

"Do you mind if I eat? I'm starved."

"Of course not, go ahead."

Malachi opens his parcel and draws out a sausage roll. "As you can imagine I've been going over and over the last time I saw Ashleigh, which as

269

I understand it, was the last day he was seen alive and there's one thing I want you to check on. When I last set eyes on him he was in his pony and trap. Did that pony find its way home that day, or has that vanished?" He bites into the pastry and savours the delights of Flora's legendary baking.

"That's a good point, Mal. I'll put this to the detective who's now running the show, as soon as I get back. I'll also check with Lucy. If the pony and trap are still missing, maybe the villains took it to sell in lieu of his debts. If the police can track them down it should lead to whoever did the deed."

Malachi is thoughtful as he picks flakes of pastry from his prison uniform. "Ashleigh's body was discovered close to home, so unless the pony and trap were stolen, the animal should have found its own way home."

"Is there anything else you can think of, that might help your case?"

Malachi sighs. "Unfortunately no, except that if the damned fellow had serious money problems, there must be far more people out there who have a grudge against him than I do."

Joshua rubs his forehead. "I'm convinced it's something to do with the thugs who attacked him on Boxing Day, so take heart, I'm sure the police will soon be making progress. In the meantime, I'll be hectoring them all the while, until they find and arrest these true villains and prove you're blameless."

"Thank you, my friend. How is Rosa and my little uns doing without me?" His voice becomes husky and his eyes brim with tears.

"They're doing fine. Rosa is kept busy with us and the children are busy with school. Of course they're missing you and cannot wait to have you back home. They don't understand the reality of prison, which is just as well. Do you have any messages for them?"

He runs the back of his hand across his eyes. "Please assure them of my constant love and tell them I'm in good spirits."

"Of course I will, and I'll speak to your sister about the pony and trap; she's staying at Home Farm at present, I believe."

"Thank you, my friend. I'm so relieved to see you and so grateful for your help."

"I intend to get you out of here as soon as I can, Malachi, you have my word on that." They shake hands. "Time is of the essence. I must make haste to investigate and will report back to you, the moment I have any relevant intelligence."

That evening, having rested after his journey, Joshua wanders over to Home Farm. He knocks on the door and is admitted by Beth Warren. The kitchen still holds the aroma of the family meal and he can hear music coming from the parlour.

"Welcome, my lord, how wonderful to have you back home."

"Thank you, Beth. I wanted to tell you, I went to see Malachi today and he's in good spirits, considering where he is. He was very pleased to see me, and he had some salient questions, which I was hoping Lucy might shed some light on. Is she here?"

"Yes, she is. She and little Frankie have been staying with us for a few weeks now. Come through, my lord, everyone will be pleased to see you."

"Thank you." He follows her into their parlour where he finds Lucy playing a Brahms lullaby, with

Frankie asleep in a crib in the corner of the room. Bunny is playing draughts with Toby Boucher, and Jacob is chatting to Isaac, who is leisurely smoking his pipe and the fragrant aroma of Erinmore tobacco fills the room. They all stand up.

He goes to Lucy and, taking her hand, he says, "My sincere condolences, Lucy. I'm very sorry, both for the loss of your husband and for the injustice of Malachi's arrest."

She dips a curtsey. "Thank you, my lord."

He turns to everyone and bids them, "Please, sit down. I've come to let you know that I saw Malachi this morning and I left him in good spirits. There was one question however, that he asked me to investigate and I was wondering whether you might be able to help me with it, Lucy." He pauses, "Do you know if the pony and trap returned to Bingham Manor after your husband visited you here that day?"

Lucy looks thoughtful, but shakes her head in frustration, "I'm sorry, I don't, my lord. So much happened, it was all so confusing and distressing... but now you come to mention it, I haven't seen them lately. Robshaw brought us here in the brougham."

"Don't worry, Lucy, I'll go tomorrow to Bingham Manor to check with your in-laws. If the pony and trap are missing, it does suggest they were stolen, which could well be the motive for the murder."

Isaac says, "Thank you, my lord. This is what we've been praying for, something that will point the finger to someone other than our Malachi."

"You're very welcome. I will intrude no longer. I'm looking forward to spending some precious time with my wife and family, and there will be another early start tomorrow. Goodnight, all."

"Goodnight, my lord."

The next day Joshua goes to Bingham Manor to speak with Jeremy Seymour. Robshaw answers the door and Joshua realises it might be more appropriate to ask him instead. "Good day to you." He hands the manservant his card. "I'm Joshua Dryer, the Justice of the Peace from Alvington Manor. I'm acting on behalf of Lucy's brother, Malachi Warren, and I was hoping to speak to the master of the house, but I believe there is no need to trouble him, if you could be of assistance?"

"I will do my best, my lord."

"I'd be most grateful if you could tell me if your master's pony and trap returned to the manor, on the night that he went to fetch his wife home, which as I understand it, was the last time he was seen alive?"

He shakes his head. "No sir, it did not, and she's greatly missed. A gentle little filly she was, and a beautifully fashioned trap made by Hill's Carriage Works of Kingston in Ivell."

He sighs with relief, "Does the detective superintendent know this?"

"I don't rightly know, sir. No one has spoken to me about it."

"Can you describe the pony for me?"

"Yes, sir. She was a brown Exmoor pony, about twelve hands, called Dolly."

He smiles. "Thank you. I've no need to disturb your master, you've answered my questions. Good day to you."

After supper, he and Louisa are relaxing on the terrace listening to the birdsong and enjoying a nightcap just before the sun goes down. He breaks the companionable silence by saying, "I went to see Detective Superintendent McKinley today and told him about the pony and trap. Apparently, John and Sophie Hill always initial their workmanship on the back plate and so it should be easier to track the trap at least. I suggested that this information is released to the press, so people will be on the lookout, but the detective believes that this will alert the robbers to the fact that we're on to them and they'd destroy any evidence, so he's keeping it quiet at present."

"They should be checking on all the markets and horse fayres."

"I am sure they will be now."

"I just hope it isn't too late."

"The villains may well be waiting until the heat dies down, before they try to sell them on. Who knows?" He thoughtfully takes a swig of his brandy.

As the sun slants low in the sky over Odcombe, tiny bats begin to flit around, dodging each other and chasing the bugs.

Louisa changes the subject. "Luke came down to see Aurora today."

He smiles to himself. "Oh yes, and how did that go?"

"Well, Grace stayed with them the whole time and Aurora told Luke all about her adventures."

Joshua grins. "I bet she didn't tell him about the two young Welsh bucks who were in attendance!"

"What do you mean?"

"Well, it seems that both Lewys Davies and Rhys Thomas were rather enamoured of our Aurora."

Louisa looks pleased. "Ah! Well, that at least has shown her there are more fish in the sea."

"Yes, but the distance between our seas is pretty expansive! I only hope that she hasn't left her heart behind in Bendigo."

Her pleasure dissipates. "Oh, my darling, please don't say that."

Upstairs, Aurora is sitting in her bedchamber thinking about what she should say to Rhys. She picks up her dipping pen and begins to write to him:

Mr Rhys Thomas
Brecon Valley Mining Company
C/O Bendigo Post Office
Sandhurst
Victoria
South Australia

My dearest Rhys,

We have arrived safely back home in Somerset and it is with sadness that I put pen to paper to let you know how dreadfully I am already missing you and how I regret not being able to stay in Bendigo longer, so that we might get to know each other better. During the brief period we spent together I admit to being blissfully happy, but the time was far too short to be able to decide on the course of a whole lifetime. Cruel fate has decreed that we should be parted too soon, and I dearly miss your strong arms around me, those wicked twinkling eyes and your loving kisses. Please write, for I feel it is important that we should keep in touch, for who knows what the future may hold.

My mind has been going over and over what happened between us and how I involved poor Gwyneth in our conspiracy, and I fear that she too holds a candle for you. I hope that we have not unintentionally hurt her, but I do think you need to be aware of her possible attachment to you, Rhys, so that you might deal with her sympathetically.

I must close now, as I also promised to write to Gwyneth and Camira, but please remember I am thinking of you always, longing to hear from

*you and praying that one day we might be together
again.*

   Your loving sweetheart,
   Aurora.

There are tears running down her cheeks as she puts down her dipping pen and blots the writing paper and yet confusingly she thinks about earlier that afternoon when she had covertly passed Luke a note, without her governess, Grace, noticing, requesting that he should meet her at the top of Pound Lane the following evening. She is not going to tell him about her affections for Rhys, because she doesn't wish to hurt his feelings and wants to put them to the test of time. Surely it wouldn't be practical for her to imagine a life with Rhys in Australia, leaving all she has ever known and loved, behind her here?

   She settles down to write to Camira and tell her of the close encounter with the whale, the leaping dolphins and the albatross she saw on their journey home and to Gwyneth, asking her to thank everyone for caring for them so well, during their stay Down Under.

The following evening, when no one is looking, she sneaks out and makes her way to the top of Pound Lane. She can see Luke waiting for her, impatiently slashing at stinging nettles with a stick. The instant he sees her, he throws away his cane, eagerly takes her hand and they set off towards Odcombe together.

   He looks a little anxious and then he asks her, "You've happily told me all about your trip with your papa, but you've said nothing about your feelings for me. Did you miss me at all, Rora?"

"Of course I did, but there was so much going on all the time, I suppose it was easier for me than it was for you, left here with everything mundane as usual."

"Not exactly mundane, Rora, with a murder in the next village, affecting the manor more than most households, with the victim being married to our own Lucy and poor Malachi being arrested!"

"No, no, you must have all been terribly worried, but apart from that, life went on much the same, didn't it? Whereas life was incredibly novel for us and exciting too."

"But despite all that was going on here, I missed you dreadfully, Rora. I'm so relieved that you are unharmed and back home with us again. I was worried about your safety, not only on the crossing, which was risky enough, but also in that uncivilised, lawless place, where everyone is so desperate for gold."

"You had no need to worry, Luke. The family we lodged with were Welsh chapel folk and could not have been kinder or more hospitable. We were very well looked after."

They reach a small area set off the road under three fir trees and Luke leans back against the trunk of one of the trees and pulls her towards him for a kiss. She is pleased he wants to kiss her and she kisses him back, enjoying his strong arms around her, but his kisses become more urgent. She tries to push her mother's words of caution from her mind, warning her of the risk of falling for the wrong man, but the fear of what happened to her own mother, fills her head. Why did she not think of this when she was with Rhys?

She pulls away slightly, reluctantly resisting his charms and she feels his frustration and

277

disappointment. She hears a carriage approaching and quickly pulls him back out into the open, recognising one of the local farmers and they both wave as he passes by.

"I hope he doesn't tell on us," she says to Luke giggling.

"There is not much to tell, is there?" he replies sadly.

"What do you mean by that? Look, Luke, you're my very best friend. I cannot imagine living here without you, but…"

"But, what? I know we're both friends, but I need more. I want you to be my sweetheart."

"I'm happy to be your sweetheart for now, but I'm not sure that I want to be promised to you for ever, Luke. It is such an important decision."

"I see." He looks so sad. "Well, I suppose I must make the best of it. Come here." He pulls her towards him and kisses her again, exceptionally tenderly this time and her lips tingle with pleasure, but the memory of those distant twinkling eyes fills her with guilt.

CHAPTER SEVENTEEN *(April–May 1870)*

ITCHY FEET AND ITCHY FINGERS

Billy is getting itchy feet, as the Easter celebrations loom. He is sure they will want to race Bay Rum on Easter Monday and he badly wants to return home and be a part of it all again. He decides to go to His Lordship and ask him when he is next going to see Malachi.

"I hadn't planned to go just yet, but if you'd like to hitch a ride, I can drop you off at Podimore on Wednesday and then go on and take a food parcel for Malachi and update him on the latest developments. Although there's not much more to tell him at present, he might be relieved to learn that Ashleigh's pony and trap are still missing."

"So they were stolen?"

"Yes, Billy, a little brown Exmoor pony called Dolly, and a Hill's Carriage Works trap made by John and Sophie Hill of Kingston in Ivell, with their initials carved in the back plate, but please keep this information to yourself, so the villains are not alerted to the fact that we're on the lookout for them."

"Of course, my lord."

When, on Wednesday, Lord Dryer is ready to leave, he sends Gareth to fetch Billy, who rushes over with his haversack and climbs aboard the gig.

They set off together, Billy feeling a little tongue-tied being seated next to His Lordship, but Lord Dryer asks him about his time at Hatherleigh Farm. Billy proudly tells him of the races he has won on Bay Rum, about training with Queenie, and his friends Wally, Noah, and Florica, all the time growing more excited at the prospect of being reunited with them, and his new-found family.

Eventually, Lord Dryer pulls in the reins and draws the gig to a halt at the road junction at Podimore. He takes out his purse and counts four guineas into the palm of his hand. "I haven't forgotten that you've been working for me since Christmas and so here are your wages for the four months." He hands Billy the gold coins.

"I don't know what to say, my lord. It was for my benefit not yours that I turned up like a bad penny."

"No, Billy, never a bad penny. You've always been a hard worker and you deserve to be paid for your time. Take it with my blessing."

"Thank you, my lord." He wraps the coins in his handkerchief to prevent any jingling and puts them in his pocket. He doesn't want to be robbed by a footpad. Then he jumps down, shoulders his knapsack and sets off purposefully, waving cheerily, while Lord Dryer flicks the reins and Capella trots off in a northerly direction towards Shepton Mallet and the prison. He manages to hitch a ride with a Wincanton farmer and is eventually back in his little cottage at Hatherleigh Farm. He drops off his knapsack and immediately goes to the farmhouse to see the family.

Victoria is feeding the pigs with some vegetable peelings when she spots him walking towards the house, and she drops her pail and hurls herself at him, her pleasure at seeing him again, obvious. He hugs her back, enjoying the novelty of the unfamiliar womanly feel of her in his arms.

"It's so good to have you back home, Billy. We've all been missing you. Come on in; Ma will be so pleased to see you again."

He flushes bright pink at the unexpected joy of such a warm reception and follows her shapely figure into the house. He has developed tender feelings for her, over the last four years. He finally realised, during their recent meeting, that he and Lucy are no longer suited and that he has been missing Victoria's happy disposition dearly since January. *Could it be possible that she feels the same?*

He is surprised to find Noah sitting at the kitchen table along with Bob, Don and Jake.

"Hey, Billy! It's good to have you back."

"Good afternoon, everyone. I'm more than happy to be here, I can tell you. How are things on the farm?"

Bob grins at him. "Things are fine, lad. Noah here has been a great help, repairing stuff and generally lending a hand with the horses. His *vardo* is behind the stables. He's even been exercising Bay Rum, occasionally, along with our Don."

"I'm glad. But where is Florica?"

"She's still with her *day* and *dat* in Wincanton. Our Romany rules are very strict. She must remain chaste until we are wed."

Bob adds, "But you're back in good time, because he and Florica don't have much longer to wait; they're planning to wed in August. All their family are meeting at Priddy Fayre and with the gathering of the clans, they'll be married there."

Noah grins. "Working here for Bob, has enabled me to save up more money towards our wedding celebrations and Florica's *dat*, Leon, has been creating metalwork for Bob, which has also contributed towards Florica's *darro*."

"*Darro*?"

"Er... dowry?"

"That's grand. My hearty congratulations, my friend." He shakes Noah's hand.

"Florica asked me to invite you and Vicky to our *abijav*... er, as you say, wedding party."

"Really? That's wonderful!" He turns to his boss. "But what do you think, Bob? Will you be able to manage without us for a couple of days?"

"Well, we've managed for nearly four months without you, lad, so a couple of days shouldn't be a problem, providing Jake doesn't mind helping out again."

Jake grins. "Of course not, Bob. Me and my Maud could do with the extra cash."

"Thanks, Bob and you, Jake." He turns back to Noah. "I'd love to come; what do you think, Vicky?"

Vicky looks delighted. "Of course, it promises to be a wonderful diversion."

Billy grows grave again. "I suppose it's no surprise to you that Ashleigh Seymour's body was found, not long after I left here?"

Bob Yates answers for them. "No, we read all about it in the *Western Gazette* and we've been so worried about you, Billy. Did the heavies come looking for you?"

"No, thank heavens! I was quite safe at the manor and I've informed the detective superintendent of what happened here, so I believe those louts will be under lock and key by now."

Lillian passes him a mug of tea. "That's a relief, Billy. Let's hope they'll get their just deserts."

"I really want to put all that behind me now. I've done my duty and I trust the consequences all fall on the heads of Pocket and his minders, Snodgrass and Blakely, and not on me."

Jake clears his throat. "Did you say Pocket?"

"I did, Jake, why?"

"It's just that my missus pawned her cameo brooch, that once belonged to her mother, before Christmas. She doesn't know that I know, but now I'm worried, she'll likely not get it back."

"I'd be worried, too, Jake, because the interest will go up the longer he has hold of it. He should be called Jarvis *Deep* Pocket. You ought to go and redeem it before he's arrested."

"I'd have fetched it back immediately if I'd had the money, Billy."

Billy thoughtfully puts his hand in his pocket and feels the handkerchief and the golden coins. "Do you know how much is owed?"

"My lad said he thought he heard three guineas."

He pulls out the handkerchief and unwraps it. Leaving himself one guinea piece, he hands the other three coins to Jake. "Here, I can loan you this. Lord Dryer gave it to me this morning for my time with him. I hope it covers it, Jake. Unlike Pocket, I won't be charging any interest. Just pay me back in dribs and drabs when you can afford it. I don't have a family to feed like you; not yet, anyway." He looks at Victoria hopefully, but she has her back turned from him towards the sink.

"Thank you, Billy. That brooch means a lot to my Maud."

"Go now, Jake," says Bob Yates. "You can't risk waiting any longer, if he's likely to be arrested and the shop closed down."

"Thanks, boss." He grabs his jacket and rushes off, with Billy's guineas clutched in his hand.

"Good luck, Jake." Billy takes a swig of tea. He looks at the others. "I hope he isn't too late."

Don looks at him and says, "That was very kind of you, Billy."

Billy grins. "Glad to be of help." Then changing the subject, he asks them, "What are the plans for Easter Monday? Do you know if Queenie is running?"

"Yes, Mortimer Bathhurst has entered Wally and Conker Queen, so you'll be seeing them both next week."

"I'm so looking forward to being reunited with Bay Rum. How is she doing?"

Don and Noah eagerly both answer at once and they all laugh, as they go over all that has happened during her training since Billy left them.

Later that day, Jake returns triumphant; he has redeemed the brooch. He had to pay a bit more of his own money, but he is so happy to have it back for his Maud.

He finds Billy in the stable. "Look, Billy, I got it back for her." He shows Billy his wife's family heirloom, an attractive shell cameo portrait, set in gold.

"I'm glad, Jake. Your wife will be thrilled. So, he's still in operation then?"

"Yes, he was large as life behind the counter."

"What about Blakely and Snodgrass? Did you see any sign of them?"

"No, Billy. The shop was empty, besides him."

Billy sighs in frustration. He is relieved that his friend has retrieved the brooch, but if Pocket is still in operation, what progress have the police made?

On Easter Monday, all the preparations are completed and the family gather for a quick lunch before the racing begins. Billy is impressed with Bay Rum. The lads have obviously kept up his programme of training and she is looking superb. He doesn't want to eat anything, he is far too excited, but the others all tuck into a tasty ploughman's.

At half past twelve they all set off together, following behind him riding Bay Rum, in their purple and gold colours. The usual members of the race committee are milling around and he spots Lucky Joe Mintern immediately. He will always be grateful to him for warning him about Jarvis Pocket.

Then, to his horror, he spots Blakely and Snodgrass leaning against Pocket's bookie stand. He leans down to Bob Yates and tells him, "Those bastards are here! So much for the police arresting them!"

"Don't worry about them, Billy. Just you make sure you're always in the public eye. They won't risk any trouble here with what is at stake for them if they get caught by the police. You concentrate on the race. Don't forget, Midnight Rambler only just managed to get by you on Boxing Day; we don't want Lucky Joe to win again today."

"I'll do my best, Bob, you can depend on that."

He can now see Wally and Queenie among the horses in the riders' enclosure and he trots off to greet them.

"Hey, Billy, it's good to see you. I see you're in the first race against Lucky Joe's Illicit Liaison. We've drawn Midnight Rambler this time. Good luck, my friend."

"Thank you. It's wonderful to be back and reunited with Bay Rum. I've missed all this excitement so much."

"I bet."

He sniggers. "But you don't, do you, Wally?"

"Don't what?"

"Bet."

He laughs. "No, not as a rule, but there have been rare exceptions."

"Did you win?"

"Did I heck! 'Tis a rich man's hobby, not for the likes of us."

"I agree, Wally, I certainly don't have enough spare gold to risk being fleeced by the tic-tac men."

The announcement is made for the horses to make their way for the first race and Billy falls in line with the rest. He observes Illicit Liaison in the red and yellow colours of Lucky Joe Mintern's stable. She looks to be a worthy opponent and he braces himself for the competition.

Then he notices Lord Dryer, sitting with some dignitaries on the grandstand. *What the devil is he doing here?*

Joshua is impressed with the set-up here at Hatherleigh Farm. The race committee seem to have everything well organised. He just hopes his little plan will also go like clockwork. He is itching to get those two rogues in custody. In the meantime, he has backed Billy by putting some money on Bay Rum to win with Uriah Levi. He is not a betting man, but as he is here, he may as well make it a little more interesting. He has also taken the advice of Jock McKinley and put a small bet on each of the other races.

The day is warm and dry and, between the light clouds, hot in the sunshine. The background noise of the optimistic racegoers and happy hawkers escalates. A young barmaid serves them with ale. While supping the beer, which is going down rather well, he is enjoying the unfamiliar spectacle; all the folk dressed in their Sunday best and the eager jockeys in a variety of racing colours. He is absolutely thrilled for Billy and for himself when he wins the first race, nail bitingly, neck and neck, against Illicit Liaison.

When Billy goes up to accept the prize with Bob, Joshua beckons to him to join them in the grandstand. Billy excuses himself from Bob and strolls over, easing himself past the other gentlemen seated in the same row, all patting him on the back with their congratulations, as he squeezes past. They return to their conversations.

Billy recognises the man seated next to Lord Dryer. He bows. "You wanted to see me, my lord?"

"Yes, Billy. I wanted to congratulate you in person. I've won a little money, thanks to your Bay Rum."

"I'm pleased, my lord."

Lord Dryer lowers his voice. "You'll remember Detective Superintendent McKinley."

"Yes, my lord. Good day, Superintendent."

"Good afternoon, Mr Riddick. Congratulations on your race."

"Thank you, sir."

"As I'm sure you've guessed, we're not only here to enjoy a day's racing, Mr Riddick, but we're planning to arrest the two men you described to me, who accosted Mr Ashleigh Seymour. Are you able to point them out to me?"

"I am, sir. However, I've no need to draw attention to myself by physically pointing to them, as they're both, at this very moment, leaning against the betting booth of Mr Pocket."

Lord Dryer smiles reassuringly. "Thank you, Billy. We can take it from here. Please go on back to your friends and relax and enjoy the rest of the afternoon."

"I will now, my lord. I'm indebted to you. Thank you."

"Just leave things to us."

"I will gladly, my lord."

He bows and makes his way back the way he had come, hurrying over to stand with Bob and Noah, near the track to the farm, where they might have a good view of the proceedings. Fred Meaden announces the next race and the horses line up near to where they are standing. The flag goes down, the horses are off and all attention at the course is on the racetrack, but at the same moment, Billy observes a line of constables moving towards the betting booths. He holds his breath, as the two bullies are taken by surprise and a struggle ensues. Snodgrass legs it and is brought down in a rugby tackle by one of the constables, but Blakely is held fast by two burly policemen, presumably especially chosen for the task, and finally they are both efficiently handcuffed and marched off to the horse-drawn Black Maria already waiting in Clemmy's Field. He also notes with some satisfaction, the indignant look of horror and astonishment on the face of Jarvis Pocket.

CHAPTER EIGHTEEN *(May 1870)*

THE ROBBERS' CODE

Blakely and Snodgrass are held in the lock-up at the police station in North Street, Wincanton to await the Western Circuit, midsummer court of assize, held in Salisbury.

A few days later Jock McKinley calls at Alvington Manor to tell Joshua, "I've decided that those two ruffians deserve to be kept in custody, while my officers are busy searching their homes for any evidence that might be forthcoming pertaining to either of the murders. From what Billy Riddick tells us, they're far more likely to be guilty than Malachi Warren, but we need evidence."

Joshua shakes his hand. "Of course; in the meantime, it will be a relief to Billy that they will not be able to intimidate him."

"Exactly, and maybe others may come forward, if they are securely held."

"I do hope so. Can I offer you some afternoon tea?"

"That is most kind, but I've an appointment in Ivell shortly and sadly I'm unable to spare the time today."

"Well, thank you for letting me know. I'll probably see you at the quarter sessions."

On 21st May in the early hours of the morning, Louisa goes into labour with her second baby. Aurora knows her mother is anxious, but she has also told her how relieved she feels to have her and her papa near at hand and not on route from Australia, as might have been the case. Her papa fetches the midwife from Montacute and remains at home ready for instructions should the help of Dr Gillingham be required.

Once the sun is up, Gabriel is too anxious to stay inside and goes outside onto the lawn to play with his boomerang with Dottie and Dash. Rosa remains with Louisa to fetch and carry for the midwife and Aurora is along the passageway in her bedchamber attempting to focus on her letter to Rhys, while trying not to listen to the moans and groans emitting from the master bedchamber.

Eventually, she hears Gabriel being called inside for lunch, but still Mama's cries continue. She goes downstairs to join her papa and brother. "Don't you think we ought to send for Dr Gillingham?"

"I sent John Moore to fetch him ages ago, my dear, but he must be on another case. I'm sure he'll be here the minute he can be."

"Well, I hope so. I don't remember it being this bad when Gabriel was born."

"You were only a small child then, Aurora, and we kept you away in the nursery, with Nanny. You mustn't worry, this is quite normal."

"I'm never going to have any babies, if this is what you have to endure."

Joshua smiles. "We'll see."

Louisa's labour continues in much the same vein throughout the day and they are halfway through their supper when Dr Gillingham arrives and rushes upstairs to attend to his patient, without preamble.

At about eleven o'clock, Aurora hears the mewling sound of a new baby, gradually increasing in volume to a wail. "It's here, Papa, the baby is finally here. May we go up to see it?"

"Rosa will come and tell us when your mama is ready to receive us, but when that happens, I will be going up first, then you and Gabriel may follow afterwards, if all is well with your mama."

It is about another half an hour before Rosa comes downstairs and tells him that Louisa is ready to see him. He jumps up eagerly and strides from the room and up the stairs, with Aurora and Gabriel, dressed in their nightclothes, but too excited to go to bed, following close behind. They wait patiently in the passageway while he goes in to see his new baby and Louisa.

Outside the door they can hear the mumbling of voices and Aurora unsuccessfully strains to hear what is being said, then finally the door is opened and they are allowed inside.

Their mother looks absolutely drained, but full of smiles as she says, "Come and meet your perfect little baby sister. Your papa and I have agreed we're going to call her Lydia May. Lydia, after my grandmother and May because she has arrived in May. What do you think?"

"It is a lovely name, Mama. She looks so like you, she even has a hint of red in her fine hair."

"She will resemble both of us, Rora. I hope you're not disappointed, Gabriel. I know you were hoping for a little brother."

"No, Mama, she is so adorable. How could I be disappointed? I love her already and I promise I'll always take care of her, as her big brother. Besides, it is quite nice being the only man of the house, after Papa of course."

When Superintendent McKinley goes to Wincanton Police Station to check on the progress of the two murder cases, the desk sergeant there greets him cheerfully. "Good morning, sir. I believe we have good tidings for you."

"I'm pleased to hear it, Sergeant. Pray tell, what is this good news?"

"Well, we've discovered some incriminating evidence in the form of a golden pocket watch, with Ashleigh Seymour's initials engraved on it, hidden among clothing at Blakely's home. Furthermore, Snodgrass has his silver hip flask and owns boots that exactly match one of the clearer footprints preserved at the crime scene."

"That is excellent work, Sergeant. This means, however, that we are holding an innocent man at Shepton Mallet Prison and must secure the release of Malachi Warren, post-haste."

"I will arrange it, sir."

"I have to say that I find it hard to believe that those two knuckleheads are the brains behind this murder. I feel certain that their boss, Pocket, is the one who makes the decisions and gives the orders, but I cannot see how we can prove it."

"He's a sticky customer, make no mistake, sir."

"While I'm here, I'd like to look over the evidence box you hold for the earlier murder of Raymond Baker, if you please, Sergeant."

"Of course, sir." He presses a buzzer and another policeman enters the foyer.

"Ah, Constable, would you please take Superintendent McKinley to the evidence room and show him the box pertaining to the Raymond Baker case."

"Of course, Sergeant. Please follow me Superintendent McKinley."

The box contains the clothing and personal effects of the murdered man and McKinley shudders, as he fingers through the dirty, stained clothing, until he discovers there is something hard and rectangular, sliding around within the jacket lining. He manages to slowly draw it out, through a split in the stitching, revealing a small, swollen water-stained notebook. The writing within is water-smudged and difficult to make out, but on the cleanest pages, he can discern columns of numbers, separated by commas, on the left, and sums of money on the right. The columns of numbers are in two groups and vary in length, but none is higher than the number twenty-six. He is mystified. It must be some sort of coded tally book. The oldest records have lines drawn through them, as if the amount owing has been settled. If he can break the code he may be able to work out who and what the records are about.

He pulls up a chair and takes a piece of paper and pencil from the desk. *There are twenty-six letters in the alphabet, so the numbers must relate to that. Maybe it's a list of people's names. As it would link both murders, let's start with ASHLEIGH SEYMOUR.* He prints his full name on the piece of paper. *If the numbers relate to the alphabet and Ashleigh Seymour is on the list, then there should be a group of eight numbers relating to Ashleigh and a group of seven numbers relating to Seymour. The third number and the last number of the first group should be the same, and the fifth number in the group of eight should be the same as the second number in the group of seven.* He scans the most recent pages until his eyes are going bleary, then he nearly whoops with joy as he finds what he is looking for. H = 2 and E = 25. He writes down the alphabet and puts down the numbers 2 and 25 against H and E. Then he completes the alphabet starting at G =1. The seemingly random numbers relate to a forward-seven code: A=21 S=13, H=2, L=6, E=25, I=3, G=1, H=2.

He neatly rewrites the alphabet and the corresponding forward-seven code and takes the notebook and the code out to the desk sergeant. "Sergeant Barrett, I want you to work your way through this tally book and make a list of the names therein, according to this code. Then, I want these folks interviewed, as to why they feature in this record. The fact that we have their names may loosen their tongues. I've a strong feeling it was our moneylender's record, but maybe now we can find out for sure who the moneylender was and why it was in the pocket of our victim."

"Yes, sir."

"Have you arranged for the release papers for Malachi Warren?"

"I have them here, sir."

"Thank you, Sergeant. If you'll just witness my signature, I'll take them with me. I'm returning to my digs in Ivell, and I'll drop them off at Lord Dryer's home, so that he can arrange to collect his friend, forthwith."

When Joshua opens the envelope, and studies the pages within, he is overwhelmed with relief and gratitude to Detective Superintendent Jock McKinley. He shows the evidence of the glad tidings to Louisa and then rushes over to Hamlet Cottage to tell Rosa that her husband will be home by tomorrow.

"You must pack some clothes for him and we'll go together to fetch him in the landau first thing tomorrow morning. I've asked Gareth to give the staff the afternoon off to celebrate his release from incarceration and Flora is arranging a homecoming buffet supper for us all."

"Do you think he knows he'll be free tomorrow?"

"I doubt it, Rosa. I'll let you be the one to give him the good news."

"Thank you, my lord. I'm so grateful for your help and support. It's dreadful to think that some poor folk might be left to rot in jail, or even hang, despite being innocent. It doesn't bear thinking about."

Malachi is aching with the repetitive effort of walking the treadwheel, ten minutes on, and five minutes off for eight hours daily, climbing the equivalent of 8,000 feet, along with forty other prisoners. He is aware that the wheel is used to generate a grain mill, situated outside the prison wall. It seems unfair that they don't get to see much of the bread that results in their hard labour. He has a painful lump in his groin because of this constant effort and longs to be taken off this task and given oakum picking, or breaking rocks for a change.

When one of the guards orders him off the wheel before his time, he is surprised to be singled out, but relieved to be getting a longer break from his labours. He follows the guard through the prison to the governor's residence, where the guard knocks on the door.

The door opens. "Prisoner number 361 is here, sir."

"Thank you, Warder, that is all. Come inside, Mr Warren, I have visitors for you."

Malachi steps into the governor's office and is stunned to see Rosa there alongside Joshua. "Rosa!"

He cannot hold back his tears. Rosa rushes forward and into his arms at last.

He holds her tightly to him. "My darling, I've missed you so much."

"Me too. But it's all over. You're free again. We've come to take you home."

He is stunned. "Today?"

Joshua steps forward. "Yes, Mal, you're coming home with us right now. They've arrested two Wincanton men for the deed and you are, my friend, officially off the hook."

Malachi sinks to his knees completely overcome. "Thank the Lord in heaven! This nightmare is at last over!" He buries his head in Rosa's skirts and they both weep with joy and relief.

CHAPTER NINETEEN *(August 1870)*

PRIDDY FAYRE

Noah has encouraged Bob Yates to allow Billy and Victoria to go with him to attend his wedding to Florica and they plan to set off together in his Romany wagon. Don isn't bothered about the wedding and will remain behind with Jake to help with the farm. Lillian always helps her husband with the milking and they are both more than happy to let Victoria and Billy have some free time together.

On the day before hitching up and moving on, Noah washes the *vardo* down, cleans the harnesses, polishes all the brass and grooms Ned, his gypsy horse. As far as he is concerned, Florica will be proud of him when he meets up with the other gypsy families and no one on route will be justified in calling him a 'dirty gypsy'.

When he leads the horse and wagon around to the front of the farmhouse, Billy is fascinated with the beauty of the vehicle and impressed with his hard work. The brass gleams in the sunlight and the whole length of the *vardo* is painted brightly in scarlet and framed in Lincoln green, and over the ornate scrollwork and patterned carvings, it is sheathed in shimmering gold leaf. The design includes large wheels set outside the body, whose sides slope outwards considerably, as they rise towards the eaves. The attractive wooden bow roof extends over the length of the wagon to form porches at each end, and it has a small skylight, or mollycroft, to let in more light.

Billy and Victoria climb inside to stock the cupboards with Lillian's baking, before loading up their small bundles of clothes, and are both stunned by the ornate beauty of the decorations. The body of the *vardo* is made from beaded tongue-and-groove matchboard, like the exterior, painted scarlet and picked out in gold and green. The far end of the wagon is carpeted and partitioned off with an ornate wooden half door with a curtain above, to form the sleeping accommodation, equipped with a wardrobe, a double bed, and a chest of drawers with a hole cut out, in which to sit a wash bowl. On either side of the bed space, are quarter-inch-thick, bevelled mirrors, lavishly decorated with images of birds and flowers, and cupboards and locker seats have been built in to prevent movement while travelling.

The other half serves as the kitchen and contains built-in seats, a closet or larder, a large pitcher and bowl for water, some cooking utensils and crockery hung upon the walls, or within a glass-fronted china cabinet. In the centre of the left-hand wall, seated within a wooden fireplace, is a small cast-iron cooking stove, whose chimney passes through the bow-shaped wooden roof to vent the smoke. There are curtained windows on the left-hand side of the *vardo*, and at front and rear. A bracket for an oil lamp is mounted over the chest of drawers opposite the fireplace; the chest top functions as a table. The whole thing is neat and clean and both Billy and Victoria are impressed.

Before they leave, Bob comes outside with a flannel belt in his hand. "Here, Billy, Lillian made this for me for when I go into Salisbury. You may think I'm being over cautious, but there'll be a lot of light-fingered folk at this here fayre and you can't be too careful. Put your money in here, Billy, and strap it around your middle where it will be safe from opportunists."

"Thank you, Bob, that's very sensible. Not that I've much to steal, but all the more important to look after it." He takes it and places his money in the pockets, folding the flap over it to keep it safe and fixing it in place around his waist.

"The idea is that you take out what you need, so it's handy, but leave the rest safely concealed."

"Thank you, Bob. It's a good idea; you have a clever wife."

"I know and a beautiful daughter, too. Please take good care of her."

"Of course I will. Don't worry. We'll see you anon."

They stow their belongings and are finally ready to set off. The weather is warm and dry, and they hope to get to Priddy the night before the sheep fayre, to make camp and enjoy the spectacle, before preparing for the nuptials taking place on the day of the horse fayre.

It is a long journey from Hatherleigh Farm, but Noah's little gypsy horse, Ned, does well and they relax to the slow, steady pace, the jingle of the harness and the clip-clop sound of his hooves echoing along the country lanes. They pass through Castle Cary, Ansford, Ditcheat, and Prestleigh, covering about two and a half miles an hour, high hedges giving way to dry stone walls, as they move towards the Mendip Hills. When they see the impressive Gothic towers of Wells Cathedral, Noah decides to pull over onto a wide, firm verge and they stop there overnight, to rest Ned. Victoria cooks some eggs, sausages and bacon and then they retire for the night. Noah and

Billy sleep on bedrolls under the wagon, allowing Victoria to have the bedchamber.

They set off again at first light, eager to get to Priddy. They pass through Wookey Hole and are joined by many other itinerant folk along the way, taking their sheep and woollen produce to the market.

At last Noah spots the Norman tower of the church of St Lawrence in Priddy. "The village green is close to the church." He reassures them. "Not much further now."

Billy and Victoria are seated inside, looking out through the front window, surprised at the huge influx of farmers, wool traders, spinners and weavers along with their families, their children excitedly skipping along beside them. Noah finds a place to set up camp, against a hedge at the far edge of the common and they each have a drink of cider. He then unharnesses Ned and tethers him at the back of the *vardo* so he can graze more freely, before they set off to find some breakfast at the hostelry known as the New Inn. They pass farmers and shepherds busy dismantling the thatched stack of hurdles in the centre of the green, to form folds for their sheep, and folk setting out their wares, beautiful shawls and all manner of colourful woollen items, dyed with blue woad, yellow weld and red madder.

The noise of the protesting sheep, excitable children and people already selling their goods adds to the crazy atmosphere and Billy grabs hold of Victoria's hand in the excitement. Whatever is he thinking of? *It's too late to let go and she seems to be happy, so what the heck?*

Even though it is only half past six in the morning, the New Inn is already crowded with hungry folk looking to breakfast. They each pay their shilling and join the queue alongside the inglenook fireplace, waiting to be served with slices from a small hindquarter of beef, while it and the young fellow turning the spit, slowly roast in front of the huge fire. The landlord carves the meat with a three-foot fork and knife and Billy remarks on the size of his implements. The man takes the opportunity to brag, "Oh aye, lad, this here knife was fashioned from a sword once used by my ancestor against the Russians at Balaclava." He holds up the knife and the meat juices run down it macabrely, making them all shudder at the thought.

To go with the beef, they are served turnips and potatoes that have been boiled in two huge coppers, each batch being removed within nets, and placed in serving dishes. Once served they find a settle in the corner of the room where they can sit together and enjoy the nourishing food. It is a well-appointed thatched inn, with practical blue/grey flagstone flooring, black beamed ceilings and brass oil lamps for night-time.

Noah has been keeping an eye out for his relations, even though most of them will be arriving the following day. "It's a good job we left yesterday. I was worried it might be hard to find a place to pitch camp with there being so many people attending," says Noah.

Victoria replies, "I hope Florica and her parents will be as lucky."

"I did tell her where to find me, so hopefully it won't be a problem. All the sheep farmers will be finished and moved on by then."

Billy is amazed to be among so many strangers, some even with north-country accents, they have travelled so far to be here. He feels sure it is the perfect place to get rid of the pony and trap, but he has secretly been looking at every rig he has come across, to no avail. Nevertheless, he is convinced that Jarvis Pocket would think this an ideal place to fence them, as he would have travelled far enough away from the scene of the crime. But who will he enlist to do his dirty work?

When they have eaten their fill, Victoria is keen to go outside and peruse the craft stalls. It is a relatively warm, late-August day, but being on high ground, the breeze holds the promise of autumn soon to follow. She wraps her brown woollen shawl around her, as they leave the inn and move back onto the green.

Billy can see she is drawn to a brightly coloured, red madder cloak and matching mittens. When she has moved on to the next stand with Noah, he asks the vendor quietly how much they cost.

"I made all these myself and that set is two weeks' work. I'd be happy with six shillings, sir. They'll suit your lady friend well, as the colour will complement her dark hair."

He pays the lady and she wraps up the parcel for him. He will give it to Vicky later, when she will likely be feeling the cold.

He can hear a lot of shouting, booing and jeering coming from over the fence in the adjoining paddock. Between the stalls he can make out crowds of supporters surrounding six pairs of local maulers, all stripped to the waist and bare-knuckle boxing, with their different families and friends yelling encouragement. Billy immediately thinks of Malachi. *He'd show them all a thing or two. Though I doubt he'd be up to it just now, after what he's been through!*

Suddenly, among all the strange faces, he thinks he may have spotted 'Lanky', one of the ne'er-do-wells, head and shoulders above the others, moving swiftly among the crowds with sleight of hand, up to his old tricks. He is sure it is him and keeps his eyes open then, for the other three. He is rewarded with a sighting of 'Ginger'. This is who he must keep track of, for they could well be the ones tasked with selling on the pony and trap.

He grabs hold of Noah. "The ne'er-do-wells are here, Noah."

"Ah, that's interesting. They're a long way from home."

"Can you see 'Ginger' over there?"

"Yes."

"I think they'll be up to their usual mischief, pickpocketing. I'm going to tail 'Lanky' discreetly with Vicky. Can you keep an eye on 'Ginger', and let us know if you see anything untoward? We'll meet you at the wagon at noon."

"All right."

They set off after their quarries, keeping a safe distance and hidden among the crowds. Billy spots a constable talking to some children and is pleased to see there is a police presence there. Later he spots another one, standing beside the hurdling and chatting to a farmer, watching over his sheep. He may well have to call on their services later. He could alert them to the pickpocketing, but he wants to catch them red-handed with the pony and trap. If he is right, they must have travelled from Wincanton in it, in which case it will be tethered here somewhere already. He decides to go around the perimeter of the common to see if he can spot it.

"Vicky, would you be happy following 'Lanky', or would you rather stay with me?"

"I'd rather stay with you, Billy, if you don't mind. Why, what do you think he has in mind?"

"I'll explain everything to you, if I'm proved right, but in the meantime, stick close to me."

"What if he recognises us?"

"Then my plan will be ruined. Come on, let's go around the edge of the green and see if I can find what I'm looking for."

They go around the boundary, but he cannot see it anywhere. *Maybe it is further along the verge side.* They leave the crowded common and progress a little way along the road until they are roughly opposite the New Inn and here they find a small brown Exmoor pony tethered and grazing beside a trap. Billy's heart starts to thump, in case any of the ne'er-do-wells are around, but he summons the courage to go and inspect the back plate on the trap.

"You keep a lookout, Vicky."

He is rewarded by finding the initials, 'J. & S. H.' carved there as plain as day. He moves quickly away, whispering, "We must fetch the constable, Vicky."

"Why, Billy? What is it?"

"That is the pony and trap that was stolen when Ashleigh Seymour was murdered and therefore evidence in the murder case."

Victoria looks stunned. "Oh, my goodness!" They rush back through the people, wary of bumping into 'Lanky' or 'Ginger'. They find the policeman still chatting to the farmer and Billy approaches him.

"Excuse me, officer."

"Yes, sir. How can I help you?"

"Well, I'm hoping I'll be able to help you with some important information. Is there somewhere we can talk freely and confidentially?"

The constable shakes his head. "Not really, sir. I'm supposed to be on duty here."

"Would you mind standing behind one of the stalls? I don't want to be seen talking to you if I can avoid it."

"Of course, sir." The constable follows them to the nearest stall and they sneak behind it to talk unseen.

Billy clears his throat. "You'll be aware that there was a murder some time ago in Wincanton and more recently another body was found near Ivell."

"Yes, sir."

"Well, the police in Ivell have been looking out for a pony and trap, stolen at the time of the murder. It has the tell-tale signature of the people who manufactured it, 'J & S Hill' carved in the back plate and I've found it here, on the verge opposite the New Inn. If you're prepared to keep an eye on it, I believe that tomorrow, it will be put up for sale in the horse fayre. I also believe that whoever sells it, will lead you to the person behind both murders."

"I can see this is a very serious matter, sir. Can you give me any further authority to act on this information?"

"Detective Superintendent Jock McKinley is the officer in charge of the investigation and if you telegraph him at Ivell Police Station, he'll corroborate all I'm telling you. Otherwise, the Justice of the Peace, Lord Dryer of Alvington Manor, will also confirm what I'm saying is true."

"Unfortunately, the nearest station where I can use a wire is at Wells, and I'll be honest with you, sir, I'm reluctant to leave my post here. There are only three of us policing the whole fayre."

"I understand, Constable, but if you don't have the authority, or confidence, to arrest these men on my say so, I can assure you they'll have valuables about their person that have been filched from the folk at the fayre, because they're well-known pickpockets in the Wincanton area. One of the chaps is extremely tall with a receding hairline, and the other one is a ginger, freckly lad. However, we need them to be in possession of the pony and trap, to link them to the murder of Ashleigh Seymour. If you could hold off arresting them, until they are in the act of selling the pony and trap, you may well have them for both fencing stolen goods and theft."

"I understand what you're saying, sir. Leave the matter with me. I'll do my utmost to achieve the desired outcome."

"Thank you, I'm obliged to you, Constable. It's a relief for me, to be able to pass this information on to you and to leave the conclusion in your capable hands."

Billy looks up at the sun, now high in the sky and turns to Victoria. "It must be around noon, Vicky. We'd better go and find Noah."

They wend their way back to the *vardo*, all the time vigilantly looking out for the ne'er-do-wells. They manage to avoid them and by the time they reach their wagon, Noah has already made a brew. Billy explains to him about finding the pony and trap and what he suspects 'Lanky' and 'Ginger' are up to. They have some of Lillian's pigeon pie and a cup of tea.

Once they have eaten their fill, Billy looks out over the common from the vantage point of the top of the *vardo* steps and he can see another contest starting up in the paddock where the local maulers had been. He remembers seeing an advertisement for 'single-stick fighters'.

He says to Noah and Vicky, "There's a single-stick contest just starting, where prizes of a golden guinea, a wide-awake hat and a gold button are offered. This seems to have encouraged quite a few knuckleheads to have a go. Shall we go and watch them for a while?"

"Why not? We're not likely to be buying any sheep today are we!" she laughs.

They hear the rapid cries of an auctioneer. The farmers bid for the sheep and they skirt the area, making for the paddock. The lads are recklessly waving their sticks about and ducking and diving to avoid being hit around the head.

After a while, Vicky is tired of cringing on behalf of the brow-beaten and says, "I'm sorry, Billy, but I can't bear to watch them anymore. I'm sure someone is going to get badly hurt."

"Come on then, we'll go along the stalls again; maybe there is something we can take back for your family."

"Thank you, Billy. How about you, Noah, do you want to come with us to the craft stalls?"

"Yes, I've seen enough of this foolishness, and I might find something for Florica."

Noah cannot find anything he likes for Florica, but Victoria buys some wool and a pattern for some fingerless gloves. Her mother will find them useful for when she is milking through the winter. She chooses some darker wool for her to make some scarves for Don and her father for Christmas.

The sun disappears behind dark cloud and the breeze strengthens, so Billy decides it is a good time to give Vicky his gift. He opens his package and gently places the red madder cloak around her shoulders and hands her the mittens. Her wide smile beams up at him. She draws the soft woven material around her. "Oh, Billy, it's beautiful and really keeps out the wind. I'm truly snug and warm in it. Thank

307

you so much. You're very thoughtful." She plants a tender kiss on his cheek. He blushes with pleasure; he is crazily in love again, but this time more hopeful of a happy ending.

They return together to the wagon for a rest. It has been an eventful day. Finally, they hear the last of the auctioneer and the sheep are all sold and the flocks shepherded away. The organisers are busy packing up the hurdles and stacking them under the thatched roof in the centre of the green, aware the lord of the manor could refuse the right of the fayre to take place, if the hurdles are not all returned after each annual event.

Suddenly, there is a lot of whooping and hollering, and a small army of lads come careering onto the common, chasing a squealing pig.

Noah calls to them, "Come quickly and look, they're hunting the 'greasy pig'!"

"Oh, my goodness, the pig is so slippery they'll never catch hold of it!" cries Victoria laughing heartily.

Each time some brave fellow rugby tackles the well-oiled and larded pig, it shrieks loudly, slithers away and changes direction. The young lads are all so enthusiastic, even the pig seems to enjoy the challenge. It is extremely funny and entertaining to watch and the three of them are in hysterics, before the animal is finally grabbed, rolled over the lad's belly, upside down and thus his trotters are lifted off the ground and he is unable to escape.

"That was so funny, the images will remain with me forever!" says Billy. "Perhaps on your pa's next birthday we should do it with one of your pigs, Vicky."

"Oh no, I couldn't do it to Porky and Podge; they'd never trust me again."

"Would anyone like a bacon butty?" suggests Noah.

"Oh dear, that's rather cruel, don't you think?" says Victoria, cringing.

They return to the New Inn that evening to join in the merriment there, all the time wary of bumping into the ne'er-do-wells. They have a few drinks and when Noah goes up to the bar to order his round, Billy becomes bolder and he whispers to Victoria, "You must realise by now, I've become very fond of you, Vicky. Will you consider being my sweetheart?"

She smiles happily and whispers back, "I thought you'd never ask."

When Noah returns with the drinks he finds them holding hands and kissing. "Well, this is a turn-up. What do you think your ma and pa will make of this?"

"I'm sure they'll be thrilled. They all like Billy; he's already one of the family."

"I'm very pleased for you both. This has turned out to be a rather romantic trip."

"It depends on your point of view. I doubt 'Lanky' and 'Ginger' will agree with you by this time tomorrow."

"Hopefully not."

CHAPTER TWENTY *(August 1870)*

ROMANY WEDDING

The following day Billy is awoken early, by the sound of the gypsy travellers arriving on the common. He peeps out from under the wagon and the place is filling up with the *vardos* belonging to Romany families with their lively young horses and colts for sale. He nudges Noah, "I think your bride may have arrived, Noah."

They slide out from under the wagon and Noah immediately spots Florica's family and makes his way over to say hello. Billy decides to go inside the wagon and prepare some breakfast. As he goes up the steps, he spots 'Lanky' driving the pony and trap onto the common. There is a 'For sale' notice tied to the trap. He ducks inside before he is spotted and peeps out through the window. There is no sign of the constables.

He ponders, Noah and Florica's wedding is to take place in the church of St Lawrence at twelve noon. He ardently hopes the ne'er-do-wells are arrested before then, so he can finally relax and enjoy the celebrations. He decides to stay inside the *vardo*. It is a good vantage point and he can keep watch from there.

He hears Victoria stirring and calls to her, "Would you like a cup of cocoa, Vicky?"

"Yes, please," she replies.

He stokes the stove, puts the kettle on to boil and lays out three beakers, all the while keeping a close eye on 'Lanky' and 'Ginger'.

Victoria comes out of the bedchamber dressed in her long white nightgown. She looks beautiful, with her thick rich brown hair, tousled from sleep and the pupils of her hazel eyes, huge as she leaves the darkened room. He kisses her softly, "Good morning, sweetheart."

"Good morning, Billy. Did you sleep all right with all the noise from the night owls?"

"I did, thank you. How about you?"

"I slept very well, but I was disturbed before I dropped off, by thoughts of where Noah and Florica will be sleeping tonight."

"Hmm, I must admit, I hadn't thought of that. Perhaps we should take a room in the New Inn?"

Victoria looks shocked. "I don't think that would be proper, Billy. I don't think my parents would approve."

"But two rooms will be rather costly, Vicky. We still need to consider the cost of the tolls on our return journey. I should have thought this through, before giving my money away to Jake."

"Or buying a beautiful cloak for me."

"Not at all, Vicky. I don't regret that one bit. You remind me of 'Little Red Riding Hood' in it, and I want to spend my whole life protecting you from big bad wolves." He holds her close and kisses her hair.

"You are a softie, Billy."

"I know I am, but I'm so happy to have found you, Vicky." He glances through the window, keeping vigil, instantly spotting three constables making their way towards 'Lanky' and 'Ginger' and the pony and trap.

"Oh, my goodness, Vicky! They're about to arrest them!"

Victoria stands beside him and together they watch the two dumbfounded lads being handcuffed and led away.

Billy muses, "I wonder what they're going to do with the pony and trap?"

"Well, I suppose it will be returned to the Seymours."

"Yes, but in the meantime, it's evidence. I think I may offer for us to drive it back to Wincanton to the police station there."

"Do you think they'll let us?"

"I don't know, but it is worth a try. Noah offered to take us back to Hatherleigh tomorrow, before setting off to join the rest of his family on their way to Bridgewater Fayre, but it means he'll have to double back, which isn't reasonable. It will add at least two days to their journey; besides, he has a new bride and won't be wanting us two in their way. I'll go and find the sergeant and ask him."

He finds the policemen pushing 'Lanky' and 'Ginger' up into their Black Maria. As he approaches, 'Lanky' turns and spots him. "You! You're the snitch. You wait, when the boss hears about this! Your days are numbered, blabbermouth."

Billy turns to the policeman. "You heard that, Sergeant, please make a note of what he said. It's evidence that they're following someone else's orders."

The sergeant slams and secures the door, then takes out his notepad and pencil and writes down the comment. He looks back at him, "What can I do for you, sir?"

"I was hoping you might allow me to take charge of the pony and trap and drive it back to Wincanton Police Station, so that they might photograph the evidence, before it is returned to the owners, the Seymours."

"I don't see why not, as you're the person responsible for us catching these villains, but I don't have the authority to make that decision. Tomorrow, if you'd care to follow me back to Wells, I'll attempt to get authority from the superintendent there to allow you to go on unaccompanied to Wincanton."

"Thank you, Sergeant, I'm much obliged."

"You were quite right, sir. Many stolen items were found in their knapsacks and about their person, which have obviously been pilfered from the folk at the festival. Some of the items were reported stolen yesterday and we'll be able to return those. The remainder we'll keep as evidence for the court case."

"It's a great relief to me that this evidence has been secured and I'm honoured to be given the opportunity to return the pony and trap to Wincanton. Hopefully, when 'Lanky' and 'Ginger' realise they're both implicated in a double murder enquiry, they'll come clean and give up the person who, I'm sure, is behind it all."

"I'll meet you here at 8 o'clock tomorrow morning then, sir. We have our hands full with these two reprobates, who'll be taken to Wells by my two colleagues today, to be held and charged. I'll liaise with Wincanton, of course."

"I'll be here tomorrow morning, on the dot of eight with my travelling companion, Victoria."

"Right you are, sir."

Billy decides to pop to the New Inn to ask how much for a room for Victoria for the night. He'll be quite happy under the *vardo* as before. But the landlord tells him he is fully booked, unless she would be prepared to share. "How much to share?" he asks him.

"Two shillings for bed and breakfast."

"I'll take it. Her name is Victoria Yates and she'll be here after the wedding celebrations."

Billy hands him the coins, relieved to have found somewhere safe and relatively comfortable for Vicky to stay. Then he makes his way back to the green to lead the pony and trap to the water trough for Dolly to drink and then on, to tether her next to their *vardo*. He finds Vicky has dressed in her deep blue, taffeta, Sunday-best church costume. "I didn't make the cocoa. I was waiting for you to come back, so I dressed instead."

"You look very smart. I suppose I ought to change into my Sunday outfit too."

"Let's have a drink first."

The kettle bubbles as it comes to the boil and Victoria pours them both a beaker of cocoa. "What did the sergeant say?"

"He said he doesn't have the authority to let us take it back, but he'll accompany us to Wells, where the superintendent will be able to give us his decision."

She frowns. "But if he says no, we'll be stuck in Wells and Noah and Florica will have already gone on to Bridgewater with their relations."

"I know it's not ideal, but I cannot see why he'd refuse us. It means he'll not be losing any police manpower, after all. Don't worry, Vicky, we'll cross that bridge when we come to it."

She smiles, seemingly happy to put her life in his hands. "Well, if nothing else, it'll be quite an adventure for us. I just hope Ma and Pa can manage until we get home."

"In the meantime, I've found a place for you to sleep tonight at the New Inn. I'm afraid you'll have to share, but at least it will be more comfortable for you, than under the wagon."

"Thank you, Billy, that was very thoughtful."

Billy has changed into his Sunday best by the time Noah returns to prepare for his nuptials. Victoria has already left the *vardo* to give the men some privacy and to go to find Florica and her family. Ablutions completed, Billy assists Noah donning his colourful wedding attire. First Noah pulls on his long, wide, dark green trousers, with a broad red band down the outside of each leg. They are decorated with gold coin-shaped sequins, ribbon, and thread. Next, he passes him his loose-sleeved cream shirt, also dotted with large gold sequins and while Noah does up his shirt buttons, Billy is waiting ready with a red waistcoat that matches the bands down the trouser legs. Noah winds a scarlet scarf around his head decorated with gold coins and ties another around his waist, allowing it to hang down on the left-hand side. Billy is reminded of a bold and handsome pirate. Finally, he puts on his polished black shoes.

"You look amazing, Noah. Florica is going to be enthralled."

"Do you think so, Billy?"

"I know so. You make me feel very dull by comparison. You certainly know how to dress up!"

"All the Romany relations will be dressed this way for the celebrations. There'll be a lot of gypsy families there. I'm to be waiting inside the church when Florica and her *dat* arrive there on horseback. Her *dat* will carry her over the threshold. I ought to be there fifteen minutes before noon so we might as well all leave together."

"Hopefully Vicky and I will be able to find a pew somewhere near the back of the church. I'm not really sure what to expect."

"Well, after the church wedding, everybody gathers for the traditional union. We use the Romany rites and speak in the Romany language, so

315

you may not understand all that is said, but I think you'll enjoy the *abijav*."

Victoria then turns up. "Wow! You look amazing, Noah."

"Thank you, Vicky. You look smart yourself."

"You're too kind."

"Shall we set off, then?" he asks them.

"Yes, if you're ready?" says Billy.

They walk with Noah to the church, passing village folk, who stare at the bridegroom in awe. There are many Romany relations milling around the churchyard to witness the arrival of the bride and groom, and several gypsies call out to Noah and pat him on the back as they go by. Billy and Victoria follow him inside, to find a discreet pew at the back of the nave.

Soon the church is filling up with the colourful, gregarious Romany people and Victoria realises that Florica is about to arrive. She enters the church, held in the arms of Leon Petulengro, revealing several layers of red petticoats, underneath a long, tiered green skirt, each tier, banded with gold ribbon. Her light cream blouse has elbow-length, layered, lacy sleeves, decorated with coin-size sequins, and showing off her many gold bracelets. A small red waistcoat, also decorated with gold sequins finishes off her costume and matches her outfit with her groom's. The final feminine touch is an elaborate golden tiara, seated among her dark curls, with a fine chain of gold coins dangling from it and falling from behind ears that are adorned with gold earrings, to join more golden necklaces. Victoria has never seen her look so happy. She watches over the heads of the rest of the congregation as the gypsy father and daughter walk arm in arm down the aisle, to pause and stand beside Noah, and the ceremony begins.

When the official ceremony is over, the happy couple leave the church to the lively traditional music of a gypsy band. Noah mounts a fine piebald horse, held steady for him by the head of their clan, King Dufferty, and Florica mounts behind him. Then all the wedding party set off in a colourful procession for the village common and the traditional Romany wedding, the fiddlers and accordionists, all dressed as part of the wedding party, still playing as they go.

Once everyone has gathered around the elders on the dais, with gentle violin music in the background, King Dufferty puts the question, "Are there any among you who shall say that this *chal*, Noah Boswell, shall not be *Roma* in the true *Zingali* fashion to Florica Petulengro?"

There is a resounding 'No'.

The bride is then presented and Leon Petulengro answers for her, "There are none, King Dufferty, who can say that these two cannot be Roma by the rights of the Zingali, and by mingling their blood."

King Dufferty then cuts the skin on their left hands until the blood flows and he binds their hands together with a silken cord. Noah and Florica kneel before him, put their right hands to their brows and bow their heads, while the chief offers up a Romany prayer, that neither Victoria nor Billy understand. At the end of the prayer, Noah kisses his happy bride.

In the meantime, a campfire has been lit in front of the dais and, accompanied by the rousing music, Noah runs and jumps through it. To show that she will go anywhere with her husband, Florica follows him. Then, symbolic of their life to come, they turn back and holding hands, jump the flames together

317

to the swelling sound of the gypsy band. The ceremony is over and the dancing begins. Florica rushes over to Billy and says, "Come, Billy, you must join in dancing with Vicky."

"Congratulations, Florica. How do you like being Mrs Boswell?"

"I am most happy, Billy." She grabs his hand. "Come, you must dance around *yog* with us."

Victoria enjoys learning the gypsy dances with Billy, giggling and blushing when they trip over their feet and go wrong.

For the wedding feast, the ladies bring out cauldrons of stewed rabbit, squirrel, hedgehog and game. They serve the meat on slates, with fried potatoes, boiled cabbage and rice and this is followed with fruit pies and custard and plenty of cider.

After they have all eaten and everything has been cleared away, Leon Petulengro, who is an expert with a bull-whip, challenges Noah to stand before him with a cigar in his mouth.

Billy can see that Noah is in a difficult position; he must appear brave, and he needs to show trust in his new father-in-law. Knowing that Leon has had quite a few ciders, Billy, Victoria and Florica, along with everyone else, watch in horror, as he flexes and cracks the whip in practice.

Suddenly he cries, "*Stanya!*" and the cigar is suddenly whipped expertly from Noah's mouth from twenty yards away.

Everyone claps at the showmanship, and Noah sighs with relief.

More cider is passed around and more dancing, until Billy breathlessly suggests to Victoria that they might discreetly leave. "We've an early start tomorrow and I'd prefer to be settled, before Noah brings Florica back to the *vardo*."

"I've really enjoyed tonight's merriment. What joyful people they are. It's been such a pleasant diversion, but I agree, I too am tired now, Billy, and ready to go. It will be near midnight by the time we get to the New Inn."

They set off together, skirting around the edge of the revellers, until they can see the gold leaf of the *vardo* glimmering in the moonlight. Billy pats and strokes Ned while Victoria collects her belongings together. She removes from her valise, a small corn dolly fertility charm, that she made especially for Noah and Florica and a bottle of honeymoon mead that her mother had purchased from Wincanton Market, as a gift from all of them and she places the presents beside the bed. Then she refills her bag with all her belongings and Billy escorts her to the New Inn.

Outside the hostelry he takes her in his arms and kisses her tenderly. "Goodnight, my sweet." He strokes her hair away from her face. "I hope the other occupant of the room is quiet and friendly and doesn't snore and you sleep well and awake refreshed tomorrow morning."

She laughs and kisses him. "Goodnight, Billy. Thank you for a wonderful day today. I hope you also sleep tight under the wagon and I'll see you tomorrow after breakfast."

She quietly steps inside and Billy returns to the *vardo*, excitement and optimism coursing through him.

Unaccustomed to consuming so much cider, Billy is fast asleep by the time Noah and Florica return and he sleeps well, until an inquisitive, shaggy-haired lurcher nuzzles him awake at dawn. The animal lays down beside him and keeps him company for a while and together they listen to the stirrings of life around them, but all is quiet within the *vardo*. Finally, Billy rouses himself and, using some of the rainwater from the decorated pale, hooked to the outside of the wagon, he swills his face and hands and brushes his teeth. He combs his hair and rolls up the canvas bedroll and places it on the top step, beside the *vardo* door where Noah will easily find it and sets off with his haversack over his shoulder. Looking back, he sees the lurcher forlornly watching him go, but then wandering off to look for another companion.

He can smell bacon cooking, and his mouth waters as he approaches the New Inn. Inside, he finds Victoria eating her breakfast and she offers to share it with him. He has half a sausage and some bacon, but leaves the egg for her.

"How did you sleep, Vicky?" he asks her quietly.

"Not too badly; the bed was comfortable, and I was very tired after the celebrations, but I've been bitten and so awoke early with the itching."

"I'll ask the landlord if they have any basil or peppermint leaves." He goes off to find him and returns with a sprig of basil.

"If you squash it between your fingers and rub it on the itchy spots, I'm sure it will help."

"Thank you, Billy. I'll go and do that and meet you outside in five minutes."

Billy finds the constable waiting for them outside the New Inn and so he rushes off to fetch the pony and trap.

Noah and Florica are up and about when he reaches the wagon and they both come out to say goodbye to him.

Noah says, "*Sastimos*." They shake hands. "Thank you for the gifts, Billy. Florrie loved the mead. Please thank Vicky and her *familia* too."

Florica smiles. "Yes, it was *cushti*, but what is meaning of little corn figure?"

Billy grins. "It's a fertility symbol, to encourage the production of babies."

"Oh! I see! It's a *draba*, Noah," she giggles.

Noah raises his eyebrows. "I don't think we'll be needing that, Billy, do you, Florrie?"

"Not if we go on as we've started, Noah." She giggles again.

"I'm very pleased for you both. I came to tell you that Vicky and I are setting off for home now and returning the stolen pony and trap. I hope that you'll both call in to see us all again in the future."

"I'm sure we will, but we can't say when. We wish you *cushti baxt*. You've a *lungo drom* ahead."

"Thank you, my friend. Farewell for now, from me and Vicky." They shake hands again and Billy gives Florica a hug, before jumping up into the trap and setting off to collect Victoria.

She is waiting patiently outside the New Inn chatting to the constable. He hands her up into the trap beside Billy and they set off towards home, with the mounted policeman riding ahead of them. His name is Fred Oatley and he has some amusing tales of his life as a policeman to entertain them as they go. When they reach the police station in Wells, Fred goes inside to speak to the superintendent and they anxiously wait outside with Dolly and the trap.

It is not long before he steps outside again. "My superior has granted you permission to continue, my friend. He appreciates the help you have given, that led to the arrest of Maurice Feltham and Ivan Hockey and believes you deserve the honour of delivering the evidence to Jock McKinley yourself."

Victoria lets out a sigh of relief. Billy grins and shakes hands with the policeman, glad to be granted this accession. They say their goodbyes and make tracks again, taking some refreshment in a tavern, just outside Wells, recommended by Fred. The small beer quenches their thirst and they set off once more, thankful to be on the last leg of their journey.

They reach North Street at about five o'clock and the desk sergeant sends a runner to summon the photographer. He tells them, "He has already been primed of his duties, since a wire was sent by the sergeant at Wells informing us you were due this evening. Also, Superintendent McKinley has instructed us to allow you to continue your journey and deliver the pony and trap back to the owners."

Billy smiles. "Thank you. It will be my pleasure."

"You will also be pleased to know that the two men caught in possession of the horse and trap have spilled all and pointed the finger to a well-known bookmaker and pawnbroker in the town."

"Would that be Jarvis Pocket?"

"How did you know?"

"I've had suspicions for a long time, but proving it is a different matter."

"Well, we now have sufficient evidence to convict them all and I must say we're most grateful for your considerable help in us accomplishing this."

"You're very welcome. It was a personal challenge for me and I am most gratified with the outcome."

Finally, they set off for Hatherleigh Farm where Billy will rest overnight, before heading off again to Sutton Bingham.

CHAPTER TWENTY-ONE *(August–September 1870)*

SETTLING THE SCORE

Billy looks out for Bay Rum as they drive along the farm track and spots him in Square Mead, grazing contentedly. His head goes up when he hears the clip-clop of hooves and he whinnies at the sight of Dolly, who tosses her head and snorts back.

Victoria helps him unload their things, while he unhitches Dolly and leads her into one of the stables for the night, making sure she has food and water. When they enter the farmhouse, he is pleased to see that Bob, Lillian and Don are all delighted and relieved to have them both safely back home again. He is being welcomed with kisses and hugs just as warmly as Victoria.

Lillian cries, "Come in, come in, what a joy to have you back home. Sit down; we've had our supper, but there's some rabbit pie left and plenty of cheese and pickle." She puts out plates and cutlery and serves up the food for them.

"I expect you're hungry after your long journey," says Bob. "How did you get on?"

"Well, we found Ashleigh Seymour's pony and trap and I've been given permission to return it to the family."

"Well done, my lad. That's great news!"

"It was two of the ne'er-do-wells who were trying to sell it; apparently, Maurice Feltham and Ivan Hockey, or 'Ginger' and 'Lanky' as we knew them. Anyway, the policemen arrested them and when 'Lanky' saw me there, he made some comment, about his boss not standing for it, and my days being numbered, indicating there was someone else orchestrating their crimes, which the policeman obviously witnessed. We were then told at Wincanton Police Station that they had both talked, under police questioning, and given up Jarvis Pocket."

"That's grand news, lad, well done."

"I must say it's a huge relief it's all over at last."

Lillian asks, "Would you like a cider, or some cocoa?"

"Cider please, Ma," says Victoria.

"Me too, please," says Billy gratefully.

Lillian pours them the drinks and then asks, "How did the wedding go?"

While Billy takes a large mouthful of the rabbit pie, Vicky tells her, "It was amazing, Ma; so colourful. Noah and Florica were both dressed beautifully in their traditional costumes. There was music and dancing and lots of interesting things to eat, like hedgehog pie. It was great fun."

He swallows his food and adds, "The whole event, including the sheep fayre, was entertaining and most successful, wasn't it, Vicky?"

"It really was." She looks up at him and giggles happily, "Remember the hunting of the greasy pig? It was so funny, wasn't it, Billy?"

Billy nods enthusiastically and laughs with her. Then he spots Bob and Lillian sharing a knowing glance.

Lillian notices him watching them and she says, smiling, "I'm very pleased you've both enjoyed your time together. I also like your new cloak very much, Vicky."

"Thank you, Ma. Billy bought it for me."

A twinkle in her eye, she says, "That was very kind of him."

Billy changes the subject. "Noah and Florica were pleased with the mead and the corn dolly and they asked us to thank you all."

Lillian smiles. "I'm glad. It was very difficult to know what to give them, they have such strict rules."

"Well, they're married now, so hopefully not quite so restricted and both are really happy. Florica's father, Leon, is a strong character. He's excellent with a bull-whip. He flicked a cigar from Noah's mouth with it."

Don is impressed. "Wow!"

Victoria remembers their friend's expression. "Poor Noah looked absolutely stricken and was most relieved when it was over."

They continue to eat and chat until Victoria yawns, "I am utterly exhausted. Will you all excuse me, please? I'm really looking forward to getting a good night's sleep in my own comfortable bed."

"Of course, my dear. Goodnight." Her mother kisses her on her cheek. "I'm so pleased to have you back home with us, but I'm glad you had a good time, too. Sleep tight."

"I'm sure I will. Goodnight."

Billy finishes his meal and his cider and gets up to go to his cottage. "Thank you for the meal, Lillian, that was most welcome, and the rabbit pie was delicious."

"You're very welcome, Billy. Goodnight."

He turns to Bob. "I'll be off first thing tomorrow morning, if that is acceptable, Bob."

"Of course, lad. We'll look forward to seeing you on your return."

"Would you mind if I take Melody, hitched to the back of the trap, ready for my return journey?"

"No, that's fine, we have Samson and Delilah if we need to go anywhere."

"Thanks, mate. Goodnight to you all."

There is a chorus of 'goodnights', as he leaves their parlour.

The following morning, he hitches Dolly into the trap, tethers Melody to the back, chucks in his haversack and they set off west towards Sutton Bingham. The weather is changeable and he expects it to rain at some point on the journey. His suspicions are realised when he turns off the road at Sparkford towards Queen Camel, and he pulls his cap on more firmly and lifts his collar to protect his neck. It isn't cold, but it is damp and uncomfortable. The rain lasts until he has passed through Ivell and then the clouds disperse and the sun shines down on him, making his clothes steam. A rainbow has formed bridging the dull rainy side, with the bright sunlit road ahead.

He is stiff and tired by the time he drives through the gates of Sutton Bingham Manor. He pulls up outside the front door and clambers down, stretching his limbs and putting his collar back down. He pulls on the doorbell and shortly the maid answers the door.

"Good day, sir. How may I help you?"

"Could I please speak with your master? I've returned his stolen pony and trap."

"Oh my! They will be pleased. I'll fetch him for you, sir."

"Thank you."

Then he hears the noise of wheels approaching on the gravel driveway and Lucy appears, looking charming beneath her parasol, with her nanny, pushing Frankie in his perambulator. "Hello, Billy. Whatever are you doing here?"

He points towards Dolly. "I've returned the missing pony and trap."

"Oh, my gracious, that's good news."

He can hear within, Colonel Seymour calling, "Robshaw, Dolly and the trap have been found and returned, come quickly."

Colonel Seymour and Robshaw find Billy standing on the doorstep with Lucy, Mercy and the baby.

Billy steps forward and holds out his hand. "Good day, Colonel Seymour, I have great pleasure in returning Dolly, and your rig."

Colonel Seymour inspects the trap, checking the back plate and also the bench seat. "This is definitely our trap. You see here on the front of the seat?" Billy looks at the marks and realises it is the initials R. S. scratched there. "My eldest son's initials; he got a good ticking off for that."

Billy smiles and clears his throat. "I travelled all the way from Wincanton to the Priddy Sheep and Horse Fayre in the express hope that I might spot your pony on sale there. I was extremely fortunate that they chose this market and that Lord Dryer had told me about the John and Sophie Hill's mark on the back plate of the trap. I didn't know about your son's marks, but, I was nevertheless able to inform the police there and get the two men responsible for trying to sell them, arrested."

"Well done, sir. Please, step inside. Robshaw will settle Dolly and look after your pony for you in the meantime."

"Thank you, Colonel. I'd be grateful for a small break; I've been travelling for days."

"Come inside and dry off. Gladys, would you please organise some refreshments for Mr…"

"Riddick, Billy Riddick. Thank you, Colonel."

He wipes his feet on the large doormat and is shown into the drawing room, where he sits down in an armchair. Lucy follows them in, while Mercy disappears with the baby. He continues, eager to tell the colonel why the Wincanton police authorised him to return his goods, personally. "I asked permission from Superintendent McKinley to be allowed to deliver Dolly back to you, sir, as I've been involved in helping the police in tracking down your son's murderer." He glances at Lucy to gauge her reaction, but she simply looks stunned.

The colonel responds, "Have you, indeed?"

"Yes, Colonel, and I'm pleased to say, they've arrested the two thugs responsible, Blakely and Snodgrass, and have found evidence that will convict them. Also, they now have evidence against their boss, the bookmaker, moneylender and pawnbroker, Jarvis Pocket. They are being held at Shepton Mallet Prison to await the next assize.

"The two men charged with selling on the pony and trap were both pickpockets, local to Wincanton, who used to work in cahoots with the pawnbroker and they are being held at Wincanton Police Station at present."

Lucy sighs, "That's a huge relief. I know it won't bring back my husband, but at least my brother is no longer in the frame."

"This is true. Malachi has been released and is now safely back home with his family."

Gladys enters with a trolley of sandwiches, cakes and tea and passes from person to person, handing out tea plates and serviettes and offering the selection of food.

Billy continues, once he has been served his plate of sandwiches, "I can honestly say that I don't believe they would have caught them, without my help. You see, I work at the Hatherleigh Racecourse and I saw your son being beaten up by Blakely and Snodgrass. I reluctantly interceded, but this enabled him to get away on that occasion, and it was because of this, that I suspected they were responsible, and thankfully the police worked on that assumption. Hopefully, they will all be convicted. The police believe that Jarvis Pocket also ordered the murder of the other man, Raymond Baker, found around four years ago."

"Well, we will never recover from the shock of losing our son at such a young age, but I'm exceedingly grateful for your fortitude in helping the police with this matter. I don't know if you are aware of this, but I offered a reward for the safe return of Dolly, in the hope that her discovery would lead us to the murderer and I'm pleased to be able to offer this reward to you, Billy Riddick. I can see it is well deserved."

He stands up and goes off into his study, returning moments later with a pouch of gold coins. He counts out fifty sovereigns into Billy's outstretched hand, as he sits there open-mouthed.

"Thank you, Colonel. I didn't know there was a reward, but I couldn't be happier. This will go a long way towards my plans to wed."

He notes the surprised look on Lucy's face. "You're getting married, Billy?"

He looks her in the eye. "Yes, I am, Lucy. To Victoria Yates and I'm delighted and extremely contented."

She smiles sincerely. "I'm very pleased for you, really I am. I wish you all the best of good fortune."

"Thank you, Lucy." He glances at the sovereigns and at Colonel Seymour. "This is an excellent start. Thank you, sir."

Later, he sets off towards Alvington Manor, thinking about Lucy's reaction to the news of his marriage and although he knows she was never interested in him, he feels she may have been a little hurt by the obvious loss of his once well-known love for her.

When he reaches the manor, he hears cheering and cries of encouragement coming from the paddock beside the orchard and steers Melody towards the sound. He finds all the staff enjoying a cricket match and, pausing at the paddock gate, the happy scene will be etched in his memory forever. The ladies are all dressed in their colourful gowns and sun bonnets, seated in deckchairs or serving the refreshments, while the Alvington men, dressed in their whites, are sitting in line on a bench, waiting for their turn to bat. A visiting team, who he doesn't recognise, are fielding.

He notes the Alvington team consists of all the younger members of staff, including: Lord Dryer and Gabriel, Malachi and Jacob Warren, John and Luke Moore, Harry Sandford, Thomas Hawkins and his cousin Raymond, Toby Boucher and Edwin Proctor, with Frank Hawkins and Robert Sandford in reserve, while the older members of staff are seated behind them wistfully remembering days gone by. Malachi's children are seated on a picnic rug waiting impatiently for their father's turn to bat. The batting is part way through and Toby Boucher and Edwin Proctor are currently in bat. Edwin is the striker and Toby the non-striker. Gareth is their scorer and Reverend David Phelps is the umpire.

Then Lettie spots him by the paddock gate and runs over to greet him. "Billy, what are you doing here? Not run away again, I hope."

"No, Lettie, nothing like that, but I did wonder if I might stay overnight to break up my journey. I've just returned the stolen pony and trap to the Seymours and I thought I'd pop by to see you all."

"Well, that's good news. We're celebrating because we have Malachi back home again and Lord Dryer has arranged this friendly match with the St Ivell Cricket Team."

Suddenly, there is a loud thwack and a burst of applause as Edwin hits a boundary shot scoring six. The fielders retrieve the ball and Edwin proceeds to hit another boundary, scoring another six. His sisters are jumping up and down cheering wildly when astonishingly he scores two more boundaries in his over.

"Four boundaries and a total of twenty-four notches, before handing over to Toby. He is doing very well," says Billy, impressed. He tethers Melody to the paddock gate and wanders over with Lettie to join everyone. They stand beside Ruth Proctor. "Your Edwin is doing a grand job."

"I know, we're all so proud of him."

They watch as Edwin and Toby swap ends and Toby prepares to be striker for the next over.

Billy checks the scoreboard. In the first innings, the St Ivell Cricket Team scored a total of 360 runs and, with Jacob bowling, the home team managed to take three wickets. So far, the Alvington team have scored 148 runs, with still six more players to go.

Toby does nearly as well, hitting one bouncing boundary, scoring four notches and between him and Edwin they score another fourteen runs. Then they swap again and Edwin hits two more boundaries for six, before being caught out by one of the St Ivell lads. At that moment Billy recognises the triumphant fellow who caught the ball, as Bobby Tompkins and then he spots his brother, Harry, there too. Edwin leaves the pitch and hands the bat over to Malachi and everyone cheers, Billy as enthusiastic as everyone else, both for Edwin's success and to encourage Malachi.

Billy watches optimistically, but in his weakened state, Malachi does not do as well as expected. He manages to make a few runs with Toby until Toby is caught, leg before wicket, and Luke takes his place. Luke appears determined to show off to Aurora and keeps hitting near boundaries and together they make another twelve runs with Aurora shouting encouragement. Then Malachi is striker again and with his children yelling louder than everyone else, he seems to have warmed up. He goes on to hit three bouncing boundaries for four and one for six before it is Luke's turn again. Not to be outdone he also hits a few boundaries and one good shot making the fielders run and, in the process, making a total of seventeen notches. Malachi keeps up his good form scoring a further fifteen. Then Luke decides to switch hands, confusing the bowler and scoring twenty-four.

"I didn't realise Luke was ambidextrous," says Louisa to his mother.

"Oh yes, he's very able with both of his hands."

Aurora blushes, when both mothers glance in her direction. She drinks some lemonade and looks away.

Louisa says, hastily, "Well, it certainly seems to be serving him well here! He's doing us proud."

Billy smiles to himself, wondering if Aurora feels for Luke, as much as he feels for his Vicky.

Louisa says to him, "Billy, help yourself to some sandwiches, we had our refreshments after the St Ivell team's innings. There is plenty there."

"Thank you, my lady. I must admit to feeling rather hungry."

"Please go and help yourself."

"I will, thank you." He wanders towards the picnic table, weighed down with platters of tasty food, prepared by Flora, Ruth and her girls. He picks up a plate and fork and selects a variety of sandwiches and a slice of pie, an apple and some pickle. Then Elsie offers him a glass of cider, which he accepts gratefully. "Thank you, Elsie. How are you?"

"I'm very well, Billy. Are you enjoying your job at Wincanton?"

"Yes, I am, very much. Actually, I'm so happy there, I'm planning to wed my boss's daughter, Victoria."

"Wow! That's good news. Does Lettie know? She will be so pleased for you."

"I haven't told her yet, but it's no secret. I plan to buy an engagement ring in Ivell tomorrow morning, given that Edwin, or Lord Dryer, don't object to me kipping down above the stables again."

"Here's Edwin, you can ask him now."

"Hello, Billy, to what do we owe this pleasure?"

"I'm on my way back to Wincanton, after delivering the stolen pony and trap to the Seymours, and I decided to call in and see you all, especially to see how Malachi is doing, and I was hoping I might be allowed to kip down with you again, just for tonight?"

"Of course, pal, you're always welcome. I'm sure His Lordship won't object, but we must check with him first. I'll go and ask him now for you."

"Thanks, Ed."

"No trouble."

He returns shortly. "No problems, Billy, but Lord Dryer wants to see you after the match."

"Well, I can relax here, now I don't have to get back to Wincanton before dark."

Malachi is finally caught out and wanders over to fill his cider beaker. "Billy, my friend, I believe I've you to thank for my eventual release from prison."

"I regret it wasn't sooner, Malachi. Was it really bad?"

"It was dreadful, Billy. The only thing that kept me going, was the thought of Rosa and my kids back home and the knowledge that I was innocent. I prayed every day that they would find the real culprits and I'm so grateful to you for your help in that."

"I never doubted your innocence, Malachi, and I couldn't be happier to see you here enjoying your freedom once more."

"I was lucky in that I was fit and strong when I went inside, because the treadwheel was relentless, day in, day out. It takes its toll and the food was minimal, not the good fresh farming produce I'm used to, but thankfully I survived and I'm beholden to you, my friend."

He pats him warmly on the back and they shake hands.

Then Rosa comes up and throws her arms around him. "Billy, thank you so much for what you've done for us. I was almost at the end of my tether, when Lord Dryer came to tell me he was coming home. It's such a relief to know the nightmare is over."

Billy looks at Malachi. "It was what you said to Lord Dryer about the pony and trap, that led us to the real killers, so you helped yourself as much as anyone, Malachi. I was just the one who tracked it down. Being in the Wincanton area was also an advantage to me, as I knew a bit about the gambling fraternity and the characters of the men involved."

"Well, our family is indebted to you, Billy. If ever you need any help, you know where to come in the future."

"Thank you. I'm just glad it all turned out well in the end."

Once everyone sees that Billy is there among them, they all, in turn, wander over for a chat, and he is thankful to have such good friends among his old work colleagues.

The cricket match is over when Gabriel is run out and the final score is St Ivell Cricket Team 360 runs to four wickets, versus Alvington Manor 355 runs to three wickets. It was a close call and a good match and even though the more experienced team won, the Alvington Manor staff especially enjoyed a wonderful afternoon.

Lord Dryer finds Billy chatting with Edwin. "Edwin tells me you're here, having returned the pony and trap to the Seymours. How did you manage that, Billy?"

"Well, my lord, you told me about the missing rig, and I thought the most obvious place to sell it would be the Priddy Horse Fayre. When my two gypsy friends decided to get married at Priddy and invited myself and Victoria to their wedding, I accepted, with the possibility of finding it there always in the back of my mind. As luck would have it, I spotted it with two fellows I recognised from Wincanton and informed the police, who arrested them. Then I asked permission to bring the rig back to the Seymours. The police may have known there was a reward, but I didn't, so it was a wonderful surprise when Colonel Seymour gave me fifty gold sovereigns for my trouble."

"It sounds to me as if it was well deserved, Billy. I'm very pleased for you and I've also heard mention among the staff that you've found yourself a bride?"

"Yes, my lord, and I couldn't be happier."

"Well done, Billy. I wish you much delight in your marriage union."

"Thank you, my lord. You gave me good advice when I was at a low ebb."

"Think nothing of it. You are of course welcome to stay here with Edwin whenever you wish."

"Thank you, my lord."

"You're welcome, Billy." He turns then and picks up a cider bottle and bangs a metal spoon against it to get everyone's attention.

"I would like you all to show your appreciation for the St Ivell Cricket Team who were successful in defeating us here this afternoon." He starts to clap his hands together and everyone joins in. "However, I think we gave them a good run for their money and I would like you all to show your appreciation for Alvington Manor, our very enthusiastic losing side."

Again, everyone claps. Then he continues, "It has been my pleasure to host this cricket match in celebration of our good friend Malachi's release from prison, so I would like a big hand for Malachi; also, for the person mainly responsible for his release, our old friend, Billy Riddick. The wholehearted applause is most gratifying and there are cries of 'well done, Billy' in amongst the clapping. Billy blushes at all the attention.

"Finally, I would like you all to show your appreciation to Beth, Flora and her girls for the wonderful spread of food they have prepared for the occasion, and to Isaac for supplying the cider. Thank you, Flora, Beth and Isaac." More applause follows.

The next morning, Billy wakes when he hears Edwin preparing for work, but the moment he moves, a pain shoots through his head. *I've drunk too much cider and now I'm going to pay for it!* After he had stabled Melody, he had enjoyed the rest of the afternoon chatting with everyone, but especially Lettie and Elsie, Edwin and his sisters, Bobby and Harry Tompkins, Toby and Raymond and together they had sunk quite a few pints of Isaac's home brew. The amber liquid had gone down well, but now he feels dehydrated, his mouth as dry as a desert.

He stirs himself and fetches a bucket of water from the pump, eagerly downing a pint of water, before swilling his teeth, washing and dressing. Edwin is, by this time, already mucking out the horses. He descends the stairs and finds him to say goodbye. "I'm just popping to the kitchen to say goodbye to everyone and I'm off into town to buy an engagement and wedding ring."

"Have you already asked permission of her father?"

"No, I haven't, but I'm sure he will be happy for us. I intend to ask him, the instant I'm back."

"Do you know her size?"

"I do, actually. I tied a piece of horsehair around her ring finger, just messing around, but I've kept it to give to the jeweller."

"Well done, Billy, good thinking. Well, good luck, pal. Let us know the date and maybe some of us will be able to attend."

"I will. Bye for now, Ed. Thanks for putting up with me last night."

"Any time, dear boy. Any time."

They shake hands and he sets off towards the kitchen. Flora gives him a huge hug. "Can I tempt you to some breakfast before you set off, Billy?"

"No thanks, Flora. I'm still overfull from yesterday. I just popped in to say farewell to you all."

"If you're sure."

"I'm sure, thank you. I'm eager to set off, because I want to find a jeweller in town to buy my sweetheart an engagement and a wedding ring."

"You're in an 'urry, all of a sudden. I 'ope there's no shotgun involved."

"No, nothing like that!" he laughs. "But, between you and me, I was given a reward for finding and returning the pony and trap to the Seymours and now the money is burning a hole in my pocket. I can't wait to spend it on my Vicky, she'll be so amazed. I wondered if you could recommend anywhere in town."

"I don't 'ave much to do with jewellers, but I know there's Frederick Dobel's, a clockmaker, silversmith and jeweller at 'endford, opposite Stuckey's bank, and I believe, another in the same trade in Middle Street called 'ancock and Cox."

"Thank you, Flora. I'll try them both and see if there is anything I think she'll like."

Elsie and Hattie, say in unison, "Good luck, Billy."

"Thank you, please say goodbye to everyone and I'll let you know when I fix a wedding date."

"We will. Bye."

"Bye." He leaves quickly, before any more staff turn up and delay him further.

He finds Dobel's on the corner of Hendford and the High Street, and as he enters the premises a bell rings to summon an assistant. The shop is beautifully laid out with wooden, glass-fronted display drawers and units and around the room stand a variety of grandfather and grandmother long-case clocks, all ticking in harmony with different tones. He discovers exactly what he is looking for, in a rose-gold diamond-cluster, betrothal ring, with a matching wedding band. He is thrilled and convinced Victoria will love them. Mr Dobel checks the size against his horsehair, slots them inside a velvet-lined gift box and his assistant gift wraps them for him. He surreptitiously places his remaining sovereigns, some small change and the gift box containing the rings, into Lillian's money belt around his waist thinking to himself, *hidden here they'll be safe from the threat of footpads*. He leaves the shop, on cloud nine, eager to be home speaking to Bob and putting his plan into practice.

Melody is waiting patiently, tethered to a gas streetlamp outside the bank opposite and he unties and mounts her, setting off feeling well pleased with himself. The day is warm and dry, but overcast; fair travelling weather in fact and they trot along at a good pace, passing through Mudford, Marston Magna, Queen Camel and Sparkford, only stopping to pay the tolls on the route.

As he approaches Lawrence Hill he notices two figures loitering at the entrance to Hatherleigh Farm. He is immediately suspicious, still wary of footpads, and slows a little, until he believes he recognises their faces, but they turn into the farm lane and disappear. He suspects it is the remaining ne'er-do-wells, 'Shorty' and 'Beefy', but at that distance he cannot be positive.

His heart is racing by the time he reaches the entrance to the driveway and turns to go along the track. Suddenly, the pocket jockey jumps from the bank and tries to pull him from the horse. Melody bucks in fright and catches the idiot, as he falls backwards, with a hoof on his chin, making him cry out in pain.

Immediately, 'Beefy' catches hold of the reins and tries to drag Billy to the ground. 'Beefy' is strong and more muscular than he is, despite his young age. Melody turns sharply. Billy can feel himself losing control of her and being dragged from the saddle. He slides down landing heavily on his shoulder in the lane, but his right leather riding boot is twisted and still caught in the stirrup. He attempts to free it, but 'Beefy' punches him around his head and face. He tries to ward him off, his arms flailing. His head pounds, he tastes blood, but he's unable to defend himself in this prone position with his leg suspended, caught by the stirrup.

Melody side steps and prances nervously all the while. Billy steadies himself with his left hand on the ground using his right to protect himself, but 'Shorty' has now recovered and joins the attack by stamping on his left hand. He howls in pain causing Melody to bolt and she gallops off down the road towards the farmhouse with him sweeping the ground behind her. His head thumping along the track, he blacks out.

'Shorty' and 'Beefy' brush themselves down and wander off, score settled.

CHAPTER TWENTY-TWO *(September 1870)*

A PERFECT FIT

Victoria wanders the yard, trailing chicken feed in her wake, with the fowl clucking and pecking at the ground around her. She is impatiently looking forward to seeing her beau and looks up at the sound of horse's hooves approaching. Melody is rider-less and trailing something in her wake. Then she realises it is poor Billy being dragged along like a limp effigy. She screams for help.

"Ma… Pa, come quickly! Billy's hurt."

Her father and Jake are quickly at her side. Jake calms the fractious pony, while her father carefully untwists and releases Billy's right boot. Don arrives on the scene and her pa asks him to take Melody to her stable.

She watches anxiously as he checks Billy's pulse and then gently removes his ripped and filthy Sunday-best jacket, before he and Jake carry him inside and lie him unceremoniously on the kitchen table.

She bursts into tears. *He looks like a dead body.*

Her pa calls upstairs, "Lillian, come quickly! Billy's badly hurt."

She can hear her descending the stairs, as tearfully, she prepares a bowl of warm water to wash his wounds.

Her mother enters the parlour from the stairway door. "Whatever's all the commotion

341

about?" She looks stunned at the deathly, bedraggled sight of Billy. "Oh, my good God, whatever has happened?"

Her pa looks worried. "We don't know, but Billy wouldn't have ended up like this without some foul play. He's unconscious, but still has a pulse. I doubt he'll have escaped without any broken bones though, and, going by the scored leather on his right boot, his ankle could well be shattered."

Lillian steps forward. "Here, let me bathe his wounds. Vicky, please pull yourself together, my dear, crying isn't going to help him. Go and fetch some bandages and the arnica cream and then go into the garden and bring me a bunch of feverfew. You'll need about a tablespoonful. Then steep it in a cup of boiling water for me."

Vicky delivers the bandages and arnica cream and leaves the room still crying hopelessly and Lillian takes control, bathing his puffy eyes and gently removing the mud and blood from his battered face and hands. In the meantime, Bob has eased off his boots. His ankle is red and swollen.

Once the worst of the mud and blood has been removed, Lillian looks at her husband. "We can't leave him here on the kitchen table, Bob."

Don volunteers, "He can have my bed, Ma. I can kip on the sofa for tonight."

Bob responds, "Thanks, lad. Can you help me carry him upstairs, Jake?"

"Of course."

Bob takes him under his arms and Jake takes his feet and they manage to manoeuvre him up the narrow stairway and place him on Don's bed.

Lillian pats her husband on the shoulder. "Thank you, I can take it from here, Bob."

They leave her to it and she unbuttons and removes his trousers and his moleskin waistcoat, which must have helped protect his back from being cut to pieces, when his jacket became rucked up behind him. This discloses her money belt and to make him more comfortable, she gently unbuttons and slides this from under him. She attempts to roll it up and in doing so she notices the gold sovereigns and the small gift box. She decides to hide this in a drawer in her bedroom. Curious as to how Billy came by them, but knowing him well, she is sure it must all be above board. But if this is what the villains were after, she doesn't want to take any chances.

She returns quickly and applies the arnica cream to his bruises, taking particular care of his left hand and right ankle, which she also bandages. Then she covers him with the bedding; knowing that shock can kill, she wants to keep him warm and comfortable. Victoria arrives with the feverfew.

"He hasn't come around yet, Vicky, but sit and talk to him; I'm sure it will help. When he comes to his senses, let him sip the infusion a little at a time. Call us when he opens his eyes and don't worry, he'll recover in a few days, I'm sure."

Billy wakes up to throbbing pains in his head, hand and ankle and at first, he is unable to open his eyes and thinks he has gone blind. He groans, immediately alerting Victoria.

"Billy, you're safe. I'm here with you; you're going to be fine."

His throat is parched and his voice croaky, "Vicky, I can't see."

343

"Don't worry, it's just your eyes are still swollen over. You really took a beating."

He is confused. "I did? I can't remember."

He tries to move and a pain shoots through his back.

"Just try to lie still, Billy. I'll get another pillow so you can sit up a bit and have a drink."

He lies there trying to recollect what happened. He had been in such a happy mood coming home from Ivell. Then he remembers 'Shorty' and 'Beefy' ambushing him. He shudders recalling the beating he took, but how did he get back to the farm?

Vicky returns and tenderly lifts his head and slides the extra pillow underneath him. He feels a cup against his lips and he thankfully takes a sip of the drink.

Huskily he asks her, "How did I get back home, Vicky?"

"You were dragged here by Melody. Your boot was twisted in the stirrup and you were in a dreadful state. Ma says there's no way she can invisibly mend your Sunday-best jacket; it was ripped to shreds!"

He suddenly realises his right hand is resting on his undergarments. "Who undressed me, Vicky?"

"Ma did."

He flushes at the thought, then he feels for the money belt and realises it is gone. He feels nauseous. *They must have robbed me.* All his dreams come crashing down, his plans ruined. *How could I have let them get the better of me?* His eyes become sore, tears build behind the swelling, then he finds he can see out of one eye.

"Here, Billy, take some more." She presses the cup against his lips again and he drinks some more.

"Where am I?"

"You're in Don's bedchamber. You've been here for three days."

"Three days!"

"Yes, Billy. I've been so worried about you. We all have, but now you've come round I'm sure all will be well. I'm going to go and tell Ma and bring you something to eat. Would you like some soup?"

"Yes please, Vicky, I'm parched."

He lies there going over what he can remember. His left hand is exceedingly painful and this reminds him of how 'Shorty' had stamped on it. He cannot help wondering if he will ever be able to race again. *I suppose this is the price you pay for getting involved with criminals.*

Lillian enters the room with a tray of food for him. "Oh, Billy, it's good to have you back in the land of the living."

"Thank you for looking after me, Lillian."

"You're welcome. How are you feeling?"

"Like I've been in a bullring!"

"Well, we called out the doctor and he said it was mostly bruising. He strapped your hand to reset the bones and he believes in time you'll recover full use of it. He says your ankle was simply twisted and strained and should also recover completely given time, but you may get a bit of arthritis in it as you get older."

"Thank goodness! Arthritis in old age is the least of my worries."

"How is your head?"

"Thumping, but I'm very thirsty, so that can't be helping."

"Here, have some more of Vicky's infusion. It should help calm things down."

"I'm so grateful to you for looking after me so well."

"Of course we would. You're part of our family now, Billy."

"I was hoping to be, but now I've been robbed I don't have the means to continue with my plans."

"If you're talking about the money belt, I have it in a safe place."

"You do?" Relief washes over him.

"Yes, Billy. I removed it so you would be more comfortable and I hid it in my bedroom, in case your attackers were after its contents."

"Bless you, Lillian, that's a load off my mind. It's thanks to you and Bob for loaning me the money belt for the fayre that I had it with me still. The fellows who attacked me couldn't have known about the reward."

"Reward?"

"Yes, for returning the pony and trap, Colonel Seymour gave me fifty gold sovereigns."

"Well done, Billy!"

"Could you let me have the contents of the belt back. I need to speak to Bob, before I'm able to continue with my plans."

"Of course." She goes to retrieve Billy's treasure from her bedroom and, on her return, he places it all under his pillow.

There is a twinkle in her eye as she says, "I'll send him up to you when he comes in for his lunch."

Later, Bob enters the bedchamber. "Good to see you're back with us again, Billy."

"Thank you for looking out for me, Bob."

"No problems. Jake helped me carry you inside and upstairs, once Lily had cleaned your wounds, but you were in a hell of a state, lad. Do you remember who did this to you?"

"It was the remaining two of the ne'er-do-wells, 'Beefy' and 'Shorty'."

"I see. Look, lad, I never told you this, because I didn't want you to feel uncomfortable, but the fellow you call 'Shorty' is the younger brother of the chap who used to ride Bay Rum for us, before you came to work here."

"Ah! That makes a lot of sense; he had a double grudge against me then."

"Sorry, Billy, I should have warned you, but I never thought it would come to this."

"I don't hold it against you, Bob, but I hope he has got it out of his system now and there's an end to it." He is eager to change the subject. "Anyway, I wanted to discuss something else with you. I know I'm not a pretty sight, but I want to speak to you about me and Vicky."

"Oh yes." He smiles, which Billy finds encouraging.

"Before this happened, I was planning to ask you for her hand in marriage. Lillian tells me that, according to the doctor, I should recover fully and so I respectfully ask you, may I become betrothed to your beautiful daughter. I love her with all my heart and I will cherish and take care of her until we are old and grey together."

"It's my pleasure to give you our permission to marry, Billy. We can see how much you mean to each other and I'm sure Lillian is as happy as I am to have you for our son-in-law. Welcome to the family, lad." He holds out his hand and Billy shakes it with his good hand.

"Keep it between us for now, Bob. I want to look more myself when I pluck up the courage to ask her. I have the rings ready and I have some extra money given to me as a reward for returning the pony and trap."

"Don't worry, lad, your secret is safe with me, but I wouldn't keep her waiting too long. My Lillian will be hankering after grandchildren soon."

Billy blushes with pleasure at the thought.

347

After a week of complete rest, Billy is up and about and looking almost normal again; his bruises have faded from red and purple, to yellow and fawn and he only gets pain when he catches his hand awkwardly or twists his ankle.

Victoria keeps saying he should report what happened to him to the police, but he feels too much time has gone by for the police to take him seriously. His wounds are now all healed, so there is no evidence anymore. It would just be his word against theirs.

He decides to put it all out of his mind and look instead to the future by taking Victoria out for a picnic lunch. Lillian has helped him prepare a hamper of goodies and he has hidden the gift box underneath the serviettes. It is a beautiful autumnal day and they set off together in the pony and trap, rust coloured fallen leaves, caught in the backdraft, fluttering in their wake. They travel up Lawrence Hill with the sunlight glimmering through the trees and enhancing the green, red and golden rainbow colours of the leaves.

Billy is excited and anxious at the same time, his heart thumping at the thought of what he is going to say, while Victoria chatters away happily, obviously relieved to have him back beside her and virtually recovered from his ordeal.

He points out to her a flock of curlews taking off from a field on their left and swirling together up into the sky in a ballet formation. She spots a hare leaping through the long grass and then stopping statue-still as they go by. It is peaceful as they trot along, passing the occasional coach and four and the odd pedestrian. They turn at the fingerpost to South Cadbury.

"Are we going to Cadbury Castle, Billy?"

"Well, I've never been there before and it seems a fine place for a picnic, don't you think?"

"Yes, I've never been there either. The legend of King Arthur, Lady Guinevere and Lancelot and the court of Camelot has always fascinated me."

They reach Castle Lane, its hedgerows draped with the creamy fronds of traveller's joy and Billy finds a suitable place to leave the trap. "You stay there a moment, Vicky."

He clambers down, unharnesses Melody and lays the picnic rug across her back. Then holding her steady, he invites Victoria to mount her from the cart. He passes her the picnic hamper and leads his Lady Guinevere along the leaf strewn lane, through the shedding trees, up the ramparts and onto the summit of Cadbury Castle. He takes the hamper from her and helps her down, allowing Melody to graze.

He smiles at her. "It seems we have the place all to ourselves."

She scans the plateau. "It is hard to imagine this was once a bustling Iron Age hillfort, with warriors' dwellings and livestock and folk like potters and metalworkers, all living in close proximity."

He agrees. "The surrounding earthwork terracing, with its banks and ditches, made it very difficult to attack and an ideal defensive position against the Saxons for King Arthur and his soldiers," says Billy with admiration.

She marvels at the panoramic views of the colourful autumn landscape, trying to pinpoint the different villages around them. It is a magnificent spectacle and he is pleased with his choice. He removes the picnic rug and spreads it on the ground for them to sit down. His ankle is aching now and he sits down gingerly and begins to lay out Lillian's

349

food. Victoria comes running back to him her face animated and rosy from the breeze.

I'm in too much suspense, I can't wait any longer. I think now is the moment. He kneels on one knee before her, takes the box from beneath the serviettes and looks up into her smiling face. A face filled with anticipation.

"My dear Victoria... I think you must know by now, how much I care for you. I'm aware I'm not the most handsome of men, but nevertheless I promise to love, protect and care for you, to the best of my abilities for as long as we both shall live. If it should ever become necessary, I'd give my life for you, my darling. Please, will you be Lady Guinevere to my King Arthur and do me the honour of becoming my wife?"

"No! No! No!"

He is astonished, but then he sees her smile.

"Guinevere loved Lancelot; you cannot be King Arthur, you must be Lancelot!"

He grins back at her then. "Will you be my beautiful Lady Guinevere to my ever-constant Lancelot?"

She looks like she is holding her breath. He hands her the gift box. Her eyes sparkle with tears. "I will, my dearest. I will."

Her hands are shaking. She rips off the wrapping and opens the box, discovering, not only an engagement ring, but the matching wedding ring.

He gently takes the box from her, removes the rose-gold cluster ring and places it on her finger.

"Oh, Billy, I love it. It's absolutely beautiful. I couldn't have chosen better myself and it's a perfect fit."

He takes her hands and, pulling her down onto the rug beside him, he kisses her passionately. They lie together contentedly for a while, then he tells her, "I was given a reward of fifty sovereigns for returning the rig to the Seymours. I have the money for us to wed now and so you may pick the date, my love."

"Oh, Billy, it's so exciting. I cannot wait to tell Ma and Pa."

"They already know, my sweet. I asked your pa's permission, when I was recovering in Don's bedchamber."

"Well! They never let on."

"I swore them to secrecy. Of course, Don doesn't know yet."

They enjoy the picnic and afterwards stroll around the circumference of the castle, recognising certain landmarks and chatting about their wedding plans.

Before they return home, back to normality, they stand arm in arm enjoying the splendid views, both engrossed in their own private thoughts. She is planning her wedding in the spring and how she will make the cottage into a loving home for Billy.

He is thinking how his past lady friends, Lucy and Beth, had both been taller than he is, whereas Victoria is small and neat and fits in his arms perfectly, fits in his life perfectly and is held in his heart forever. He sighs with satisfaction. He cannot believe how lucky was, when he was at such a low ebb, and Lettie discovered the advertisement in the *Western Flying Post* that led him to Hatherleigh Farm and such a new and wonderful future.

THE EPILOGUE *(December 1871–March 1872)*

1ˢᵗ October 1871

Mrs Lucy Seymour
Bingham Manor
Sutton Bingham
Ivell
Somerset
England
Great Britain

My dearest Lucy,

    I am sending season's greetings from South Africa and wishing you all the very best for the new year 1872. I am also the bearer of good news in that we have dug down and discovered a kimberlite layer that looks promising enough to make all three partners a fortune. Please do not discuss this with my father. I will be writing to him separately, but I am in a position to fund both a fine ranch and your voyage over here with young Frankie if you are so disposed. I have befriended a Dutch builder who has already constructed some fine homesteads in the area and he is drawing up plans for me.

    I am writing to you in the hope that you have had enough time to give my offer serious thought and I trust that by now you may have come to a decision.

    I have been unable to think of anything but you, my dear, since we spoke together at Ashleigh's funeral and I know we could have a wonderfully adventurous life together, here in South Africa, if you are prepared to leave your family behind and give us a chance.

If you are willing to come, I would recommend that you wait until the autumn, perhaps September, when Frankie will be over three years old, the journey by sea less hazardous and you will be arriving here in time for our summer. My ranch may well be completed by then.

Please let me know as soon as you have decided. I eagerly await your decision.

I realise we don't need to marry, you already have my surname and we could continue with that pretence, but if you do join me, I would like you to do me the honour of becoming my wife and I will adopt young Frankie as my own.

With fondest wishes,
Rupert
xx

14th March 1872

Rupert Seymour Esq
The Hopetown Hopefuls
C/O Hopetown Post Office
Hopetown
Pixley ka Seme
Thembelihle
Northern Cape Province
South Africa

My dear Rupert,
I have given your offer a great deal of heartfelt consideration and I am delighted to tell you that I am inclined to accept your proposal of marriage. I am honoured that you think I will make a worthy wife

for you and thrilled that you wish to be a father to little Frankie.

I believe it will be sensible for us to be betrothed as soon as I arrive, but not to make any marriage plans until I am sure I will be able to accept this new life and that both Frankie and I are happy with this arrangement.

I believe you are quite right, my dear, it will be the making of the boy and I cannot help but feel excited at the prospect of the journey to an unknown land and to a very different lifestyle.

I am, however, loath to break it to my family and especially reluctant to tell poor Clara. I think I will just inform them all I am going on a visit in September; in this way, I can disclose it to them gently over time.

I will start preparations for our emigration and eagerly await receipt of the tickets.

With fondest love,
Lucy
xx

ACKNOWLEDGEMENTS

I would like to take this opportunity to pay tribute to the following people whose meticulous work all helped enormously with my research for *The Heart of Stone Saga* series:

BRANDY ROW

Firstly, the legendary *Stuart Morris*, who has written many books about Weymouth and Portland, and played a large part in the plot of my first novel, *Brandy Row*.

Secondly, *Roger Guttridge* who wrote the book *Dorset Smugglers* from which I learned the likely prison sentences for smuggling offences and a variety of other useful information.

Thirdly, *Eric Ricketts*, and his little book, *The Buildings of Old Portland*, which I also found useful, particularly his sketch-map of Chiswell, circa 1860.

DAWN TO DEADLY NIGHTSHADE
 LEGACY OF VAN DIEMEN'S LAND
 THE GOLDEN FLEECE

For the books set in the Yeovil area, I want to thank our wonderful local author and historian *Bob Osborn* for *The A to Z of Yeovil's History*, for all the information he has gleaned about Yeovil and its past characters and the history of the town, which I am sure he will recognise sprinkled throughout this story and my other two novels set in and around Yeovil.

Secondly, *Robin Ansell* and *Marion Barnes* for their book, *Around Yeovil*, a volume in the *Images of England* series, which as well as many images of old Yeovil, also includes interesting old advertisements from *Whitby's Almanack*.

Thirdly: For information on the Hatherleigh Farm Races: The helpful staff of the Wincanton Library and Mrs Lilian Elson of the Holton Heritage Trust. The late Puffy Bowden's map of the old racecourse and the letters and map sent to Mrs Mary Sweet from Mr Norman Leeks was also invaluable.

In addition to these eminent people, I would like to thank my family and friends for their support and encouragement. My husband, Barry, for his patience when asked to help with deliveries to my local outlets and for reading and vetting my manuscripts. Also, for reading and commenting before publication, my two sisters, Maddy Sams and Bridget Overd; my daughter, Nicky Smith, daughter-in-law, Charlie Smith, and my friends Angela Hart and Pamela Dudley; their help is much appreciated.

Lastly my thanks and appreciation go to all the staff at Matador, but particularly Heidi Hurst, Production Controller, Jonathan White, Marketing Manager, Hannah Eveleigh for her very thorough copy edit and Chelsea Taylor for her work on the Cover Design.

POETIC LICENCE

In a subsidiary story line, Bingham Lake was mentioned in *Legacy of Van Diemen's Land*, where I ignored the fact that Sutton Bingham Reservoir was not formed until the 1950s and made the reservoir a natural lake for poetic reasons. Thus, in this story I have continued with this fiction. Also, the position of the real Sutton Bingham Manor is hidden behind the church, but in *Legacy* I placed it opposite the railway bridge facing the smaller part of the lake. I trust that I will be forgiven for these small anomalies.